The Ring of Betrayal

ISBN 978-1-62806-478-0 (paperback)
ISBN 978-1-62806-479-7 (ebook)

Library of Congress Control Number 2026904367

Published by Salt Water Media
29 Broad Street, Suite 104
Berlin, MD 21811
www.saltwatermedia.com

SALT WATER
MEDIA

Cover background image used via license from istockphoto.com; image of girl in the water with the ring provided by Burt Allman using Google Gemini AI

The Ring of Betrayal

Maria Sundy

Acknowledgments

I want to thank Dina Simoni who not only helped me with many good ideas but kept me honest with grammar and punctuation. Thank you to Burt Allman for his artistic ability to create the cover image for this book. To professor Frank Tatone of Robert Morris University for wonderfully editing my book. His knowledge and insight for the characters was an immense help. To Thomas Testa for his inciteful financial advice. To the Scribes Writers Group for all their helpful ideas. Most of all I want to thank Stephanie Fowler and her wonderful staff at Salt Water Media who made this book possible.

Prologue

Patrice Elyse Traffortelli sat there at her desk, elbows resting on the soft upholstered arms of the wingback chair. In her left hand, she held a glass of white wine. Her heart felt heavy as she stared at the blank piece of paper and a pen; a letter to her parents needed to be written. It was 2 a.m., and still the right words would not come to mind.

The earlier conversation with Alistair and Fiona upset her. Alistair harassed, she defended, and Fiona pleaded.

She heard his words over and over in her head. "Come back, lass, where ye have family. Ye' no business in the city where folk behave like heathens, roughin' ye up in unsavory neighborhoods. That foreigner could a killed ye! Don'a ye know that? And then to be caught up in a rape trial by the same scoundrel! 'Tis no good, Pet. Never would me kin do a thing like that! I should na' give me consent for ta marry either!"

"It was not my fault, Father. You know it wasn't. My life is not always going to be terrible. Did I know my husband Neil was going to divorce and kick me out of the house I loved? Did I know he was going to die in a stupid car crash?"

In the background, she heard Fiona crying, "Oh, my baby."

"Father, why is she crying? Let me talk to her."

"Pet, me angel, just do what ye father asks. 'Tis not a hard thing. Or maybe I should send Uncle Mike to protect ye."

"No, no, Uncle Mike, Mother. Really, I can take care of myself. You have to understand this fact. I will be okay."

Fiona cried louder. Alistair grabbed the phone again. "Yer upsettin' Fi now. Come home, and we will have a talk, lass. We love you, Pet."

"I love you both, and I will…" Before Pet could get another word in, Alistair hung up.

She growled, "He always does that. Just once, I would like to end a conversation!"

Then, with renewed resolution, Pet looked at the empty page, walked over to the secretary's desk, and began to write. She would make them understand that she was no longer a helpless young girl but an intelligent grown woman. With one more sip of wine, she started writing.

Dear Mother and Father,

This past year was frightening and challenging, but the outcome of the trial made me realize I can stand on my own two feet. Jari Slobomon was an evil man, and he scared me to death. I wanted to run away from the trial, but I knew it was he who raped that poor girl and assaulted me. I stayed because it was the right thing to do. In the end, I was glad he was convicted and taken off the streets for good!

During the trial, I met people from all walks of life. My eyes were opened to a whole new world. I began to see that some people are a bunch of crooks who think only of themselves, while others are generous and kind, helping anyone who needs a hand up. My friend Harry Trotter taught me that human nature is a fascinating subject to study.

One good person I have met is Anthony Prattmore, Neil's lawyer. Consequently, he became my lawyer too. I think I told you about him, but I didn't tell you he's also become a very dear friend.

Another was Grace Rutherford Traffortelli. She was Neil's grandmother and was responsible for giving me the grandfather clock. Grace was a very loving person. I want to learn more about her. Like, how did she live as a young girl? Where did she go to school? How did she meet her husband? She was like you, Mother, kind, generous, and very smart. I want to learn about her past. It broke her heart when Neil turned to drinking and gambling. His stupidity got him killed on the highway. We were in the middle of the divorce when it happened. And that situation was interesting because I never officially signed the divorce decree, so, technically, I was still married to Neil when he was killed. That is how I inherited the furniture company.

I learned true friendship from Grace. She owned Briar Town Furniture Company. She was also very smart in the business world. She made the furniture business sound exciting. There was so much I could have learned from her, but she died before I really got to know her well.

Anthony told me that if I can be patient, good things will come my way regarding this company. So, I hope you can understand why I must stay here. I cannot leave knowing I will have a place in this town to continue Grace Traffortelli's Legacy.

A good life is in my future. Please trust me, Mother and Father, I want you to be proud of me.

With love and affection,

Your loving daughter,

Pet

Chapter 1

Grace and Howard

Grace loved Hitherton Valley, especially in the summer, even though tonight the atmosphere was hot and humid. The sweltering heat of the day had become a heavy blanket of steam, its vapors rising on a sluggish evening breeze.

She watched nature's events as fireflies came alive, blinking erratically in the trees, and listened to the crickets drone a low, sultry tune. Over the trees, the sunset faded into a pale bluish-gray line streaming across the horizon, shrinking her valley into mist and shadows.

All this beauty surrounded her and normally would have been appreciated, but something more important was happening. Grace's life was about to change. Her concentration was on Howard. She was absolutely lost in his deep brown eyes.

On the wide oak porch, shadows of the young lovers were silhouetted by the moon rising behind the gabled Victorian house. Soft voices and the steady squeak of a swing were only a small part of the players in this tranquil scene.

His voice was pleading, trying to persuade her that he was right. As the pleading continued, his curly red hair became damp, and tiny beads of sweat trickled along his hairline. Finally, he took out a big white cotton handkerchief and dabbed his forehead and neck.

"Grace, you know I love you. I wouldn't dream of being apart from you. In fact, I couldn't live the rest of my life without you. I'm going to be somebody, and you'll be there beside me forever, but I must do this. I'm going to prove to my Old Man that I can be somebody without the name of Hyde helping me. The Army is the way to go. With my college degree in

Business, I'll be able to apply for OCS. We can get married as soon as I graduate." He hesitated for a split second. "Maybe even after basic training. Who knows?"

Grace looked away when he said OCS. She smoothed the soft pleats of her white organdy dress, adjusting the satin bow around her waist. Her full skirt draped over the swing as it swayed gently with each push of her heel. With a dainty hand, she dabbed her linen hanky around the corners of her eyes and above her upper lip. She knew Howard was watching her. She couldn't look at him now, not at this moment. Tears would surely well up in her eyes if she did.

Out of frustration, Howard said impatiently, "Are you listening to me, Grace?"

She nodded slowly. "Yes, Howard, but when did you decide to enlist? Why did you get my hopes up, thinking we could start making our wedding plans and that we would marry this fall? You said as soon as you got your first paycheck from Bennington Steel Works, plans would be made!"

Howard took both of her hands in his. "Honey, I know I said a lot of things. I might have even said the word 'promise', but we will have a whole lifetime together. What is eight or nine months apart? It will be over in a flash, and then I will be home. You'll see, I won't disappoint you! Don't you see, I have to be better than Al."

With a tear in each eye, she whispered, "When are you going?"

Before any other words could be spoken, a Ford convertible roared up the driveway. Aloysius Hyde screeched the brakes to a stop and jumped out of the car.

"Hey, Sport, I've been lookin' all over creation for you. I thought you stood me up on tonight's poker game."

Aloysius looked at Grace with a big smile on his face. "Evening, Grace. You look pretty tonight. Can I grab this old coot from you for a little while? We're running a little late! I 'll have him back to you soon, and maybe even richer than when he left."

Howard got up from the swing. "Yeah, guess I forgot. Are Froggy and Jim going to be there?"

"Yup, it's their payday, and they got a lot of cash on them. Let's go!"

Howard gently pulled Grace up from the swing and kissed her tenderly on the mouth. Then he pulled back slightly from her, cupping her face in his hands. "I'll be back. I'll only play a couple of hours with the guys. I promise. I could possibly win enough to put a down payment on an engagement ring for you. You'd like that, wouldn't you?"

Pouting, she said, "If it's honest money, I'd like it. Are you good at poker?"

"Yes, I could really beat the pants off these clowns, but I'm a nice guy and keep it fun. Aloysius goes in for the kill every time. He's a real serious type. I would like to beat a new guy named Shorty. He thinks he's Mr. Las Vegas. He needs to be cut down a peg or two. I can take him. Don't worry."

Howard kissed her again quickly and headed for the car. Aloysius had already turned the car around and was beeping the horn for Howard to hurry up. Grace waved to him and thought to herself, "Oh, no!" She ran down the steps after him, calling. "Howard. Howard, when are you leaving?"

Howard leaned out the window laughing, "Sometime tomorrow morning, sweetheart! "

Two seconds later, the Ford convertible was out of sight. The memory of Howard's smiling face had to last Grace forever. She never saw him again. The only tangible memory was a short letter from boot camp, Fort Dix, New Jersey.

Chapter 2

The Wait That Never Ended

Grace bounded down the stairs like she did every morning since Howard went away. Her eyes were happy, a smile on her face, and hope in her heart that there would be a letter from Howard today.

Her mother came through the screen door, clutching many envelopes. "Bills, always bills, no catalogs, or periodicals, just bills. There are no letters of importance," she sighed.

Grace reached for them, "May I?"

Adeline shook her head, going over the envelopes again. "As I said, dear, you won't find any letters today. I was expecting at least a note from my sister, Anna Lee. I wonder what's gotten into her these days?"

Grace sighed, "You are right, Mother. Gosh, why won't he write to me? He promised." She then went outside and sat down on the porch swing. She really wasn't concerned about Aunt Anna Lee. Howard was her priority now.

Still talking, Adeline Briar came out and stood on the porch near the swing.

"Well, what do you think, Grace? I am right, after all. She did mention bringing the coat."

Grace looked up, "Hmm? I'm sorry, Mother, I didn't hear a word you said. I've got to know what happened to Howard. Do you think it would be improper to visit his home and speak with his mother? Howard must have told her about me, and I know where the family lives."

"I would wait a little while longer, dear. You mustn't seem anxious or be a pest. You don't know them that well. Give it another week. Maybe you will get a letter by then."

Grace let out an audible sigh. "Okay, just one more week."

At the end of the week, Grace was glad she had taken her mother's advice. Preparing for her first day at college was filled with shopping, visits to the registrar's office, and buying books. The days that followed were filled with assignments and adjusting to a very hectic schedule. She met new people and was fascinated by the professors. She excelled in exchanging ideas on economic theory.

Howard soon took a back seat in her mind until one day she saw a young man in uniform at the post office. Instantly, she felt a pang of loneliness. She thought to herself, "Oh, Howard, why couldn't this young soldier be you!" She vowed to herself to see Mrs. Hyde that evening.

Grace walked up the sidewalk to the Hyde residence with confidence. She was hoping with a naive prayer that he might even be home this very night. She pushed the door buzzer with her right index finger. It made her jump. It was a loud, irritating buzz.

A very heavy-set woman with a thick, woven shawl wrapped around her disheveled dress opened the door. Her right hand wiped unruly bangs away from her eyes as she peered at Grace in an angry grimace.

"What do you want?"

Sheepishly, Grace sputtered her request, "Are you Mrs. Hyde, Howard's mother?"

"Who are you, young lady? How do you know my Howard?"

Grace braced herself for the strength to ask more questions. She didn't like this woman. "Well, you see, Ma'am, we, I mean Howard and I, we were going to get engaged, and when he left, he said—"

The woman rudely interrupted her. "That doesn't matter now. Leave! Howard is never coming back. Do you understand? Nothing matters now. Don't come back here again!"

The front door slammed in Grace's face. The sound of the door slamming was so loud she almost fell backwards down the concrete steps. She didn't know what to do.

She just stood there. Dare she knock again? Then she heard a male voice. "Mother, you were very rude to the girl. I think I know her."

The next sound Grace heard was a woman's hysterical voice. "No one is going to talk about my Howard. I don't want anyone in this house wondering about my Howard. You can't make me ask them in. Too many have come already!"

Grace turned around and ran down the steps. She ran all the way home, confused and frightened that something very bad had happened to Howard.

The next afternoon, coming home from class, she passed by the drug store. People were gathered in front of it. One man held a newspaper.

Grace heard whispers. Women were saying, "Oh no, not him," and "Poor dear." She won't accept this well. She tried not to be obvious, peering into the crowd, but she had to see what was wrong. Then she saw it, the bold headlines: "LOCAL BOY, KILLED IN JEEP ACCIDENT AT FORT DIX."

For some odd reason, the headlines had meaning for her. She walked into the store and bought a paper, even though she knew there would be one there for her father at home. She wanted to digest all the details privately. Doom and sadness fell over her while a slight hope stirred in her heart that this incident had nothing to do with the love of her life. The glimmer soon faded into a harsh reality. Howard was dead.

The next day, Grace was in a state of inertia. Her tears never stopped streaming from her eyes. Her head sank down into her pillow, and thick brown curls tangled on her wet cheeks. Adeline Briar had a morning routine. It was bright, cheery, and conversational. When she entered Grace's room, her lilting voice spoke of happy little things to lighten Grace's mood. "Isn't it a beautiful day out there, so bright and sunny?" She pulled up the window blinds of every window in Grace's room.

Grace rolled over and pulled the covers over her head. "Oh, Mother, please, I just can't get out of bed today. Maybe I'll never get out of bed. I'm not going to classes either. My life is over. It's the end of the world. Without him, I will never be happy again."

Adeline sighed, realizing her cheery efforts were fruitless, "Suit yourself, dear. I don't know what else to say to comfort you. I am terribly sorry for your loss. Howard was a wonderful boy. Surely, he is among the angels in Our Father's Heaven Above."

Grace wailed from under the sheets, "Oh, Mother, please! Howard was a man, not a boy! He was everything I ever hoped for in life, and now he is gone! Please leave me alone!"

With that, Adeline Briar left, softly closing the door behind her.

Grace realized each morning the sun rose, and the day began anew, even without Howard. She came to the obvious conclusion, after much soul searching, that life would go on about her. One day followed another, and she had to succeed at something to make her beloved proud of her. She imagined Howard looking down from the heavens, watching over her. She physically felt a pain in her heart as she thought of him. Silently, she said a prayer and vowed never forget him as long as she lived.

Chapter 3

Aloysius Steps In

Aloysius rolled the tightly wadded piece of paper into a ball and sent the tiny projectile forward. It sailed easily downward in the amphitheater seating and landed on the back of Grace's cascading brown curls. He waited for a reaction. She made no movement. He volleyed another, hitting her higher, right above a blue gingham bow.

Without looking back at the rows of students, she brushed the top of her head as if brushing away a fly and continued taking notes. He quickly made one more ball, flicking it harder from his thumb. This time it grazed her left ear.

"That is game, set, and match, Mr. Hyde. Your opponent is obviously not interested in your energetic serves. On the other hand, were you experimenting with Einstein's theory of relativity since this is a Physics Class?"

The young men around Aloysius roared with laughter as he put his hands to his side.

"No, Professor Rossetti, I wasn't. It won't happen again."

"Be sure that it doesn't, Mr. Hyde," the professor admonished, and he continued his talk.

James Wingate leaned over to Aloysius and whispered, "You blew it again, Al. I knew you would. Didn't you see the prof? He caught your actions the second time you aimed the spitball at her. Who is she anyway? She's not a bad-looking gal."

"First of all, that girl is off limits to you. She's mine. Her name is Grace Briar. I aim to marry that girl."

James sat up straight in the hardback chair and took notice of her. Aloysius rarely made a statement that profound unless he really meant it.

"Have you gone out with her before, Al?"

"No. Now shut up. He's giving us the eye."

The Physics Class ended with Professor Rossetti calling out page numbers and chapters for their next assignment. The mass exodus of young men and women left the room, with the thunder of moving desks, dropping books, conversations, and giggles from girls getting a closer look at young Mr. Hyde.

Grace couldn't wait to get out of there. She walked quickly down the hall and out of the building. Her friends ran to catch up to her. How embarrassing, she thought. Now her friends would want to know all sorts of things that she had no answers to. Aloysius ran faster than they did and was right at her side in a minute. Grace kept walking but slowed her pace.

"Hello! Sorry if I embarrassed you. I've been trying to get your attention all week, but you haven't given me the time of day. My name is Aloysius Hyde. Remember? My friends call me Al. It sounds less formal, don't you think?"

"Frankly, Mr. Hyde, I don't have an opinion on that right now. I really don't know you that well to call you by a nickname. Have we met formally? And, for your information, I was a little uncomfortable. I don't like being the center of attention."

Aloysius laughed, trying to lighten the atmosphere. "Well, you might say I was the center of attention, Miss Briar. You have seen me before. I came and picked up my brother Howard at your home the night before he left for Boot Camp."

Grace stopped in her tracks. She looked Aloysius in the eye, studying him carefully. "Oh, you are the one who took Howard away from me that night. I never saw him again. I do recognize you now. You have grown taller and more muscular. Your hair is darker."

She turned away from him and continued walking a little faster toward the center of town.

Al caught up with her again. "Um, Miss Briar. I'm awfully sorry things turned out the way they did. I had no control over the events that took place later. We're all sad over Howard's death."

Again, she stopped. "Well, I suppose you didn't have anything to do with his death, but you could have left us alone and not taken him to a poker game."

She stunned him with her curt remark. Immediately, he lowered his head. His eyes looked to the ground. He didn't know what to say, but he wasn't about to defend himself to a girl he hardly knew. He didn't want this meeting to end badly, so he swallowed a smart remark and said, in the sincerest way he knew how. "Miss Grace, had I known the future, I surely would have left you two alone. Heck, I kick myself every day. I should have brought him home so my own mother could have time with him. She hasn't been herself lately. She drinks all the time. My father goes to work and comes home drunk most days, and they argue the rest of the night. I don't know where it's going to end. I try to do the best I can, but it's hard living in a house that's all broken apart." Aloysius backed away slightly. "Good day, Miss Briar. I'll try not to bother you again."

His story brought tears to her eyes as she watched the young Mr. Hyde walk away from her. Maybe she had been a bit abrupt with him. Should she give him another chance?

Chapter 4

Aloysius Goes Courting

Two days later, Aloysius found Grace in the library. Four books were opened in front of her. She was feverishly taking notes, flipping back and forth through a thick chemistry book that showed the atomic periodic table.

Aloysius addressed her as if their last conversation never existed, "My, you look studious. Cramming for an exam?" Aloysius asked as he sat next to her.

"No, we aren't having final exams yet. You should know that. Professor Rossetti is very strict on the completeness of our assignment. I want to make sure I have some of the element values correct. I don't know why I'm even telling you this. Where are your books? Do you have the assignment done already?"

"Oh, don't worry about me. I don't panic over homework, but I would like to know something else important."

"Oh, something about the periodic table?"

"No. It's more important than that."

Grace gave him a curious smile. "Well, what is it, Mr. Hyde? Our next class begins in ten minutes."

He gave her his most sincere smile and looked intently into her eyes. "Will you, ahem, would you like to go to the movies with me this Saturday night? It would mean a lot to me, Grace."

The question caught her by surprise. The idea of going out with someone so soon after Howard's death never occurred to her. Would he have the same warm, fun-loving personality that her Howard did?

"I would like to think about it, Aloysius. Could I give you my answer tomorrow?"

"I guess I have no other choice, do I? Please call me Al."

Grace looked at her watch and quickly gathered her books. The idea of going out and having some male companionship did give her pleasure. She wanted to say yes right away, but her independent thinking said, "Don't make it too easy for him." After all, she really didn't know if she liked this persistent young man. A twinge of guilt played on her emotions as she remembered Howard's last kiss.

Grace hurried to class. She formed a plan on the way. She would go out with Aloysius just once, and it had to be with another couple. She would keep this a casual affair, nothing serious. She felt Mother would approve of her judgment. She didn't need gossip floating around town that she was a loose woman, dating men so soon after her Howard died.

Chapter 5

Grace and Aloysius

The fact was that Grace liked Al. He made her laugh with a feigned ridiculous grin. Sometimes his language was a little coarse, but he had such a way with words to fit the situation that Grace couldn't argue with him. If she frowned, Aloysius apologized profusely, begging her pardon if his wit offended her.

She tried not to compare his looks with Howard's, because the differences were too extreme. Howard was tall and athletic with deep blue eyes. Aloysius was stocky and well-built. His eyes captured the female gaze and held a stare that mesmerized a girl's soul. His voice, when he wanted to, could be soft and entreating, telling stories and giving compliments to entertain a woman's affection.

The demands of college studies and work engulfed Grace and Aloysius' time. Both of them had part-time jobs. Grace took an easy job at Kline's Drug Store. She loved working in retail, but it limited her from seeing Aloysius whenever she wanted to.

In their free time, they went to dances, pep rallies, or any excuse to laugh and have fun. With each meeting, her feelings got stronger for this handsome young man with a business head on his shoulders. Grace felt she had attained a high social status among her peers. One day, Grace passed a crowd of friends. She heard a girl say, "They are an item, you know, going steady and all, the son of a Macy's executive." A smile was on Grace's lips all day long when she heard that expression. It gave her goosebumps.

Aloysius worked at Krauss' Jewelry store, helping Cornelius

Krauss with the books and waiting on customers. The workings of a business interested him very much. The prominence of money and its lucrative advantages gave him many ideas and personal gain. He learned a lot about the value of various precious stones and about the different weights of gold, silver, and platinum. Mr. Krauss instructed him on categorizing the weekly shipments of jewelry from countries around the world.

One day in May, Aloysius got a call from Cornelius. "Aloysius, do not be alarmed. I am not myself today. I have the grippe. I am very sick. I cannot work today. I know you can help me, yes?"

"Yes, Mr. Krauss, I can help you. The shipment is coming in today. I know it will be a large one," Aloysius said anxiously.

"Yes, yes, this is true, but I showed you many times. You know what to do. Write down everything as I told you, in both ledgers, weight, and description. It must be exact. You call me when you finish. You can do this, yes? I will price them tomorrow, or the next day on my return."

"Yes, Mr. Krauss, you won't have to worry."

"Good boy."

Aloysius remembered the owner's instructions. He would perform the same ritual Mr. Krauss did with every shipment. He studied the old man's technique many times, savoring the meticulous routine of categorizing each precious item. Aloysius couldn't wait to go to the back room and spread the mounted jewels on the special wooden counter. He would use the velvet cloth to protect them from any dust particles or debris. He loved the touch of the stones on dark blue velvet cloth. It was a tantalizing anticipation.

As Mr. Krauss said, the shipment arrived exactly at eleven a.m. Aloysius signed for them and quickly took a rather large wooden box to the shop's back room. All day long, he hoped to close early, but the customers kept coming in looking about, and buying sale items. Finally, at exactly five p.m., he pulled down the shade and flipped off the OPEN sign in the window of KRAUSS' JEWELRY STORE. As he headed to the backroom. He had a satisfied smile on his face. "Now you're all mine."

He performed the ritual, opening the box very carefully. The precious cargo was encased within a case. Rings, earrings, and bracelets were separated by thin balsa-wood trays in the box, and each item was in a small felt envelope. He took each one out and laid them in front of him. The soft light of the jeweler's lamp enhanced each stone, showing off its incredible brilliance.

It took him quite a long time to write down every piece. Each one was a marvel in design and beauty. The gold and silver were awesome in weight and purity, but the brilliance of the diamonds, sapphires, and rubies tested his appetite for valuable luxuries. To keep one or two of these precious trinkets for himself tortured his conscience. He wanted one, just one to treasure. Perhaps he could put one of these rings on Grace's finger. She would see it as a rare thing of prestige and power.

Just as he was about to close the lid, he double checked the box, feeling around each corner. His finger touched another felt envelope. Why, it's another ring, he said to himself, and immediately took it out of the soft tan felt. He was amazed at the weight of the ring, and quickly reached for the jeweler's magnifying eyepiece. He had never seen a stone like this before. It was a brilliant oval pink stone, set in a wreath of four round diamonds, with an eighteen-carat white gold shank woven with diamonds. The attached tag read Pink Tourmaline, Afghanistan.

Aloysius consulted the original manifest for a more precise description of the ring, but found none. How odd, he thought, how convenient. It was meant to be mine. "If it wasn't on the list, surely it can't be worth as much as the other jewelry. He'll never miss this little trinket. It will be a perfect gift for Grace.

That night, he placed it on her finger, pledging his undying love.

Chapter 6

The Unexpected Call

Two days later, Mr. Krauss came back to work a little weakened by his illness, but ready to see what his young apprentice had accomplished. All seemed in order as Aloysius gave details of his entries in the ledgers. With every page turn, Aloysius held his breath, ready for an accusing question of something missing. Nothing happened. Mr. Krauss seemed satisfied, and business went on as usual.

For a week, Aloysius made sure each one of his transactions was perfect. He sometimes listened to the phone calls Cornelius received. Fortunately, he detected nothing out of the ordinary. He mentally screened professional-looking men who came through the door as potential detectives ready to haul him off to jail.

Little by little, the paranoia lessened. Disaster was not in the future, and he enjoyed his work at the store again. He felt so good one evening that he decided to go over to Grace's house unannounced. She wouldn't deny him. He was a young man on his way to greatness.

The following Sunday, Cornelius got a call from Herr Gustav Reichstein, his jewelry broker and importer from Gilderhaus Ltd.

Gerda's voice was hesitant when she called Cornelius. "I'm sorry, Cornelius, I know you don't take business calls on Sunday, but a Mr. Gustav Reichstein is very insistent and says he must ask you something important."

"Not to worry, Gerda, Herr Gustav is a businessman, he doesn't make chit chat mit little things."

"Cornelius Krauss, guten tag."

"Ah, Gustav Reichstein, guten tag."

"Now, Herr Krauss, I am glad to know you are good. I have something on my mind. I don't have much time, so I won't waste time on pleasantries. I must say I am curious about your omission in the shipment."

"Herr Reichstein, you never waste time with riddles, but I'm puzzled. I don't know what you mean about an omission."

"Herr Krauss, I thought you would mention the Pink Tourmaline ring in the shipment. Such a beautiful ring deserves notice and appreciation. I wanted to hear how you liked it. You know some are of great value. This one can certainly be listed as much as $800.00. You will find it, ja?"

"Ja, some are very precious and rare. I would have surely noticed it and called you immediately. I will check the shipment box again and question my young clerk. I will get answers and call you tomorrow, three o'clock at the latest." It was good talking with you, Herr Reichstein. Guten Abend."

Cornelius put the receiver down slowly. His angry expression gave Gerda evidence that the conversation wasn't a good one.

She came to him and led him to the sofa. "Cornelius, I think you'd better sit down here. Your face is so red. You must be careful of your blood pressure. Tell me, Papa, what is troubling you?"

His troubled face looked at her lovingly." You see, Gerda, I had so much hope for this young man, who works for me, and now I find out he is not the person I thought he was. He is so bright. I didn't expect him to be so dishonest. This boy's father gives such a good impression. He's well-spoken and a good community citizen. Why would his son discredit him? If this ring is not there, then he is truly guilty of theft."

"Cornelius, you are scaring me. I don't know what you are talking about."

"I'll tell you later, Momma. Young Mr. Hyde has some explaining to do. I will be back later. I must go to the store now."

Chapter 7

The Shame

Monday morning arrived with a downpour. Cornelius arrived in a foul mood, and the rain didn't help. He started checking every item in the inventory. His mind kept going over the events of Sunday. Herr Reichstein was obviously disappointed. If the ring was there, it would have been interesting to discuss the tourmaline's possibilities.

It was eleven a.m. when Aloysius came whistling through the door. He gave a friendly "Hello. Good morning, Mr. Krauss!" as he hung up his hat and jacket.

Cornelius was at his desk behind the jewelry counter and gave Aloysius a curt professional, "Morning, Mr. Hyde."

"I'll empty the trash and tidy the back room up before I sweep the front of the store, Sir, then I'll start my work."

Still not turning around, Cornelius said, "Yes, you do that."

Aloysius barely got to the back room when Grace walked through the door. The bell above the door clanged loudly. Its abrupt sound was so startling that Cornelius practically fell to the floor. He righted himself and came to the counter. He smiled at her. He couldn't be angry at such a beautiful, innocent girl. It was her despicable boyfriend who was the criminal.

Her stride was bouncy, half skipping and half walking. She could hardly contain her happiness.

"Good morning, Mr. Krauss. How are you today? It's really raining out there, isn't it, but it is just lovely in here. You have such a beautiful store, Mr. Krauss. Aloysius really loves working here. In fact, he bought this ring from your store." Grace jutted the ring out in front of her and laid her hand on the counter.

"Mr. Krauss, Aloysius proposed to me last night with this ring. It is the most beautiful ring I've ever seen in my life. Don't you think it is magnificent? Aloysius said it had to be a special one. No, he said it had to be a perfect one."

Very gently, Cornelius took her hand in his and admired the ring. "So, the perfect ring is for a perfect lady, eh? It is a very special ring and an expensive one too, I think." He took out his jeweler's loop. Now he knew why Herr Gustav wanted him to make a comment on it. The color and facets were flawless.

He put Grace's hand slowly back down on the counter, and in a quiet, formal voice, Cornelius called Aloysius to the front counter. Grace busied herself getting a slip of paper out of a black velvet box and attempted to show it to him. Cornelius looked at it, knowing it was a meaningless, made-up receipt, and brushed it aside. "I understand you want to show me this, but it is not necessary, Miss Grace."

When Aloysius heard that controlled, cold, authoritative voice, his heart stopped pumping, and his knees buckled under him for a second. He wanted to bolt out the back door. He wanted to run far away and not look back. He'd been found out. All the excuses in the world would not help him now.

He could barely walk to the front counter and stand before his executioner. Grace was oblivious to the potential horror and embarrassment that was going to take place.

Cornelius didn't say anything. Grace gave Aloysius a big smile. When the two didn't speak, Grace started speaking rather rapidly.

"Oh, Aloysius, I couldn't contain my joy. I had to see you again and say hello. I wanted to show Mr. Krauss my beautiful ring. I also thought you might want to keep this receipt, being that you helped Mr. Krauss with his books."

Cornelius solemnly looked at them. "The receipt at this point is immaterial, young miss. An engagement ring is an investment between two people. The buyer knows the value of the ring, and the receiver knows the value of the man who purchased it. Don't you think so, Mr. Hyde?"

Aloysius' voice was barely audible. "Yes, Mr. Krauss, you are right."

He waited for Aloysius to say something, anything for an explanation, any utterance of apology or excuse for why he did such an unbelievable act of deceit. But no words came.

Grace started the conversation again, turning to Aloysius, telling him of her wedding ideas. Aloysius held her hand. His pale face wincing with every happy giggle.

Cornelius couldn't stand the pretense any longer and abruptly interrupted their conversation. "I'm closing the store early today, Aloysius. See that you cover the front and back counters. I will close out the register. You can see your young lady out now. Call your father and tell him to meet us here before you go home."

"Yes, Mr. Krauss, I will."

Grace looked at Aloysius. She had a worried look on her face. "What's the matter? Is everything all right?"

Aloysius walked her to the door. "It's okay. It's just business. I'll see you later, Grace."

Chapter 8

The Confrontation

Cornelius stood before the young thief. "I should call the police for this act of stupidity and greed. How could you be so insensitive to my kindness toward you, Aloysius? But you will pay. You will pay dearly, and by my rules. Your disgrace in my eyes will always be there. You will no longer be working in this store, but you will be working, doing hard manual labor. You will dig ditches, garden, and do anything I see fit to make you physically exhausted. You will know the meaning of shame. You will work whether it rains or shines. You will also work on a farm, mucking out my good friend Herr Gernshaltar's livestock stalls. You will do anything he tells you to do.

"Your father will know of this. You will apologize to him for disgracing your family. And you will pay off this ring in full. I will not give you any consideration or leniency for jobs well done. Do I make myself clear? As of now, you will be out of this store. Monday morning, you will report to my house. Also, your lovely fiancée, if she will still have you, will keep this ring as a remembrance of the once-upstanding young man you were. She is young and impressionable. I wouldn't do anything unkind to her. The ring is perfect in every aspect of its design. Let her life from now on be as perfect and beautiful."

The expression on Aloysius' face was sullen, his voice quiet. He didn't argue, just uttered a lame excuse. "I do understand. I'm awfully sorry, Mr. Krauss. I don't know why I did it. The ring is so beautiful, I had to have it. It was all for her." Aloysius said nothing else.

His voice trailed off to silence.

When Mr. Hyde arrived at the store, his demeanor was

cordial. Cornelius greeted him with a polite "Good Afternoon, Mr. Hyde." There was no handshake. Mr. Hyde followed suit with the same, "Good afternoon, Mr. Krauss." Aloysius said nothing. Then the damaging conversation began. The facts of the incident didn't take long to present. Cornelius didn't pull any punches. His father couldn't believe his ears as Cornelius told him of the theft and value of an $800.00 ring.

His father looked hard into Aloysius' eyes, seeing a thief and a coward. Howard Sr. exploded into a barrage of foul language, berating his son for his stupidity. He didn't want to hear an apology. Howard Sr. screamed and punctuated his curse words with jabs to his son's shoulder and face. The more he cursed, the angrier he got. He pushed him to the floor.

The boy got up quickly, ducking and weaving like a prize fighter, almost egging the old man on. Aloysius was inching himself to the door when Howard lunged forward. Cornelius caught Howard Sr. and pulled him away, getting between the two.

Cornelius, visibly shaken by this physical outrage, held up his hands. "Enough! No more of this hitting and fighting. You should deal with him at home."

Howard Hyde changed his fighting stance and put down his fists. "You are right, Mr. Krauss. Excuse my conduct." He turned to Aloysius, "Now, boy, get out of my sight. I'll deal with you as soon as I get home, and you better be home when I get there."

Aloysius ran out into the rain with no jacket or hat. Mr. Hyde excused himself, muttering his apologies. He got into his car and was out of sight in two seconds flat.

Chapter 9

The Demise

When Howard Hyde Sr. got home, the yelling started all over again. "You rotten no-good son of a bitch. Get down here so I don't have to come up there and get you!" Howard screamed at the top of his lungs, banging the front door wide open.

Margery came running from the living room. "Don't talk that way to the only son I have left! Shut up!"

Howard Sr. tore off his coat and headed upstairs. Margery grabbed him, pulling him off the second step. He lost his balance and fell on her, toppling down to the floor.

"Get outta my way! I'm gonna kill him!" He scrambled to his feet and tried for the stairs again, but Margery held on to his legs.

"No, go in the kitchen. Tell me what's going on. What happened? Why are you so upset?" She hung onto him, grunting and moaning. Howard Sr. bent down and offered her his hand. "Aw, come on. I'll tell you what that big shot college boy did, then I'm going to beat the hell out of him! First, I need a drink."

A few minutes later, Aloysius heard his mother cry out in disbelief. "No, not my Al!"

Aloysius didn't bother listening anymore. He threw shirts, pants, socks, and other clothes in an old duffel bag as fast as he could. He was going to blow this town. He wasn't about to work for that pompous old German any longer. He wasn't about to dig ditches either.

His mother barged into his bedroom.

"Why did you shame us? How could you steal something so valuable? You're no thief! I didn't raise criminals. Didn't your poor brother teach you anything?"

Aloysius threw the duffel bag on the floor. "Aw, Ma, Stop! Stop! I've had enough of Howard! Can't you talk about something else besides him? Yeah, he's dead, but I can't do anything about that, and neither can you! I'm the only son now. Think of me! Talk to me! You don't care if I live or die! It was always Howard, the fair-haired brother who walked on water, for Christ's sake. I'm getting out of this town!"

Margery started to cry as she lumbered to the bed and sat down. The three gin and tonics she drank this afternoon were taking their toll. Her crying turned into loud sobs. "Oh, Aloysius, I love you, don't you know that? If you leave, no one will care for me."

Aloysius sat down beside her and took both of her hands in his. In a soft pleading voice, he said, "Aw, Ma, don't do this to me. You'll be okay."

Her crying subsided to a whimper, and Margery leaned against his shoulder. He sat with her, patting her hands, realizing the runaway plans were shot to hell. For the first time in his carefree life, entrapment became a sickening reality. There was no chance of escaping a very dismal future.

Aloysius wasn't sure how long they sat on the bed, but it seemed like a long time. Margery finally stopped crying. After a few more minutes, Aloysius turned his head in the direction of the open bedroom door. He strained his ears and listened for another outburst downstairs. Evidently, his father's loud rambling had stopped.

Suddenly, he heard a bottle fall to the floor and shatter. A chair fell over, and Howard was swearing. Then Aloysius heard the hall closet door open and close, and footsteps stomping back into the kitchen. The next sound was the drunken roar from Howard, "Hey, assholes, I'm not living in this Godforsaken world any longer. I can't depend on that worthless thief of a son or a stupid, drunken woman. I don't need nothin' from any of you!" The next sound was the back door slamming shut.

The house became very quiet. Aloysius wanted to execute

his next move without waking Margery, but her head leaned heavily on his shoulder. He stayed on the bed, waiting anxiously, contemplating a plan B.

Suddenly, the unmistakable sound of a gun going off echoed for a few seconds in the garage. Aloysius recognized it immediately and headed for the door. Margery woke from her stupor, reaching for him.

"Aloysius, what was that loud bang? Don't go. I'm afraid."

"I'll be back, Mother. Stay here. Please, just stay here!"

He walked quickly down the hall, down the stairs, and into the kitchen, but he stopped at the kitchen table. He figured out the obvious scenario. His father always kept a full bottle of his favorite whiskey on hand, and it seemed his intent to consume it all was complete.

He saw tiny puddles of whiskey surrounding a glass tumbler where his father drank himself into a mindless rage. On the floor, the broken bottle of Jack Daniel's lay beside the chair. The scene was disturbing.

Aloysius grimaced, wondering what to do next. Should he call the police and let them see the bloody mess? Deep in his soul, he knew Howard Hyde Sr. shot himself. He cursed his father for being a coward.

His thoughts turned to the gun. Where did he get it? He was no hunter and didn't appreciate them. The situation was puzzling.

"Aloysius, where are you? Where is your father? What happened?"

Aloysius began to panic. "Mother, please, I'll be up in a minute. Stay upstairs. For God's sake, do as I say!"

He took a deep breath and headed for the garage. He opened the side door and peered in. The overhead lamp above the workbench showed a grisly sight of a man slumped over the wooden bench. What had been a human being was now a lifeless body with parts of a head hanging from it in a pool of reddish white goo.

The surreal events that followed would haunt Aloysius, leaving him with little emotion for the rest of his life. He called the police. They arrived right away, sirens blaring. They found the gun next to the paper bag. Captain Horace Mueller said it was a military issue Colt 45 M1911 pistol.

There was an inquest because it was a sudden death at home. After a thorough search of their house, no other guns were found. The detectives told him that Howard must have kept the pistol hidden and hadn't touched it since the war. The incident was an open-and-shut case. It was ruled a suicide.

The city paper ran the story of the shocking event. In bold headlines, reporter Ed Hatch caught the attention of Hitherton Valley's town folk.

MACY'S DEPARTMENT STORE EXECUTIVE COMMITS SUICIDE WITH AN ARMY PISTOL.

The next evening, Grace waited until her mother and father were occupied in the kitchen and sneaked out to the parlor. Her plan was to call Aloysius, but instead, that very night, he caught her by surprise.

"Grace! Come here," he whispered hoarsely, grabbing her from behind the living room drapes.

"How did you get in my house? Father will kill you barging in like this!"

"I slid in through the open window," Aloysius pulled her further behind the drapes and held tightly to her wrists.

"Aloysius, are you sure no one saw you?"

Aloysius impulsively brought her hands up to his chest, pleading with her. "You gotta believe me, Grace. I'm not a criminal. I took it for you. You deserved it. I was going to pay him. You know that, Grace. Say you love me."

Tears welled up in her eyes. The only thing she could manage to say was, "I do, Al. Now, please let me go. You're hurting me. I must go. I don't want them to catch us."

The words were no sooner out of her mouth when the drapes were pulled aside. Her parents stood before them. Her father saw how tightly Aloysius held onto Grace's wrist. His eyes met Robert Briar's angry stare.

It may have been the coward's way out, but Al made no excuses or words of apology. He released her wrist and wasted no time exiting the living room, slamming the door behind him. He felt a twinge of guilt leaving Grace to fend for herself, but at that moment, he knew her parents wouldn't believe anything he said anyway.

His logic proved to be correct. Grace did try to defend Aloysius, but her father didn't want to hear flimsy excuses. His lecture was brief and explicit. She had disappointed them. As a young lady in society, her life choices must improve from now on, starting tonight. Aloysius Hyde would never enter his home again, and that was final!

Chapter 10

The Final Resolve

Aloysius didn't shed a tear during his father's funeral service, nor did he have sympathy for his mother's hysterics. She sobbed loudly during the Reverend's sermon of hope and life after death. The only thing he felt was the burdening yoke of responsibility hanging heavily around his neck. Knowing that he was the cause of his father's death, shame would be the bitter pill that he would swallow every day of his life.

One day after the funeral, Aloysius sat on a park bench and thought about what to do next. So much was on his mind, and all of it depressing. Seeing Grace was the only highlight of the last few days. He missed her desperately. Over and over, he told himself she must believe in him again.

He also thought of his former job. He made good money at the store. Now he didn't know what his wages would be for doing physical labor. It took all that was in him not to run from his fate.

Cornelius took pity on Aloysius and let him have two days off before digging the drainage ditches around the house. This made Aloysius even more bitter. "Two days off. Big deal. I could have made it out of here if he had given me three days off, the old cheapskate!"

On his last day of freedom, Aloysius decided to take one last chance and try to see Grace. Doubt was eating him alive. He wanted to hear that she totally believed in him. He didn't care if her old man was there or not.

He knocked rather loudly on her front door. Several minutes went by, and he was about to turn around and leave when the door opened. Mr. Briar stood in front of him.

"Good afternoon, Mr. Briar. Would it be possible to talk to Grace? I also want to apologize for the other night. The last few days have been awful for me."

"I understand. I am surprised, Mr. Hyde, that you are standing at my door now. But be that as it may, please accept my deepest condolences to you and your mother."

Although his tone of voice was polite, his manner was not cordial and did not invite the young man in.

Aloysius was shocked by his change in behavior. He pressed on, hoping to cross the threshold. To avoid an awkward moment, he asked again. "Please, Sir, I am begging you. Is she home?"

Robert Briar spoke with a firm voice bordering on irritation, "I'm sorry, Grace and her mother have gone to Europe for a well-deserved vacation. She will not be back for a long time. Now, if you will excuse me, I have business to attend to, so Mr. Hyde, it would be best for you never to call again. Thank you." He immediately shut the door in Aloysius' face.

Chapter 11

The Dream

For the last two months, Patrice Elyce Traffortelli has been trying to get her life back on track. Paranoia crept into her thoughts, wondering what people thought of her front-page notoriety. After all, being assaulted and a witness during a rape trial was not her fault, but sometimes the newspaper articles put a very negative slant on everything! Also, the Whalen Press reporters called her at least once a day for any sensational tidbit about Neil's fatal auto accident. Was he mad about the divorce? How will it affect the furniture company? How would it affect the community?

The restlessness of these days had finally taken its toll. Night after night, snippets of sleep were all that she seemed to capture. One afternoon, her best friend, Judy, laughed at her for not being able to finish three words without yawning out loud. "Good grief, child, get some ZzzQuil before you turn into a total zombie! You know you've had a lot to cope with these last few months. You can't prioritize everything at once. The assault, the rape trial, Grace's dying, and Neil's being killed are more than enough to send a normal person to the funny farm. It's a lot to handle. YOU deserve a chill pill and a good night's sleep."

Pet decided the very next night to take Judy's advice. She popped the small oval sleep aid capsule into her mouth and swallowed it with a glass of water. Soon, a warm drowsiness came over her. A dreamy numbness closed her eyes, and she felt her body drift, far, far away. She felt light as a flower floating on a quiet pond.

For a while, nothingness was her friend, and time stood still.

She felt herself floating aimlessly on what became a wooden raft. Soon, she noticed that the edges of the pond disappeared. The waters flowed and swirled, making the pond bigger and deeper until she could no longer see the shoreline.

She felt the soft wind on her back and imagined her skin as a sail being pushed along by the rhythmic waves. She lay down on her stomach, feeling the cool, wet raft and listening to the water lapping against the edge of it. It didn't bother her that she was totally alone.

High above in the clouds, she thought she could see some gulls, but none came close. The sun was warm, and it felt good. Oddly enough, she didn't know if she was wearing a bathing suit or nothing at all, and that was okay too. She felt contented, free, satisfied to stay there drifting forever. Her hand dipped in the water, startling some goldfish swimming around the raft. Pet laughed. You are adorable little fish.

Suddenly, the waves rolled higher and faster. Sea spray splashed her face. She felt the churning water beneath the raft. A clipper ship appeared and headed straight toward her as it crashed through the waves. The ship's wake was strong, pitching her small vessel in all directions. The motion was exciting.

The clipper ship was in full sail, tall, massive, and majestic. Her three masts leaned into the wind as the rigging hung taut from them. It came close enough to make out the sailors manning the sails. Then it turned ever so slightly with the wind. Pet reached out, beckoning it to come closer. She could see the name *SEA DREAMER* painted on her bow.

She watched its slender hull dip and rise into the white-capped waves. With every rise of the starboard bow, it gained speed, carrying it faster along the horizon. It came closer to her. Men climbed the masts, calling out orders she didn't understand. A young sailor waved to her. She wanted to get on it, to be part of its excitement, its adventure, its beauty.

Then, as quickly as it appeared, the clipper ship turned into the wind and gracefully slipped away. She cried out to the crew,

"Come back. Come back. I want to come aboard your ship! Help! Help! Don't leave me!"

A swift wave splashed onto the raft, catching Pet off guard. She rolled to the edge of it. She tried to pull herself nearer to the center, but she kept slipping. Another wave crashed on the raft and threw her into the sea. Down into the water, sinking lower and lower into a watery womb, she sank, surrounded by little fish and bubbles. Her body stopped sinking. Then, looking about her, she felt a light skirt about her legs. And was transformed into a delicate ballerina. She moved gracefully, with a newfound joy, executing a perfect pirouette. Her body was light, swirling softly, dancing, suspended above a watery stage.

Her eyes became accustomed to the shimmering effect of the water. She began to swim like a fish, darting back and forth, taking in the wonders of her new surroundings. Soon, a large silvery mackerel with large black eyes came close to her. It opened and closed its mouth in a contorted smile. "Why, you look like Anthony Prattmore, but you don't look like any lawyer I've ever seen." It must have understood her and quickly squiggled away.

Next, a huge sea turtle swam toward her. He nodded. His eyes looked at her intelligently. She thought to herself, "My goodness, you resemble my good friend, Harry Trotter!"

No sooner had the turtle left when a dolphin swam up to her. His body bobbed up and down playfully, doing somersaults in front of her. He looked like Detective Iverson.

She moved about, swimming parallel to the ocean floor. The fish were fascinating, and she wanted to see more. Suddenly, an eel with a large gaping mouth and paunchy cheeks snaked its way out of the seaweed. His eyes were a menacing red, and he didn't take his eyes off her. Pet did not like this fish. It scared her. She tried to kick it, but its hungry mouth got bigger and closer. It wouldn't leave no matter what she did.

Out of the corner of her eye, she saw a golden koi swimming toward the eel. The koi nipped at it, darting with quick movements, striking its body. He poked it until the eel left. The koi stopped and winked at Pet. She smiled at him, "Why, he's flirting with me just like Officer Jones does. How cute!" Then, the golden koi quickly spun around, disappearing into a cave.

She felt relieved and smiled, "Well, that was an experience!"

Pet thought, "It's fun and so beautiful down in the sea. I feel like the Little Mermaid! Would it be bad to stay down here? I would have no worries on the sea. I could play and have fun the rest of my life in this fantasy world."

With a sudden jerk, something was pulling her deeper into the watery abyss. Her dreamworld became a nightmare. To her horror, she looked down and felt the strong tentacles of an octopus around her feet! It yanked her legs further into the murky darkness. Where was her beautiful fantasy world? She panicked. "I'll be eaten by a monster! I must swim out of here!" She kicked, thrashing her arms upward with all her strength to free herself from this demon.

With long upward strokes, Pet strained her arms and body to move forward. At the same time, she kicked and twisted her legs, fighting with all her might to free herself. Finally, she saw the sunlight coming through the water above her. She was close! Her lungs burned as she felt precious air escaping. She prayed. I gotta get to that raft, Lord! I can see it. Please let me get to safety! No one else is going to help me! Then, with one last kick, her legs were free!

She was almost to the surface when a brilliant ring floated before her. A beautiful pink and gold ring. Tiny diamonds surrounding the stone sparkled in the watery sunlight. Pet grabbed for it again and again, but she could not reach it.

She desired that ring, and yet she didn't know why. In an instant, she wondered what was more important, the ring or the safety of the raft. In one last desperate attempt, she came within inches of grabbing this prize, but a huge grouper fish had other plans. His gaping mouth opened and snatched the ring in one big gulp, swimming away into the deep.

She felt herself screaming in anguish, clawing at the emptiness. With one last hard kick, she reached the surface. Her face felt the waves and breathed in the salty air. She climbed onto the raft for safety.

Then it was over. No water, no waves, no raft. She woke up with her head under the pillow, the sheet was on the floor, and her pajama top was off, lying beside her. She wriggled out from under the pillow and cleared her throat with a hoarse cough.

"Gawd, that was weird," she said out loud. "Was it a nightmare or a fantasy at sea? The ship was so beautiful. I wasn't afraid." She looked at her hand. It was empty, no ring. She felt a sense of loss. Pet smiled at the thought of surviving, fighting her way back up to the raft. "I've got to tell Judy about this dream. It was fantastic. I bet she'll laugh. I wonder what it all means."

She didn't have long to ponder because her cell phone rang. Grabbing it quickly from the night table, she caught it on the third ring.

"Hello?"

"Hello, Pet. Hi. It's Anthony, your favorite attorney at law. How are you this morning?"

"Hi, Anthony. Well, to answer your question, I'm not sure exactly. Okay, I guess."

"Oh, how come?" Anthony chuckled a bit. "I like the sound of your voice, but sometimes you answer like you are asking a question. Is there any legalese I can help you with, or are you puzzled about something?"

"Well, not really. I was sort of in a daze and not fully awake when I answered. I've had the most bizarre dream. I'm not sure if it was a good one or a bad one. I dream a lot and…"

"I'm not trying to cut you off, Pet, but I'm a little rushed for time. I am scheduled to be in court in a few minutes. Don't lose that thought. We will have all the time in the world to discuss that dream when we go to the Shelburn Room next Thursday, remember?"

"Yes, I'm looking forward to it. Formal, right?"

"Black tie, the whole works. Since Neil's death, so much has happened to the company, and as you are intimately aware, his death has changed your life as well. I can't wait to tell you what has taken place, and for you to meet the board members. But enough said for now. I will keep in contact with you, Pet. I will pick you up next Thursday evening, eight sharp!"

She hung up the phone quite stunned. Her brain wasn't ready to process what had just happened. Out of the fog of a very vivid, weird dream, she had to confirm an important date with her lawyer that could change her entire life. Emotion and indecision always waged war with her logic. The 'what ifs' drove her nuts, and the countless insecurities of 'I just don't know' made her feel immature. This had to stop, but she still wondered if she was going in the right direction toward happiness.

She mused, "Just go. You're committed. Yeah, but I don't like change." She pondered a few minutes longer in her usual state of inertia. She got up off the bed and stretched her arms to the ceiling. It felt good to be standing. She stretched again as far as her arms could reach. The third time, she brought her arms down and forward. The motion relaxed her.

Pet tried to rationalize again. "What could go wrong meeting a lot of strangers in an unfamiliar atmosphere, in unfamiliar territory, rubbing elbows with 'hoity toity' snobs. Don't be a turtle! Get that head out there! Follow what Anthony suggests." She grabbed her robe from the cedar closet and headed for the shower.

With determination, this time she said out loud, "Okay, now, I will go. I should call 'my best bud' in the whole wide world for a coffee this morning. Yes, Harry Trotte will have some sage advice for me."

At the coffee shop, Pet and Harry giggled and laughed like school kids over Pet's new prospects.

Chapter 12

The A Line Dress

Her mood was happy with anticipation. No matter what happened tonight, she would remember this event forever. Then she wondered, what would this fancy meeting place look like? Would it be huge and impersonal, or intimate with soft lighting? She had seen the impressive white marble restaurant many times from the outside, but never the elite Shellburn Room from the inside. The imminent possibilities were exciting.

Sliding the black lace dress over her head, her skin tingled as the dress slowly fell into place. The A-line skirt flared slightly at the hem, and the sheer black lace overlay barely brushed her knees. It was a perfect hemline to show off her shapely legs.

She pulled at the strapless bra and made sure she was tucked in snugly. Pet had no desire to fall out of this dress in high society. She was pleased with the fitted bodice and short sleeves, richly decorated with lace and beading. The subtle décolleté neckline caught her attention in the mirror. The cocktail dress exposed her as a woman to be desired, yet at the same time accentuated a delicate sophistication.

Before she pulled up the zipper in the back, she ran her fingers ever so lightly down the lace, making sure none of the bra hooks showed through. Her fingers met the open V dipping down her back. "Yes," she thought, "everything was in place." She smiled at the thought of men looking at her. Maybe it was a bit naughty, but it would certainly give them something to talk about.

Judy came into her bedroom. "Stop fussing with it. It's perfect. I told you that in the store. You're doing Gucci, or whoever, proud."

"It certainly cost enough, even if it is a knock off. So, you really think this looks okay? Are you sure my bra isn't riding up in the back?"

"No, it's not. Just don't do any toe touches! Your dress is divine, blah, blah, blah! You're also making me jealous. I wish I could go with you."

"Oh, yeah. Anthony would enjoy that. I can see us meeting him at the door. How's this for openers? Oh, good evening, Anthony. You don't mind Judy tagging along tonight, do you? She'll be my bodyguard for this event. Do you like these old rags?"

"You are definitely insane, woman. By the way, how did you get invited to this dinner?"

"Anthony thought it would be nice to meet some of the members of the board informally before the actual legal transfer next month. About every two months, senior members have a formal dinner party downtown at the Shellburn Room. Tonight, they are calling it a Fall Gala."

Judy gave her a little snicker, "Mmm, sounds deelish, and a bit upper class. My, my, we're steppin' out to the big time. Do you think you're ready to assume all this limelight and power?"

"Oh, please, don't make me more nervous than I am now, Jude. I am looking forward to this event, but with mixed emotions. I've got enough phobias buzzing in my head. Don't put any more doubts in there! I wonder how they will look at me. Will they be friendly and accepting? Am I overdressed for this affair?"

"There ya go again. Pet, don't second-guess yourself. I've told you twenty times already. Sensuous sophistication is your look tonight. When they see you, their minds won't be on business. Men's tongues are going to drag the floor tonight! You'll give those old geezers a heart attack!"

Anthony approached Pet's apartment door and knocked casually three times. He felt just a tad nervous, wondering what the night would bring. What would this young woman be wearing? Was she ready for this important social affair? A nervous tickle formed in his throat as Pet opened the door. But when he saw this vision of loveliness, it took his breath away. He was speechless. His gaze was on her for several seconds, taking in her elegant cocktail dress. His eyes started from the tip of her soft blonde curls resting on her shoulders, down her plunging neckline, skipping to her slim waistline and legs, then up again to her peek-a-boo cleavage. He couldn't stop staring at her.

"Pet, you are beautiful! And that dress is exquisite. Black becomes you. I think we'd better go now, because if we stay too much longer there's no telling what I will do next." He gave her an impish grin.

Judy came into the living room. She gave him a wink. "Oh, hello, Anthony. You might have to fight some young studs off Pet tonight. She looks fabulous, doesn't she!"

"Yes, she sure does," he said, taking Pet's hand in his as he drew her closer.

"I just might have to do that." He cleared his throat. "We'd better be going now. Don't want to keep the board waiting."

Helping her with her evening wrap, they were out the door in no time, on their way to the Shellburn Room.

Chapter 13

The Shellburn Room

The ride over to the restaurant was pleasant. Pet listened to the hum of the Jaguar's engine as Anthony maneuvered the sports car through the city traffic. He was telling her an amusing incident involving a nervous court clerk who spilled water all over the DA's briefs. His description of the calamity kept her laughing, which made the ride even more enjoyable. Her uneasiness completely subsided by the time they pulled up to the door. She decided not to talk about her simple insecurities and absolutely nothing about the dream. She didn't want to put a damper on anything connected with tonight's excitement.

She smiled to herself, thinking, 'Would he always be this attentive and amusing?'

Anthony Prattmore broke her train of thought and looked over at her. "Pet, you will be meeting a lot of people tonight. Most of them will be members of the board of the Briar Town Furniture Company. These men and women have been with the company for many years. The President is Aloysius Hyde. You will also meet some of the division managers.

"Do not feel bad if you can't remember everyone's name. You will get to know them in time. I do know for a fact that you won't forget Mr. Hyde's name and face once you've met him. He is a big presence in a room and makes his authority felt. His business sense is outstanding, and it shows in making the company what it is today. I just wanted to give you a heads up." He gave her a reassuring smile and a pat on the hand.

A tall valet came to the car. Waiting attentively for a few seconds, he then opened the car door and took Pet's hand, helping her out of the car. She felt like royalty, and yet, at the same time, a little like a fairy princess.

Once inside, Pet stood for a minute to take in the grandeur of the Shellburn. The large semi-circular building had two floors. The marbled ground floor was a large foyer. An elevator was to the far left, where two huge potted ferns stood on either side of the doors. Her eyes roamed to the right. A dark walnut-framed doorway led to the hatcheck room, where two women stood ready to receive patrons' coats. Immediately, a young woman approached them and asked to take their wraps. He tipped her generously. She gave him a warm smile and spoke softly, "Thank you, Mr. Prattmore, have a nice evening."

Anthony indulged himself in thinking about how good she looked at his side. He smiled at her wonderment as she gazed about the foyer. At this moment, she was Disney's Cinderella wrapped up in a woman's body, but he also wanted her to have the strength and courage of a lion.

He casually ushered her to the right towards the carpeted stairs. He leaned in close and whispered in her ear, "Let the games begin!"

As they ascended the stairs hand in hand, Pet chuckled to herself, I wonder how well he knows Miss Hat check? It seemed like a knowing smile to me, but tonight I'm not going to think about that insecurity. I am a strong, confident woman with a handsome man at my side. Her footsteps were muffled on the thick red carpet as she ascended the stairs.

The restaurant's table area was enclosed on all sides by tall glass windows. Tiny LED lights were spaced several inches apart, outlining each of them. At some windows, large ceramic planters festooned with Peace Lilies added color and warmth to the spacious room.

Men and women were standing about, talking with drinks in their hands, some near the windows taking in the city's view, and some near the bar.

Pet leaned closer to Anthony, whispering in his ear, "This is a beautiful restaurant, very elegant. Any woman would feel like a queen in these surroundings."

"Yes, and tonight, you are my queen. You're not hiding a tiara anywhere, are you?" She laughed and gave him a playful nudge.

"Let's mingle, Pet. I want you to meet the senior board member of Briar Town Furniture Company."

"Okay, here we go, into the lion's den," she said with all the bravado she could muster.

Chapter 14

Gibbie and Aloysius

Gibbie was pulling on the bottom of his white waiter's vest, mumbling to himself. "I feel ridiculous in white. The vests should be black for this occasion."

Aloysius pulled him aside behind the coffee station. "Look, Gibbie. I don't care if you're wearing purple with gold braid trim. Just do what I asked you to do! Keep your ears open. Be attentive to the attorney. If he speaks to Marshall Kochmann over there, give me a high sign. Marshall might want to fill Prattmore's ear about the possible judgment against him. I don't know how many of the board members know about it. Also, listen to what the newbie has to say. See if she asks a lot of questions."

Gibbie, short for Gilbert, was getting huffy with Aloysius' demands. "Do you want me to serve these jerks, or do you want me to take notes? I can snoop just as easily at work. You'd be surprised how much gossip goes on at the docks on A Deck of Briar Town Furniture Company." His upper lip curled in an evil grin. "A lowly clerk like me is a wonderful confidant to disgruntled employees in the shipping department."

Aloysius was losing his patience, but he let Gilbert Seetholder rant a bit because he didn't want the fickle little man to quit on him now.

"I'm only here as a favor to you and to Chef Thompson. Poor man, he was so short-handed. I think he's coming down with a cold. You're lucky I'm very talented and have two professions. I could have been very big in New York City at Sari's, you know. I was a godsend to Chef when I called and offered to help this evening, with your urging, of course. Anyway, I think you're getting paranoid over nothing."

Aloysius nudged him to go,"Yeah, yeah, grateful, too. Just get out there and do your job. I don't want to hear any more of your problems, or anyone else's, tonight. Remember everything you hear. I'll see you later tonight in the back of the restaurant."

"Oh. No cognac, and whispers at the apartment? You're such a shit. You'd better appreciate this."

Gibbie deftly picked up a silver tray of crystal glasses filled with champagne and began serving the guests. He glided around the small groups, smiling and offering drinks. He mentally critiqued the women's makeup and hair. Some young bloods just didn't know how to apply eyeliner and shadow these days. Too much color, he grimaced.

He thought to himself, "Look at these old hag wannabes trying to look ultra-sophisticated. What a nightmare! Is this a freak show or what?" He gave an older woman a drink and offered her a napkin. "Hmm, your liner brush was too thick, sweetheart, and too high on the lid, not fine enough to the edge. Girl, you need tweezing. Oh, my, you really have some Brooke Shields eyebrows going on, and those bangs. Uh, you have no forehead at all! I should really open a salon of my own."

He was as graceful as a reed in the wind, gliding about the crowd with dexterity and aloofness, hearing bits of conversations without flexing a muscle. All the while pretending to be part of this elite group, he loved his job. His tray empty, he went back to the galley area and selected a large platter with shrimp canapés and caviar toast points. He lifted it to his left shoulder and was about to circulate again.

Aloysius came up behind him, "Did you hear anything? Have you served the lawyer and his escort yet?"

Gibbie nearly lost his balance as the heavy tray dipped downward. "Christ, whatta ya doin'? I almost dropped this! No. I'm not even sure who he is."

"Look, Gibbie, I told you. He's the tall one with black hair and the strawberry birthmark at the edge of his hairline. You can't help but see it. I pointed him out to you at the last dinner. Now, do your thing and circulate!"

Before Gibbie left the service station, he adjusted the platter on his shoulder and uttered a half-hearted threat.

"I'd better get compensated for this, and it definitely will be more than money. I could be doing other things, you know. I'd better get that armoire you promised me."

Chapter 15

The Meet and Greet

He brought the tray to serving level and weaved about groups of twos and threes until he caught sight of his target. Extending the platter to a beautiful blonde, he smiled, "Canape, Miss?"

Pet quickly took one, and Gibbie handed her a small damask napkin.

"Thank you. These look delicious." She smiled at him. He nodded politely and smiled back. He did a quick summation of her in his head before he moved to Anthony. "Let's see, eyes, foundation, blush. Yes, you are perfect. Mmm, and that perfume smells divine. You could be on a 'Catwalk' in that dress, fabulous. Just fabulous."

Anthony also took a canape and continued to talk to Pet, "I think the one thing you'll learn about this company is that Grace put together a well-oiled machine. Each man is a perfectionist in his job, but he isn't afraid to share his knowledge on any project."

"Anthony, now I'm really beginning to feel intimidated. Everyone knows so much. I know nothing."

He chuckled and whispered a reassurance in her ear while guiding her to another section of people. Gibbie casually followed a few paces behind them, swinging the platter left and right so people could grab the tasty morsels. He tried to keep within earshot of the two without being an obvious listener. Gibbie cursed Aloysius under his breath for needing him here tonight. This feat was not easy.

Anthony caught James Wingate's eye and nodded, "Hello, James."

The smile on James' face was wide as a Cheshire cat's gleam, all the while appraising Pet as he approached them. "Ah, and who do we have here? Is this the beautiful woman to be added to the knights of the Round Table?"

Anthony said light-heartedly," I think she will definitely be the 'Queen Presiding', don't you?"

Pet blushed. "Gentlemen, you make too much of me. I haven't even perused the kingdom, nor the castle's inhabitants!"

James couldn't take his eyes off Pet's face, but then his eyes slowly took in the rest of her, savoring every detail from head to toe.

With a feigned bow, James said, "I will be honored to be the knight to escort m'lady around the kingdom."

Then Anthony formally introduced James. "James Wingate, I would like you to meet Mrs. Patrice Elyse Traffortelli."

"Mrs. Traffortelli, it is a pleasure meeting you tonight. What a beautiful name. Your presence will truly enhance our company. Welcome."

Pet's blush added to her beauty and heightened James' attention. He would be on his best behavior the rest of the evening, but his male imagination would be running wild with fantasies.

They walked slowly to Aloysius Hyde and Harold Blocker. "Good evening, gentlemen. Nice night for a get-together, isn't it? Aloysius, Harold, may I introduce you to Mrs. Patrice Elyse Traffortelli."

The gray-haired, portly man eyed Pet for a second or two, cleared his throat, and then held out his hand. "Good evening, Mrs. Traffortelli. I am Aloysius Hyde, acting President and Senior Board Member. It's nice to meet you. We will have to make you feel most 'Welcome.'"

Pet gave him a warm smile. "Good evening, Mr. Hyde. It's nice to be here. I'm looking forward to meeting everyone at this company, and I hope to learn more about this fascinating industry of fine furniture. I've already done a bit of research on Briar Town Furniture's Website. I found it very interesting. The presentation was informative and invited the viewer to explore the elegant design of period furniture. The furniture's fabrics looked fabulous. I would like to talk to the committee that worked on this project, unless you subcontracted it to an advertising agency."

Aloysius let out an annoyed cough. "I'm glad you liked it. The whole layout was brainstormed here a few months ago, when companies were expanding their social media ad campaigns. In time, I will present these people to you, Mrs. Traffortelli."

Pet nodded her head politely in agreement. "I would enjoy that very much, Mr. Hyde. You must be proud of your team. Are there many women on it? I've heard that women are exceptional in this realm of advertising because we are born shoppers and we admire expensive things. Whether they are looking for a gown or a piece of furniture, we love that touch of class."

Aloysius strained to control his mouth from blurting out an expletive to cut her down to size. He bowed to her, slightly taking a drink from the circulating waiter, and mumbled as he turned to go. "Yes, I see, shoppers. We will be in touch, Mrs. Traffortelli."

Anthony casually steered her away from Aloysius. "Why did you question him like that? Don't be aggressive with these men right away, Pet. Everything you say tonight will be analyzed three different ways. Don't make them think you've scrutinized the company, or that you will change things right away. Sound interested in what they have to say and nod politely. Don't piss these guys off, especially Aloysius Hyde! "

Going further into the room, they met Harold Buford. Anthony smiled cordially at Harold. "Good evening, Harold. I would like to introduce Mrs. Patrice Elyse Traffortelli."

He immediately held out his hand, giving a jovial chuckle. "My, this is certainly a pleasure." His tone of voice was friendly and confident. It put Pet at ease quickly, and she returned in kind with a smile and a handshake.

Anthony continued, "Harold is second in command, Mrs. Traffortelli. He makes being Vice President of this important company look easy." With that, Harold's round face beamed. His youthful appearance belied his age and experience.

Her voice was energetic as she kept her hand in his. "I'm very pleased to meet you, Mr. Blocker. "

Anthony gave Pet's elbow a little nudge. "We are going to mingle with the other members, Harold. She has a lot of people to meet tonight. Excuse us," Anthony said ever so slightly, steering Pet onward.

Harold took a sidestep to ease their retreat while keeping his full focus on Pet. "Of course, I'm looking forward to an after-dinner schmooze, councilor." He grinned, studying Pet's bare back as they walked away. James Wingate came up to Harold and looked in the same direction. "Beautiful woman," James commented.

"I would say, a blonde bombshell, compared to you, ole boy." Harold Buford said.

James let out a low whistle before Pet and Anthony disappeared into a crowd. James grabbed a cocktail. "She sure looks good from what I saw of her. She has a real fancy name too, but I think I'll call her gorgeous."

In a gruff voice, Aloysius volleyed a warning to James. "Keep it in your pants, whore monger. It's Mrs. Traffortelli, to you. You should know that, asshole. Don't finger the merchandise, either! She's nothing spectacular. That attorney has had many a chippie on his arm before, only this one has a bit more clout." Aloysius gulped down his drink and headed into the growing crowd.

In the next hour, Pet was introduced to so many people that her head was swimming with names and faces. Some people were openly friendly; some were reserved and polite. The wives eyed her cautiously as their husbands tried not to drool into their martinis.

When Pet was introduced to Catherine Hartwell, the

corporate secretary, her manner was cool. Catherine looked upon Pet with the eyes of a serpent studying its prey. There was no warmth in her handshake. She quickly said, "Good evening, Mrs. Traffortelli," in an expressionless tone of voice and didn't try to engage in any welcoming banter. Instead, she reached for a cocktail, sauntering away like a professional snob. Awkwardly, Pet stepped sideways to give Catherine an exit and inadvertently bumped into an attractive blonde-haired young man. The glass of beer he was holding immediately fell to the floor.

"Oh, my God, I am so sorry!" Pet exclaimed. "I hope none of it spilled on your suit."

The young man looked at her and smiled as a busboy came rushing to clean up the spilled beer. He brushed his suit jacket casually. "No, not at all. Don't worry about it. You just made the evening a little less dull."

Embarrassed that she had caused a scene, Pet stuck out her hand to him. "I'm Mrs. Patrice Elyse Trafforelli."

"Nice to meet you, Mrs. Traffortelli. My name is Charles Franklin. I'm in the finance department."

Pet felt Anthony by her side. "Oh, do you know Anthony Prattmore, Mr. Franklin? I imagine everyone knows this gentleman."

Anthony gave Pet a quick look of annoyance, then offered his hand quickly to Charles.

"Nice seeing you, Charles."

"Likewise."

Charles made a graceful move to the bar.

In a low, stern whisper, Anthony leaned into Pet's ear. "What the hell was that all about? Are you purposely trying to make a spectacle of yourself? I told you not to be overly friendly. Nod politely, remember?"

"Accidents happen, Anthony. Yes, nod politely."

"You're a little imp, you know that? I won't be mad at you if you promise to be a good girl from now on." He gave her a big smile and an affectionate squeeze of her hand.

A minute later, Bunny Haskel sauntered up to Anthony and Pet. With a broad smile and her hand extended, she greeted them. Bouncing long curls fell about her face and shoulders. She laughed energetically, whisking a few strands of her hair away. "Good evening, Anthony. It's very nice to see you! Isn't this a beautiful room? I just love coming here, mixing with the upper crust. Who is this pretty woman at your side, Anthony?"

Anthony laughed softly and shook his head at Bunny's informality. He liked Bunny and shared a short bio about Pet. "She is the head of the IT department. She is very computer-savvy and a very intuitive problem solver. The B. S. behind her name in computer science proves it." Bunny gave everyone a big hello and made them feel welcome.

Anthony smiled warmly. "Bunny Haskins, may I introduce to you Mrs. Patrice Elyse Traffortelli. Bunny is our head information systems analyst. She is very good at her job, but one of her best qualities is making people feel at home."

"I'm very pleased to meet you, Mrs. Traffortelli. Your dress is exquisite, and those suede pumps are heaven. I don't think I've seen such an elegant dress anywhere. May I ask where you bought it?"

Pet smiled at her. "Thank you, Bunny. I got it at the new Sashay Shop on 5th Street. It's nice meeting you too. I hope we will see a lot of each other, maybe even at the Sashay Shop!"

Bunny laughed as she brushed her long brown curls over her shoulder again. "I do too. I'm sure we will get to know one another very soon."

Anthony slowly edged Pet away, saying, "Before I become second fiddle to you two fashionistas, I think we should go and meet some more people, Mrs. Traffortelli."

As they walked away, Pet looked back at Bunny and gave her a wink and a friendly nod.

"I hope everyone will be as friendly as she, Anthony. She is so pleasant."

"Most everyone is, Pet. There could be some exceptions

down the road, but for now, I'm sure they will be on their best behavior."

Not five minutes later, Gibbie walked up to Aloysius, spoke a few words, and left him. Aloysius immediately played the host, generously opening his arms wide, saying, "Ladies and Gentlemen, I've been told dinner is ready. Please join me at the assigned tables for a wonderful dinner."

The evening proceeded with pleasantries, French wines, pâté de foie gras, and a sumptuous standing rib roast was presented to this elite group. Pet was impressed.

Finishing the dinner was an elaborate dessert of flaming Lemon liquor poured over crepes. Delicate demitasse cups filled with espresso complemented the ending of a perfect meal. It was the most elegant dinner Pet had ever eaten. She wondered if royalty supped this well.

Chapter 16

Different People Different Stories

Pet was about to politely excuse herself from the table as quietly and unobtrusively as she could, but Anthony gently touched her wrist before she fully got up. “Don’t be too long, Pet. Introductions and announcements are about to start.”

She leaned down near Anthony’s ear, close enough for her bust to lightly touch his shoulder. “Don’t worry, I’m just going to do what is absolutely necessary.” She was gone in a second, but every man at their table had a tempting view of her creamy white cleavage.

Anthony’s gaze followed her. Under his breath, he said, “You’re such a tease, Pet. If I weren’t such a gentleman, I’d do things that would make a pimp blush right here and now.” He knew he was falling in love with her and schemed to be alone with her. These meetings lately have been making it very hard for him to be a refined public servant.

James Wingate, sitting directly across from Anthony and Pet’s table, stopped talking mid-sentence. The view of Pet’s cleavage hit him like a thunderbolt. He almost let out a boyish, ”Wow, will ya look at that!” but he bit his lip instead. The pain of it brought his eyeballs back into his head. “Oh, my God, she is incredible! How did this arrogant lawyer get so lucky to be escorting her tonight? I must have a piece of that.” His brain went wild with different scenarios to draw her into his bed. He admired beautiful women and somewhat respected their professional status, but she startled him to the point of near distraction. He hadn’t been struck like this in a long time.

Marian grimaced, “Are you having a heart attack, James? Your facial expression is weird. You have a look of excitement and pain all rolled up in a potential belch. I've never seen you at a loss for words." Marian Kochmann had her back to Anthony's table. She didn't have the view James just had, but she enjoyed needling his agitation. Then, she immediately turned around, catching Pet as she walked out of the room.

"Hmm, she is very pretty, isn't she?"

James' voice sputtered as he coughed and put a linen napkin to his mouth. He patted his lips quickly and answered her casually. "No, Marian, no heart attack for this boy. My eyes just beheld a vision of exquisite loveliness."

Marian's husband, Marshall, said in a fatherly voice, "One of these days, James, your constant occupation will either land you in jail or the hospital."

Marian chuckled, "Probably both! Sorry, James. You asked for that one. What makes this woman different from the dozen or so you've entertained in the past?"

James struck back but kept his sense of humor. "A bit harsh, ole man. You'll give Marian the impression I don't have a sensitive bone in my body. My intentions to the fairer sex are always honorable."

He looked toward Marian and gave her a boyish grin, entreating her sympathy.

"You wouldn't hate a sincere man in love, now would you, Marian? Where was that kind of beauty when Aloysius and I were growing up? If she had lived in my neighborhood, I would have never left her side."

Marshall Kochmann got up from the table and headed for the men's room. He knew Marian loved a good game of give-and-take and was glad she was enjoying herself. Her upper-class sophistication was authentic and could handle these shallow youngsters with no problem. He was proud of her family's history, tracing back to the very beginning of the Whalen Falls founding fathers.

Pet's approaching smile brought him back to reality as Marshall ambled out to the hallway. He noticed what a graceful walk she had, slow and easy. She held herself erectly like a model, but not aloof.

She spoke with a soft voice, "Good evening."

"Good evening, Mrs. Traffortelli. Are you enjoying yourself?"

"Yes, I am Mr...."

He held out his hand. "Marshall Kochmann, Productions Manager, formerly Corporate Controller. You are at a disadvantage tonight, Mrs. Traffortelli. This group of people must seem like a wave of dignitaries and heads of state without cue cards to help you out. You've probably heard this phrase a lot tonight, but don't worry. I am sure you will put two and two together very soon. You can call on me anytime for a who's who."

She laughed slightly, "I wish I had those cue cards now, Mr. Kochmann. I am afraid of putting the wrong title to the wrong person, or putting a Miss to a Mrs. I hope these people give me a wide learning curve. Have you been with this company very long?"

Pet immediately put her hand to her mouth. "Oh, I'm terribly sorry. I have no right to ask you that. Please pardon me, Mr. Kochmann. I hope I didn't offend you."

"None taken, Mrs. Traffortelli. I can see you are a very sincere person. Your empathy will go far in the company, but don't let people take advantage of this, especially in the business world."

Marshall looked up for a second and caught Aloysius coming into view. He was coming toward them hurriedly, and his expression was not cordial.

"I hope you are not boring our lovely Mrs Traffortelli with a lot of shop talk tonight, Marshall."

"Didn't enter my mind at all, Aloysius. I wouldn't want to ruin her dinner," Marshall said sarcastically. Before he distanced himself completely, the next utterance was more of a warning than a casual observation. "I imagine she will learn the inner workings of corporate America soon enough and know exactly when to weed out all the BS too."

Aloysius smiled stiffly at Marshall and slowly turned away.

Marshall offered his left arm to Pet, showing the way to the dining area. She dreaded going back into the room. All those strangers would be staring at her again. Her eyes scanned the room. She wanted to see friendly faces she knew, but the only one she saw was Anthony's. She hunted for Bunny. She wanted to catch her eye and say, 'Help me. I want to get outta here!'

Still searching for Bunny, she looked over to the bar area. No one was there except the young man she had met earlier before dinner. He was extremely good-looking. She was glad the Armani suit jacket sustained the beer spill. He was rather tall and tan; his sun-bleached hair was wavy and short. His face exuded the look of a GQ Magazine's front page. He looked somewhat bored with the whole event, but dutifully stayed as if waiting for the right time to be dismissed from duty. She wondered what was going through his mind.

* * *

Charles' left elbow relaxed on the bar, and he watched the crowd. He sipped the draft beer with a satisfied stare. He had no intention of mingling with any of them, especially after meeting the over-anxious newbie.

James Wingate abruptly came up to the bar and ordered a double Maker's Mark over ice. Looking at Charles, he said, "Ah, Charles, are you joining us for dessert and brandy?"

"No," he said with a frown.

James took the drink and put a five-dollar bill in the tip glass. "I understand. I am tired of these formal dinners, too. By your expression, you don't look that enthused either." He lifted his glass to Charles. "This will help!" James left and quickly joined the others.

Charles' plan was to excuse himself to the men's room if anyone approached to start a conversation. He was glad that Wingate kept it brief.

He hated these affairs and the people who attended them.

They exuded friendship to everyone but, with a refined finesse, spoke their lines with true art of lip service.

To him, he saw the dinner crowd as cattle lumbering aimlessly about, looking for a watering hole. He watched them with disdain and mentally conjugated the groups in degrees of absurdity. There was the loud false bravado of the social climbers telling off-color jokes to get a rise out of Aloysius.

It made his skin crawl watching the darting eyes of insecure lackeys, wondering who was going to whisper lies about them. But the most insidious ones were the braggers sucking up to division managers, bragging about their golf scores and the perks of newly acquired shares of Fortune 500 stock.

The scene was a painful reminder of his adolescent years watching his mother play queen of the court with ne'er-do-wells at the country club. Endless dances there demanded his presence so he could drive his inebriated mother home before she got sick on the dance floor.

Charles erased the scene from his memory as quickly as he could and ordered another draft beer, thinking that if it weren't for the free booze, he would've left long ago. He made a mental note to finish this last beer and head for the door, but then someone else caught his eye.

He noticed the blonde newbie watching him as she passed by. For an instant, their eyes met. He smiled at her. She smiled at him. Charles thought, "What's her game? Is she a flirt like all the other bimbo's here? Aw, hell, I'm out of here." Charles dug a five-spot out of his pants pocket and left.

Pet watched Charles leave as she walked back to the tables. She didn't see Aloysius approach her.

"Did you enjoy the dinner, Mrs. Traffortelli? The Shellburn has the best chef in town," Aloysius said.

Pet answered abruptly, "Oh, um, yes, Mr. Hyde. Ah, here we are at our table. Thank you."

Aloysius returned to his table, and the speeches began. Pet looked back at the boy. The young gentleman had vanished.

She thought about how young he looked to have such an important position.

Pet began to feel fidgety. She couldn't wait to call Judy and tell her everything that happened. What a "Baptism" by fire!

Chapter 17

The Board Meeting

Anthony Prattmore lifted the cuff of his shirt to check his watch. It was ten a.m. He cleared his throat softly and smiled at the men sitting around the huge boardroom table. Then he pushed the legal-sized papers that were in front of him over to his right and rested them in front of Aloysius Hyde's folded hands. Rising from his chair, he waited for a few seconds and then began to speak.

"Gentlemen, good morning. It is nice to see you all here today. As I promised Mr. Hyde, I have brought the Official Charter of Briar Town Furniture Company and Grace Traffortelli's final Will and Testament. Later, I will go over these papers with you when Mrs. Traffortelli arrives. Aloysius, since you and I have gone over them briefly, you will be familiar with the wording. You will see for yourself that not much has changed from the previous year, except for the new clauses of ownership and decision-making with that authority. Since you are president, I will leave them here for you to show these gentlemen. I have the original. When I return, I will read the important clauses that pertain to the chain of command for everyone seated at this table. Once they are read, if you have any questions or want to discuss anything, please feel free to ask. I am at your disposal."

Aloysius gave Anthony a curt nod. His posture was defensive and rigid as he took the papers. His facial expression likewise gave no hint of cordiality. Anthony waited for him to comment, but he didn't.

Anthony continued, "I am sure you will find the contents clear and self-explanatory. Everything has been outlined in accordance with Grace's specific orders in her last Will and Testament.

"I must stress, Gentlemen, that we can't linger in uncertainty about the company's ownership. It would not be good for our stockholders to wonder who the new CEO will be and if policies will change. We must make this transition quickly to prevent any fear that our stock will waver.

"I hope you will see the new ownership as a good corporate move. I'm sure, after meeting Mrs. Traffortelli the other evening at the Shelburn, you will agree that she seems very capable of assuming her entitlement. I know she will have your utmost cooperation to help guide her in maintaining a financially prosperous atmosphere for Briar Town Furniture Company.

"I have asked her to come here today to attend this formal 'Rite of Passage,' so to speak. I also wanted all the board members and top supervisors of our plant to meet her. I will be back shortly and reintroduce her to you and to those of you who weren't present at the dinner."

Anthony looked again at his watch. "She will be here at 10:30. Thank you."

After he finished talking, Anthony walked out of the boardroom.

Aloysius watched him leave and waited until the door was completely closed. He sat there in thought, slowly rubbing his jaw with his left thumb while his right hand still clutched the documents. His eyes darted back and forth to each man sitting around the table. The low rumble that started in his throat grew into a menacing growl.

"This will not happen! No skinny little twit is going to take over my company! I expanded Briar Town to where it is today. Grace knew I deserved that honor."

Harold Buford and James Wingate watched him expectantly. They sat back in their chairs. Harold shook his head, looking straight at Aloysius. "Yeah, Al, it is a line of bullshit. He must really think we're going to believe him."

Aloysius looked at Harold. "I've had some dealings with Anthony Prattmore. He has handled some business matters for me. I do not think it will be too hard to change Anthony's mind if the price is right.

"As for this little bitch, she is not going to win! She is a gold digger with no qualifications. I will take her down in a heartbeat."

The more Aloysius thought, the angrier he got. He rose from the table and paced a few steps around it. His eyes darted to Catherine Hartwell. "Catherine, I want you to do a background check on Mrs. Traffortelli. See if she has any credits to her name. I doubt that she would have any, but check anyway, and see if you can find a financial background, too."

Catherine said with a vicious grin on her face. "A pleasure, Mein Herr."

Aloysius stopped pacing and sat back down. "You know, I've run this establishment for thirty years with an iron fist, kept it profitable, mind you, and got it to a Fortune 500 company on the NYSE for the last ten years." Aloysius hissed, "I never agree to an ultimatum!"

He coughed and pulled at his tie, loosening it from his stiff collar. Sweat trickled down his cheeks as he held the document tightly in his hands. Aloysius huddled among his cronies; Charles Wingate and Harold Blocker looked on nervously. They thought for sure Al was going to have a stroke.

This agitated state showed a malevolence in him they had never seen before. His bushy eyebrows raised up and down while his white mustache fluttered with each syllable that spat out of his mouth. His fat cheeks flushed red.

Aloysius chewed his last sentence, pounding his fist on the table. "I'll prove Mrs. Traffortelli to be incompetent and easily discredit her."

Harold Buford leaned over to Aloysius. He spoke in a firm, steady voice in trying to appease his agitated associate. "Easy, Al. Listen. Grace was the heart of this place. We know Robert

Briar taught her the ropes. The firm is sound. We believe you know what is best for the company. Nothing can change the history of her alcoholic son and that idiot grandson, Neil. He was just a drunken puppet while he was here. We can't help the fact that he was killed. You'll always be the brains and decision maker, no matter who's appointed. We'll find a way to keep this Traffortelli witch away from the inner workings of our company.

"You told me yourself; our hands are legally tied because Neil was too dumb not to sign the divorce decree. We'll get over this, trust me. She can try to change anything she wants, but we don't have to approve it. She'll never get a majority vote."

* * *

Anthony met Pet in the lobby. She looked radiant and ready to meet the world head-on. She dressed like a young executive in a Yves Saint Laurent powder-blue suit. Her white crepe shell underneath draped nicely into a V neckline, showing a wee bit of cleavage. A small diamond cluster brooch on the right lapel, which Grace had given her, added an elegant sophistication.

Anthony greeted her with a light kiss on the cheek and took a deep breath of her perfume. He had a mischievous grin on his face and whispered in her ear.

"Mmm, you look scrumptious!" Then he smiled warmly and gave her a cheery, "Hello."

Pet immediately blushed and coughed slightly. "Well, hello yourself! Do you always like unnerving women in public places?"

"Not always. Only the exceptionally beautiful ones. Ready to meet everyone?"

With their little fun time over, Anthony brought Pet up to

speed as to what the morning would be about. He told her he would also be reading certain clauses of Grace's Will and what had transpired since Neil's death. As they got closer to the boardroom, Pet strained to hear what was going on inside the room. She looked at Anthony.

"There are a lot of people talking all at once. How many people are in there? What did you say to those men?"

Chapter 18

The Real Aloysius Hyde

While Anthony was out of the room, the atmosphere changed. Department managers were called into the boardroom. Aloysius excused himself and went to the men's room. By the time he came back, the mood of the room had lightened. He even forced a smile and greeted the other employees.

Harold Buford and James Wingate breathed a sigh of relief for now. There was even a soft hum of conversation. When Anthony and Pet entered the room, they were surprised to see so many people.

Anthony played the Master of Ceremonies and introduced Pet to the board members again and to the associates in other departments. When he stumbled on a name, Catherine Hartwell helped him out. Everyone exchanged the 'How Do's' and 'Welcome Aboard' salutations. Then Catherine nodded to them for their cue to exit, and although they would have given anything to stay, these minor characters acknowledged her as they left the room to return to their duties.

After Grace's Will and the rewritten Briar Town Furniture Company Bylaws were read, silence came over the room. No one spoke. Paranoia set in, and Pet had the gnawing dread in the pit of her stomach that these men and women would suddenly get up and leave, or worse yet, start yelling at her all at once. After a minute or two, she looked around the table to see if she could read any signs of negativity.

Two members were talking quietly to each other. One pointed to a certain clause. She recognized Harold Buford and studied him as he took out a small notepad and began making notes in it.

Then, with an abrupt clearing of his throat, Aloysius looked up and immediately addressed Pet. "Mrs. Traffortelli, did you understand everything that was stated in Grace's Will?"

She looked at him without blinking an eye. "Yes, Mr. Hyde, I believe I did."

"Do you realize that you will be responsible for this entire company? You will answer to the workings of our manufacturing plant, promoting our product, its employees, our board of directors, and their combined welfare?"

With an assertive voice, Pet answered slowly, "I think it will be a big responsibility, sir. It is a lot to comprehend right now. I hope I will have committee members to assist me in these matters."

Aloysius' voice got extremely harsh. "I don't want you to misunderstand my line of questioning, Mrs. Traffortelli. I am not angry with you. But, from your answer just then, you don't sound sure at all. There is no time for hesitation. When the president of a company talks to buyers and sellers in the corporate world, thinking is like guessing. Knowledgeable information must be at his or her fingertips at all times. Using the phrase 'I don't know yet' instantly costs the business money. You must know what to do and act swiftly. I can't stress this enough. But, Mrs. Traffortelli, for now, let us not change any policies. The board will continue doing its job, and you won't have to worry about a thing. All will be fine."

Pet felt her face burn. The emotions of humiliation and indignation hit her all at once. Still looking at him, she lifted her chin with a slight defiance. The action prevented her quivering lips from breaking into a cry. She took a shallow breath to quell the rising bile in her throat. Her mind was racing for something intelligible to say. Nothing came. So, she said the only sentence that made sense, even though it showed defeat.

"No, Mr. Hyde, I'm sorry I don't."

James Wingate looked at Pet and raised his hand slightly off the table, indicating he wanted to ask her a question, but

Anthony came to her rescue. He stood up and put his hand gently on her shoulder.

"Gentlemen, I think we should give Mrs. Traffortelli a little leeway here. After all, this is an exceptional amount of information to take in all at once. Even a Harvard Graduate with an MBA would be intimidated by such an awesome responsibility. I'm sure you, Mr. Wingate, and you, Mr. Buford, could set up meetings with Mrs. Traffortelli to ease her into the workings of this company before anything is released officially to the press. For expediency, though, her assumed title will stand for the sake of the stockholders. Any further questions, Gentlemen?"

Each one gave a solemn 'no' with a shake of the head. Anthony had taken the wind out of their sails for now and made a deliberate move to get her out of the room.

After that harrowing experience, Anthony took his time on the way to his townhouse. A block down the street, he stopped at a Starbucks and got two lattes for them. She drank it appreciatively.

"I needed this," she said, relaxing into the plush leather seats.

Anthony gave her a few minutes to herself. Then he looked over to her. "Ready?" She nodded. "Good. I have another trick up my sleeve."

He started the car and got back into the traffic. She was expecting him to take the next left to Commerce Street to his home address, but he took a quick right and went down three blocks to River Road Drive. He knew she liked that area. The road followed the high riverbank overlooking Murtaw Dam.

Pet and Anthony got out of the car. The mid-September day was gently winding down, cooling off the city with a slight Fall breeze. They walked along the walking path until they were in full view of the spillway. Taking Anthony's hand, Pet walked him to one of the park benches. She motioned him to sit with her.

"I love this place. I can breathe here. The world doesn't close in on me. I can hear the rushing water and listen to the birds. Everything here makes sense to me." She leaned back on the bench and became part of it.

Almost to himself, Anthony said, "I know, Pet. Just unwind."

The quiet scene was a visual aspirin. A soft breeze rustled leaves below a Sycamore tree. She laughed at the squirrels as they chased each other. The constant sounds of the dam seemed to wash away all the ugliness of the board meeting. She thought to herself, "Too bad business couldn't be conducted here instead of stuffy board rooms."

There was no need for conversation. It was nice just being alone with him. After a few minutes, he gave her a nod. It was time to go.

He wanted to surprise her with a home-cooked meal he had prepared earlier. His objective was for a celebration, but after the way Aloysius grilled her like a Jesuit, he would have to make it a consolation dinner.

As they came through the door, Anthony watched Pet throw her jacket onto the arm of his couch, then sat rigidly. Her mind returned to reality and the boardroom. "Why do they hate me? What crime did I commit that was so horrible? Are they afraid I'll fire them? Hell, I don't even know them! I felt like a dartboard."

He walked slowly to the couch and sat down beside her.

"Pet, don't worry. They are angry that somebody took their 'fire truck' away. It has been a toy that they have had full control over for a long time. Nobody, meaning the board, can take Briar Town Furniture Company away from you. It is in the Will. Take it home with you. Read it. Take notes. Everything is explained. Things will settle down. Trust me."

"Yeah, but what if they think I'll deceive them and go to you anyway?"

"Now, you're just being a smart ass."

"Yes, but Aloysius Hyde scares the hell out of me. And that phrase, 'trust me' will go only so far, ya know." She looked up at him with her arms folded on her chest.

Anthony just shook his head, pulling Pet closer, surrounding her in a bear hug and a long, loving kiss. But the mood for loving was not there. He sensed it quickly and was disappointed. Removing his lips from hers, he said gently, "As much as I want you tonight, I'm not going to push the envelope. I think you need time to mull things over, and I know right now you're not in the mood this evening. My good intentions would certainly be bruised." He ended those last words with a little smile.

"Bruised? I think you are trying too hard, Anthony, but I will take a rain check. I've got to sort things out. Could you take me home now?"

He nodded and kissed her softly on the cheek. "Sure, Pet."

Chapter 19

Harry's Visit

The days following the board meeting, Pet was lost in thought. Walking around her neighborhood for several days gave her ideas, plenty of doubts, and a blister on her left heel, but no solutions. How was she going to get the board's respect? She needed a friend. She decided to call Bunny for suggestions.

One day, while deep in thought, she began talking to herself. Judy came over and found her in total conversation with the kitchen cabinets.

"Whoa, girl; I don't like the looks of this at all. Who are you talking to? What is going on? You didn't even hear me come in. Your apartment door was open, too."

Pet looked at Judy sullenly. "This doesn't look good, does it? I've really been thinking, Jude. Just when I think I've got a plan in my head, I back down, thinking it's stupid. I must earn the board's confidence. I should have done more research about this company and been more persuasive. They must think I'm an idiot. I know Aloysius Hyde would love to take everything away from me."

They sat around the kitchen table. Judy made her coffee.

"Pet, you have to ask yourself if you really want this company to be your own."

"Of course, I do, Jude. You know I want it!"

"Then fight for it. Call Harry Trotter. He's helped you sort things out before. I don't think he would steer you wrong. Didn't he have a business of his own? Surely, he could give you good advice."

Pet called Harry the very next day. She smiled when he said,

"Of course I'll come over." She felt sometimes that she could trust his experience more than Anthony's.

He greeted her with a big bear hug with all the strength a 77-year-old man could muster.

"Harry!" she hugged back. "It's so good to see you again!" She ushered him into the apartment. "Come in and sit down. I have so much to tell you. Wanna cinnamon Danish?"

"You know, I do and make my coffee in a nice big mug."

It was good seeing him again. She missed their down-to-earth talks. They sat at her kitchen table. "Now, Pet, what's going on? You said something about a Mr. Hyde being mean, the board, the Will, and Briar Town Furniture Company. It didn't make a lot of sense over the phone."

"The problem is, I don't understand all the legal wording. Grace's Will says I own the company now, but Mr. Aloysius Hyde, the CEO, knows I don't have the experience to run it, and he will try to take it from me. I'm intimidated by these people because they are professionals and know a lot more than I do. What can I do?"

"Pet, I have a business adviser who has helped me tremendously in my own line of work. He showed me how to invest and keep the books in order. His instructions were straightforward and easy to learn. I had no trouble filing my business returns with the IRS. In less than a month, I knew what I was doing. If he can teach me, he can certainly teach you. I know he could give you pointers on selecting sound business advisors if you wanted to replace some of those board members."

She gently touched his arm. "And, to think I was scared. Harry, you are an angel! Once again, you have come to my rescue. Oh, I almost forgot to tell you, my parents want to come for a visit. Don't you know? For the last year and a half, I have begged and pleaded for them to come down. So now, at the most inconvenient time, they have decided to come in ten days! I can't say 'not now,' or they'll never want to come again."

He sat back in the chair and chuckled, letting her unwind.

He told her, "One crisis at a time, Pet." He urged Pet to read the Will. She read it slowly and became familiar with the legal phrases. With Harry's explanations, she finally felt confident in understanding the important document. Grace knew what she was doing with carefully chosen words. They protected Pet and the company's future.

He also gave her instructions to start taking classes in Business Management, then Basic Economics. He said, "Pet, taking the little steps is the easiest. From now on, don't be afraid to go to the big guy's office. Be affirmative in asking for a position at Briar Town, possibly in advertising. That is an important department for a furniture company. Get in there and learn the ropes. You are smart and imaginative. I know you can do it. Let's face it, Pet, you'll have to take command sooner or later."

She thanked him with a home-cooked meal. Judy came over, supplying the evening with sidesplitting laughs and ridiculous stories. Judy could make returning a book to the library a hilarious event.

Finally, the evening came to an end. Pet and Judy gave him a big goodbye hug, and he promised to come back very soon. As Harry left the apartment, both women watched him walk slowly down the hall to the elevator.

"Gosh, that was fun, Jude. I needed that. I haven't laughed that hard since high school. I wish Harry were my real grandfather. He is such a loving man. I could have learned so much from him in my growing-up years. He did help me tonight, though. He also touched on something I hadn't thought about since Neil died. He mentioned Grace's mansion. He was surprised that I'm not living there yet."

Judy had a puzzled look on her face. "Is it empty? I thought people were still living there?"

"So did I. In our conversation before you came over, I told him about living with Grace at the manor house. He knew exactly where it was. Then Harry told me that he passed by the Rutherford Manor the other day, and it looked empty. The grounds around the house looked a bit shabby and unkempt. He said the grass was high and the bushes needed trimming. He said snakes love to live in that kind of environment and hoped they wouldn't be in the high grass."

"Yuck! I hate snakes! I wouldn't want to find one there all by myself!"

Pet scrunched up her nose. "I hate them. They're just a wee bit more loathsome than spiders. I'm going to call Anthony and ask him what's up with the house. If nobody's in there, you can bet your ass I'm going to be! Funny, he didn't mention it."

Chapter 20

Gibbie Helps Himself

"What do you mean I can't have it? It's already done, my dear man. I make out shipping order forms all the time. You know that. It's marked special delivery, per A. Hyde cc G.S. to said destination, and out the door it goes. Besides, you owe me that piece of furniture. It's little compensation for one grueling night of pure hell at the Shelburn. I was exhausted for two days. You'd better never do that to me again. You told me yourself the time is right. The store inventory is full, and a few pieces going here and heading there won't be missed. So don't play me, Al. Your boys will never think twice about it. If they question the inventory, I'll say the Boss authorized it!" Gibbie exclaimed.

"You, flaming meathead. I told you to wait until the big lumber orders and the overseas cherry wood secretaries arrive in the loading area. During that time, the dock workers will be so busy they wouldn't notice one armoire being sent to a private home address. You couldn't wait one more day!"

Aloysius shouted so loudly over the phone that Catherine popped her head into his office to see what the commotion was all about. He wanted to grab Gibbie's scrawny little neck right through the phone.

Al's red face alarmed Catherine as he rubbed his forehead. She got him a small paper cup of water and some Advil from the desk drawer and motioned for him to take the two tablets she held in her hand.

Gibbie continued, "I tried to get you all day yesterday, Al. You're not an easy man to find. Those dock workers aren't that smart, anyway. Who's going to miss one little ole armoire?"

"Manny isn't stupid. He's the only one down there who can put two and two together. Let's hope he doesn't have time to check it out.

We do have one item to discuss; the hundred tons of raw material and finished merchandise will be on the foreign manifest docket tomorrow for sorting and pricing. Make sure you keep Manny busy. He will have twenty men and forklifts moving wood all morning. Now, don't bother me again and don't screw this up!"

"Okay, okay. You're such a crab. I just wanted to tell you it was here. You wanted this armoire, too, you know. It will look so special next to the dresser."

"Aw, shut up!" Aloysius slammed the phone down and popped the Advil into his mouth. He looked up at Catherine, who was still standing by his side.

Her voice was calm and soft when she spoke to him. "Al, you'd better start winding this whole scheme up soon. You have too many things going on at once. If you stroke out, we won't get a thing. And, you'd better keep that little man friend at arm's length, too. I hope he's worth the trouble, if he ever..."

"Yeah, yeah, I know. Don't worry about him. He will be fine. Harmless but important. He's my ears on the docks. I need him. It's all going to come together soon. Plans like these must be foolproof. You know that, Catherine. I'm not going into this half-cocked. We'll get rid of that Traffortelli pest. Don't worry."

Chapter 21

Registration

"Please fill out the first three pages back and front. Print your name, then sign your name right underneath on the next line on each page. You can use that counter over there. Then bring them back to me when you pay for your courses, Mrs. Traffortelli. The student advisor, Mr. Applebee, will see you. His office is down the hallway and to the right."

"Thank you," Pet said politely and followed the administrative secretary's instructions exactly. She looked around the lobby as she filled out the forms. Her attire of linen slacks and a white blouse screamed "clueless" to the college scene. The college dress of choice seemed to be sweatshirts, ragged jeans, and Sketchers.

Students milled about the lobby. Groups of fives and sixes came in at once, asking questions, laughing, and filling out forms just like she was doing. She felt as if she were in a foreign country, not knowing what to expect next. Would she understand their slang words? She was so removed from the college scene. For an instant, she felt a bit old.

With the sudden influx of students, she quickly signed her name to all the forms and gave them to the registrar. Pet knocked softly on Mr. Applebee's door.

A voice in the inner office said, "Come in. Have a seat. I will be with you in a moment."

Then he looked up at her in surprise. By his look of amazement, Pet could tell he was expecting another college kid. She handed him her papers and schedule. He didn't say anything until he studied them completely.

"You are very lucky, Miss Traffortelli. You just made the cut-off date," Mr. Applebee said, extending his hand to her.

"Thank you. It was a last-minute decision, but I'm glad I chose to enroll here now. My title is Mrs., but I am divorced. That's why I marked single. "

"Pardon me, Mrs. Traffortelli. I am sorry. My mistake." Handing the papers back to her, he said, "You will see your courses pretty much follow each other. Business Math and Accounting are in the same building behind the Visual Arts Lab. Sales and Marketing are in another building, room 4131, next to Human Services. It is just left of the Library behind Administration, which is right here. So, you almost make a perfect square."

Pet looked at him, a little confused.

He smiled reassuringly, looking down from his horn-rimmed glasses. "Not to worry, Mrs. Traffortelli. There are signposts in front of all the buildings. I am sure you will find your way around in no time."

She thanked him and departed the busy administration area. She took her time walking back to her car. It was a beautiful Fall Day. She felt young and carefree until she saw a police officer standing in front of her car. Pet grimaced. "First day on campus and I'm committing a parking violation!" She quickened her pace immediately.

She got to her car a little out of breath. The officer had his back to her, checking her license plate. "Is something wrong, Officer? Did I park in the wrong place? I'm not familiar with the college yet."

Turning around, Officer David Jones got a big smile on his face. "Not if you are a handicapped person, or you have a handicap card hanging from your rear-view mirror."

"Uh, nope. I don't even have a cane to help me." Then, recognizing him from the assault trial, Pet got a big smile on her face. "Why, Officer David Jones. What a surprise! I'm happy to see you! Do you work here at the college too?"

"No, Mrs. Traffortelli, I don't usually. I had a meeting with the Security Administrator. The station has an affiliation with campus police for stadium events and such. Your sports car caught my eye, parked here without the correct ID. There are more than a few senior citizens and disabled students taking courses. Some people just aren't considerate of the situation. If the same person continues doing this, the car is towed away without notice. I try to help the security guys out. I just can't stop being a cop, ya know."

Her expression was serious as she looked at the offending car. Only now did she see the HANDICAP PARKING ONLY sign staring her in the face. How could she have been so preoccupied and not seen it?

"Oh, I am so sorry. I was hurrying to register for classes. I really wasn't paying attention to parking signs. I will be more careful where I park next time, Officer Jones. And by the way, please call me Pet. I do consider you my friend. I hope you will think of me as your friend too."

She broke off suddenly, seeing the notepad. "Am I getting a ticket?"

David put it in his back pocket. His half-smile and light-hearted tone told her he was most likely bluffing. David Jones would have believed anything Pet said. That gorgeous smile and expressive eyes melted every bone in his body. His thoughts were less professional and more carnal every time he saw her. He paused and collected his thoughts. He mentally praised himself for acting like an officer and a gentleman.

"I'm not going to write this up now, but you will have to be more careful in the future, Pet. And on the same level, you can call me David when I'm not on duty. I would like that a lot."

She looked at him and smiled warmly. "I'd like that, too."

"Hey, how about a coffee sometime real soon?"

She looked up at him with an even bigger smile and was about to answer him when her eyes caught Anthony's Jaguar pulling out of the lower parking lot. He drove slowly down the road, then sped up, crossing the lane into heavier traffic.

Without realizing it, her face turned completely away from

David, and she continued watching Anthony's car. Her answer to David was rather vague. "Yes, that would be nice sometime. Uh huh. I've really got to go now, bye."

Pet's change in behavior didn't bother him that much, but he followed her gaze, wondering what was up with the jag. David gave her a noncommittal, "Okay, I'll be seeing you, Pet," and walked away.

Chapter 22

Anthony and Alyosius

"Why all the cloak and dagger, Mr. Hyde? You could have met me in my office in town. I wasn't expecting a cement bench at Whalen Community College for a talk."

"This was a last-minute decision on my part, Mr. Prattmore. I had to meet the college president about an endowment from our company. So, the timing suited me. I hope it wasn't too inconvenient for you."

"No, not at all. The fifteen-minute wait on a concrete bench was fine," Anthony said, with a bit of sarcasm in his voice.

Aloysius continued, "Well, Mr. Prattmore, after much consideration, I do believe we have a situation here ever since Mrs. Traffortelli arrived in our midst; if something isn't settled soon, it could seriously affect our wallets. My main objective is to serve the best interests of Briar Town Furniture Co. I think you know this for a fact, too. There is no way she can assume full responsibility now. I will not allow her to make any financial decisions at our board meetings. She can be a figurehead, or a puppet, or whatever you want to call her, but most definitely not a governing member in this company. She is immature, a child, and wouldn't survive in this cut-throat world. The pressure would kill her. I'm only thinking of her welfare, mind you, Mr. Prattmore. Draw up a contingency plan for a five-year period to keep her in the outer circles. Bury her in some menial job. Just keep her out of my hair. If you do this, I could make it well worth your while, Anthony."

Anthony was somewhat surprised by the informality but interested at the same time. His eyebrows drew together in thought. Finally, after a minute or two, he said, "I won't demean or take away her privilege of not being able to physically come into the Briar Town building, Mr. Hyde. It wouldn't be ethical or good business practice to do that. On a financial level, I see your point. Let's make it two years instead of five. I will think about this and check into the legalities of your idea. By the way, what kind of compensation are we talking about? May I call you, Aloysius?"

Aloysius stood up. "Yes, certainly, Anthony. I think we can come up with a suitable amount for your trouble. I will be in touch. Oh, one other thing. I must go back to Rutherford Manor. I want to find a small cameo picture of Grace. It belongs to me. See that Mrs. Traffortelli doesn't get into the house for another month. I don't think she would like me searching for some picture after she moves in."

Anthony looked at him in surprise. "Was it in the Will?"

"No, but it has a great sentimental value to me. I would like to find it as soon as possible."

Anthony nodded. "Hmm, I see. I'm pretty sure I can make that happen, Aloysius. I will call you with the arrangements." They did the perfunctory handshake. Aloysius walked away with a limp. Sitting on the hard cement was killing his left hip.

As Aloysius drove home, he congratulated himself on the quick lie. There was no way he'd tell the truth about the ring. It has to be there, somewhere easy to find. Grace loved games of hide-and-seek. Now he just had to find it! He'd be damned if he was going to let that woman get her hands on it.

Chapter 23

Alistair and Fiona Arrive

"Fi, now, wait here. We've gotten this far. All will be good. Don't ye worry. I'll find the porter back inside and ask him if they found your knitting bag. Of all the things ye had to leave on a train! There'll be no more travelin' wi' small bags agin,' woman. Stay here. We don't know what's about this town. I'll be just a bit."

Fiona obediently stayed where Alistair planted her, amongst the luggage. After he left, she looked about in awe. The scene before her was fascinating. She heard police sirens blaring down the street, cab drivers honking their horns, and pedestrians disappearing into various buildings.

She stood against the building, trying not to look so conspicuous with big suitcases at her feet. She clutched her purse tightly because Alistair warned her about muggers. Not ten minutes later, Alistair came back muttering to himself about lost knitting bags. He was about to say something to Fiona when Pet came into view.

Frantically, Pet burst open the doors of the train station. She looked out into the street and caught sight of her parents. "Mom, Dad, why are you out on the sidewalk? I thought I lost you! I told you we'd meet inside the station. It's not safe. There is low life all around here."

Alistair held up his hand, "I know me, darlin'. We'll have to watch ye mother every minute in this big city of yours. She can't even keep track of her knitting bag. I tried to fetch it back, ye know."

"But, Dad, that doesn't explain why you are out here on the sidewalk," Pet said exasperatedly.

"We had to get away from the train. Too many people around us, Pet. We're country folk. We need the breathin' room."

Pet rolled her eyes, bit her lip, shook her head, and ushered her parents back into the train station. She kept telling herself not to argue with Alistair's logic. He was going to do things his way, even if he was wrong. On the way to the car, she chuckled to herself, "This is going to be some visit."

The rest of the way home, she was fully engaged in the conversation. She found out who was still single, divorced, and who was going to have a baby. Her parents enjoyed relaying all the town's gossip. It turned out to be a good day after all.

Chapter 24

The Disappointment

"So, how is it going, Pet? I'm glad I finally caught up with you. I can't tell you how many times I've called. You must be very much in demand!"

"Oh, Harry, you wouldn't believe it. Every day I'm going somewhere, looking at rare exhibits, or eating in the city's well-known restaurants. They've commissioned me as their personal guide to the Pittsburgh region and its surroundings. Thank God, I have GPS, or I would surely be a very lost lamb."

She told him that Fiona wanted to see the historical Strip District of Pittsburgh, which PBS showcased this past summer. Alistair decided he wanted to check out a dinosaur exhibit at the Carnegie Museum. Then the Andy Warhol Museum was added to the list. After those places were checked off the list, Mom said the Phipps Conservatory was a 'must see', exactly in that order. "I'm spending a fortune in gas and parking fees," exclaimed Pet.

Harry laughed. "It is fun learning a city by sightseeing. I know you love it. It's nice of them to take an interest in where you live."

"Yeah, but Harry, I don't live in Pittsburgh!"

He said, "I know, but you probably wouldn't have gotten to see all those places on your own if they hadn't come down to see you, right?"

"I guess you're right. I am having a good time with them. You should have seen my Dad's face when he saw the Campbell's Soup picture. He couldn't understand why it was even put up there."

"I'm glad, Pet. I'm going to see my sister tomorrow afternoon. Do you want to stop by for coffee with us?"

"Gosh, Harry, I start classes tomorrow. Sorry, I can't."

"No problem. How about the next evening? I want to show you that new car they have at the Dodge Dealer on Route 51. It's the perfect color and model you were interested in, remember?"

Pet's voice sank. Again, she had to disappoint him. "Oh, Harry, I'm going to be very busy tomorrow night. I'm surprising my parents with a fancy dinner at the Shellburn Room and a concert at Lincoln Center. I even splurged on front row seats. I think it will be a night to remember. I miss you, Harry. I thought after the trial we would have a lot more time for morning coffee, or evening strolls to Starbucks on Third Street. We haven't had the chance to be together since the night Judy came over. Why does everything have to happen at once?"

"Now, don't worry yourself, Pet. Sometimes things just happen that way. I just thought you might like seeing that car. I've done some research on it, you know, performance-wise and all. This old man will give you some good advice, but it can wait. Maybe I'll hang with my son tomorrow or just rest."

"Are you sure, Harry? I'll make it up to you, I promise."

"That's going to be a wonderful evening for them, Pet. You are a good daughter."

"I wish I could be a better friend to you, Harry. You have helped me overcome many of my fears in so many ways. You have the comforting voice and advice of a very wise man; maybe I should say, like a loving grandfather." She had to stop talking that very minute, because a lump was forming in her throat and she was about to cry over the phone.

"Now, now, don't go getting soft on me, young lady. I know how you feel. We will have more time together. I'll let you go. Call me soon. I'd like to meet your parents before they leave for Minnesota."

"I will, Harry, real soon. Bye."

Chapter 25

Anthony's Dinner

"Hi, Pet. How are you? I've got a surprise for you. What are you doing tomorrow night," asked Anthony.

The question caught her off guard, because she was just about to put a luscious piece of her mother's cinnamon Danish into her mouth.

"Oh, nothing really. No, not yet, Mom." Pet moved her plate closer to her and waved her hand over her coffee cup.

"What? Do I look that old or feminine?"

"No, silly. My Mom and Dad are here, you know. I told you they were visiting for a week. She was offering me some more coffee."

"Oh, yes, I remember now. You know I was just teasing. Anyway, what are you doing tomorrow night?"

"Um, let me think. We have done so much in the last few days. Goodness, how could I forget? I'm taking them to a cantata at Lincoln Center tomorrow evening and then dinner at the Shellburn Room."

Anthony's voice became animated and insistent at the same time. "No, no no! All of you will come to my house for a wonderful, intimate dinner before you go to the theater. You know I make a mean soufflé. They might get a kick out of my expertise in French cuisine, don't you think?"

Pet was halfway disappointed and halfway elated. She really wanted to show her parents the elegant restaurant and what Whalen Falls had to offer in fine entertaining. In some respects, though, she liked the idea of them meeting Anthony.

She asked Fiona, who had been listening to every word they spoke, "Mom, would you and Dad like to meet my friend, Anthony Prattmore, for dinner at his house before we go to the theater?"

Fiona's eyes lit up. Alistair stopped reading the paper for a second. Without looking up, he said, "As long as me stomach won't be a growlin' from too rich a fare. You know how it reacts to highfalutin' foods and the like."

Fiona countered his worries immediately, "Now, Alistair, mind you, you'll be fine. Ah, won't that be lovely, dear, an elegant dinner in a bachelor's home."

She grinned at them. "It's unanimous, Anthony, we will be at your house promptly at six. Thank you. Your invitation is very gracious."

She could hear him laugh, "Your parents sound like a fun couple, Pet. I'm glad you are coming."

She was a bit disappointed not to go to Shellburn, but maybe this would be an opportunity to ask him about Rutherford Manor. How could he deny important information in front of her parents? Maybe he could show it to them before they left. Then her parents would know what a grand place she would be living in and no longer worry about her future.

The following night, after dinner, Pet found it hard to concentrate while driving to Lincoln Park. Yes, it was nice, but something was different. She was annoyed with his fastidious obsession with details. She had never seen him act that way before. Did the forks really have to be exactly a half an inch from the plate? Another annoyance was her mother's prattle. It was a constant drone about Anthony this and Anthony that.

"Oh, my what a lovely house he has. Wasn't his silverware elegant, and the damask tablecloth immaculate? It accented the beautiful plates and crystal goblets perfectly. Why, it was a picture out of *House Beautiful,* it was. Don't you think, Alistair? Everything shone so!"

Alistair finally chimed in, "Yes, Mother, like a new penny, it did. The beef and potatoes with the pot liquor gravy were fit too. I'll wager that spread set him back a day or two. Does he always eat like that, lass? Did he cook it, too? Seemed too perfect for a man to be putting on airs with fancy wines and table dressings and all. Do ye eat often with him?"

Pet made a quick right onto Eighth Street. "What, Dad?"

"Does he feed ye all the time now?"

Pet suddenly slammed on the brakes. Traffic came to an immediate halt. A crowd had gathered near the E Street Police Station. An ambulance pulled around the car in front of her.

"Could ye give us a blessed sign before ye slammed on the brakes to send us through the windshield, lass!"

"Sorry, Dad. I didn't want to ram into the guy in front of me. I HAD to stop fast. Something's going on. Someone's in trouble."

She watched the crowd part to one side as the paramedics took out a stretcher and hurried toward a man lying on the sidewalk. She automatically craned her neck to see if she recognized anyone.

Scanning the crowd, she noticed an older gentleman out of the corner of her eye. He walked quickly toward one of the paramedics assessing the patient. He looked vaguely familiar to Pet. She watched the older man gesture wildly as he approached the scene.

A light bulb went off in Pet's head. "Hmmm, blue jacket, khaki slacks, slightly balding, oh, my God! That is Jack Oberti, a friend of Harry's." Her next realization startled her. "Where's Harry?"

She unfastened her safety belt and put the car in park. "I have to go. I have to see if Harry is in trouble. I'll be back."

"But, lass, stop! Do ye think it sensible, now? "

"I have to go see, Dad. I'll be back. Wait here, please."

She gave them no time to argue and bolted out of the car. She walked quickly into the crowd, saying excuse me several times. The onlookers moved aside reluctantly and let her reach the paramedic.

Pet moved in closer. "Please, Sir, I think, OH HARRY, WHAT'S WRONG? WHAT HAPPENED?"

Harry made no acknowledgment of her presence, or if he had even heard her voice. He lay there very still, and a slight moan came from his lips.

The paramedic was kneeling over Harry, opening his shirt as he did so. He was about to put the stethoscope on Harry's neck when he felt Pet close to him and looked up.

"Are you a relative of his, Miss? If not, step back. I don't have time for hysterics right now. "

"No, I'm not a relative, but I'm a close friend of his. His name is Harry Trotter. He has a sister," she blurted out.

"Do you know how old he is or any medications he might be taking?

"He is about 75 years old, I think, and I don't know what medications he is taking. He should have his wallet with him."

Pet was about to kneel down beside Harry when the paramedic suddenly told her to move.

Without looking to see if anyone was behind her, she bumped into another person in the crowd.

"Scuse me," the male voice said, "Pet? What happened? "

She turned to face a police officer.

"Oh, David, I mean Officer Jones. I'm sorry. I don't know much, Traffic stopped. I got through the crowd and saw Harry lying on the sidewalk. I recognized one of Harry's friends."

Jack Oberti was standing nearby and approached them. "Can't tell you much, Officer. We were walking, see, an' Harry grabs his chest. All of a sudden, bam! He falls to the sidewalk. Didn't say a word. Didn't tell me he was gonna quit breathin' on me!"

Pet shot a quick glance at Harry. Did his eyes just open? Did he see her? For an instant, she thought he winked at her. Then, paramedics lifted him onto the stretcher and proceeded to put him into the ambulance. One of them turned to Pet while he talked. He adjusted the oxygen mask over Harry's mouth.

"We're transporting him right now to St. Vincent's ER. His pressure is dropping fast. You and that other gentleman can follow. If you know any of his immediate relatives, you'd better call and get them to the hospital without delay."

For a minute, Pet felt helpless and torn over what to do next. She desperately wanted to follow the ambulance, but obviously couldn't because of her parents. She should go to his sister's apartment when she gets home. What if she wasn't home? How could she get in touch with his children? Surely, Harry would have something written down in his wallet as to next of kin.

Officer Jones saw the anxiety in Pet's face and lightly touched her arm. "Pet, I'm going to give them an escort to the hospital, so the traffic won't snarl up again. If there's anything I can do, let me know."

She nodded her head and walked quickly to the car. Her silent prayers were intense: "Dear God, let him be okay. Harry looked so bad. I must go to him. I wish I hadn't asked Mom and Dad to come down to visit me now. God, let his sister be home."

Chapter 26

Cubicle Three

By the time Pet got to the car, traffic had cleared away. She didn't waste any time heading down E Street.

"What is it, lass? Who was lying there? Was he dead?"

"Dad, please! I know that man, and he's a very dear friend! You shouldn't talk that way about people you don't know."

"Sorry, Pet, my dear lass, don't get yer panties in a bunch now. I'm sure the good docs over there will fix him all up. Maybe ye shouldn't go. Don' na be in their way now."

Pet shook her head in frustration. Alistair Teaseling had a way of simplifying a grave situation. She would have to be very direct with him so he would understand her concern for Harry. Alistair always tried to protect his little girl from frightful situations.

The rest of the way home, her parents spoke more about the happenings in her old neighborhood. Fiona giggled when she related the scandal between Mrs. Monahan and Clyde Harrison. Alistair hushed her quickly, saying, "No good comes from spreading trash about the streets." But Fiona just kept laughing at Alistair's indignation with it all. It was a brief distraction, and it helped Pet calm down.

Once inside her apartment, Pet half-apologized for having to rush off again. "Mom and Dad, do you think you could entertain yourselves for a bit while I go to the hospital? I must see if Harry's sister is home and wants to go to him."

"Pet, dear, doesn't he have a wife or children? My goodness, surely, he lives with someone. From what I could see, he looked awfully old," Fiona said, gently patting her daughter's hand.

"Seventy-five isn't that old, Mom. And no, his wife died

several years ago, and he lives alone. His children live somewhere around here, but I never met them. He never got around to telling me about all their particulars."

"Sounds a bit fishy to me, girl. What do ye mean by carrying on with an old gent like that? He's not one of those sly buggers a goin' after the young ones, now, is he?"

Pet groaned out loud, "Aw, Dad, please listen to me. Harry was the second truest friend a woman like me could have. He helped me get through that awful trial with wisdom and the tenderness of a loving grandfather. He stopped me from running away from this city. With his help, I grew up and faced my fears. So, don't judge people you don't know."

Alistair was taken aback and humbled himself. "Hmm, I guess my girl knows her mind. I didn't mean to judge ye, lass. Okay, go. See to this man named Harry. May the Lord keep him in good grace till ye get there. We'll be fine. Ye might even be back for us to catch the last part of the concert."

She stopped short in the middle of the living room. Her eyes got wide as saucers. "Oh, my God! I forgot all about the Whalen Cantata tonight! Damn! I promised to take you tonight. I would hate for you to miss this. Let me think for a second."

Pet hated to impose on Anthony, but who else would take them? Judy would rather gulp down turpentine than listen to anything classical. Well, Anthony, looks like you're up.

"Mom, Dad, you wouldn't mind going to the concert with Anthony, would you? I'm going to ask him now."

Fiona answered with a girlish grin. "Why no, dear. He is such a handsome man to be escorting us two to the theater, and he is so gracious. You can tell him we would be pleased if he would oblige. That is all right with you, Alistair?"

"I guess yer mind is made up. There's no goin' agin' ye girlish ways."

"Good, I'm calling him now. I just hope he doesn't have other plans."

Anthony picked up the phone on the first ring. Relief

couldn't have been sweeter when he said yes to her request. He had planned to go over a brief for court tomorrow, but he understood her predicament.

"I'll be over in twenty minutes or so, Pet. Don't worry. Harry has been good to you, and he's a good client of mine. You need to go to him."

"You are a lifesaver, Anthony. I am in your debt. I will give Mom my ticket for you. If all goes well and Harry is stable, I will meet you at the theater door after the concert. Thank you so much. I... I will see you later."

Alistair could never refrain from giving her advice, "Pet, me lass, don't be speedin' now. I know that lead foot of yours. Ye give a speeding bullet competition!"

Walking out the door, she assured Alistair, "I'll be fine. I promise I won't drive too fast. I'll be back as soon as I can. I love you both." She also mentally forgave his blunt assessment of Harry.

She walked down the hall to Clementine's apartment. She knocked, and Clementine hesitantly opened the door. Pet told her who she was and explained the situation simply without emotion. When she finished speaking, Clementine neither spoke nor indicated that she understood what had just happened. She just stood there.

Finally, a look of recognition came over her face. "Harry? Oh my, is my brother, Harry, sick?"

Pet said urgently. "Yes, Clementine, how can I help you? Do you want to come with me to the hospital? We must go quickly. The hospital needs a lot of important information."

At this point, Pet gently opened the door wider and walked with Clementine into her living room. She ushered her to a couch. Still, she showed no sign of wanting to go with her.

"I have to call Fred. He'll know what to do."

"Who is Fred? Is he Harry's son? Can I call him for you? We mustn't waste time."

"Yes, his son."

She pointed to a large white notepad on the end table beside the phone. Pet reached for it. Phone numbers with their corresponding names were printed in bold. Pet found Fred's name.

"This one, Clementine?"

"Yes, dear."

Pet dialed. After several rings, she was ready to hang up.

"Hello."

"Hello? Is this Mr. Fred Trotter?"

"Yes. Who is calling, please?"

"Mr. Trotter, I am Mrs. Traffortelli. I live down the hall from your Aunt Clementine. I hate to ask you this so bluntly, but has St. Vincent's hospital called you about your father?"

"No, I just got in the door as I answered the phone."

"Mr. Trotter, it is important that you go there. Harry has taken ill. He collapsed on E Street while he was walking with his friend. I don't know his exact condition, but it seemed very serious. I know that Clementine is Harry's sister, and I came to see if she wanted to go with me. "

"Thank you, Mrs. Traffortelli, you have been very kind, but do not take her with you. She is afraid of crowds and unfamiliar places. She is very unsure of her footing and falls easily. I will call my two brothers and sister to go to the hospital. Fortunately, they live close to the hospital and will get there quicker. Tell my aunt I will be there shortly. Thank you. Goodbye."

Feeling stressed, Pet arrived at the immense ER facility of St. Vincent's Hospital. Patients in wheelchairs in all states of calamity were everywhere. She asked a nurse for directions and the whereabouts of Mr. Harry Trotter. Pet was directed to the cardiac trauma unit. When she finally found it, there was another huge waiting area. Families were seated, or stood, huddled in clumps everywhere, waiting to hear news of their loved ones.

The area was separated from the trauma unit by large, automatic glass doors. A reception desk was to the left, about six feet from the doors. She came to a complete stop when she read AUTHORIZED PERSONNEL ONLY.

Behind the glass doors, she watched orderlies and nurses push carts and IV poles into the cubicles. Doctors were being paged overhead to go to the Cardiac Trauma unit immediately. The clerk at the registration desk answered one call after another, totally ignoring Pet's effort to get her attention.

Finally, the clerk looked up. "Can I help you? Are you looking for someone, or are you a patient?"

"I'm looking for a patient by the name of Harry Trotter."

The registration clerk looked at her screen. "He's in cubicle three, ma'am."

"Can I go see him? Is he okay? I am a good friend of his. Has his family arrived yet?"

"I can't answer any of your questions now, ma'am. Let me check with the nurse first."

The registration girl answered three more calls. A matter of at least ten minutes had gone by. Pet was about to go through the door herself when the clerk finally got up and headed for one of the nurses. She watched the clerk speak briefly to one of them. Suddenly, the nurse broke off the conversation and rushed into cubicle three. As the big doors opened, she saw two men and a woman emerge from the area. They walked hesitantly to another door marked FAMILY ROOM.

Overhead, a loud, piercing voice announced CODE - ONE - CARDIAC - TRAUMA - THREE, CODE - ONE - CARDIAC - TRAUMA - THREE. Another orderly and a doctor ran in. A respiratory technician followed, pushing a cart with syringes, tubing, and resuscitation equipment.

Pet strained to see beyond the partially open door. The people standing in the room held onto each other. The woman was sobbing. Pet thought they must be his children. She wanted to go to them, but what could she ask them except the obvious? What happened? Or something worse, like, is he okay? Duh, of course he ISN'T OKAY! How lame.

The doctors and nurses worked on him for at least twenty-five minutes. No one came out of the cubicle. No one came to give information. They just heard orders: IV push, bag him, one, two, three, four, five, paddles, contact, clear, again, again. The succession of orders was repeated three times. Then there was an agonizingly long silence. Minutes later, footsteps were heard as equipment was moved back to the cubicle wall. An authoritative voice asked, "Time?"

"7:45 pm, Doctor."

Finally, a nurse emerged from the cubicle and headed to the family room. She put on a weak smile for them as she entered.

Pet looked at the clerk in desperation, "Can I go back there with those people? I am a good friend of Harry's. I must find out what happened." With tears brimming in her eyes, she asked softly, "Is he dead?"

The clerk sighed an irritated hiss. "Let me get the supervisor. Don't follow me. You can't come in unless you are given permission. Wait here."

Pet was losing her patience, too. "Yeah, yeah. I understand. Please tell her that I'm his good friend."

She got up from her desk and went through the door. Over her shoulder, she said curtly. "Yes, ma'am, heard you the first time."

Pet stood helplessly at the desk. She felt out of place, yet was afraid to go anywhere else. She muttered in a low voice, "What an insolent little brat. She doesn't belong in this unit. She has no compassion at all!"

David Jones walked into the area looking for someone when he caught sight of Pet and walked up behind her.

She immediately faced him, "Oh, David, she won't let me go to them. It's just that..."

Then the strain of impending doom caught up with her. A flood of tears poured down her face. She sobbed and talked at the same time. "She doesn't care. I don't know if he's dead or alive. The family was sent to a special room. I must see if..."

Very subtly, David guided her to a chair. He had decided he was going to be all kinds of happy with funny jokes and cheery smiles for Pet the next time he saw her. Now, those ideas were dashed. He must console her and act in an official capacity rather than as a lighthearted acquaintance. He directed her to that all-too-familiar FAMILY ROOM.

"Wait here. Let me see what I can do."

David knew this unit. He had brought too many gunshot wounds to this place and walked too many parents to that special room. He walked through the doors without question. An authority had its privileges. He was greeted by a very tall, attractive nurse. She smiled at him immediately and nodded her head as he explained the situation. She followed him to the waiting area, where Pet was sitting.

"Mrs. Traffortelli, I understand you know Mr. Trotter. Do you know his family?"

"No, not personally. But Harry told me so much about them that I feel I do know them. Please, can't you tell me about his condition?"

"Since this is an unusual situation, Mrs. Traffortelli, I think I can make an allowance here. I'm the nursing supervisor for this floor. Let me ask the family if I can tell you what has happened, and then if they wish, I will let you go back to them. Please wait here. I will return. The doctor is with the family now. "

Pet let out a sigh and gave her a weak smile. "Thank you," she said softly. She was at least more compassionate than that other person.

"This is awful. Harry is too young to die. He's such a good friend. Sorry about being familiar. I should've said officer when I addressed you since you are in an official capacity."

"Don't worry about official stuff now, Pet. This situation is a little different. You can call me David, Pet. I think we know each other well enough by now. What do you say, hmm?" He gave her his best smile and sat down beside her.

Pet studied his face. "You know he's not alive, don't you, David?"

"Pet, I can't tell you until she comes back. She'll be here soon." Just as he finished his last word, Miss Cuttsbeth was in front of them. By the look on her face, Pet knew. She knew the awful truth.

"I'm sorry, Mrs. Traffortelli. We did everything possible. We just couldn't save him. If you would like to talk with his family, they are still in the family room waiting to see Mr. Trotter before the funeral director comes. You may go back and see them if you wish."

Sobbing, Pet stood up and nodded yes. David stayed back. Miss Cuttsbeth knocked on the door and opened it. The woman came toward her and said softly, "I'm Harry's daughter, Amy." Then she opened her arms, and they embraced, crying together.

Amy patted Pet softly on her back. "There, there, Mrs. Traffortelli. It's alright now. He knew his time was coming."

"He kept walking, though. He never told me how bad he was."

"My father wouldn't have told anyone anything, even one of his closest friends like you. Yes, Dad told us all about you, Mrs. Traffortelli. He liked you. He said he adopted you as another loving granddaughter."

"He was so gentle and kind. I thought of him as my special grandfather. He endeared himself to me, and I to him. I don't understand why someone so good and loving had to die. I feel lost. I didn't get the chance to say goodbye. I will miss him."

She tried to stop crying. Her daughter was being so nice to her and so brave, trying to cheer her up. The two walked to a couch and sat down. The two brothers stood against a wall, speaking softly to one another.

A few minutes later, Miss Cuttsbeth softly knocked on the door.

"The gentlemen from Mattingly Funeral Home will be here very shortly. You may go back into the cubicle before they come."

His sons stopped talking and immediately followed Miss Cuttsbeth. Amy rose and followed her brothers. Pet looked up to Amy, pleading with her eyes for permission to do the same. Amy nodded..

Solemnly, as if in a procession, the four of them entered the cubicle. Pet did not know what to expect. She was a bit apprehensive and wondered what went on during a cardiac arrest. What did they do to Harry to bring him back to life? Would his face be ashen and distorted? Would he have a painful look about him?

The scene that they beheld was soft and serene. Instead of a face contorted, his expression was peaceful, as if he was sleeping, perhaps dreaming a lovely dream. His skin was a soft pink, and his hair was combed and smoothed. Harry was wearing a blue hospital gown. A white sheet and a thin blanket covered him from his chest to his feet.

For a bizarre minute, she thought he was alive, and it was just a mean joke the hospital was playing.

Disbelief made her want to ask, "Are you sure he's dead?"

With respect for the moment, she didn't utter a word. She had cried enough and submitted to death's reality. The next thing she heard were footsteps and low voices.

"In here, gentlemen, cubicle three."

Chapter 27

The Resolve

Still sniffling, she blew her nose and slowly walked into the hallway. She heard someone cough and looked up to see David standing a few feet from her.

A bit surprised, Pet asked, "David, why are you still here?"

"I wanted to see if you would be okay. Even though I don't think he was a close relative of yours, he must have meant an awful lot to you. Death's emotional shock sometimes strips away rational thinking, not paying attention to things. I didn't want anything to happen to you on the way home. Are you by yourself?"

"Yes, I am. You are so kind and thoughtful. It is good to see a friendly face in front of me right now. Got a minute?"

She didn't wait for his answer. She just walked over to a bench a short distance down the hall. David followed without answering. Her gaze was random. Her eyes were glassy-eyed, staring out into space; when she talked, it was to the floor, half mumbling, half whispering.

"I feel like I'm stuck in a state of inertia. My feet feel like lead weights. My mind is in slow motion. Even though this place is where he died, I don't want to leave. Maybe if I stay here long enough, these last few hours will change. Nurse Cuttsbeth will come out and tell me I can go in and see a smiling Harry Trotter."

She stopped abruptly, biting her lower lip, trying not to cry. Then she blurted out, "Oh, David, do you think they tried everything to save him? I don't know, I'm not a nurse. I didn't have a chance to say…"

Then a flood of tears started once again. He moved closer

to her and held her in his arms. Professionalism be damned, he thought. This is an exception to the rule.

Pet clung to David until she emotionally accepted the fact that Harry was gone. It felt good to be in the arms of a strong young man and feel secure in his embrace. David patted her back, softly talking to her, reassuring her that it was going to be okay. Finally, he told her he had to leave. They exchanged phone numbers.

She watched him walk down the hall, liking him more every time she saw him. Sighing, she came back to reality. Pet had to move on and prepare herself for another sad event, the funeral.

Chapter 28

After Talk

"I was waiting, hoping you would be able to meet us at the theater, Pet."

"I know, I couldn't bear to tell you or Mom or Dad what had happened. I was so emotionally drained, Anthony. I went straight home. I really appreciate you taking them to the performance and seeing them to my apartment building. I hope you enjoyed it."

"Yes, yes, I did. Fiona is a prize. She was interested in Whalen Falls and thinks it is beautifully quaint. She has even told her brother back in Minnesota about our fair city. I think she referred to him as Pet's Uncle Mike. So, I told her as much as I knew from my ten years here. She also kept the conversation going by asking many questions about my professional background. She made me laugh, because she has such an endearing way to find out personal information too."

Pet grimaced at the mention of Uncle Mike's name, the lovable but loose cannon of the family. "Oh no. Uncle Mike. I hope she didn't tell him too much about Whalen Falls. Uncle Mike is very curious. Oh, what does my mother know about attorney Anthony Prattmore that I don't? I hope you did not feel interrogated. Mom is good at getting secrets from the unsuspecting ones."

"Well, I won't go into it over the phone, but she asked if my parents were still living, where they resided, and how many brothers and sisters I had, or if I was an only child."

"Goodness, she may know more than I do. You will owe me some prime time, Mr. Prattmore. But anyway, both Mom and Dad said it was an enjoyable evening. Mom said you were her prince, her knight in shining armor. She loved the attention and your gallantry. She couldn't stop talking about your knowledge of classical music and the different composers. Dad was impressed by how you handled the Mercedes in city traffic. He likes fast cars, too."

"Do you know the funeral arrangements yet?"

Pet sighed audibly, taking a long time to answer him. She spoke slowly, "No, but his daughter, Amy, said she would call me sometime today."

"Pet, what else is going on? You don't sound sure of yourself."

"Well, besides the funeral, I have a lot of planning to do. My parents were going to leave on Thursday, but they have decided to stay for another week or so. Mom said they would stay a little while to cheer me up. Besides, she says, it wouldn't be fittin' to go on such a sad note.

I'm going to be pulled in about five directions in the next few days, and school is going to take up a lot of that time. I thought I was going to have at least two days to myself, but now with everything that has happened, I won't get that luxury."

"I can understand. Family can be wonderful until they get in the way. Listen, I have to go. I'll be in my office this afternoon. Call me. Don't worry, Pet. It will work out."

"Yeah, I know. Call you soon. Bye."

Chapter 29

On a Whim to Briar Town

Precisely at the stroke of twelve, the solemn sound of the bell in the tower of Christ Church First Presbyterian echoed throughout the town of Whalen Falls. The pallbearers on each side slowly rolled the casket up the aisle. The family followed in silence. The church was almost filled. Pet had never seen so many people paying their respects to a good friend.

Although emotional, the service was uplifting. The minister praised Harry's good works to the community and spoke of the love he had for his family. The music couldn't have been more fitting. The first hymn was "How Great Thou Art," and then the funeral choir sang a beautiful rendition of "My Shepherd Will Supply My Every Need."

As the familiar hymn was played and the choir joined in, Amy sobbed on her husband's shoulder. The music was so beautiful that no one could be immune to its influence. Even her two brothers broke down, but only for a few minutes. Pet guessed that there wasn't a dry eye in the church because her own emotions were overflowing, too.

Pet stayed for the luncheon afterward out of politeness for the family. Sitting alone at a table in the big church hall, she regretted it instantly. She didn't know a soul there except Harry's family, and that was just by happenstance at the hospital. A few of the church women offered her coffee and asked if she was new in the congregation. Pet answered immediately that she was just a friend of Harry's.

She rose from the table and scanned the room for Amy. She wanted to give her a good-bye hug. Out of nowhere, she heard a male voice. "Mrs. Traffortelli, I didn't know you knew the family."

Pet froze in her tracks, looking directly at a tall, handsome man. She said a soft "Hello."

"Excuse me. I'm sorry if I caught you off guard, Mrs. Traffortellli. I'm James Wingate, vice president of Briar Town."

She put her hand to her mouth. "Oh, forgive me, Mr. Wingate. This is the second time I'm meeting you. I should have recognized you, but I wouldn't expect to see you here, knowing Harry. How did you know him?"

"Harry and my father go way back. They played golf for a long time down at Lake View Country Club. When Dad stopped playing, I filled in for him. Harry was a great golfer in his day."

Pet continued to search for Amy. "Oh, that's nice. I think Harry must have done everything well, even a game of golf."

James smiled and put on the charm. "Yup, that was Harry. Could I get you a cup of coffee, or a piece of pie?"

"Thank you, Mr. Wingate. I feel rather out of place. I think I'm going to leave. I really don't feel comfortable talking to people I don't know very well, especially at a funeral luncheon. I must find Harry's daughter, Amy. Have you seen her?"

Their eyes searched the room together. James saw Amy first.

"Wait here, I'll bring her to you." James walked over to Amy. They conversed for a second or two, then they came to Pet.

Both women fought back the tears as they embraced. Amy and Pet found an instant camaraderie in the death of Harry, the loss of a loving father, and the loss of a good friend. They hugged. Pet spoke first.

"Oh, Amy, you've been so kind to me. Thank you for letting me come to the luncheon, but I'm afraid I must be going. My parents are in town and I…"

"You don't have to say another word, Mrs. Traffortelli. Go. Every minute will be precious with them."

"Yes, I know that now, Amy. Thank you again."

She turned slowly, picking up her purse from the table, and walked toward the exit. A minute later, James Wingate gave Amy a quick peck on the cheek and hurried to catch Pet.

"Mrs. Traffortelli, let me walk you to your car."

"Thank you again, Mr. Wingate, for your kind consideration, but I really am fine."

"You don't sound very convincing. I have an idea. Why don't you come back to Briar Town with me? I canceled a meeting today because of the funeral, and I have some free time. Would you like to get a physical feel for this big company you have acquired? You will understand the roles of our employees and associate names with their work areas. Of course, you did meet some of them at the board meeting."

Pet smiled weakly at James as they walked to her car. "That would be nice. That board meeting didn't end well. I was embarrassed. I hope the other members will get to know a more competent Mrs. Traffortelli soon."

James gave her his best smile. "Yes, that was a bit intense, wasn't it. Don't worry about Mr. Hyde, and the others will forget all about that. It looks like we are parked very close together. You can follow me, right now."

Her mood changed instantly from sadness to absolute joy. She thought to herself, "In just twenty minutes, I will be walking through the door of my company."

Pet was about to put the key in the ignition when her cell phone rang.

"Hello, Dad, what's wrong? Who are you talking about? Uncle Mike? Oh no. You are talking too fast, Dad. Slow down. But I was going to do something. Oh, all right, I'm coming."

Then, before she ended the conversation, Alistair said, quite upset, "Hurry, lass, someone higher up is gonin' t'call back."

"Okay, Dad, I'll be there in less than ten minutes. Don't talk to anyone till I get there."

She looked at her watch, mentally preparing herself for impending doom, and quelled her disappointment in forgoing the tour with James Wingate. Pet got out of her car and explained the situation to him. He looked disappointed, too. He said tomorrow, around eleven, would be a good time for a short tour if she would like to come. “Thank you, Mr. Wingate. I would like that very much.” He gave her his card and drove off.

All the way back to her apartment, Pet wondered why Uncle Mike put Alistair into such a rage.

Chapter 30

Uncle Mike Arrives

It was eight o'clock in the morning when Michael Yoderman walked out of the sliding glass door of the airport to idling taxi cabs. Since he didn't know Whalen Falls or its surroundings, he decided to take a taxi from the airport instead of renting a car. He wanted to surprise his sister and brother-in-law. The main reason, though, was to show them he could leave the little town of Shoban, Minnesota, and find this big city all on his own. He made no promises about when he would arrive there. He just told Fiona, "I'm comin' for sure, you betcha!" Even though Alistair and Fiona's protests were many, he told them not to worry. He would figure it out.

Carrying two big suitcases, he lumbered over to a waiting taxi and stuck his head in the window. With a loud, gruff voice, Mike Yoderman said, "Hey, can you take me away from this airport and find Whalen Falls for me?

The cabbie was so startled he dropped the newspaper and jerked his head back on the headrest. He shouted back at the huge man whose head and chest were halfway into his cab.

"No shouting, please! I can hear you! I can take you anywhere, but you must move. Get out of my window! Get out of my window! Step back. Where is your luggage?" The man opened the back door and was seconds away from hoisting the suitcases into the back seat.

The cabbie got out of his cab. "No. No! Suitcases in the trunk, please. We cannot do this. All luggage must go in the trunk!"

The excited cabbie opened the trunk quickly and tried to lift the large leather suitcases.

"That's okay, feller. You'll fall on your keester tryin' to lift these bags."

"This is no problem. I can do this. It is my cab." But his efforts were in vain. Mike's big arms latched onto the cumbersome objects. In two seconds, he heaved them into the trunk of the compact vehicle before the cabbie knew what was happening.

Then he crammed his six-foot-four-inch body into the backseat of the small car. He tugged and twisted at his long coat to get it out from under him. Mike's belly and long legs hit the front seat several times before Mike settled down. The gyrations of his passenger tried this cabbie's patience. He looked to heaven for calm inspiration.

Once inside the vehicle, he turned to his passenger. "Are we ready to go, Sir? Are you comfortable now? You must buckle up. Safety is important in my cab."

"Sure, I'll try, but these straps ain't gonna fit around my big chest." After about three tries, he quit. and let the buckle retract to the top of the seat. "Do you know where Whalen Falls is? My sister told me it is in Carrollton County."

The cabbie nodded and drove away from the bustling airport. Still using a booming voice, Mike started up the conversation again. "HEY, now that we're getting away from that airport, which way are we headed? I want to find Whalen Falls. I hear it's a big city."

The dark olive-skinned man chuckled to himself before he answered. "Oh, maybe compared to a small village it is big, but to Pittsburgh, it is very small, very small indeed."

"Ya mean it's a one-horse town? Won't a guy be able to wet his whistle with maybe a drink, or two?"

"Oh, I think it has a restaurant, maybe one or two. One is very nice."

"NO, man, a bar. A place you can relax in, toss down a couple of beers, you know, a beer garden with lots of people, laughin', music, and stuff. I don't want nuthin' fancy."

"Well, maybe there is such a place in that city," the cabbie assured him. "Now, Sir, what is the exact address of your destination?"

Mike reached into his coat pocket and found the crumpled piece of paper with the address. "Let's see here, 112 Queen Anne Lane, Castleton Apartments. Hey, by the way, what's your name? I don't like callin' people "hey you" all the time."

The cabbie was hesitant and mumbled under his breath.

"Say what, fella? I didn't hear you, unless you were coughin'."

"I don't give my name to strangers. They are not in my cab that long to form a relationship. If you are that interested, my picture and taxi license number are on the dashboard."

Then Mike leaned closer to look at his picture and heard him issue a command to a dashboard device.

"Please find 112 Queen Anne Lane, Whalen Falls, Pennsylvania."

The computerized voice of the GPS came on, "Make a left on ramp to Route 376, continue to follow Route 376 for nineteen miles."

"Well, yeah, I can see your picture, but that doesn't tell me your name. And I guess we'll be in this here cab for a while, seeing how we'll be driving some nineteen miles or so. So, what's your name? I'm Mike Yoderman."

He sighed a heavy sigh, "If you must know my name, it is Amir. That is all I will tell you, and all you need to know."

Mike chuckled, "Okay, I'll take that. Ammer it is."

Amir said indignantly, "It is Amir, Amir. If you must know my name, say it correctly, Amir, not Ammer!"

He drove in silence and tried to ignore this huge man in the back seat of his cab.

Finally, the exit sign to Whalen Falls came into view.

Gliding down the off-ramp, the commercial activity that loomed ahead seemed very appealing. The city of Whalen Falls spread open to Mike like a picture postcard. It was studded with shops, a pharmacy, two banks, and multiple little restaurants with inviting window fronts on either side. He scanned both sides of the main street for a down-home watering hole.

Amir broke his concentration. "We are nearing Queen Anne Lane. I will be turning onto your street now. I must tell you the fare. It will be $45.00 exactly. I can take credit cards or cash. I will pull over to the apartments now."

Mike kept looking around. "No, keep on going."

With an alarmed look on his face, Amir stared in the rear-view mirror at Mike. He spoke angrily and quickly, "I don't want any funny stuff! You must pay me! Don't try to run away, or I will call the police! I take credit cards or cash. I should have taken the money before we left, but Amir is a good cab driver, an honest person. Don't!..."

"Hold on, man, don't jump to conclusions. Mike Yoderman never stiffs anyone! I mean, just keep going, I wanna find a bar. Let's try a street off the main road. Go down this street to the right."

"Then you will pay me," Amir said vehemently.

Mike strained his neck to see if he could find a likely place.

Suddenly, he pointed out the window. "Hey, stop. Look. Down there, Scotty's. That there sounds like a bar to me, you betcha!"

Amir pulled up to the curb with a jerk right in front of Scotty's Bar and Grill. He kept the cab running and turned around to face his burly passenger. "That will be $45.00 exactly, Mr. Yoderman. I will not charge you for the extra tenth of a mile to find this bar."

Mike laughed out loud and leaned back in the seat to fish his wallet out of his back pocket. "No problem, my good man. Never let it be said that Mike Yoderman doesn't pay his bill. I'm even gonna give you a ten-dollar tip to show you I have a good heart."

With a feigned expression of gratitude, Amir held out his hand. "Thank you, Sir. You are most kind. We will get your bags out now."

Looking into the rearview mirror, Amir watched Mike standing beside the suitcases on the pavement. He drove away quickly. The cabbie didn't care how this man would get to his original destination, or how he was going to fend for himself in this strange city. It was not his problem. He just hoped his patience would not be tried by another fare like Mr. Yoderman.

Chapter 31

The Bar Fight

He lugged his suitcases through the bar's door. One of the suitcases slammed against the door frame on the way in as a young couple pushed by him on the way out.

"Watch it, buddy. You gotta big load there!" They laughed and kept on going.

Mike smiled at them while pushing the baggage. He searched for a table, squinting his eyes as he adjusted them to the softer light of the bar. He plopped himself down into the closest empty seat.

Putting the suitcases closer to the table, he ambled over to the bar. He saw a man standing behind it near the cash register. Mike called out to him in a loud voice so he could be heard above the jukebox's blaring music.

"Hey, do ya think I could get me a couple of beers?"

The bartender nodded and poured two glasses of draft beer. When he came over to Mike, he looked up at the mountain of a man facing him. "There you go, big guy, that will be seven dollars."

Mike reached into his pocket and took out a wad of dollar bills. "Thank you. Nice place you got here. What is that crazy music? It sure is loud!"

"I don't know, some noise the kids dance to." The bartender laughed.

Mike smiled back, "I'll have me a couple more of that draft beer and I'll sit over there. Is that okay with ya?" He motioned to a table nearest to him.

The bartender shouted back, "Sure, Mac, no problem."

While Mike was at the bar, he caught the attention of two

men. They watched him struggle with the glasses of beer, trying to sit without knocking over his suitcases. One of the men snickered at him. "What a jerk. He doesn't know his ass from third base."

The other man spoke up, "Shut up, Clay. Don't go pissing off guys bigger than you."

Clay Deeter was a scrawny, mean little man and got meaner the more he drank. He didn't like strangers and liked to pick on them, no matter what size they were. He took a pack of cigarettes out of his soiled shirt pocket and, with his left hand, searched for a lighter in his pants.

Joe glared at Clay, "Put those things away. You know you can't smoke in here. I've told you that a hundred times."

"Shit, Joe, I could take him. Those big guys are dumb and easy to roll; 'sides you could finish him off."

Clay slouched his elbows on the table. He looked at his drinking buddy as if he hated the whole world and everyone in it.

"I ain't doin' nuthin' of the kind, Clay. We've been here all afternoon, drinkin'. Now let's go. I'm going home."

Clay scratched his oily brown hair, grinned, and gave a nod to Joe. With a sudden move of his work boot, he kicked the nearby chair hard, causing Mike to spill some beer on his coat.

Clay smirked, "Kinda clumsy, ain't ya, dipshit."

Giving him a sideways glance, Mike quickly brushed off the suds and continued to drink. He said nothing.

A waitress walked up to Mike's table with the other beers. She sat them down with a smile. He immediately picked up one and drank it down. "This sure tastes good, pretty lady. I'm gonna pay you right now," again pulling out a wad of five, ten, and twenty-dollar bills. "Here's the seven I owe ya and a ten for you." He folded the money back into his pocket, and she thanked him, walking away with a big smile on her face.

Clay crudely asked her if she liked the fat guys now, then asked for another beer. She told him to get lost and get it himself. The exchange between Mike and the waitress caught the attention of the two men. The instigator immediately nudged his pal.

"Did you see all that cash?! He's easy pickings. We could take him."

Joe looked at him as if he had two heads. "You're nuts! He's huge! He could wipe the floor with your scrawny ass."

Clay kept watching Mike drink his beer. His grimy thumb and forefinger stroked his chin. A minute later, he whispered to Joe. "Not if you help me. This guy is gonna drink another one, you watch, and then he's gonna hafta take a leak. We'll jump him in the men's room. That jerk won't know what hit him. Come on. First, let's grab a smoke outside. We can watch him from the door."

As they got up from the table, Joe whispered back, "I'll go out with you, but you're going about this half-cocked."

They both lit their cigarettes. Clay peered back into the bar.

Joe looked behind him to make sure no one was around them. Then he leaned into Clay's face. "That shitter is too damn small. It only has one stall, and you can't move easily. I don't wanna get pinned against the wall trying to make a quick move on him. You should know ya can't move in there. The lighting in Scotty's isn't that bright. He'll be searchin' for his table. Why don't you wait until he comes back from the john? You can trip him again as he tries to sit down. We'll start a fight. I'll jump him from behind while you punch him in the ribs. I'll grab the money from his pocket and run out the door."

Clay thought about Joe's plan for a minute. He smiled and looked in the bar again.

"Yeah, I like your idea. Look, there he goes gulping down another beer. He's gonna take a piss soon, I know it." Clay's voice was getting excited. "There he goes. He's getting up. That dumb jerk is lookin' all around for the john. He spotted it. Let's wait till we see him come back out; then we'll jump him."

They waited outside, trying to look casual. He lit another

cigarette, taking quick puffs, ready to make a quick entrance back into Scotty's.

Clay talked in an authoritative voice. "It's getting busier in there, a lot of distraction going on. People won't even care what's happening. Remember, Joe, make your moves deliberate and quick. We can be out of here in a couple of minutes. Darkness will be on our side. We can cut back into the alley and get in your car from the side street on 3rd. Look, there he is."

Mike walked out of the john mumbling to himself that these kinda bars never had enough paper towels. He shook his hands slightly and wiped them on his pants.

The two threw their cigarettes to the cement sidewalk and walked back inside. Clay came up on Mike's right side, staggering as if he were drunk. He deliberately fell onto his right side, stepping hard on his right foot. Then, with a forceful jab, Joe hit Mike in the back.

"Hey, son of a bitch! What's going on?" Mike yelled out, and before he could turn around, Joe hit him again in the back with his left fist and reached for Mike's pocket. Clay lowered his body and threw a punch into Mike's stomach.

Once this big man caught on to their plan, he whirled around and caught his assailants off guard. He reached down and picked up the scrawny one and threw him against the table while he quickly jerked his body to the left, throwing the other man off balance. His big left arm reached behind, catching Joe by the shirt and bringing him in front of him to hit him in the face. Joe went sailing to the floor, bringing another patron down with him. Obscenities flew about. Pushing and shoving ensued, but that ended quickly. Clay got up and lunged for Mike's right pants pocket. Mike was beginning to enjoy this. He flicked him off easily. His powerful blow sent Clay backward into another table full of college boys drinking beer. They immediately started fighting with Clay.

Finally, this got the bartender's attention, and he called the police. Carl Mikus had enough of Friday night fights. He used to try to break them up himself, being a heavyweight boxer in college, but after several boxer fractures and a broken nose, he let the police have the fun now. Carl came from around the bar and started yelling at the men. NO one listened to him.

While Clay was entangled with the drunken college kid, he tried to bring the ruckus closer, hoping a stray punch would land in Mike's kisser. He still wanted to get his hands on the money. That plan failed, too.

Joe wouldn't give up either as long as the fighting was going on. Fists clenched, he made one last lunge at Mike's ribs in an attempt to get at his pocket. Mike's meaty hands grabbed Joe's collar and, with a right hook, hit him in the nose. Blood gushed from both nostrils, and Joe was down.

Outside, a police siren was heard, and two big men in uniform came in with nightsticks in their hands, yelling orders.

Chapter 32

Mike Meets Joshua Iverson

The next thing Mike Yoderman knew, he was in the back seat of a police car trying to explain himself.

"All I aimed to do here was to protect myself, ya know."

"Save it for the judge, Mac. I don't want to hear your lousy excuses."

Officer Clancy was tired of the routine. He had no patience with anyone involved in a bar fight. He put the car in gear and drove to the station.

The second policeman, Officer Stevens, shoved the two men through the door and led them past the desk clerk. To the left of the foyer area, there were three jail cells of heavy chrome. The cell doors and bars were high, reaching the ceiling. With each heavy footstep of the men, the sound on the marble floor echoed throughout the station. Jack Kelly, the officer of the day, got up to open the doors.

As soon as they got near the cells, Joe and Clay started shouting obscenities at each other. One foul name led to another. Even with his hands handcuffed behind his back, Clay attempted to show Joe who was boss and tried to head butt him. He clumsily lost his footing and fell to the floor. Another officer ran to pick Clay up before anything else happened. He jerked Clay up by the shoulders and pushed him hard into the cell. "Stay there. You miserable ass wipe and shut the hell up. I don't want to hear another word out of you!" He looked toward Joe as he was being dealt with in the same rough manner.

Then, with a loud slam of the station door, Clancy brought in Mike and pushed Mike toward the cells, but Mike kept trying to turn around and talk to Clancy. Mike towered over Clancy, who himself was a little over six feet. His voice was getting louder and louder, "I'm telling ya, yer not listening. I'm not the guilty one here. A fella has a right to defend himself, he does. I'm a peaceful l man! Ya can ask anyone who knows me!"

Clancy prodded him in the back with his nightstick. "No one knows you here, Pal."

The officer who put Clay in his cell looked over to Clancy and headed for the third cell door. He started grinning because Clancy was beet red, about to lose his patience in a hurry.

"Can't you handle your new friend there, Clancy?"

"Aw, shut up! Just open the door. He's not talkin' to anybody until all of them settle down!"

Mike wouldn't let up. He stood there facing the other two. His loud voice boomed throughout the station while he raised his fists at them. "I woulda had your asses down cold if these fools hadn't stopped me. Ya know that! Yer nothin' but stupid jerks, lookin' ta bust their heads against sumpthin'."

Clay limped closer to Mike's cell. "We coulda taken you, asshole. Yer too dumb to know when to quit. Where the hell did you come from, anyway? Ya sound like a real hick."

"Oh, yeah? I'll wipe the floor with ya, for sure!"

Then the obscenities started again.

Clancy had it. He faced the jail cells from his desk and drew his taser, ready to fire. Joe saw it first and backed away. He slumped down on the bench against the wall. Clay shut his mouth in a hurry.

"I'M NOT GIVING ANY WARNINGS FROM HERE ON IN. THE NEXT ASSHOLE TO MAKE A NOISE GETS IT SQUARE IN THE CHEST. IS THAT CLEAR!?!"

The men nodded.

Immediately after that, Joshua Iverson walked out of his office, slamming the door behind him. He stood in front of Clancy's desk. "What in the hell is goin' on here? I could hear you guys all the way from my inner office! Clancy Stevens, one of your duties, in case you've forgotten, is to maintain order at all times on these premises. Why did you bring them in here, besides the obvious drunk and disorderly?"

"It will probably be simple assault, too." Clancy said.

Joshua sized up the men, starting from Joe, then Clay, then Mike.

"Let me guess. The two small guys against that 'mountain' over there."

"You got it, " Clancy said, rubbing his forehead.

"What's the big guy's name?"

"Mike Yoderman, your honor!" Came a loud booming voice.

Clancy spun around in his chair. "Hey! I told ya to button it! And he's not a judge, stupid."

Mike gripped the metal bars with both hands. His once white shirt was sticking out of his pants. Some buttons had popped off during the scuffle, and his big belly bulged between the bars. He looked the perfect picture of a clown in a circus act. But in this situation, he didn't want to come off as a buffoon. He wanted to plead his case and get out of there. He cleared his throat and started talking in a normal voice.

"Hey there, sir, beggin' your pardon, but do you have more authority than these here cops? Maybe I can get you to understand my problem."

Clancy was ready to roar back at Mike, but Joshua raised his hand slightly to stop him. He had the faintest expression of amusement on his face. He leaned down to Clancy and spoke softly.

"I'll handle it. I want to see if he can tell me what happened to cause all this mess. He does look a little bit more intelligent than those other bozos."

Joshua started by grabbing a chair and sitting down beside Clancy's desk. "Do you live around here, sir?"

"No. I'm not familiar with these here parts."

"Then, why were you in the bar?"

"Well, ya see I got this here niece, and she's been through a real bad time, and her old parents come to see her, don'tcha know, and, well, they're on in years, and I come t'help."

"That doesn't explain to me why you were in the bar, Mr. Yoderman. Were you planning to meet her at the bar?"

"Aw, heck no. Pet doesn't even know I'm here yet. I just needed a beer. I was parched, ya know. Ain't no law against tossin' down a few, is there?"

When Mike said Pet's name, his heart skipped a beat. "Oh, my God, he thought, a connection to Pet. This guy is going to be the perfect excuse to see her again! I haven't seen her in months."

Joshua cleared his throat and tried to remain calm. He didn't want to ask any obvious questions about her.

"No, Mr. Yoderman, there's no law against having a beer as long as you act like a law-abiding citizen."

"Well, I was trying to. Those monkeys sure didn't help matters. They come on me like hungry badgers after a field mouse. I was just trying to wet my whistle, and then go to Pet's apartment. I was gonna surprise her, I was."

Joshua looked over to Clancy. "Get priors on all of these guys, and if the big one doesn't have any, send him into my office. I'll be finishing up some paperwork before I go home."

About thirty minutes later, Clancy buzzed Joshua. "He's clean."

"Send him in."

Then Joshua heard a rap on his door. "Yes."

"It's me, sir, Mike Yoderman. Can I come in?"

"Come in."

"The guard said I could talk to you. He's not very nice to the public, ya know. He makes people mad for no reason. He needs more people skills. He needs to..."

"Enough about my Senior Officer, Mr. Yoderman. I'd like to know if I let you out of my jail, do you have a way home, or a phone number to contact a family member? I don't want you to go back to the bar."

Mike feverishly began to dig in his pockets. He was mumbling to himself, "It's here somewhere, I know it." Then he started throwing the contents of his pockets on Joshua's once neat desk. Soon, things started appearing in scattered bunches. It began with crumpled-up dollar bills, a thick wad of money in a brass clip, assorted change, an airline boarding pass, a candy bar wrapper, chewing gum, a cellophane wrapper with two cheese-and-peanut-butter crackers, a flip cell phone, and a used handkerchief. Then he dug deep into his back pocket and got out his wallet.

His beefy hands went through the mess, sending some of the debris to the floor. "It's here. It's gotta be here. Now, where do you suppose...?"

Joshua didn't want to make a hunting expedition out of this. The total disarray was getting on his last nerve. He had to get the man to focus.

"Mr. Yoderman, do you have a phone number for a family member? If not, we can look up the person's number for you."

Then Mike opened his wallet, and immediately he shouted, "Yes! Here it is. I found Pet's cell phone number!"

"Good, Mr. Yoderman. I think you should call her now. What is her name? You never told me."

"It's Pet! My niece! I told ya that."

"Mr. Yoderman, that sounds like a nickname. I'm at a disadvantage here. Being a law officer, it would be improper for me to be so informal. I have to write in the report who I released you to. What is her formal name?"

"Oh. You can call her Mrs. Traffortelli, I think."

"You don't know her real name? I thought you said she was your niece."

"Yeah, she is, but I don't know if she changed it back to her maiden name, Teaseling, yet. It's a long story."

Joshua knew the story, but he had to be sure it was the only woman he wanted to see.

"You can use this phone at my desk."

"Thanks."

As he picked up the phone, Joshua noticed how small it

looked in Mike's hand. He said to himself, "Mike is never going to handle this simple task." He watched as Mike stood, weaving slightly, trying to focus on a wrinkled piece of paper. He squinted and started punching numbers on the keypad. His big fingers hit two at a time.

"This doesn't work. You got tiny phones here. Could ya call this number for me? I can read numbers and all, but this here thing's impossible."

Joshua smiled. He took the paper from Mike. "The last four digits are 7489?"

"Yeah."

Joshua nodded, punching in the last four digits. It started ringing immediately.

"Hello?"

"Hello, Mrs. Traffortelli? This is Detective Joshua Iverson at the E Street Police Station. Do you know a Mike Yoderman?"

In a hesitant voice, Pet said slowly, "Yes. He is my uncle. What has happened to him?"

In a reassuring voice, Joshua said, "There's no need to worry, Mrs. Traffortelli. You remember me, don't you, the trial and...?"

"Yes, yes, Joshua, I mean Detective. I do remember you. Is my uncle okay? Why is he at your police station?"

"He's fine. I'm sorry if I startled you, Mrs. Traffortelli. Mike had a slight problem, which I can explain to you as soon as you get here. Will you be able to come to the station now?"

"Yes, of course, I'd rather my father and I come right away. We'll be there directly."

Joshua turned to Mike. "Sir, I'm going to put you back in the cell. I can't let you roam around the jail until your niece comes for you."

Mike let out a moan deep from within his gut, "Aw, for the love of.... I can't go back with those monkeys; besides, I think I'm going to be sick.

Joshua quickly opened the door and yelled at Clancy. "Show

this man to the bathroom now! Make sure he gets it in the shitter!"

Clancy rushed toward Mike, grabbed his shirt, and pointed the heaving man toward the men's room with little time to spare. He pushed him in and immediately closed the door. What happened next was Mike's audible elimination of undesirable stomach contents from the last three hours.

Joe and Clay started laughing. Clay hung onto the bars. "That hick can't hold his liquor. What a dumb shit. Listen to him moan. He's puking his guts out."

"Quit laughing, or I'll give you something to moan about in a second if you don't shut up, now!" Clancy yelled at them.

Ten minutes went by, and Clancy was still making out the report. He looked over to Stevens. "Stevens, will you kindly look in on our sick guest and make sure he hasn't fallen in the shitter or something. He's awfully quiet."

Steven returned the request with a scowl and reluctantly got up, mumbling, "You always give me the shit jobs. One of these days, I'm going to refuse your stinkin' orders, ya know that? I'm tired of wet nursing drunks and old men. I should have been Captain by now if it wasn't for you."

"What's that, Stevens? Do you have something to say? Go on; see if he's okay?"

"I'm goin,' I'm goin."

Suddenly, the big doors opened with a bang. Pet walked briskly toward the front desk with her father in tow. A lively conversation was in progress. "No, Dad, I don't know how this works, and I don't know if there is money involved. I've never gotten a man out of jail before. Detective Iverson didn't give me any particulars. Please don't make a scene."

"A scene, what would be the reason to make one? Although I'd like to box his ears in, I would. The man's been in trouble every day of his life. He just can't act normal like everybody else!"

Pet grimaced, retorting back at her father, "And you wanted

to send him down to protect me during the trial? There is no doubt in my mind that he would've been in more trouble than the rapist, and I know his mug would've been on the front page of the papers, more than the poor victims themselves."

Clancy was about to stand up and greet them, but Joshua came forward and stood before them.

"Mrs. Traffortelli, it's nice to see you again. Thank you for coming down so quickly." Joshua extended his hand.

She knew she wanted to be friendly and open to him, but she couldn't relax. Her handshake was perfunctory, and her tone of voice was formal when she introduced her father to him.

"Detective Iverson, this is my father, Alistair Teaseling. I hope my Uncle Mike hasn't been too much of a problem."

Alistair chimed in, "He's a good man, Detective. A stalwart citizen, even though he has a penchant for trouble."

"Dad, please, he doesn't need a character witness."

Joshua walked them to his office and ushered them to some chairs. Alistair sat, but Pet stood beside him. Joshua talked casually, helping her relax, but her stance was rigid.

"There is no fine, Mrs. Traffortelli. This incident occurred because Mr. Yoderman was trying to defend himself, according to my officers, and I guess it got extremely out of hand. I would impress upon him, though, that he can't engage in bar fights when he decides to have a beer or two in a strange city."

"I agree, Detective Iverson. Can we see my uncle now?"

Joshua opened the door slightly. "Officer Clancy, could you bring in Mr. Yoderman, please?"

Mike came through the door quieter now, looking pale and tired. His eyes were bloodshot from vomiting. He was tucking the back of his shirt into his pants.

Alistair got up immediately. "Are ye among the living, Mike Yoderan? Ye look like something the cat dragged in. Did ye have to drain the whole barrel of ale?!"

"Ally, don't start with me. There were circumstances, ya know."

"Always the excuse, Mike, I..."

Pet got between the two of them, looking embarrassed that the men would start squabbling in front of a law officer. A bit of her formality faded, "I'm sorry, Joshua. These men just don't know when to be quiet. You said there will be no fine. Will there be any charges against my uncle? If there aren't, I would like to take him to my apartment now. I think he's had quite a day in Whalen Falls."

He looked at her face and was lost in her blue eyes. He took in the light scent of her perfume and wished the circumstances were much different. His loss of the right words at that moment made the next sentences perfunctory and cold. "Certainly, Mrs. Traffortelli. As I have said, due to these circumstances, there will be no charges. You may take him to your home. Have your uncle pass by the Desk Sargent and sign for his release."

The two men left the office. Pet followed them. He wanted to touch her on the shoulder and whisper "It was wonderful seeing you again. You look beautiful. I've missed you." Instead, he silently ushered them out.

Pet awkwardly turned to close the door. Joshua touched the doorknob at the same time. She looked up and gave him a slight smile. "Oh, sorry."

He smiled back, "Are you going to be okay? Your uncle might be a handful."

"Oh, don't worry. I'm used to this man. My father certainly is too. Thank you, Joshua." In a few seconds, the three of them were out the door.

* * *

Officer David Jones walked into the station just as Pet and her entourage of men were walking out. The next day, he confronted Joshua Iverson.

"You had her right there. Why didn't you talk to her or ask her out? You had goo goo eyes all over your puss. I've never seen you smile so much since her day in court."

For a moment, Joshua Iverson had a pleasant smile on his face.

"Yes, it was nice seeing her again, but I don't operate that way, Jones. You should know that by now. The situation wasn't right. It would have been very unprofessional to ask her out while she was dealing with her uncle. I think he's going to be a real handful. I did get a chuckle out of that mountain called Mike Yoderman."

"So, call her now. It's only one day later. You could ask her how everything is going and then ask her out. Simple. Go for it!"

"Do I look like I'd take any orders from you? I stopped taking orders from my mother thirty years ago."

"I think you're scared she'll turn ya down. That's what I think."

Chapter 33

Pet Makes Promises

The next morning, Pet quickly got into her car, still excited to see her company. "Well, let's try this again." She smiled to herself, remembering what James Wingate told her.

"When you come to the third traffic light, get into the right-hand lane after you get out of the city limits. About a mile past the high school, you will see the entrance to the office and factory buildings." James gave her further instructions. "Pull into the administration parking area, Mrs. Traffortelli. You can park right beside my space. I will tell the head guard you are the new owner. He'll take your license plate number."

It was an easy drive through Whalen Falls. She thought about how many times she had passed by this factory and never had given it a second glance. Now it loomed large and impressive. She liked hearing him say, "You are the new owner." Yes, it was hers, all hers. Pet could hardly contain her joy. She also felt an immediate sense of power. I'm going to talk to my employees. I'm going to see what they do. I'm going to express myself and let them know I have ideas for this company. I can do this. I know I can.

Just as he had said, a uniformed guard greeted Pet politely. "Good morning. How can I help you? I am Emerson Bellows."

She smiled at him. "Well, Mr. Bellows, I am Mrs. Traffortelli. Hello."

"I will remember who you are from now on, ma'am. I've been here many years, and I know who goes in and out. Also, there will be no trouble with your parking space. Your name will be painted on the curb in front of it. It is nice to meet you, Mrs. Traffortelli." He went to the large desk in the foyer and used the phone to announce her presence.

Pet watched this kind gentleman. She liked his warm greeting and hoped everyone would be this cordial. Putting down the phone, he pointed the way to the lobby. The lobby was full of people. Employees were coming and going, looking busy with file folders or legal tablets in their hands. Pet headed for the wide marble steps leading up to the second floor. James Wingate appeared at the top waiting for her. He smiled as he extended his hand to greet her.

He gave her hand a polite, familiar squeeze, and she gave a friendly nod back. Pet looked to the right and saw immediately where the executive wing was. She recognized the ominous sign on the Board Room door. James could feel her uneasiness as her steps slowed at the top of the stairs.

In a low voice, he said, "Don't worry. We are not going right. Walk straight ahead to the administrative wing." He deftly put his arm on her back, ushering her through the double doors. He then smiled at her and whispered, "Nervous?"

"Well, maybe a little, but excited too."

It was a beehive of activity. She could hear many conversations at once coming from the cubicles. There were more people milling about, laughing and talking. It was everything Pet imagined a busy company would be like. She wanted to be part of this right now. She fantasized herself in a business suit carrying a legal-sized folder full of furniture designs.

Suddenly, a joyous squeal of delight pierced her ears. Bunny Haskell came walking up to them. "Mrs. Trafforteli, you've come to visit us. This is fantastic! Have you come to see our operations? If you have, I hope you have more than just a minute to be with us today."

Pet gave her a broad smile. "My goodness, Bunny. It is good to see you again. Yes, I do have a minute or two, and I would like a tour of my furniture company."

James Wingate saw right away the mutual enthusiasm these women had for each other. He saw that he was going to lose Pet to Bunny while touring Briar Town. There was a sparkle in

Pet's eyes at the mention of being guided by Bunny, and she could see that she would be more comfortable with this vivacious young woman.

Bunny batted her long eyelashes at James and gave him a big smile, saying, "Mr. Wingate, would you mind if I showed her around? I think she would be more relaxed with me. There is so much to see here and many people to meet, but I will be careful not to overwhelm her, I promise."

"What can I say? I've been ambushed by a pro. I would keep the tour to the second floor, Miss Haskell. That territory alone should take you an hour." James barely finished the last sentence when Aloysius came up to them. He looked at them with wary curiosity.

James spoke first, avoiding an embarrassing inquisition about why people were just standing around in the administration area, especially during an unannounced visit from Pet.

"Afternoon, Aloysius. Mrs. Traffortelli is honoring us with an impromptu visit. She is about to have a tour of our second floor and all its many wonders. Miss Haskell has offered to be her guide."

Aloysius looked a bit peeved, not offering any cordial greeting. "I hope you will excuse us for not having a presentation ready for you on the different departments, and what they do, Mrs. Traffortelli." He then turned to Bunny, saying almost in a warning manner, "I'm sure Miss Haskell would be delighted to give you a brief tour."

He coughed and turned directly to James. His raspy voice was slightly above a whisper. "Did Keller Brothers get in touch with you the other day? Your secretary didn't respond to me."

"I attended the funeral, remember?"

"No. Anyway, I need you to call Phil Keller right away. I'm going back to my office. Catherine will fill you in. Talk to her before you call Keller."

James was visibly annoyed with Aloysius' interruption.

"Well, ladies, enjoy your tour. I will join you as soon as I can."

Bunny turned to him. "I'm sure, Mr. Wingate, we will do fine without you."

In a matter of seconds, Bunny was steering Pet to the Productions Wing. Her mouth was going a mile a minute, laughing a lot to punctuate her narrative. Pet was in awe of the workings of Briar Town. Never had she realized what it takes to run a furniture company. Colorful layouts and materials caught her eye as Bunny talked about each machine and art sketches of the furniture.

Bunny continued talking as they moved from one department to the next.

"So, as you can see, there are many specialists involved here. Even advertising is an important campaign for a large company like this."

The whole time she talked, a little voice in Pet's head kept saying, "My, my. Just think you own all of this!"

Bunny introduced each supervisor to her. They were welcoming and seemed to like her. Some of them asked questions about whether anything was going to change. Bunny laughed and told them to give her a break.

Pet looked at her watch as she and Bunny stood in the very spot where they began. Pet started asking her own questions about the advertising division. She found it very interesting and wished they could have spent more time there. An employee she met from advertising came up to her. He was holding a pamphlet with a sofa on it.

"Mrs. Traffortelli, you asked if these fliers circulate to Whalen Falls' homes every week. I checked with the manager, and they do. Do you think that it is too many times a month?"

A woman quickly approached Pet. "Hello, Mrs. Traffortelli. Excuse me, but some of us in the art and design department were wondering, will our work be transferred to another city or country?"

Then an older man questioned, "Oh, yes, how about our advertising department? I heard they are thinking about Mexico City for that."

Pet looked surprised. "Oh, my, I should look into these situations."

Another man sneaked up from behind them. "Are our parts and assembly going to be transferred to Canada? What about our P.R. staff? Will that be dissolved and handed over to India?"

Before Pet had a chance to answer, employees came up by twos and threes. Soon, five people were standing around her, talking and asking questions. Then another curious employee called out, "Hey, Stevens, ask her if there's gonna be layoffs. Are we gonna get that raise we never got, or that stinkin' little bonus?"

After that, the office atmosphere exploded into raucous laughter and loud voices. They were all curious about her and even started asking personal questions about her life.

"Where are you from? Did you always live in Whalen Falls?" Pet was enjoying this immensely.

Aloysius came out of his office, wondering why he heard so much commotion. He wasn't prepared for the growing scene before him. He put down the coffee cup he was holding on a nearby desk. Watching the crowd escalate, he headed toward them.

James Wingate also heard the disturbance and came out of another office. He saw Aloysius' glaring look and anticipated the older man's mood. He intercepted Aloysius just before he came within earshot of the employees and quickly cut him off.

"Wingate, get these people out of here and back to work! This isn't a kid's day at the circus! Get that bitch out of here now. Why didn't you keep an eye on her?"

"Don't panic, Al. I'll have her out of here in a jiff."

"See that you do."

James Wingate hurried to the noisy crowd. He eased through directing them to go back to work, but not before he heard phrases that made his blood run cold. The unsettling bits of conversation were danger signs. Phrases like bargaining committees, better representation, new policy changes, raises, and time off for overtime were echoed by more than one person.

He kept his cool with her until they reached the parking lot.

"Mrs. Traffortelli, that was quite a circus you had going on there. I've never seen so many employees talking in the administrative office at once. How did all that get started?"

Pet had a guilty look on her face after hearing his rather stern voice. "Gosh, I really don't know. Maybe it was just curiosity on their part. I guess my name has been a current topic at the lunch table. Do you think there is any unrest in the departments?"

"There shouldn't be. I haven't heard anything from the department managers. Don't encourage any talks of this kind, Mrs. Trafforelli. Briar Town Furniture Company has been running like a well-oiled machine. Don't screw it up."

"But I am now the owner of this company, Mr. Wingate. I do think I have the right to listen to these employees."

"Yes, in a sense you are correct, but since you have no working experience with Business Management, I don't think it would be wise to say anything concerning any suggestions employees would make now. Is that understood, Mrs. Traffortelli?"

Pet's tone of voice was soft but professional. "I'm sorry, Mr. Wingate. I wouldn't do anything to undermine what Grace has established with the workers. That scene won't happen again."

He smiled at her as he opened the car door for her. The perfunctory departing remarks came spilling out of his mouth. There was no charm or warmth to them as before. "It has been a pleasure seeing you again, Mrs. Traffortelli. I hope your visit to Briar Town Furniture Company was enjoyable. Take care, now. We'll be seeing you again, I'm sure."

She smiled politely and quickly got in her car. In a matter of seconds, she was out of the parking lot. The more she thought about James Wingate's warning, the angrier she got. She grumbled, "What right does he have to scold me? Wait till I tell Anthony what happened!"

* * *

"I thought I told you to keep a leash on her. Can't you control that woman, Prattmore? I won't deal with a loose cannon. Tell her to keep her yap shut about raises and anything to do with time-off shit. I do not want to see her in this administration area at all. She is to say absolutely nothing to anyone!. Do I make myself perfectly clear? Did you draw up a tentative timeline for her indoctrination? I'm not going to be rushed. She is not going to call the shots in this."

"Yes, Aloysius. I did. I have written a rough draft and sent it to your office yesterday. Didn't your secretary show it to you?"

"No. Maybe. It could be on my desk. I didn't have the chance; I've been on overseas conference calls all morning. I will call you when I've read it thoroughly. It better be written to our advantage. Don't make me regret this agreement, Prattmore."

Chapter 34

Ecstasy Gone Awry

Throughout dinner, Pet was animated as she told Anthony about her first visit to Briar Town. She told him every word the employees said and how interested they were in her. "Oh, Anthony, they wanted answers; they wanted my opinion. They looked up to me. I reassured them that I would run this business with a policy of honesty, integrity, and fairness. I also told them they could come to me with any problems that might arise."

During dinner, he was smiling, lighthearted, and attentive. But as they drove on, he was deep in thought and annoyed. It was partly because of her ineptitude in talking too much at Briar Town, and partly because of the tirade Aloysius brought down on him.

He knew the dinner was a total pretense of goodwill. He couldn't berate her just because Aloysius chastised him. How could Pet have known about their talk? He would soft pedal the evening until they got inside. He owed her that much.

She looked at him and gently put her hand on his shoulder. "You're quiet now, Anthony. Is anything wrong?"

"Oh, no. I have a surprise for you. I was just planning the right time to please you and to ask you a few questions."

She smiled and settled back in the seat. "Hope it's not serious. I'm having too much fun tonight. So, I'll be quiet and let you plan some more."

"No, don't worry. I'll keep the subject matter light." He grimaced, hoping for the best scenario to happen, preferably on the couch.

Pet was still talking about her day as they walked to the door.

"Oh, and you should have heard one guy ask if there would be layoffs or raises. After that, everyone chimed in with more and more questions. It was amazing. Bunny was overwhelmed."

Pet kept babbling on. He kept his cool until she spoke her last sentence. After that, he couldn't contain his agitation any longer. He verbally pounced on her like a charging lion.

"Pet, why the hell did you let the situation get so far out of hand? Why did you make promises to those people if you cannot keep them? You do not let a crowd dictate demands. Do not ever tell workers what you are thinking in an impromptu gathering. This is a major manufacturing company. You cannot run it like a Girl Scout Troup. In the business world, people are acquaintances, not your bosom buddies on the first meet and greet!"

As Anthony talked, he slowly unbuttoned the top button of his dress shirt and loosened his tie. The brief action slowed his anger. So, instead of going toe to toe with her, pointing out how stupid she was, he decided he had talked enough and went silent. He walked to the couch and slouched down into it. Pet, on the other hand, stood in the middle of his living room looking at him in disbelief.

"I did no such thing. I promised them nothing. I do want to get to know these employees. I want to let them know I'll be their friend. And I..."

With a look of exasperation, he got up off the couch. He came close to her and took her hand in his. "Young lady, you have a lot to learn. Pollyanna died a long time ago. You are coming across as very naive and inexperienced. Do you really think your approach is going to fly with a hard ass like Aloysius Hyde? You can't act this way. The executives will see you as a child. Hell, many of those employees have more than thirty years' experience."

She let go of his hand and turned away. She walked a few steps and then turned around, facing him. "I don't know what kind of man Aloysius Hyde is, but I'm no child! Don't belittle me! I can learn. I'm not stupid."

"I didn't say that you were stupid, Pet, just not experienced in a business sense. Another thing you said is that honest dialogue is a key to solving any problem. Retailers are backstabbers! The union and division managers will tear you apart on that one! Good God, girl, you were trying to make nice with a little girl smile. They are not your playmates in the sandbox!"

Without warning, she pulled her shawl over her shoulders, fluffed her hair, and turned for the door.

"Neil did the same thing to me that you're doing now. I HATE being told I'm not good at something before I've even started it. Why do men like to put women down? Are we not your equals, no matter how educated we are? Everything I did for Neil wasn't good enough. I dreaded making him breakfast. He picked me apart if the toast was too dark, or the eggs were runny, or the coffee was bitter. Some mornings, nothing pleased him. He enjoyed seeing me cry. I won't take that kind of behavior anymore. And DON'T call me LITTLE GIRL, I've passed that stage a long time ago!"

Her hand was on the door, ready to turn the knob, when he quickly came up behind her. He stood there quietly for a minute, leaning his head down to her neck. He smelled her intoxicating perfume. She hesitated several seconds, then tilted her head back, feeling his cheek, and smelled his Drakkar Noir cologne. The moment was sensual.

Slowly, gently, he put both hands on her shoulders, feeling her body quiver as she took a deep breath. He thought he heard the slightest hint of a sniffle. He silently admonished himself, "Was she crying? I didn't want to make her cry."

He leaned closer to her left ear and whispered softly. "Pet, I'm sorry. I didn't realize I struck a nerve. Neil really must have hurt you. Please forgive me. Don't cry. I didn't mean to belittle you. I love you."

Staying close, she turned and faced him. Immediately, their lips met. Their embrace was loving and long. Then they both stopped. Pet was afraid to go too far and seem needy. Anthony was afraid to scare her into submission, but, ironically, the moment was beautiful and tender. They stayed together, enjoying their intimate moment.

Still entwined after their kiss, Pet buried her head in his chest. He rested his cheek in her hair. He rocked her slowly like a mother would soothe a newborn, a slow movement to quiet hurt feelings.

"Let's go to the couch," he whispered. "I will join you there in one second."

Before Anthony had picked her up for dinner, he put a magnum of champagne to cool in an ice bucket on the butcher block island in the kitchen. He eyed the container now and calculated the moment he would open it for her. He decided to take off his Armani suit jacket before he sat down again.

This unmistakable sound of his tie slipping through the collar made Pet look up at him. She watched Anthony carefully drape his tie over the jacket. A slight smile crossed her lips as she continued to study his actions and mused that everything about him was falling into an easy sense of familiarity. This little distraction was just the right vehicle to defuse the last few minutes. She thought about how sometimes she even knew what he was thinking just by the look on his face, or the way he raised his eyebrows into a funny little question mark.

As she got to know Anthony, his serious exterior often gave way to light conversations and joyous laughter. He teased her sometimes about her down-home Midwestern ideology. She would counter his remarks and take the subject to an absurd proposition, making sexual innuendos along with it. She was adjusting to this kind of familiarity. It surprised her sometimes to even be able to control a conversation. Most of all, she liked being on an equal level with a man whom she was beginning to have deep feelings for.

He sat down. Getting comfortable, he opened his arms wide, entreating her to come closer. His voice was happy, but his eyes were serious. He whispered to her, "Come, I will kiss away everything troubling you. I will make it all better. Lay in my arms, my darling. Let yourself be comforted and throw your cares away. The night is ours to treasure."

She looked at him quizzically. "Are you playing me? You've done a one-eighty from the last ten minutes. Besides the bad acting, I could almost swear I've heard Cary Grant say those exact lines in one of his lesser B movies."

"No, Pet, I meant every word. I'd never mimic Cary Grant. I couldn't get his accent right. I just wanted to make you smile and relax at the same time." Then, with a more serious tone of voice, he continued. "Without rehashing the events of the day, I know you are going to learn from your mistakes. Everything will be fine. I will say, just trust me this time."

A little reluctantly, she said, "Okay, I'll believe you, but never take up acting. Anthony, you're a miserable actor."

Anthony feigned a sad expression, and she laughed again at his bad acting.

In one fluid movement, she slid over and cradled herself in his arms. He began kissing her. He kissed her hair, her forehead, her cheek. He brought her left hand up to his lips and softly kissed it. He kissed her neck and then gently brought her even closer to him. He felt Pet's body relax into his.

"Better?" Anthony asked.

"Yes," she said, slowly lifting her head up to kiss his lips.

As their kisses became more passionate, he slowly caressed her breast and inched his body lower onto hers. Their positions changed from sitting to lying down. She didn't resist while a slight dreamy kittenish purr escaped from her lips. She was ready to play. She moaned softly as his tongue sensuously explored her mouth.

Suddenly, he stopped kissing her and whispered in her ear. He said, "I want you. I'm hungry for you, Pet. Let's not waste a beautiful moment on the couch. Let's go to my bed. I have a surprise for you."

Easing his body from hers, he continued his seductive suggestion. "Pet, if you would like to make the evening more enticing, you will find my bathroom ready to accommodate your needs." Pet hunched up on her elbows, trying to read his expression. She was puzzled, and her body was still whirling from the sexual excitement.

"Uh, okay. Where is your bathroom?"

"Look to your left, off the kitchen. See the door?"

"Mmm hmm."

She stood up and immediately got a little dizzy, weaving back and forth. He quickly stood beside her, putting his arms around her waist.

"Swooning already? There's more to come; don't flake out on me now, sweetheart," he chuckled.

"You do take a girl's breath away, darlin'." Laughing, she elbowed him. He kissed her playfully and patted her ass.

Pet walked to his bedroom and found the adjoining bathroom. She slipped inside, closing the door behind her. She wondered to herself, "I feel tingly all over, wanting more. There is no hesitancy, no resistance. Would I care if I got pregnant?"

She began to undress. She kicked off her shoes, then threw her blouse and skirt on the spacious counter next to the basin. She started to unhook her bra but decided to keep it on and her panties. In the opposite corner of the counter, she found a neatly folded bathrobe. It was a soft, luxurious blue. She slipped into it. If she weren't so sexually aroused, she could easily cuddle up with this and take a nap.

There was a large mirror above the basin. She stared at herself. Her blonde hair, slightly mussed, fell to her bare shoulders. "Yes, this will do just fine. Let him have a little challenge," she grinned devilishly.

She continued to talk to herself, "I must be ovulating because I've never felt so sexually excited or want him this badly. I want to make love to him. Will he think I'm easy? Shall I ask him that? No, can't do that, but I want everything, every part of him."

Anthony waited for Pet to close the door, then quickly went to the kitchen and checked the ice bucket. He spun the bottle a few times, testing the temperature.

"Perfect, just cool enough."

He brought the bucket, champagne, and a small white towel to wrap the chilled bottle with him to the bedroom. He placed it strategically centered on the night table. He hummed a tune as he sauntered to the foot of his bed and proceeded to get undressed.

His shirt, shoes, and trousers were all neatly laid before him on the narrow cedar chest at the foot of the bed. He decided to keep his white briefs on. Then he hung up his shirt and trousers on a hanger and carefully placed them on a brass hook on the other front panel of a massive mahogany armoire. The socks were neatly tucked inside his shoes, which he placed directly in front of the armoire right below its mirrored door. He continued to hum softly as he surveyed his practically naked body in the mirror.

"Not bad, ole' boy, not bad."

In a wide exaggerated circular motion, he brought his hands together and rubbed them vigorously, "Now, let's get crackin'!"

"Pardon me, Anthony, did you say something?" Pet asked, coming out of the bathroom.

He turned from the mirror and came to her immediately. "Oh, nothing, Pet. You look so sensuous, so warm and soft. He said this as he nuzzled her bare neck, letting his tongue drift over her skin. Then, he put his left arm around her and guided her to the bed. "Lay with me."

The next second, they were on the bed. His hand was eagerly pulling the bathrobe from her body. He tugged gently until it was completely off her.

When they lay side by side, their bodies were as one, kneading and caressing each other with renewed energy. He kissed her passionately. His strength amazed her, but her drive was also there, and she responded hungrily.

Again, he stopped abruptly, putting his finger to her lips. She looked up at him, a little alarmed. "Shh, it's okay, Pet. I have something you'll really like."

"Hmm? Nicer than the last five minutes?"

Anthony got out of bed and went to the other side of the night table. With the flair of a French maître d', he lifted the bottle and put it in the towel. He began opening the bottle of champagne.

"I bought it just for this occasion, Pet. I paid a lot for this blinkin' bottle of bubbly."

After twisting off the wire, he maneuvered his thumbs under the cork. It wouldn't budge. He pushed his thumbs tighter under the cork. Nothing happened. He covered it with the towel and tried to twist it off. A little bead of sweat trickled down his temple. His cheeks were getting red. Every muscle in his biceps strained right down to the very tips of his fingers to free the stubborn cork. Anthony wouldn't give up.

Pet watched in amusement. She had never seen Anthony so physically agitated. His face became one big scowl, contorting like an angry clown trying to pull off a ridiculous stunt.

Slowly, she came toward him, trying not to giggle out loud, "Oh, Anthony, honey, it's okay. We really don't need it to have a good time. Maybe I could help. Can I try?"

He could tell she was laughing. "NO! I can do it myself," he hissed. "Just sit the hell down and be a good little girl and wipe that dumb ass grin off your face. I don't need your sarcastic giggles."

Immediately, a flashback of her ex-husband stood before her in a drunken rage, spewing obscenities from his lips. She did not need another scene like this or another Neil. She turned away from Anthony and headed for the bathroom.

Anthony stopped struggling with the bottle. "Where are you going, Pet?"

"I'm going home, thank you."

"Why?"

"After all I've been through with an inconsiderate, abusive louse, do you think I want another man just like him? You seem to have forgotten what happened and what I said in the living room. I don't need a temper tantrum from a man just because he can't pop a cork off a champagne bottle."

"Pet, it was going to come off. I just needed to apply the right pressure. Please wait, I'm sorry."

"No, Anthony. I didn't like what I saw just now. I'm going home."

For a few seconds, neither spoke. His face had softened. Hers was sad and disappointed. He looked at her and spoke softly.

"Okay, it is your call."

He was sitting in a big brown leather easy-boy recliner when she came out of the bedroom. Whatever parting words she might have had for him were immediately interrupted. He spoke matter-of-factly, his tone of voice formal.

"Pet, you might want to stop for a second and pick up that envelope on the dining room table. It's for you. It was going to be another surprise. Inside is a key with an explanation, and the address of the First Mercantile Bank. If you have any questions about the letter, you know where to find me."

She picked it up, flipped it front to back, and put it in her purse. She walked out, pulling the door closed behind her. With a loud bang, it connected defiantly with the frame. The clanging sound of the door knocker had a finality about it.

Chapter 35

Bunny and Pet

"How did you find my home phone number, Bunny?"

"Oh, it wasn't hard."

Pet chuckled at her bravado.

"Nah, silly. I just checked your personnel file. I'm the IT Department Head, remember?"

"Okay, go on."

"Before the dinner at the Shellburn Room, I saw Anthony at Briar Town. During our conversation, he talked about you, and naturally, I had to ask where you lived and all. A girl can get a lot of info from a guy just by asking the right kind of questions, you know, just casual stuff."

"UH huh, you found out a lot, I suppose."

"Don't worry, nothing personal. He told me briefly about getting the clock into your apartment."

"Oh, that was something, and naturally, he told you about the Carrolton Apartments. It is a beautiful building, but it is old."

There was a pause for a second or two. Pet had been dying to ask Bunny a question since the office mob scene, but was afraid she wouldn't get a straight answer. On a whim, she decided, "What the hell. I'll ask anyway."

Bunny interrupted her before she had a chance to ask her the question.

"Anyway, I do have a reason for calling you. After the tour, I found pamphlets about the history of Briar Town and its founders, as well as a list of departments and their managers. We give them out to potential investors and specialty crafting companies. Some of this you already know. I was thinking that these might help you by seeing names on paper. Would you like them?"

"Thank you, it would be a big help. Bunny, I really want to ask you this question, but if you'll get in trouble, don't answer it. Were the employees really angry about not getting a raise?"

"I can answer that. Oh yes, it almost caused a strike. Last Christmas, a memo was sent to all departments stating that, due to a sales slump, no bonuses would be given on December 22nd. Let me tell you, that was a bad day. A lot of rumors circulated among the office staff and hourly employees. Everyone wanted to walk out. They were counting on that bonus. We always got one. Mrs. Grace assured us that every year, Briar Town would reward the employees for their performances. More than one person said someone was cooking the books."

"I guess everyone was pretty upset."

"Yeah, that's when the shit hit the fan, and Marshall Kochmann was called on the carpet. But later it was proven that he hadn't done anything wrong, and then he suddenly stepped down as head controller. It was a big mess, but I never heard why he suddenly stepped down from his higher position."

"Did they ever get the raise, though?"

"Well, later, on January 7th, we got a three percent raise. The executives called it an incentive for the New Year.

"That must have sucked! Did anyone try to find the real reason? Was there any written proof, any investigation?"

Bunny's voice got excited as she switched the phone from one ear to the other. "Well, I have to tell you, for a while, nothing suspicious happened. Then one day last week, I heard Catherine Hartwell and Mr. Hyde whispering as they went down the hall to the boardroom. I heard him say real mean like to, Catherine, 'Make sure that all the books are at the annex factory, ready to ship, and there better not be anyone else there when you do it!'"

Pet sounded amazed, "Wow! That would be something if we could find those books, but wouldn't they also be in the controller's computer?"

"Yes, they would, Mr. Hyde is a stickler for detail. He likes to hang people out to dry over money details. He always tries to trip them up with a paper trail, so he has his own set of books."

"Ah ha. I sure would like to see them."

Chapter 36

The Annex Building

The annex building was far from the city. Bunny took the expressway to get out of town and drove like a bat out of hell for at least thirty minutes just to get to the factory. It was a nondescript building set in a low-lying valley on the edge of a forest of tall pine trees.

The inconspicuous setting of the place could be easily missed. A high chain link fence surrounded the apparent vacant factory and parking lot. One lonely work truck was parked in front of the massive steel doors. Sadly, this scene told the story of many other defunct factories of big steel's glory days long ago.

Pet looked at the area with interest and a little apprehension.

"This place is so remote. Do people still work here? Where is all the furniture made? I don't see any power lines. Are you sure this was a factory? How did they call for help back in the day?"

"You ask too many questions, Pet. Don't worry about things like that. If you must know the details, I was told once that the power lines are buried and are connected to big transformers in the woods. Satisfied? Look, I don't question how factories are run. I don't need to know details like that; it makes things simpler. What did I say before we started out here? We are going to the annex. That's what this place is now, an annex."

"But then, where is all the furniture made? The office complex outside Whalen Falls isn't big enough for production. What's really connected to MGM? Bunny, this place feels like the setup for a murder mystery. Don't you think it's a bit creepy out here?"

Bunny was getting perturbed with Pet's questions and

didn't speak for a minute or two. Then she blurted out, "Let's just say, there are things I do know that I can't tell you because it's not my place to run my mouth about what has gone on for the last five years. I could be fired for telling you a lot of shit. You must start asking your own questions from now on. If we find the right ledgers, you'll be on the right track. So, let's not say anything else about details, and we'll get along fine. I like you, and I don't want to mess that up. I will help you all I can, but I'm not going to get myself fired for it in the meantime."

After Bunny's mini tirade, Pet seriously considered what she said. It made sense. She had to keep Bunny as an ally to understand the past. This web of intrigue in what made Briar Town Furniture tick was growing thicker by the minute. Hopefully, Bunny would share her knowledge. Pet vowed to formulate a plan without getting her in trouble. Pet's attention was soon drawn to the huge building looming ahead.

Dusk was quickly descending over the area. Four floodlights on each corner of the factory came on. There was a loud hum of the neon bulbs warming up, and two front lights cast shadows on a huge white sign above the double metal front doors. The sign read:

BRIAR TOWN FURNITURE COMPANY
UNAUTHORIZED PERSONNEL KEEP OUT

Bunny drove her car slowly up the gravel road to the gate. Pet looked from side to side, trying to see around the building.

"This place is creepy. Are you sure there is an annex here?"

Bunny whispered, "Yeah, it's around back. You can't see the road leading to it because the higher-ups don't want any 'nebshits' nosin' around the place. You see, only Catherine, Aloysius, and Grace, well, she's dead, and I know what is really behind the old factory. Most of the factory workers think it's a shed for extra maintenance equipment. You know tools and stuff. It's kept under lock and key all the time."

"Well, how are we gonna get in there without looking suspicious?"

Bunny dug in her pocket and produced a big brass door key. She dangled it in front of Pet's face.

"Duh, do you think I'd come all the way out here without this? "

"How did you get it?"

"Oh, you don't need to know everything right now, my dear. Some things are better left unsaid. That way you won't be in trouble 'cause you won't know nuthin."

Her emphatic phrasing tickled Pet. She took familiar liberties with people, but she said them with such expression that one couldn't get upset with her. Pet came to realize why Anthony liked her so much.

Bunny eased the car around the back of the factory. As the daylight faded, tall pines cast ominous shadows over the old metal buildings. Their dense branches leaned down, scratching the car doors. It was a picture of seclusion that muffled any sound from the highway.

The further she drove to the shed, the thicker the trees grew and the eerier the scene became. From the light of the car's high beams, she found the big double doors. Bunny whispered to Pet, "Roll down your window; I'll do the same. Listen for any footsteps. I hope the guard isn't making his rounds yet."

They rolled down the windows and waited, searching for any signs of a security guard. As they waited, a stillness engulfed the area as if an ominous tension lingered in the woods. The whole area was silent, dead silent. An uneasy feeling hovered like a vulture waiting for a piece of carrion to chew on. Mother Nature seemed to abandon it because no sounds of birds, crickets, or wind rustled in the pines.

It felt as if an evil thing, hurtful and desperate, had happened here. She nervously looked around. The lights from the outside factory were dim. Dark shadows hung over its lower walls and the shed.

Finally, Bunny grabbed her purse and quickly got out of the car. Pet hesitated.

"Come on, let's go. I don't hear anyone or anything. Hurry up! We can't dilly dally. Grab that flashlight in the back seat, will ya."

Pet obliged reluctantly and followed Bunny to the door of the shed. She turned the flashlight on and lifted it so Bunny could find the door lock. The shed door was made of the same corrugated metal as the factory. Its edges overlapped the door, making it very heavy and hard to open. Bunny struggled with the doorknob, twisting and turning it several times to loosen the inner springs. She started to pull on the doorknob.

"Hey, Pet, pull on the edge of the door. This sucker doesn't want to move."

The two women pulled and tugged at the door until it finally opened. Pet jumped at the grating sound of metal on metal.

Bunny's fingers traveled up and down the inner wooden frame for a light switch.

"Damn!"

"What?"

"A splinter caught my fingernail, flicking the switch."

As soon as Bunny said that, a dim overhead light came on. The stale musty air hit their nostrils.

"Eck, when was the last time someone was in here? There's no ventilation. I feel like I'm in a tomb," Pet said as she followed Bunny inside.

"I never promised you a rose garden, or a *House Beautiful* tour, Pet. You said you wanted to see the old books no matter where they were."

"I know, but this place is awful. It even smells moldy. Are you sure the books are okay in a place where they can deteriorate?

"I think this was their plan all along, a place to be forgotten, the more derelict the better."

Pet didn't say anything. She followed Bunny closely. In the

dim light, Pet saw large benches lining the shed's walls. Tools were strewn all over them. Two twelve-foot wooden tables in the middle of the shed had power saws placed on the ends, but the sawdust around them looked damp, as if they hadn't been used for a while.

"You'll see," She pointed her finger. "Look, over there. See that door? We're going to go through there and down the stairs. It's kinda scary, and the lighting will be very dim, so be careful."

She walked to the steps. They turned their flashlights on and started down. Cobwebs hung from the low ceiling. She felt the side of the walls for a banister, but none was there. She wondered what could be crawling on these damp walls. They felt slimy to her, and she imagined slithery spiders or millipedes lurking in the stone's uneven crevices. The dry, rotted wood creaked with each step they took.

"Gawd, are you sure the books are down here? Surely, they can't be in good condition. Even the walls are wet and most probably moldy."

"I don't think we're gonna get too much snooping time."

No sooner had Pet said that than something ran over her foot.

"OOOOH! What in the HELL was that!?!"

"Simmer down, you Ninny. It was probably just a rat."

"How the hell did they get in here?"

"You're really beginning to whine. You know that? Don't panic over everything you touch down here. Besides, who knows, maybe some slob left a sandwich for them to munch on."

Pet flashed the light on her foot. It was an old scrap of cloth draped on the step. " Whew, that makes me feel better. I don't think I could stand a rat as part of this expedition. I'm glad you were wrong."

"Aw, what's a little company?" Bunny chided.

Finally, they got to the bottom. They peered into the room,

searching it with the flashlight. Bunny's light showed a lamp hanging above a long metal table. She stumbled over to the table and reached for the light cord. She pulled the cotton cord. Half of it broke in her hand. The other half rested on the metal shade. Fortunately, the light clicked on with a sputter. The bulb's wattage was dim, and it kept blinking on and off. It only added to the shadows in the suffocating basement.

Pet thought to herself, "What a wasted effort in light fixtures. Why put a light so dim you could hardly see anything, especially in a basement? Well, no time to worry about that now. We're on a mission. We gotta find something!"

In the dim lighting, the women squinted, adjusting to the dust-filtered shadows cast by the old light. Their nostrils breathed in the stagnant air. Bunny pointed to the two metal chairs that were pulled away from the table as if someone had just been there and left quickly.

Pet came over, too, and looked at three large, square office boxes, all marked PAYROLL/ACCOUNTS PAYABLE, resting haphazardly on the table. There were two old, grey ledger books lying beside them. These also had seen better days. One of the two was opened. The dog-eared pages were a yellowish brown, and a coating of dust lay on them. INVESTMENT CONTRACTS 1981-82 was written in bold print on top of page 57.

Pet brushed the dust away to get a better look. Pages were missing after 57. At the top of that page, the words "Banc de Cordoba/Cayman" were scrawled very lightly. The next entry started at 61. Pet didn't try to read any of it, for the handwriting was small and the ink was faded. The missing pages did increase her curiosity.

So many questions came to her. She wished she had the time to look through these boxes and the knowledge to know what needed to be found. It was too much to think about now. She closed the ledgers carefully and tucked them under her arm. She adjusted her flashlight and rummaged through some more boxes. The only other items were small scraps of paper and banking receipts. She didn't know how they would pertain to bookkeeping. Impulsively, she grabbed them too and shoved them into her jeans' pocket.

Soon, their eyes became accustomed to the horrible lighting. A little time later, Bunny called to Pet, "Hey, what's beside your foot underneath the table?"

"I don't know. Let's see." Pet bent down and picked up a very brittle book. It looked different, with the color once white or manila. The cover and binding were cloth over cardboard. In heavy ink, 1947 was written on top of the cover in scroll lettering.

"This looks like it might have been one of the original ledgers of Briar Town Furniture Company, Bunny. Someone dropped this. Why else would it be here under the table? Maybe Grace wrote in it. I'm taking this one!"

Bunny occupied herself scanning the walls with her flashlight. She soon found something of interest. Against the wall of this small room were two metal file cabinets. One of them was very rusty and had a thick layer of dust on it. Four drawers fit unevenly in the cabinet. Yellowed paper poked out of the gaps of the drawer. In the center of each drawer were slots with tabs of paper designating its contents.

Bunny mused out loud, "Man, will ya look at this. Looks like someone wasn't too careful with this old thing. Maybe he didn't like what he found or was in too much of a hurry to get out of here. What a mess. Some of the papers are really torn up."

Pet turned and put her light in the same direction. "Look, the other one beside it is new. It has a lock on the upper right corner." She went over to it and tried to open the file cabinet, but the metal lock was pushed in. The drawers wouldn't budge.

"Any ideas?"

Pet watched as Bunny dug in her pants pocket for yet another set of keys. She dangled them in front of her. The three keys were smaller than a door key. They were sturdy metal and looked to be the right width to fit in the file lock.

"Now I just gotta hope I grabbed the correct cabinet keys."

Bunny jabbed every key in the lock. Finally, the last one she held was the right one and pushed it into the lock. With a click, the top drawer opened about an inch. Bunny pulled it out further, shining the light in the file drawer. The only object in there was a newer legal-size ledger book. It still had the Wal-Mart sticker on the cover. Pet flipped the book open to the inner page. On the very top of the page in small print was Deposits FAR AWAY J. W. H.B./ A. L. H. Cayman Is. She grabbed it and was about to open the second drawer. Suddenly, a loud bang on one of the outside doors echoed through the factory. Pet jumped. Bunny screamed, dropping her flashlight and the keys on the dirt floor.

"What was that?" Pet yelped.

"Do I look like I'd know that?" Bunny countered nervously.

"Footsteps! Hurry, find the keys. I'll get your flashlight." Pet gasped and shone her flashlight on the cabinet drawer.

Bunny fumbled with the lock and pushed it in. She stooped down to search for the keys. Pet's flashlight dimmed to almost nothing. She shook it, and it got a little brighter while Bunny desperately searched the dirt floor. The footsteps became louder.

Pet bent down and found Bunny's light. "Let's go, Bunny. We'll come back if we have to. I think we have enough for now. Take my hand. Your flashlight is out."

The women turned and headed for the steps. Both stopped in panic, "The other light!" Bunny gasped.

It was harder now to get back to the table because of the very dim lighting. With their arms stretched out in front of them, they grabbed for the table. The chairs caught them in the chest. Bunny let out a groan but didn't stop. She stretched her body over the table to catch the dangling bit of cord.

Suddenly, the light went out. The batteries in Pet's flashlight were almost out, too, so now, in the darkness, they had to make their way to the steps. They held onto each other, hoping nothing was going to trip them. They inched their way to the steps as fast as they could. It was a lot for Pet to maneuver in holding the heavy books with her left arm and pointing the flashlight at the steps with her right hand.

Pet didn't care how nasty those old steps were. She ran so fast she wasn't sure if her feet even touched the wood. They huddled at the door listening intently. They heard another door close with a bang, followed by footsteps on gravel, then silence.

Bunny grabbed Pet's arm from behind and lunged her forward. "Go!"

It wasn't until they were on Rt. 376 past the Marovia exit, Pet and Bunny breathed normally.

"My God, what a rush!" Bunny exclaimed. "I wonder who was outside?"

"I don't really care at this point. It's over and done with. We got what we came for. We'll leave it at that. I hope we'll be able to go there again if we don't get the right ledgers. I wonder how much they kept from Grace before she died? How long did Grace manage the accounts? How well did she know Mr. Hyde? I would love to know how she lived and who she loved. There's a story here, Bunny; there are just too many questions."

Bunny shifted in her seat and had a very pensive look on her face. "Ya know, something doesn't smell right. These books and the two cabinets have a lot of info we need before the next board meeting. If Mr. Hyde is siphoning money, it has to be in the old books before all the computer technology started. I bet he started small with odd amounts of money so the bookkeepers wouldn't question it. I'm going to see if I can dig up anything else. Are you afraid to come back with me if necessary?"

"No, I'll come. How about next week?"

The women didn't talk to each other after their plan for another visit was confirmed. In the silence, Pet thanked the Lord for small favors in not getting caught by whoever was walking outside the warehouse.

For some reason, Anthony popped into her mind. She was still hurting emotionally from the other night. With a heavy sigh, a vision of their ugly scene vividly came to her. "Why did he have to talk down to me like that? I hate that demeaning tone of voice. He knows I hate it. I think he wants someone to dominate. Maybe he just wants a piece of ass, and that's all. Should I break off our relationship if he doesn't love me? God, I cannot stand this crap. Why isn't love simple? Also, I wonder why he was at Briar Town. Does he go there often? Who does he talk to? If it were business about me taking over, shouldn't I be involved? Something's not right. I have to find out these things."

Whether it was paranoia or a valid suspicion, the questions unsettled her. What wasn't he telling her? Pet was still in thought when Bunny pulled up to her apartment.

Pet got out of the car quickly and, with a friendly wave, said, "Goodnight. Thanks for helping me, Bunny."

"You got it. Any time. Once you look through those books, I know you'll have some questions. See you next week at 7p.m. sharp. Don't keep me waiting. Right here in front, okay?"

Pet laughed lightly, "Oh, don't worry, I'll be here, and I know I'll have questions!"

She waved again and called out, "I hope you find the answers to Grace's past!" Bunny was instantly lost in the traffic.

Chapter 37

Looking Over the Books

Before Pet spread out these company jewels before her, she made sure her mother was occupied with her knitting and her father was engrossed in a Zane Grey Western story. They eagerly offered help, but Pet assured them this job was all hers. All three books were ready. She picked up the oldest one first. As she leaned closer, the pungent smell of mold on the inside of the leather-bound book made her sneeze. She proceeded to flip through the pages of the first ledger, her finger feeling a fine dust resting on the yellowed pages. Carefully opening the long book, Pet hoped for answers.

At that moment, the only thing she accomplished was sneezing four times and knocking the book to the floor. She tried to retrieve it, but instead bumped another book that was too close to the edge, and it fell to the floor too. A fine brown smudge surrounded the books on the rug.

She moaned, "Ugh, I can see this isn't going to be easy. One thing just leads to another job." Pet got out the vacuum cleaner. Before she turned it on, she gingerly put both ledgers back on the table. As she laid them down, something caught her eye. A small bit of paper jutted out of the oldest one. It looked like a small envelope. She wanted to stop and look inside the page, but the relics had to be cleaned first.

Soon, the whining sound of the vacuum cleaner filled the room and sucked up the mess in no time. She also got a soft white cloth and wiped the loose dust from the books. Then she bent over them, anticipation in her eyes, and pulled out the paper. Sure enough, it was a small, dirty white envelope. She studied it. Grace's name was written in bold script lettering. To Pet's surprise, the ink was still dark. *It looks like a man's handwriting,* she pondered. *Could this be another piece of the puzzle?*

Pet decided she wasn't going to handle this detective work on an empty stomach, so she made herself a toasted cheese and tomato sandwich on New York rye bread. As she got out the butter, she saw a half-bottle of Zinfandel Wine on the fridge door. She took that and brought it to the table, too.

She hungrily bit into the toasted bread. Cheese oozed out of the side of the crunchy bread. Pet rolled her eyes in delight. "Mmm, now, that's good eating!"

Finishing the sandwich with a gulp of wine, she washed her hands carefully, making sure she didn't have any grease on her fingers, and put the gloves back on her hands. The paper envelope was as brittle as the rest of the books on the table. She opened the envelope, pulled out a single sheet of note paper, and read it silently to herself.

Dear Grace,

Thank you for letting me back into your life, even though it is on a professional basis. Thank you for having the confidence in me that I will be a good asset to Briar Town Furniture Co. I won't let you down. Maybe in time you will forgive me for the way our lives turned out.

Sincerely,

Al

"He was in love with her! Why didn't he marry, Grace? What a puzzle. I wonder who knows the whole story? One person at least, please!"

Her appetite for delving into the books was certainly whetted by this note. She immediately got her floor lamp and put it next to her chair. She also placed two different-strength magnifying glasses and a pair of white gloves next to her. After the prep work, she felt she was ready.

As the night wore on, Pet inched her way through the antique pages, scrutinizing the countless figures that began in 1953. She saw the entry dates of deposits, credit figures, and debit figures written in Grace's neat handwriting with her initials at the bottom of each page.

"How boring," she thought. "There is nothing exceptional here. Briar Town Furniture was always in the black. Every month showed a profit. There has to be something more than just deposits and credits. I hope the next book will show me something different."

She fought the urge to call Anthony for advice. She was afraid of his ridicule for not understanding simple banking. She just didn't want to hear it.

She was angry with him anyway. The last time she called him about moving into Rutherford Manor, he never returned her call. She waited two days and left him a voice message. Not only was she feeling paranoid, but she felt he was truly distancing himself from her after the champagne episode. Damn him. He could have called and begged for forgiveness, or sent flowers, or something more than complete silence.

Pet tried to get back to the ledger, but her eyes started to cross. The first glass of wine with her sandwich seemed to be a good idea, but now the second glass made her sleepy. She put a clean white tissue on the page where she stopped and carefully closed the book. "I'll deal with this tomorrow. Maybe I'll call Bunny."

Chapter 38

Page 57

The next day began brighter and earlier. Pet woke refreshed at 7:00 am. Armed with a fresh mug of coffee, she headed to the table. Placing the soft white gloves on her petite hands, she sat down again, peering over the brittle pages.

A thought occurred to her that didn't resound in her head last night. What part would Aloysius play in the company? Middle management? No, surely, he would have some administrative authority. Another twist of possibility caught her curiosity. Why would his note be among the ledgers? She reached for the second book, hoping this one would tell the tale.

On the front, she saw the faded title of contents: Payroll, Accounts Payable. Whole families worked for this company. Weekly wages for each job were tabulated in dollars and cents. The office workers weren't paid much more than a common laborer. For certain jobs, men were paid more than women. Pet laughed, "Well, nothing has changed much," she thought.

Several pages forward, she found the Accounts Payable section. She noticed large sums of money being paid to both domestic and foreign suppliers for specialty woods. The names of various types of lumber were listed in detail. Raw and finished metals were shipped to Briar Town also on a monthly schedule. Pet found the listings fascinating. She wanted to spend more time in this section, but she knew it would be time-consuming.

Still flipping through the pages of the ledger, an anomaly caught her eye. Halfway through the book, the handwriting changed drastically. It was bold with big curves on capital letters. The decimal points were exaggerated. Then it dawned on her that it was the same handwriting as the note. Aloysius had taken over the books.

"How interesting," she thought. With renewed vigor, she traced every column slowly with her gloved finger. The next two pages of this new handwriting remained the same, but the wording changed ever so slightly. Consulting Fees were added to the same page as accounts payable, and directly underneath payroll were written the initials A.R.H J.W.H.B., overseers in tiny print. "Man, is this print small! What was someone trying to hide." she questioned to herself.

The amount of cash flow and the year-end profits varied. She was amazed to see that, over two years, sales increased to $100,000.00. She was amazed and proud of Grace for making the company so profitable.

Then, in November, she saw a drastic decline in sales. The profit margin for the next six months showed little change. The entries were no surprise and made sense to Pet.

After finishing the second book, she got up and stretched her legs; a cinnamon Danish was calling her name. She filled her coffee mug again and drank it slowly. Before she reached for the third book, the wad of receipts caught her eye. She wanted to look at them again, wondering how they would play into this drama at Briar Town Furniture Company. Were they important or just bits of trash to muddle her search?

"Nope, concentrate, girl. You gotta get one thing done at a time," she muttered to herself. She was lost in thought, putting on the white gloves again, when her cell phone rang. She hoped it would be Bunny.

"Hello?"

A silence and then, "Pet, what's the matter? You always sound like a lost soul."

"Oh, it's you." Her voice fell flat. She was disappointed. "Why would I sound lost, Anthony? I'm home. I know where I am, and no one is bothering me, until now."

There was that awkward silence again. He cleared his throat. "Who did you think this was? Does my voice irritate you that much? I was hoping you would want to talk to me, anyway, I..."

Before he could answer, she interrupted him. She could tell he was either already upset with her before he called or angry that she wasn't pleased with the sound of his voice. In her mind's eye, she could see him patting down his hair.

"Anthony, are you in your car? Do I hear the radio? Where are you?"

Curtly, he asked, "Pet, are you going to listen to what I have to say, or ask a lot of pointless questions?"

She bit her lower lip, "No, Anthony. Sorry, I wasn't trying to be rude. Go ahead, what's on your mind?"

A little while ago, she would've giggled a bit and made it a game, but now doubt and mistrust strained their relationship.

"I am in the car and near your apartment building. I'd like to come up and see you. I've missed you."

As soon as he said apartment building, her hair stood up on the back of her neck. His last two words of endearment didn't faze her. She hissed in anger, "Yesss. I'm still in my apartment, Anthony. Still here in limbo, pining for a home of my own. Isn't it a shame I couldn't receive you in my rightful home, the Regal Rutherford Manor? I've heard it is empty, lonely, vacant, and void of human laughter and conversation. Do you have the keys to the manor house with you? Can I pack my bags tomorrow?"

"No, I don't. What's with your attitude, Pet? Don't get pissed off with me. Some things are out of my control." Then, softening his tone of voice, he said, "I have told you many times, Pet, probating a complicated Will is never easy. The papers should be ready to sign as soon as next month."

Anthony was about to utter the tried and true "trust me," but thought better of it. He was in no mood to hear another tirade from her.

Her tone was sullen, making her words sound like an order to a subordinate. "Good. See that they are. I am tired of waiting. And one more thing, Anthony. The next time I call your office, tell your snobbish secretary not to blow me off. Your hired help is lacking a lot of common courtesy."

"Sure, Pet, I'll be in touch," adding "bitch' under his breath, throwing the phone on the passenger seat as he drove to his office.

She heard the click, and their heated discussion ended. She gently put the phone down on the table. Pet was okay until her mind flashed back to the first time Anthony kissed her here in the living room. As if in a melodramatic soap opera, she wanted to scream at him, "Damn you! Why do you play with my emotions this way? You should be more sensitive to my needs. I loved you, Anthony, with my whole heart, my whole soul. I was yours until you copied Neil's ways. You know I don't want that kind of man. You make me crazy with doubt. I can't trust you anymore!"

Unwanted tears trickled down her cheeks as her nose began to run. She quickly dashed off the gloves and got a tissue. With a shaking hand, she dabbed her eyes. She felt hot and agitated. When she was this emotionally upset, her body temperature rose, and even her ears burned. She knew her face would be all blotchy from her tears and dared not look at herself in the mirror.

Fiona always told her, "Pet, lass, ye can never hide your tears with that angel soft face of yours. Now stop makin' a flood with them. Tears never helped a pretty face get better."

Fiona knew how to calm her down. She got up from the table and poured herself some orange juice from the fridge. She then refreshed herself with a cool splash of water. It felt good on her face. Grabbing a small terry-cloth towel, she buried her face in its softness and relaxed. Her cheeks felt cool, and she was ready to start again. She reached for the next book and thought, "Well, third book. Let's see what you have to tell me."

The old book was labeled differently, Corporate Contracts.

From page one to page ten, Pet saw countless contracts with plants and furniture companies. Each business included the owner's name, the amount of materials ordered, and the exact delivery date. The cost of the materials was staggering to Pet. Each contract was written for $10,000.00 or more. At the bottom of each contract were three names: the company's owner, Grace's, and Aloysius Hyde.

The next pages showed the companies ordering furniture from Briar Town. There was a huge jump in income. One contract from St. Francis Academy made her eyes bug out. Total Cost was $25,000. Ordered by John Michael Sundy, Approved Grace Traffortelli. Signed Grace B. Trafforelli, Aloysius Hyde, John Michael Sundy

"Wow!" Pet said to herself. Back in the day, this was a huge order for the company to fill. A new school was obviously being built. What a good thing it must have been to hire so many people. I bet the whole community thrived. Materials had to be bought, people had to make the desks, so on and so on. No wonder Whalen Falls is such a big town. Grace was important, and she was rich!

She turned the pages quickly, examining one contract after another. She found the construction contracts for the Brighton Warehouse, which were designated to build all those desks. How sad that it no longer has that activity. She recognized the name because it was the same building that she and Bunny explored that memorable night.

Altogether, she counted twenty-five major companies with many subcontracts for minor suppliers. A lot of money was poured into the company, but it also went out in the form of loans to buy the needed heavy equipment to build and maintain this and other new buildings. Expansion seemed to be the name of the game during that period. She flipped through pages of notes about investment planning in what looked like high-end consulting firms in the U.S. and overseas.

Piece by piece, Pet's understanding of the history of Briar Town Furniture Company was becoming clearer. There was a blank page, then she saw Acquisitions, Consulting Firms, Banks; the amount of money continued to amaze her.

She read the bank's names out loud: "First Fifth Bank of Detroit, Meryl Lynch, Pierce Fenner and Bean, etc. Good God! How many did they need?"

The next page she turned to was page 55. It was blank, but

what was between the pages made her laugh when she saw it. She pulled out a single-page advertisement for Britton Brothers Friendly Finance Co., Grand Cayman Islands. "Is this for real?" She looked at it in disbelief. The advertisement was poorly designed and amateurish. In bold gold lettering, it touted No Income Taxes! No Audits! Convenient Offshore Accounting, High Interest Rates. Under the lettering were palm trees and sunny skies. In the background, there was a picture of a bank near the shore.

"That advertisement looks ridiculous." Pet folded it back up, dismissing it, and went on to the next page.

But to her surprise, on the top of page 56, Britton Brothers Friendly Finance Company appeared again. Underneath this finance company, she saw in smaller print Revolving Line of Credit, underneath that Tourmell Consulting Grand Cayman.

New columns were added under the three new names. The tiny print reminded Pet of a child whispering a big secret so only a few people could hear.

They were just like the accounts payable ledgers set up for deposits, payments, and consulting fees. One followed the other, filling the page with different amounts. She noticed that Grace's initials were nowhere to be seen.

The very next turn revealed page 57 and a big disappointment. Nothing was there except the words INVESTMENT CONTRACTS, and the edges of ripped-out pages. "Damn! This tells me nothing. It doesn't make sense at all. What was going on? I'm going to call Bunny. Hopefully, by now, she's found something out."

Chapter 39

Questions and Answers

Before Pet even considered her next move, her cell phone rang.

"Hey, whatta ya doin'?" Bunny greeted Pet in her chirpy young voice.

"Wow! Are you psychic or what!" Pet laughed. "I was just going to call you. I went through the ledgers, and I've learned enough to know I've got a lot more questions."

"Oh, like what?"

"Well, Aloysius and Grace definitely had a past. I think he loved her deeply. I found a note that is almost a love letter. He thanks her for letting him be part of Briar Town, but his choice of words conveys disappointment and hurt. I'm thinking it was about midway into the company's history."

Bunny chided her. "Go on, Sherlock. You are making pretty good sense so far. What else? Did you get the idea Briar Town Furniture Company is a big bag of money?"

"Oh, my God, I had no idea the amounts of money I saw in the deposit columns were so huge. It was and still is a massive corporation, but then I saw these consulting fees and offshore accounts."

"Pretty sneaky, isn't it?" Bunny stopped talking and cleared her throat. "Look, why don't I come over after work. I don't want to be on the phone any longer than I have to. Since you've come on the scene, this place has become a real snake pit; don't trust anyone here."

Pet sighed. "Okay, don't dilly dally. Do you get off at 5:00?"

"Yes, straight from work, promise."

At 5:30p.m. Bunny was knocking at her door. Pet answered

it quickly and practically pulled her down the hall into the living room.

"Don't leave out any details. I want to hear it all. Sit here on the couch and make yourself comfortable. Mom and Dad are with Uncle Mike, so we'll have lots of time to talk."

"Do you mind if I take my sweater off first? Take a breath, Pet. I gotta pee before I can do anything!"

"Sorry, Bunny, patience isn't my strong suit. Sure, go right ahead; turn to your left and down past the bedroom."

Pet got out cheese, pepperoni, and two cold cans of Pepsi. Bunny came back and sat down on the couch. Smiling, she reached for the Pepsi and took a big gulp. "Ah, that's good. I needed that. I was parched. Okay, ready, Missy?"

"Oh yes, what did you find out? Anything juicy?"

"Yeah, sneaky stuff. Aloysius was smart and stupid at the same time. At first, it looked like a lot of gibberish, but after I deciphered the coding, I was able to get into his personal files."

Pet had an odd expression on her face, and she put up her hand to stop Bunny.

"Wait a minute. How did you get into Aloysius' personal files? I thought Mr. Big Shot would be more secretive than to let anyone find them."

"I had about given up on finding out where any of the older files went or even where they were buried in the computer histories. Then, out of the blue, this new kid in accounting came to me yesterday with some old bills and said he had to consolidate delinquent write-offs and needed the correct code. He didn't know how to do it. The poor kid was so nervous. He said he thought he had the right override code number, but it kept coming up ACCESS DENIED ADMINISTRATIVE PROGRAMMERS ONLY.

"He thought he had done something wrong. I thought to myself, buddy, you just handed me the golden key. I dismissed him and told him I would fix the problem.

"So, with a little fiddling around, I realized that when computers were first used, files were easily deciphered. All I had to do was repeat the number sequences and simple coordinating words back to front and front to back, and bingo, Voila! I was in Al's files! Also, the dumb shit never changed these number sequences for his firewall. Do you believe that? It was like robbing a bank with my eyes closed!"

Pet took a piece of pepperoni. "Wow! How else can we nail him to the wall, you know, money-wise? The only thing I found were deposits for several offshore accounts and payments to a consulting firm. It looked legit to me."

"Oh, that sounds interesting. What he did might look innocent, but in honest banking procedures, it wasn't. An experienced auditor will look at little hidden words that spell hidden money. I think we could get him good on something else, but I don't think I can prove it."

"Hmm? You don't sound too sure, Bunny."

"It's like this. I think Mr. Hyde and the company are involved in a serious judgment against them from bank auditors, but I can't prove it. From what I heard, the whole thing sounds really complicated."

"What's a judgment, and how did you happen upon that?"

"It goes sorta like this: Last week my goofy sister..."

Pet stopped her abruptly, "Bunny, if it's a fact, the statement you're making can't start out 'sorta like this' I want to get rid of Aloysius Hyde. It can't be some cock-a-mamie story!"

Bunny reached for some cheese and took another long drink of Pepsi, "Listen, it gets better. So anyway, my goofy sister fixes me up with a blind date in the middle of the day at Shakespeare's Restaurant, of all places. This dweeb is really trying to impress me with all his contacts at Duquesne University Administration's inner circle while we are sitting at the bar.

"He's droning on and on, and I start daydreaming until I just happen to look over my shoulder and see Catherine Hartwell, James Wingate, and Marshall Kochmann seated at the table behind me. Catherine has her back to me and is doing most of the talking, while Wingate is staring at my tight skirt. I'm surprised he didn't recognize me. That horny bastard didn't lift his eyes past my butt." Bunny continued, "So, Mr. Kochmann is nodding and listening intently. I knew it was Catherine because I could hear her raspy voice urging me to buy Alton Paint and Supply Co. as soon as possible. She said, rather excitedly, that if it wasn't grabbed up soon, in the next day or two, it was going into a foreclosure situation. Every five minutes, Wingate interrupted her by saying, "Marshall, it's a good deal. Go for it." And that really got annoying.

Then Catherine said, "Marshall, offer them $2 million for the company. I assure you, they will not hesitate to sell. You must confirm this deal today, or no later than tomorrow at noon."

"Okay, so what then?"

"So, I ordered another daiquiri and fish and chips."

"You're exasperating. Ya know that! What happened next?" Pet asked excitedly.

"Marshall excused himself briefly to go to the john. Then she and Wingate whispered together."

"Gosh, could you hear her at all?"

"Yeah, I was able to hear every word because of the hoarseness in her voice; she had to articulate slowly to be understood."

Bunny leaned closer to Pet as if she were recreating the scene. "Catherine says to Wingate, 'Get Jerry Hinkle from Federal Commerce &Loan Bank in Pittsburgh immediately. Tell him to deny Kochmann's loan and buy it for 1 million in cash. We'll call our friendly banker in the Caymans. He's on our payroll and won't bat an eyelash. The board will prove Kochmann's incompetence for overbidding and buying a worthless business for an exorbitant price.

"Remember, don't go above 2 mill. It's not even worth that. I don't want to lose it haggling over a few thousand. The debacle should get him out of our hair for a good while. Now, go quickly, I'll make your excuses."

Pet leaned back on the couch. "What a bitch! Now I understand what Mr. Kochmann said at the dinner the night I met him. No wonder he is no longer part of management. He looked so sad. Now I know why."

Bunny sat back, too. "I couldn't believe it either. He should have fought the action against him."

"More? What now?"

"Well, I overheard Catherine talking loudly late last night in the administrative conference room. She asked what Mr. Hyde was going to do about the IRS audit of the Alton Paint Company tomorrow. But you didn't hear that from me. Do you understand?"

Pet said, "Oh, yes, promise, cross my heart." Pet couldn't resist saying, "I can see Catherine, forcing words out of her throat sounding like a far-off New England foghorn."

"God, you should have heard her. She bellowed and cranked on so that Mr. Hyde told her to shut up because he couldn't take her voice any longer."

"What else did Mr. Hyde say after that?"

"Nothing," he grumbled, and said, "We'll go over it tomorrow."

Pet sat up, "Wow, sure would like to be a fly on the wall tomorrow morning. Also, I was just thinking about those old books. Those payments to Tourmel Consulting were awfully high and very frequent. I wonder if the company got anything out of it. Who was the consultant? Do you think I'm right, Bunny?"

Bunny sat up too. "Yup, also Aloysius Hyde started some creative banking practices and made it look legit at the same time. He fed a lot of bullshit figures into this system when computers first came on the banking scene. Oh, he always showed a profit because it was easy back then. The auditors didn't know enough about the new automated systems to see any discrepancies, so he kept using this ploy to make money for himself."

"And, his saying he loved Grace, while he was stealing 'thousands' right under her nose. I'm going to get him out of here. He won't be the board president for long. You'll see, Bunny. Things will change!" Pet said indignantly.

Chapter 40

Safety Deposit Box

The heels of Pet's and Judy's shoes clicked on the green marble floor of the First Mercantile Bank of New York. They passed huge white marble pillars that separated the gated area from the teller windows. A tall, distinguished, gray-haired gentleman led Pet and Judy to a secluded area as if ushering them to an assigned church pew. He stopped in front of a large floor-to-ceiling metal gate with multiple connecting bars. This cell-like door separated them from yet another room, prohibiting them from stepping into the bank's secluded rooms.

Pet and Judy were whispering to each other all the way to the vault. As they got closer to the gate, Judy looked at her in surprise. She sputtered, "You did what? What do you mean, you left?"

Pet immediately put her fingers to her lips, "Jude, please! Shhh! Not so loud!"

The gentleman turned to them, "Pardon me, Madam, did you say something?"

"Oh, no. Excuse me. I was just talking to my friend," Pet said, glaring at Judy.

"Good then. Please wait here, Madam. I will return when it is time to open the doors."

"Why can't you open the doors now? I gave you all my information. Can't you just open it? No one else is here. "

"I'm sorry, Madam. It is not ten o'clock yet. They are electronically set. It is just nine-forty-five. "

Pet sighed a bit, frustrated. "Why didn't you tell me that when we first arrived?"

"I am obeying bank policy, Madam. Unfortunately, my

hands are tied. I will come to you immediately when it is nine fifty-nine."

"Thank you," Pet said, murmuring as he walked away.

With a tone of desperation in her voice, Judy urged her to continue. "Again, why did you leave? I don't understand. Tell me more."

Pet motioned Judy farther away from any possible eavesdroppers.

"Geez, Jude, it was exactly that. I walked out of his house, slamming the door behind me."

"Well, why? Was the evening all that bad? You've got a great guy in your arms, ready to enter the threshold of ecstasy, and then suddenly you walk out the door?"

"It isn't that simple. You've paraphrased a lot, in between lying together and slamming the door, my friend."

"What was the in-between, cold feet? Have you seen him since your encounter?"

Pet sighed, "No."

"Well, come on, details please," Judy said eagerly.

"I did. I did want him. Lying there on the bed, his body heat was unbelievable. With his practically naked body next to mine, I could smell that man smell again. You know, the subtle scent of expensive cologne mixed in with the slightest bit of perspiration. It definitely intensified the anticipation of sex. He pushed all the right buttons, nuzzling into my hair, kissing my neck, and caressing my skin ever so softly with his fingertips.

"I wanted sex so badly I could taste it. Even the soft prickling sensation of his leg hair rubbing against my thighs was more than I could bear. My breathing was rapid enough to make me faint, so don't tell me I had cold feet."

Judy had a dreamy expression on her face and didn't talk for a second. She was fantasizing, waiting for more. When it didn't come, she looked over to Pet, "All that going on and you stopped? What could have gone so wrong?"

Pet spoke in a hoarse, emphatic whisper. "Him! He went

wrong, Jude. He stopped, amid tearing my panties from me, and my panting, get on top of me, you fool, you fool!"

She looked heartbroken. A tear fell from her right eye. "His plan of seduction was perfect, topping it off with champagne, but the bottle wouldn't open. We had words over the stupid situation. I asked if I could assist, and then his pride reared its ugly head. Immediately, he smarted off to me, and that was that. I'm never going to be talked to like that ever again. Neil did it, and I hated it. I won't tolerate it; I just won't."

Judy sighed, "Yeah, I can understand now, Hon, but I hope you didn't completely close the door on him."

"As it turned out, I had to go back and face him over a stupid, in my opinion, technicality. I came over here the very next day and asked to see Mr. Ernst Gernshaltar. He is an attorney at the bank in charge of these matters and the person who sent me the letter via Anthony.

"So, I'm standing right there in front of him, and this Mr. Ernst Gernshaltar gets all stuffy, asking for a legal document stating I was the legal heir to Grace's personal accounts and safety deposit box. My driver's license and this letter didn't satisfy him at all. So, back to Anthony. I went to get it all proper like, what a headache!"

"Did Anthony give you an attitude, Pet?"

"No. He was courteous and professional. He held onto the papers before he let go of them, hoping I would say something about that night. I couldn't, Judy. I didn't know what to say. His baby blues got to me, though. They were expressive and pleading. I almost caved in and kissed him goodbye, but didn't. He'll call me. I know he will. I think he's got some curiosity about the safety deposit box. He did ask me if I wanted him to go with me, but I wanted you to be with me. He would've just made me nervous."

"Oh, so I'm just a steadying factor?"

Pet huffed, "Come on, don't play games with me now, Jude. You know what I mean. Anthony would watch my every move.

I don't want to be rushed. Besides, after his call the other day, I don't think I ever want to see him face to face again as long as I live."

"Oh, did it get ugly?"

"Yeah, I yelled at him because I wasn't in my rightful home. I won't go into that now, okay?"

"Sure, do you think he'd follow you here?"

"No. Why?"

"Really? You don't think, just out of legal curiosity, he'd want to know what's in that box? "

"No. That's not his style."

Finally, the old gentleman returned and ushered them through the gate. "Follow me, please."

Chapter 41

Peak of the Past

Before he pulled out the safety deposit box from the multi-sectioned wall, Pet's curiosity got the better of her.

"Pardon me. Sir, who are you?"

"I'm Mr. Jonathan Day, Mr. Ernst Gernshaltar's assistant, Madam. Is there a problem?"

"Oh no, please, don't misunderstand. I was just wondering. Have you worked here long?"

"Over forty years now. If you are ready, I will put the box on the table after you have signed this request sheet."

Pet signed the paper quickly.

"Very good, Madam, I will be in the very next office just off to the right if you have any questions."

"Thank you."

Mr. Day retrieved the metal box from the wall. He placed it carefully on a wide wooden table. Without another word, he turned and went out the door.

Pet was excited. She never opened a safety deposit box before.

"Well, let's go for it." Her hands shook a little as she turned the key to the long, narrow metal box. As she pulled the lid up, it opened stiffly. Pet wondered. Does every executive own a safety deposit box? How important was this box?

Carefully, she looked at its contents and was immediately awestruck when she saw a gold money clip. On top was a thousand-dollar bill. She fingered the other bills and came up with ten more. "My God, Judy, look. There's eleven thousand dollars here! Why would Grace leave this kind of money here?"

Judy let out a soft whistle and whispered in a low voice.

"Fun money? Expense money? Sure is a nice little Godsend, don't cha think? Don't knock the freebees."

Pet carefully moved the money aside and picked up two envelopes. One plain, the other blue, with PICTURES of Al, HOWARD, and ME written on it.

Judy grew insistent, "Well, open them! The suspense is killing me. Why are you hesitating? There could be more money in them." Judy fingered inside the box. "Nothing else is in here."

Pet tapped Judy's hand, moving it away from the box. "Okay, okay, but look now. Seeing this money makes me sad. Maybe she was afraid I would need cash right away. I can visualize Grace putting these things in here just for me. Poor dear, I miss her so much. What was going through her mind? Wonder when she put the money in here?"

Judy's voice expressed irritation when she turned Pet around to face her. "There ya go. Second-guessing everything. You have to stop doing this, Pet. It'll drive you crazy. Ya have to start thinking like a businesswoman. You are the woman in charge. Act like it. And another thing: stop asking people you don't even know questions. They don't want to have a relationship with you. They don't care about you. They'll do their job. You do yours."

Then her voice softened a little, " I don't want to sound like a nag, Hon. I'm just trying to help you."

"It doesn't hurt to be nice to people, Judy. People are so impersonal, even snobbish toward one another these days. Your advice is probably right, though. I'll change. You'll see."

After a second or two, she reached for the blue envelope. Its paper was brittle but still vibrant. She found three old black-and-white pictures.

The first picture showed a boy and a girl standing in front of an ivy-covered wall. The boy was wearing a white varsity letter sweater, dark slacks, and white shoes. The girl was wearing a white sweater, a pleated striped skirt, and saddle shoes. They were smiling at the camera. The next picture was a girl, standing in a cap and gown with her parents. Rutgers University could be seen on the cornerstone of a building in the background.

The next picture made both women pause and say, "Aw, that's so sweet." The same couple was facing each other, holding hands. Her left hand showed a rather prominent ring. They looked happy.

Inside the ecru envelope was a single paper receipt from Kraus' Jewelers describing an engagement ring. The description was very exact.

One Brazilian Tourmaline stone, emerald cut, color pink .55 diamond, baguettes surrounding tourmaline stone totaling 1.5 carats, band, rose gold 18 carats. Value: $875.00; purchase date: December 2, 1960. Paid in full.

Pet and Judy simultaneously let out a low whistle of amazement.

"That's some ring, Pet," Judy whispered.

Pet stuck her fingers into the envelope, expecting to find a ring, but there was none. Just for the heck of it, she ran her fingers along the sides and bottom of the box. No ring was there. "Hmm, that's odd. Why would there be a receipt for this gorgeous piece of jewelry, but no ring in sight? What is pink tourmaline, anyway?"

"Don't know, Hon."

Pet's voice had a wistful tone in it, "If Mr. Day has been here forty years, I wonder if he knew Grace? Now you see, I have to ask him for more information. He might even know about Grace. Why, he could have been a 'love item' in her past."

Judy had a smirk on her face as she slowly shook her head. "You kill me. You just kill me, ya know that! I suppose you're gonna ask Mr. Day one of your nosey little questions, aren't you?"

"Damn straight! Besides, something is not right. Why would all this money be here and no ring? There is just the store receipt. I have to tell him. He has to know that something is missing."

"Pet, you could buy another ring with all this money sitting here. I wouldn't worry about it. You're reading too much into this."

"No, that's not the point. There has to be a reason it's not here. Grace was very methodical and meticulous. This ring meant something to her; why else would she keep the receipt? I think it's the ring in the picture. She loved jewelry, and good jewelry at that. No. Something's wrong. I'm going to his office."

Pet left the receipt and the money, but took the picture envelope out of the box. She locked it and put it back into the wall. She looked at Judy. "Ready?"

Chapter 42

Remembering Grace

Upon listening to Pet's question about the ring, Jonathan Day adjusted his glasses. A smile came to his lips as the corners of his mustache lifted. He took a minute staring into the past as if it were yesterday. He quelled the temptation to fantasize about the past. With a hesitant cough, he started saying, "Yes, in my younger days, I knew Grace quite well. We were all schoolmates: Howard Hyde, his brother Aloysius, and Miss Grace Briar. Master Howard and Miss Grace were sweethearts from the very beginning of their college days. Ah, they were so much in love."

In his mind, he could see the two of them standing there, face to face, and hear Grace's laughter saying, "Come on, Jona- than," Grace begged, "take our picture, pa-lease." She was fidgety and giddy, making ridiculous faces as Howard laughed at her antics. They didn't care how impatient he was, wanting to get this done. His finger ached to click the shutter button.

"Yes, I remember Grace. She was a lovely girl, and smart, too. Sharp as a tack, she was. She could make the best of us feel inadequate when it came to scholastics. We would never admit that she got better grades.

"She could hold her own in polite society, too. All the best families regarded her as an excellent choice for their sons. And her beau was Howard. He was a young man with fine aristocratic features. He had a way with people. Talkative, intelligent, and he made them feel special. Everyone knew he would go far in anything he set his mind to. They made a beautiful couple. Then, after Howard died, I could never understand why she got caught up with Aloysius. He was second-class goods, in my opinion."

When Jonathan Day saw Judy and Pet staring eagerly into his face, wanting more information, he suddenly stopped speaking. He inwardly admonished himself for lapsing into familiarity. After a moment, he cleared his throat with a gentle *ahem*. "Now, Madam, have I answered your question confirming that I knew Mrs. Grace Traffortelli?"

"Yes, you have, but something is still wrong. As I told you when we came to your office, Sir, the ring described on the receipt is not here. Do you know what happened to it?" Pet asked intently.

He gave the picture back to Pet and pretended to be busy with papers on his desk. "I'm sorry, Mrs. Traffortelli. I cannot tell you anything else, except that the day she came to deposit these items, they were in a red velvet bag. So, I couldn't have known what she placed into it. Her mood was dour and worrisome. I could see she was not herself. She quickly went about her business and left without saying goodbye. Her usual manner was always cordial." He stopped abruptly. "That is all, I'm sorry. Now, if you will excuse me, I have work to do for Mr. Gernshalter."

The two of them left without another word.

"That was a big help," Judy said sarcastically.

Pet reiterated with the same tone of voice and sentiment, "Yeah, thanks for nothing, Mr. Day."

"What are you going to do?" Judy asked as they walked out to the sidewalk.

"I'm going to the manor house, that's what."

"Fat chance, kid. How the hell are you going to do that? Does breaking and entering sound all that good to you?"

"I don't have to break and enter, my dear friend. I have my ways."

Judy looked at her in surprise as she went around to the passenger door, "What ways?"

"If I remember correctly, there is an old window well, and in it is a single pane basement window that is rusted shut. It is behind a really big bush, can't think of its name now, but I know I can get in there and pry the window open. I'll push it with my feet. It opens to the inside."

"That is a pretty sketchy plan, my dear. In fact, I think you're nuts, and it's still breaking and entering."

Pet laughed, "I'll worry about that later, Jude."

Chapter 43

The Go Ahead

"Hey, where have you been, Captain Iverson? Nice to see you, ole buddy!"

"Aren't you ever going to learn how to talk to your superiors, Jones? You are formal and, at the same time, ethically sloppy. I could get you for insubordination with that kind of greeting, not giving a superior officer his just respect."

Jones had an evil little smile on his face. "That's a bunch of shit, and you know it. I've known you too long to be disrespectful. I've been wondering where you've been lately. I have not seen you since Pet's uncle came in here, causing all that ruckus. He is some character. The look on her face when she saw him was priceless. God, it made her even more beautiful."

Joshua Iverson smiled, "You like her, don't cha?"

"Hell yeah! A man would have to be deaf, dumb, and blind not to fall for a beautiful woman like that. Pet can draw a man into her world without even trying. It is the way she talks that makes you think you are the only person in the universe. She makes the conversation interesting, yet she's vulnerable at the same time."

"Well, if you feel that way about her, why don't you make your move? Call her." Detective Iverson urged David Jones on.

"Whoa, I'm not going to get in the middle of a threesome, ole buddy. I don't play that game. What kind of statement is that?"

"I don't think I am right for her, Jones," Iverson said thoughtfully.

"Aw, come on. I see the way you look at her, remember? You love her. You've got rank, money, distinguished looks, everything a woman would like in a man. We know each other too well. Come on, gimme the truth."

For the first time in their working relationship, Joshua Iverson bared his soul to his close friend. "Well, David, this isn't going to be easy to say. I'm going to be retiring soon. My heart specialist suspects cardiac artery disease, leading to the possibility of cardiomyopathy."

"Are you pulling my chain?" David asked.

"Would I kid about something like this?" Iverson responded.

"I hope not, man. You are not that old for this kind of stuff."

"Look, Pollyanna, shit can happen to anyone at any time in his life, and it looks like I'm one of those poor slobs who gets the full load of bad. So, even though I'm only fifty-five, I'm not going to saddle Pet with a sick old fart to take care of me the rest of my miserable life."

A double whammy of emotions flooded his young mind: sadness that Joshua was sick and joy that he could pursue Pet with no regrets. He didn't speak right away. The seriousness of these medical terms weighed heavily on him. He nodded in acceptance as Joshua symbolically passed the torch to him.

Then with an air of bravado in his voice, David Jones stood up, "You've knocked the breath out of me, Joshua, but I know you ain't dead yet, and you're gonna be around for a good while longer. Hell, man, I am going to need your experience on this new case. I think we have a serial killer on our hands right in Whalen Falls. So, don't think you're gonna be 'checking out' any time soon, you hear me!?"

"Yeah, okay, now go get some bad guys, and call Pet on your way home. I'll be around for a while, kid," Joshua assured him.

Chapter 44

Saying Goodbyes

The three of them waited together on the platform. "It's really been quite an experience having you two with me. So much has happened. I don't think I could have handled Harry's death alone, Mom and Dad. You kept me busy, and I'm grateful for your understanding."

Alistair put his arms around Pet, "It's what we do, lass. Yer mother and I can na protect ye from bad times, but we can back ye up so ye won't go it alone in sadness."

She kissed him tenderly and then embraced Fiona. "I love you both so much. I'll miss you."

Alistair adjusted his jacket. "Ah, lass, it's been like a shot in the arm to be with my best girl. I'm thinkin' yer gonna have a good life wi tha' lawyer fella. Don't let this one get away. He'll keep ye in style, and I think he loves ye. I do think he's a fine catch!"

She chuckled and blushed a deep pink. "Prestige isn't everything, Dad."

Suddenly, a loud voice was heard in the crowd. "Hey, Alistair, Fiona, there you are! I had to ask three people where track 49 was!" Uncle Mike was walking quickly toward them. "I wanted to tell you goodbye!"

Alistair rolled his eyes and muttered, "Of course."

Fiona went to her brother. "'Now, Mike, are you going to be all right in that apartment? This is a strange area. You have to watch yourself and stay out of trouble, not like when you first came here."

"Aw, Fi, not now. No lectures for him. We don't have the time. He's..."

Mike butted in, "I'm going to handle myself just fine, Alistair, don't you worry about Mike Yoderman. I've even got a possible job lined up. I'll be able to work and keep an eye on my 'little Ladybug'. I can protect her whenever she needs me."

The idea of Uncle Mike being her keeper instantly put her on the defensive.

She had to diffuse this misguided Boy Scout before he planted himself at her doorstep every night.

"Now, Uncle Mike, we can talk about this another time. I am perfectly capable of taking care of myself, and I absolutely don't need a bodyguard."

A look of mild disappointment showed on the big man's face. He shrugged his shoulders in resolution. "Okay, Pet, but I'll be here if ya need me. I'll get to know this city really well. I'm smart about these kinds of things."

A conductor was calling the departure of their train. She gave her parents a big hug, sending them on their way. A porter lent his strong arm to Fiona and eased her onto the train's step with Alistair behind her. He suddenly looked back at Pet with his hand held high in a last farewell. His face took on a grave expression as if it would be a final goodbye. Then he managed a brave smile, calling out to her, "Lass, hold on to what is rightfully yours. Move into that house!"

Alistair's expression gave her pause, but she couldn't worry about that now. She had to execute her plan.

Chapter 45

Finding the Key

Pet was tired as she entered her bedroom. She could still see Alistair waving to her from the train. It saddened her because she loved them so. She would miss them. Standing in front of her dresser, she took off her watch and rings, putting them in a delicate porcelain dish. She noticed a pearl earring lying there by itself.

She quickly looked over the glass top vanity for the other earring, but it wasn't there. She traced her steps from the last time she had seen them. How long ago did she wear the earrings? She admonished herself for not being more careful. "Gads, I can be a scatterbrain sometimes," she said out loud to herself.

She went to her closet and snatched the purse off the door rack. She dug deep inside it, letting her fingers feel inch by inch for the little pearl earring. The earring had to be found. The pearls were a gift from Fiona. She would be heartbroken if she couldn't find its mate.

Her finger latched onto several coins, an individual wrapped piece of butterscotch candy, one piece of Orbit gum, a bobby pin, and a pen on the first try. She took the items out and searched again. "Ouch! What the heck is this piece of metal doing in here?" The sharp tip pricked her finger. She lifted it out and studied it carefully.

"A key? A Key! What a sharp little devil you are! That bur on the tip always did jab me!" she exclaimed. She forgot about the day Neil gave it to her. All this time, it was snuggled down in the bottom of her purse. Pet stuck her hand in the purse one last time. She unzipped a small inside pocket. Lo and behold, there was the pearl earring. The back post was stuck in the pocket lining. She chuckled to herself, "No wonder I missed it the first time. Now I can get down to business and find that ring. Ha, two problems solved already! I can't wait to tell Judy the good news."

The next morning, Pet sat, snuggling an Afghan around her, lounging in a recliner with a coffee mug in hand, talking on the phone with Judy.

"Really, in your purse all this time? This is exciting, Pet!. When are we going? I can take a day off on Thursday."

"Jude, that's two days from now. I can't wait that long. I'm going tomorrow morning around ten a.m."

"But I can't take off tomorrow. Please wait for me! You might have trouble. What if you get caught? What if people are still in the house? What if you set off a burglar alarm, and, smart ass, what if it isn't the right key? I think you'd better have a better plan."

"Jude, I've wasted two days already. I have to get over there before anyone else finds it."

"Now you're being a bit dramatic."

"Listen, this is what I have learned: A. For a month now, I have driven by Rutherford Manor and haven't seen a soul parked in the driveway day or night. B. I haven't seen anyone cut the grass or trim the boxwoods. It's looking a bit shabby. C. I see lights come on every evening, so there."

Judy shrugged her shoulders, "Eh."

Pet continued, "As far as what door the key belongs to, Neil gave it to me out of spite. He took my house keys one night after an awful row and left me this old one, saying I wasn't any better than the servants. So, I might as well come in the back way like the rest of them. He knew it was the basement key, but he didn't care. The next day, Grace gave me a new front-door key, which I unfortunately had to return when I left. I am not concerned about an alarm going off. I remember a heated conversation between Neil and Grace. Neil screwed up again. The whole manor's security system was updated and modernized except for the basement door. It was never rewired. Grace was not happy about the situation. I remember Neil shouting at her, saying, 'It is an expensive job anyway, Grace. The old door is practically encased in natural stone and mortar and would have been totally destroyed by workers drilling through all that rock,' And so, that was that. The basement was forever a forgotten entity all to itself."

"Well, Susie Sleuth, I guess you've figured out what you're going to do. I still want to go with you. You'd better call me if you change your mind, girl."

"Yeah, I will. Ya know, come to think of it, I hope I can unlock that old door. It probably hasn't been touched in fifty years."

"Duh, case in point, dearie."

"Oh, Jude, don't worry."

Chapter 46

A Chance Meeting

David found himself daydreaming and turned the squad car onto Carrolton Avenue instead of driving down 6th Street toward the station house. It was a good move because he saw Pet standing right in front of her apartment. He got a wide smile on his face just as she was about to walk up the steps. He rolled down his window and yelled at her, "Hey, good looking, whatcha doin'?"

Pet jumped at his loud voice and quickly turned around. Being curious, she bent down slightly to see who was calling her. "Oh, it's you. Hi yourself! I'm just coming home from the store." Pet was carrying a big paper bag of groceries. "What are you doing? Wanna come up for a coffee or a glass of wine?"

Officer Jones parked his squad car at the curb and got out. "I'm sorry, Pet. I'm on duty. I can't come inside unless I'm on official business or investigating a crime. I'd like to take a rain check, though," he said with a smile.

"Good. Call me real soon," she laughed.

Before she said anything else, he quickly leaned past the grocery bag and kissed her on the cheek.

"Bye!"

He turned slightly to leave her, but before he got away, Pet laughed and nudged him on the shoulder playfully saying, "Goofball!"

David didn't see the car, and neither did she. He just saw PET, but the onlooker saw them. Anthony witnessed the tender love scene close enough to catch the illicit kiss with his cellphone camera. He seethed with jealousy, uttering obscenities under his breath before driving away.

It was another infraction of his rules; the woman was a flirt. She was too free with the men. He didn't like that about her. Mother was right, younger women are sluts.

Chapter 47

Breaking and Entering

As Pet drove past the stone pillars on either side of the driveway entrance, the stately brick home of Rutherford Manor came into view. She slowed the car down and took in its splendor. A massive oak door dominated the front of the stately natural stone, and two sets of windows were on either side of it. The individual glass panels were framed in wrought iron. The same design was evident on the second story as well. This facade gave the onlooker a sign of refined power. It was built to withstand the decades, but from the looks of overgrown boxwoods, azaleas, and high grass, it was obvious that gardening had not been a priority for a long time.

Pet made a mental note to have a gardener clean up the grounds soon before winter did any more damage to the shrubbery. "On my first day in this house, I will set things straight. The grounds will be beautiful again. I love this house, and it will be my home forever," she thought to herself.

The driveway went all the way around the back of the manor house. She continued around to the back of the house, stopped in front of the double-car garage doors, and got out. They were huge, towering over her. She felt small next to them, as if she were a tiny porcelain doll placed next to a massive Victorian dollhouse.

The fine pebbled gravel under her feet was firm, but still had that dignified crunch. The sound took her back to the times she heard the limo's tires rolling down the driveway to these dark wooden doors.

Walking farther, Pet immediately identified dank, earthy smells of the old house. In all this time, nothing had changed, not even the heavy, pungent smell that belonged there, resting in the overgrowth of the old mansion. She looked around, remembering the placements of the trees and shrubs of the back gardens. The tall oaks were still surrounded by ivy that climbed halfway up their trunks. She saw the rhododendrons hugging the back wall, guarding the inhabitants therein. It all came back to her as if it were yesterday.

She also noticed that the grass was growing between the flagstones, and the ivy was still wild and undisciplined. The tangled vegetation was growing over a high retaining wall, almost obliterating the natural stones from sight. It was hard to tell if the ivy held up the wall or the wall supported the ivy.

The more she perused the area, the more evident it became that the moldy dampness was taking hold of everything. The railroad tie that separated the driveway from the flagstone walkway had a soft blanket of green moss; it was also creeping up the heavy wooden basement door, seeping inside the frame.

This door was a few feet to the left of the garage and was the only exterior entrance to the basement. Pet remembered that there was an inner door to the basement from the garage, and it was seldom used. She snickered to herself, realizing that was probably the only key Neil gave up willingly.

The door was slightly recessed from the back wall, and the lock was in the shadows. Dirt and cobwebs were around and inside the keyhole. Pet studied the door for a minute. "What a mess. I must get a cloth to wipe away this dirt; all this gunk isn't going to be easy to get off."

She went to her car trunk. Miraculously, inside it, she found an old terrycloth rag that worked perfectly. Pet brushed the cobwebs away and vigorously rubbed off the corroded metal around the keyhole.

She thought, "After this effort, I hope I have the strength to pull this thing open."

She took the key from her jeans pocket and rubbed the tip for good luck; then she slowly stuck it in, clearing any debris that might impede her quest. There was a low grinding sound from the contact of metal on metal. It didn't move easily, and Pet had to exert pressure on the key with both hands to turn it. Fortunately, she heard the satisfying click. It unlocked. She was halfway there!

Now came the hard part: she had to pull the metal knob, which was also rusty. With both hands, she twisted and pulled with all her might. It didn't move, of course. Why would this be easy? Why would years of inactivity make rust and old wood a breeze to open? She looked to see if anything was on the bottom of the door that might be making it stick. There was only a slight dirt lip against it. With her heel, she dug in and slid her foot along the width of the door, making a way for it to open a little easier. "Well, don't know if that's going to help, but it was worth a try," she said out loud.

Pet put her whole body into pulling that door again, but nothing happened. She felt exasperated and disappointed. She thought to herself, "How could I come this far and be stopped just like that? Think Pet. Think. There is some logical reason why it won't open."

She began touching the hinges, the rough door frame, and the cold stones around it. "Of course, duh. It opens inward, not outward!"

With all her might, she shoved and pushed against it. It moved just an inch or two. She shoved it again. Abruptly, the door opened with a dull scraping sound of wood against concrete. The sudden movement startled her, and she let out a shrill sort of gasp. At first, she could not see anything; then, slowly, her eyes adjusted to the dim, filtered light from the basement window to her left.

The four small windows to her left were high up in the basement wall, but outside, they were just at grass level. There was also a Rhododendron bush in front of the windows, blocking most of the sun's light. So, seeing any objects clearly in the darkness became a real challenge. In her other pocket, she took out a small flashlight. Clicking it casts immediate shadows over many covered objects.

Finally, her eyes could see in the murky darkness. She inched inside, carefully closing the door behind her. All she could make out in this area were huge containers covered with tarps everywhere she looked. Some were stacked on top of each other and taller than she was. She felt like she was in a tunnel. Pet walked a narrow pathway illuminated only by a small flashlight. She leaned to the left and to the right, trying to see if there was an open space, hoping naively that it would lead to a bigger, well-lit room.

After a few more steps, she saw a light hanging down from the ceiling above an open doorway. Quickly, she followed the light and ran right into a huge cobweb. It fell on her face, and she began brushing and clawing it away from her eyes." No spiders, no spiders, please, get off me!" She wanted to scream, but she realized if anyone was in this house, she didn't want to be seen or shot in the process!

When she got through the doorway, she could tell, even in the very dim light, that this was a large room. She moved her flashlight side to side and up and down to see her surroundings. Pointing the flashlight downward, she saw a ceramic tiled floor. Then she spied the legs of a big leather chair. Moving on, she counted another chair, two couches, and a glass coffee table.

Pet started to see more shadows in the room now that her eyes were more accustomed to the darkness. She thought she smelled burnt wood and instinctively looked in that direction. "Yes, the fireplace!" she whispered to herself, walking slowly until she felt the ebony mantle. She mused to herself, "Hey, I'm getting good at this groping in the dark."

Now what else does this room hold? I'm getting a familiar feel about it. This must be Neil's drinking hideaway when he wanted to be alone. What a nice room. No wonder he just let me peek in here once. Okay, now, steps, where are the steps?

They have to be close, just can't remember exactly which wall they were against.

Again, she shone her light in small circular motions and followed the expanse of the knotty pine walls. Suddenly, the light caught a brass floor lamp, then a huge roll top desk came into view. Two seconds later, she spied the stairs adjacent to it.

She headed toward them but stopped midway. "Do I really want to go up there now? Where do I start looking? Where..."

Out of the blue, a loud female voice spoke. A bright light shone from above, and the full view of the stairs appeared before Pet.

"Stop where you stand right now, sucka, whoever you are! I gotta shotgun pointin' in the direction of your light, and I'll shoot ya quick if you don't answer me this minute. I already called da police!"

Pet's whole body shook, and she cried out. "Don't shoot! I was just, I mean, I'm all alone! It's just me."

"Come into the light so I can see you. Stop runnin' yer mouth, girl. Tell me who you are, and you'd better be alone. I'll shoot them, too. Quick, answer me!"

"I'm a,um, Patrice Elyse Traffortelli, Ma'am. I'm alone. I used to live here. We lived here with Grace Traffortelli."

Pet stepped forward and stood at the bottom of the steps.

"Whose we?"

"With Neil, ma'am, my ex, well, dead husband. We lived here while we were married. Grace said,..."

"I don't want a story, bitch. Drop that flashlight. Turn around and let me see if you have anything else hiding in those jeans of yours."

Pet dropped the flashlight and followed the woman's orders. She turned around and lost her balance, tripping over the rim of the flashlight. As she was attempting to straighten up, a loud pounding sound could be heard beyond the open door.

Pet screamed, "Ooh! Who's that?"

"Shut up! Get up here, and don't try anything funny."

The woman stepped aside and waited for Pet to come up the steps. She walked a few paces in front of her and then stopped.

"Move! Now somebody's bangin' my door. I gotta go see, but I'll have this shotgun pointed at your ass so move it, quick!"

The pounding started again. A man's voice called out, "Are you okay, Ms. Reddick? It's the Whalen Falls police, Ms. Reddick."

Ms. Reddick walked quickly through the kitchen and the dining room entrances. She crossed the hall to the foyer and then to the front door.

"Yeah, I'm comin', I'm comin'. Stand right there, a little way to the side so they can see you too."

Ms. Reddick opened the massive door and let the officers inside. Pet had her head down, eyes on her shoes. She was so mortified. She didn't want anyone to see her face. How awful to be a real criminal getting caught breaking and entering in her own rightful home. She told herself to blot out yet another ugly experience of her already weird existence.

Chapter 48

Mortifying Experience

Detective Joshua Iverson and Officer David Jones walked through the door. Hats off, they stood before Ms. Mae Delight Reddick.

Officer Jones looked directly at Pet, then at Ms. Reddick. "Ma'am, I'm Officer David Jones, and this is my supervisor, Detective Joshua Iverson. Are you the person who called in the complaint, and what is your full name and your reason for being in the Rutherford Manor?"

Ms. Mae Delight said immediately without blinking an eyelash, "My name is Ms. Mae Delight Reddick, and yes, I called in the complaint. I'm the caretaker of this house, and I've been here for forty years."

Officer Jones continued, "Thank you, Ms. Reddick. How can we help you? Is this the intruder right here, or was there some other prowler?"

"No. I don't think so. Just this skinny little girl, havin' the nerve to come into my house. Says she used to live here. Sounds like a crock a shit to me, but I didn't hear any windows break, or I'd definitely shot her skinny little ass!"

Ms. Reddick still held the shotgun on Pet.

Joshua Iverson was starting to grin. He knew who the intruder was the minute he stepped inside the house. He controlled his emotions and professionally said, "Now, Ms. Reddick, I don't think she will do you any harm. You could probably put down your shotgun. I'll have Officer Jones take a look outside and around the back of the house for you, if it will make you feel better. We've had some break-ins lately. It is just a routine procedure."

"Thank you, Officer. Go left and follow the path to the conservatory. I want you to make sure she didn't trash my begonias with her clumsy self." Ms. Reddick said, nodding her head to David Jones.

David Jones dared not look in Pet's direction, thankful that Joshua Iverson gave him something to do, because he couldn't stand the situation. He fought hard not to convulse with laughter while maintaining a professional manner. This scene practically killed him. Ms. Reddick's description of Pet was priceless.

He chuckled to himself on his way around the back of the house. "Pet a burglar, Breaking and Entering! We'll have a rap sheet on her! Hysterical, just hysterical! Ole Josh will have a field day with this one!"

Detective Iverson asked Ms. Reddick politely, "Ms. Reddick, do you know this woman? Have you ever seen her here in Rutherford Manor?"

"Would I have a shotgun pointed at her if I knew her? No, can't say as I do, on account I never went up to the second and third floors where Miss Grace done her work. I kept to myself mostly in the kitchen. This scrawny woman says she's a Traffortelli and lived here. I never saw her. Now, it doesn't mean I couldn't go up there to the other floors if I wanted, but I'm not the nosy kind. I don't traipse in other people's space. I had work to do. I had to git breakfess, lunch, and supper on. Ain't nobody was gonna help me. That butler of Miss. Grace was no help at all. I fired him after Miss. Grace passed!"

Mae Delight slowly put down the shotgun and held it pointing downward in the crook of her arm. "Well, you might as well come into the living room and sit. I don't know what else you can ask me until that officer comes back. Go on, girl, you probably know the way to this room," Mae Delight said as she shooed Pet out of her way.

Pet hurried away from them and entered the living room, and sat down on a luxurious leather couch. Detective Iverson took a chair, and Mae Delight took another chair directly opposite to Pet.

Joshua took out a notepad and a pen from his jacket pocket. "Now, Ms. Reddick, by rights, I have to ask you because you are the proprietor of this house right now, and she did enter it illegally, even though she did have a key. Unfortunately, it was still an unannounced entry on her part."

"Ms. Reddick, let me explain the situation a little further," Joshua said in a professional yet friendly tone of voice. "We have to ask you if you are going to press charges on Mrs. Traffortelli."

Mae Delight looked her up and down. She enjoyed making this scrawny woman nervous as she stared her down. She wanted to be sure Pet wasn't about to try this stupid thing again. Mae thought before she spoke.

Pet sat there in silence the whole time she was being scrutinized. She bit her lip, too embarrassed to give any sort of excuse for this fiasco. She assumed her usual anxious position, hands tightly folded in her lap, feet flat on the floor, sitting erectly, bracing herself for another humiliation.

Before Mae could utter another word, Officer Jones came back, letting himself in the door. It was quite the scenario: the detective, the victim, and the criminal staring at each other. Although Officer Jones loved this cat-and-mouse game, he decided to break the tension as he walked further into the room. "Nobody was behind the house, Inspector Iverson, and, Ms. Reddick, your begonias were intact. Not a flower was knocked off their stems."

"Hmmpf, that's a miracle."

Detective Iverson looked at Pet, who still stared at the floor in silence. "I haven't seen you in a while, Miss, but I do believe you are a Traffortelli, correct?"

She slowly looked up at him in controlled anger. Her neck was hot. She could feel her blood rising in her neck, ready to explode. *He was enjoying this little scene. He knows exactly who I am. He knows how embarrassed I am. How dare he make fun of me,* she thought. She wanted to scream at him, but she kept her composure. She answered him slowly, looking straight at him.

"You know exactly who I am, Detective Joshua Iverson. I also know Officer David Jones. I haven't had the pleasure or misfortune of remarrying anyone since the last time you saw me approximately six months ago. Since nothing outside the house has been disturbed, I would like to go now."

Looking over to Detective Iverson, Ms. Reddick spoke up, "She has a mouth on her, don't she?" Then she turned to Pet. "I wouldn't be too uppity, Missy. You got two big men lookin' at you like a squashed bug on the floor, so I wouldn't put that mouth in gear jus yet. 'Sides, they haven't decided on your crime yet either."

David Jones watched the senior detective formally instruct Ms. Reddick on what to do. David Jones thought he was coming off as a Richard Burton type, throwing his authority around and enjoying it.

Ready to jot down Mae Delight's answer, Joshua posed in a professional posture. "Now, Ms. Reddick, we do have to ask you if you are going to press charges on Mrs. Traffortelli for Breaking and Entering. If you do, we will take her down to the station. But if you are not, we will leave the premises and go back to the station."

"Well, I don't know." Mae was still staring at Pet with coal-black eyes and a fierce scowl on her face. She waited more than a few seconds before continuing to speak. "But, I don't think she had too much evil on her mind. She don't look much like a burglar, and she sure ain't smart enough to break into a house without getting caught. So, I guess she can go."

Pet breathed a sigh of relief. She looked at Mae and gave her a meek smile. "Thank you, Ms. Reddick. I appreciate your generosity. I promise I will not break into your house, I mean Rutherford Manor, again, but I hope I will be able to come visit you very soon."

Ms. Reddick shrugged her shoulders. "Ain't no never mind to me, girl. It's been empty the las' two months anyway."

"It's been what? Why wasn't I told? What happened? It doesn't make any sense."

Puzzling questions streamed in Pet's head. "Of all the nerve. Anthony should have called me."

Soon, the situation was well in hand. The officers assured Mae that all was good and thanked her for not pressing charges on Mrs. Traffortelli. Then, Pet asked Mae for her cell phone number for the next visit. Putting the new number in her purse, she headed for the front door with Officer David Jones beside her.

Joshua Iverson also got Ms. Reddick's phone number to put into his report. He handed her his card if she needed their help again.

As Pet and Officer Jones got to her car, David stopped and smiled. "I think that went pretty well, don't you think, Pet? Kinda funny too."

Pet leaned right up to his face, "What? Are you kidding me? You want to put this into perspective, friend? Let's see, on a scale of one to ten, and ten being the worst, I'd say being caught by a woman with a shotgun, no less, breaking and entering in the basement of a house I once lived in as a ten, or falling in a mud puddle in the middle of a busy street being a one. What do you think holds water, huh? Kinda obvious, isn't it? Are you trying to make me feel like a fool?"

Officer Jones put up his hands, "Hey, now, no, no, just kidding. I wanted to see you smile. You still looked all tensed up. It's over. No harm done. You know, Detective Iverson did the impersonal inquisition thing for Ms. Delight's benefit, don't you? He's very good at that. So, there's nothing more to worry about, right, Pet? I'm not laughing at you, really."

Pet folded her arms across her chest, slowly putting down her chin, almost talking to herself rather than Officer Jones. "Well, that's easy for you to say. I'm going to be tense for a good while. I could have gotten shot, or possibly maimed, then to add insult to injury, I end up being horribly humiliated, and my reputation is shot to hell."

She shook her head as she searched for her car keys. "Why

did I think I could pull this off? Have I watched too many cop shows or adventure movies? Oh, gosh. Joshua must think I'm a real ditz."

David said warmly, "Don't go tearing yourself down, Pet. You know the old saying, 'shit happens.'"

She didn't say anything to him in return. She just gave him a scowl and got in her car. But before she could turn the key in the ignition, Joshua was right there at her car window. Pet looked up with a start. She hit the button, and the car window came down.

"Sorry to startle you, Pet. I didn't mean to add to your day. Are you really okay? You know, Ms Mae Delight Reddick is all bluff. We have dealt with her before. She's really a nice lady. It's a shame you didn't call first. But, then again, I wouldn't have gotten to see you."

"Your charm overwhelms me, Joshua. I felt like I was set up in some way, however ridiculous this happening was. And, your attitude toward me stunk."

"I am sorry, Pet. I guess I had that one coming. Can I change the subject for a second?"

She gave him an expressionless, deadpan answer, "Sure."

"Didn't you get any notice that the house had been vacated? The patrolmen in this sector were notified at least two, maybe three months ago, that the owners had declared bankruptcy and had to leave. No one would be permitted on the property after they left. You're lucky they didn't spot you. "

"No. I didn't get any notice. You'd think my so-called lawyer would tell me these things. He will definitely be on my To Do list for sure!"

Joshua got a warm smile on his face. "You still have guts. I'm glad to see that. Even though today's circumstances were a bit bizarre, it was nice seeing you again." With that, Joshua Iverson turned and walked to his car.

Pet was somewhat taken aback by his abrupt finish. She sat there watching him walk away.

David Jones took advantage of Joshua Iverson's exit and leaned into her car window. He wanted to give her an impulsive kiss, but decided not to and ended up asking her a question, "Pet, do you have a minute? I'd like to ask you a question."

His sudden voice scared her. With a jerk of her head, she turned to him, quite exasperated, "You guys are scaring the hell out of me! David, couldn't you at least clear your throat or something, and give me a hint that you're still there? You want to hear another old saying: 'Yer gittin on my last nerve.'"

David's face got instantly red. "I'm so sorry, Pet. Please forgive me. I really didn't mean to startle you. Tell me, why didn't you let me know what you were going to do? I could've saved you an awful lot of trouble. We could have gone right up to the front door."

"Well, I wanted to do it on my own. I thought it was a great idea getting in that way. Now, I just feel stupid."

"Don't knock yourself down. Learning to be independent is a gradual process. Our decisions aren't always the right ones, Pet. You will learn the ropes. How about dinner tomorrow night?"

"Whoa, that was a switch, David, first advice and then a hopeful consent. I'll call you. I do want to go out with you. I really do."

He smiled at her and held out his hand. She softly clasped his hand and smiled back. She could not be angry with him, she thought to herself, "David Jones was one of the good guys. Maybe I should give him another chance."

"Okay, I still have your number. I promise to call you, David. Thank you."

"Good, Pet. I will be waiting."

Chapter 49

Going Back for the Ring

"Pet, after everything you just told me, you are going back to that house, with that maid there?" Judy asked in astonishment.

"Why not? This time will be different if you still want to go with me. It is Thursday, isn't it? You can finally see the inside of Rutherford Manor, soon to be my new home. I followed proper protocol and called Ms. Reddick to let her know we were coming over. She wasn't friendly, but she agreed to let me in. The nerve, I'm the rightful owner, and I'm asking her permission to come inside my house," Pet said with sarcasm.

"Well, hell yes, I want to come with you. I just hope she doesn't have a shotgun in her hand when she answers the door. I'm coming over right now. Be ready to jump in the car when I pull up."

"You got it. I'll be ready."

As Judy and Pet walked up the walkway, Judy kept smiling, making little sounds of appreciation like, "Oh my, how pretty. Look at all those azaleas and boxwoods, nice, very nice. She also commented that it will look so much better when all the greenery and trees are cut and pruned.

Pet rang the doorbell. Immediately, Mae Delight opened the door. "Yes?"

Pet stepped forward slightly, "Ms. Reddick, may we come in? You do remember me, right?"

"I know your skinny little ass. I don't forget people quickly. Who's your friend?"

Judy jutted out her hand, "Hi, Ms. Reddick, I'm Judith Ann Mackie, Mrs. Traffortelli's best friend. I hope you don't mind me coming along. She has told me so much about this beautiful house. I just had to see it."

"Kinda gabby, ain't she. All right, you did call. Come on in."

They followed her into the spacious living room. Pet was more relaxed than on the previous visit two days ago. The girls casually sat down on the brocade-upholstered sofa, their eyes mesmerized by the subtle colors and rich tones of the tables and lamps. Pet admired the paintings on the walls and the accent pieces of art once again, defining Grace's appreciation of refinement and gentility. Her mind flashed back to the days of being a happy, young, naïve bride.

She remembered this room filled with people, music, champagne, and dancing. She could hear Neil's laughter and see his handsome face smiling at her. Now, her heart ached to be a part of that life again. With a silent sigh, she told herself, these luxuries will have to wait.'

Mae Delight brought her back to reality. "Are you going to sit there all day, girl? Why are ya here? I don't have time to babysit you two."

Pet came back to the present. "Oh, I'm sorry, Ms. Reddick. I came in search of a ring. Grace has left me a pink tourmaline ring, and I must find it. I know my next question is going to seem a bit weird, since I don't know you well, but I was wondering if Grace ever mentioned it or showed you the ring. The description of it sounds valuable, and I would like to make sure it is safe."

"Are you askin' me if I took it?"

"Oh, no, ma'am! I was just wondering if you had seen it or if Grace said anything about the ring to you. I don't know you well enough to accuse you of taking such a ring."

"I don't steal jewelry, Missy, or any stuff like that. You think I'm stupid? Besides, you don't look like you'd steal anything either from Miss Grace, 'cept her son and grandson. They were crooked as a dog's hind leg."

"Yeah, you're right," Pet said, a little embarrassed. "Neil was a deadbeat. I didn't know his father was, too."

"Yeah, they were bums, but she never said anything to me 'bout no ring, or them gittin' it."

Pet looked at Judy. "Well, Jude, where do we go from here? It could be anywhere in this house."

Judy looked about the room, then nudged Pet in the ribs. Her eyes were on another door across the hall. "Hey, what's behind door number two?"

"That's the library." Pet looked in that direction.

Mae Delight stood up slowly and put her right hand in her apron pocket. "Miss Grace spent a lot of time in that room 'fore she passed. She'd take tea every afternoon and sit at her favorite desk. She liked to look at old pictures over and over again."

Pet's eyes perked up. "Really! I wonder if there could be more pictures of Howard and her. I'd like to see the desk and the library. Do you mind, Ms. Reddick?"

"It's no never mind to me, girl. I have to unlock it. A while after she passed, that room became of particular interest to many people. I wanted to keep it shut, so every time they went out I closed it up again outta respect. She was so sad before she left this world. They took her out in a stretcher to the hospital, and she died two weeks later."

Judy gave Pet a puzzled look and whispered, "What happened?"

"It was a real bad time, Jude. Neil practically kicked me out of the house. We were fighting all the time. That's when I came to you for help. Remember, I needed an apartment right away? He said he was selling the house, so I couldn't get any of the proceeds. Grace put it in his name a while back. I was so unhappy. The whole situation was ugly. He didn't tell me about Grace's dying either."

"Yeah, girlfriend, you were a mess," Judy nodded in agreement.

Mae Delight had a different look on her face after Pet gave this brief insight into her life. Mae's face changed from a stern look of defiance to one of warmth and understanding.

"Hmmpf. If I'da been married to that good-for-nothin' rat, I'd a got me a gun and put him in the ground. He had no business treatin' Miss Grace like that! No, sir, that boy was plain evil."

Judy grinned, "Well, Ms. Reddick, God took care of him all right. So, no tears lost on Neil Traffortelli ever again!"

"Amen," Mae Delight agreed, "and since I feel like I know ya, now you can call me Ma Delight from now on. You hear?"

They smiled and said thanks at the same time.

"Let's go into the library," said Pet.

Chapter 50

The Secret Drawer

The room had not changed; everything was exactly the same. Mae Delight had it sealed up tighter than an Egyptian tomb. When the door opened, the air in the room was a little stuffy, smelling of old leather and Pledge furniture polish. Pet coughed, "Whoa, has this room been opened up at all, Mae?"

"Yes."

"When? Why is it still musty in here?"

"Every time those people left, I closed it back up again, had to put all those old heavy sheets back on the chairs and coffee tables and stuff. Naturally, it's gonna be stuffy," Mae retorted with a bit of agitation.

"What do you mean by 'people'?"

"People, Missy. Right after Miss Grace died, there was the lawyer, Mr. Prattmore, some big dude lookin' like a big ole owl with bushy eyebrows and a head of white hair, Hyde something,' then there were the assessors, and then carpet cleaners. For a while, this room was like the revolving doors at Macy's Department Store."

"Damn, it would've been nice if I were here, too. Why is he doing things behind my back? I should have been in this house with him, not with Mr. Hyde. It sounds like those two have a history. I wonder why?" Pet thought.

Six pairs of eyes continued to look about the room, but it was the desk that caught their attention. The beautiful cherry wood secretary dominated the room. It was the only piece of furniture that wasn't covered. Its size was not massive, but big enough to give it a presence. The well-placed secretary sat beside a lace-curtained window. The sunlight illuminated the wood's beautiful sheen. On top of the desk was a small lamp. From its mahogany base, two imitation candles held two small teardrop lights. Their delicate glass tips poked out slightly from the pale taupe shade.

Pet remembered how the subtle light from the lamp warmed the otherwise formal Library. There was a mahogany captain's chair sitting in front of it. In her mind, she could see Grace sitting at the secretary as she had so many times in the past, scrutinizing letters and the ledgers from the furniture company.

For some reason, the secretary and chair were very important to her. In fact, Pet signed the valuable life insurance policy at that very desk. After a few seconds, the girls didn't hesitate to go to it. Pet looked in Mae Delight's direction.

Mae nodded permission, "Go on, you can pull the front down. It ain't locked. I quit lockin' it since it was more interesting than anything else in this room."

Pet pulled down the lid. A green leather mat protected the inner panel. Judy couldn't resist touching the wood.

"Will ya look at this leather mat. It's so beautiful, and all those little alcoves for papers, with these cute little drawers underneath, how neat."

Pet raised her eyebrows, "I wouldn't say they're cute or neat, Jude, just the fine design of aristocratic elegance. I asked Grace one day exactly what this piece of furniture was called. She said it was an Edwardian Antique Secretary made in London, England, circa 1910."

"Oh, dig you. You sound like an English snob. Should we check the compartments, Pet?"

"Yes."

The girls slowly started pulling the drawers out one at a time. Some of the drawers contained mementos from the past. In one of them, Judy found holy cards you get at a funeral home; there were quite a few. Besides that one, she pulled out an old-fashioned round magnifying glass rimmed in silver. She thought to herself, "How quaint. I am going back in time."

The third drawer Pet drew out, and she exclaimed, "Judy, look, I found a ring box!"

Judy said eagerly,"Open it."

Pet held her breath and opened it carefully. The small black velvet box creaked softly as she pried it apart. "Oh. It's not what we were hoping for, Jude, but look, it's a man's wedding ring. This ring had to be Mr. Traffortelli's wedding band. It is engraved. 'To my love 7 20 '55' Grace.' Aw, how sweet."

Pet looked up at Judy, "Yeah, it's sweet, but no jackpot. Keep looking."

"Cynic," Judy snickered.

The rest of the drawers were empty. They went on to look at small alcoves above them. The only item Pet found was a four-by-six leather address book small enough to fit in a purse. The book held no monetary value, but Grace always treasured friends and personal contacts; that could be the only reason it was still there.

Pet was surprised that Neil didn't have the secretary shipped to his house. This was such an elegant piece of furniture. It had to be valuable. The rest of the furniture was nice but dated. She could see Neil shipping them out to some nasty storage bin until he could get a buyer for the contents of the house.

Pet looked over to Judy, who was holding a green oblong plastic box. On the lid, in gold lettering, the words "Cross since 1846" were printed. Inside, she found a silver pen and a thin mechanical pencil. They were secured in a narrow felt-covered tray.

"Nice, but still no ring."

Pet felt as if she were on a scavenger hunt, and right now, she knew Mae Delight was enjoying this entertainment immensely as she sat idly on the couch watching the girls. Judy continued rummaging through the three drawers below the writing panel.

"Aha, what have we here?" Judy's voice was excited for a second. She held up four very old envelopes. "Drats, just sympathy cards with written notes consoling Grace on her husband's death."

"Oh well, no clues or ring here, Jude. I cannot believe nothing is in this secretary, absolutely nothing. We might as well go."

"You girls don't look too good for things, do ya. Why, if I lost a dime, my momma wouldn't let me eat dinner till I found it. You're giving up too easily. That's pitiful."

Pet shot back, "Excuse me. What do you mean by that? Do you know something I don't know, like the fact you didn't tell me Anthony and Mr. Hyde had been here, too!"

"All I'm sayin' is you've only been lookin' for five minutes. I'd have torn this place apart before I left this house. Them other two men like to tear up the carpet, before I stopped 'em."

The girls looked at each other in silence and looked about the room again for the next obvious place to search. Pet still held onto the book.

"That's odd. I wonder why she wouldn't keep this in her purse? I always keep mine with me just in case I need to look someone up. I don't keep all my phone numbers in my cellphone."

Judy looked over to the book, too. "It does look old, doesn't it. And see, a lot of the alphabet is missing. The letters are worn and brownish. I would've tossed this crappy old thing." Judy was ready to toss it in the trash can beside the desk.

Immediately, Mae Delight chastised Judy, "I wouldn't do that if I were you, girl. You don't throw someone's goods away. Ain't you got any brungin' up?"

"Sorry."

Pet studied it again. She rubbed her finger on the worn letter tabs. Something odd began to happen to her: certain letters were still stuck on the pages, and she read them out loud.

"G. R. E. B. X. It looks deliberate, Jude."

"Yeah, kinda Sherlock Holmes-ish." Jude read the letters out loud again.

Pet looked up and saw Mae Delight dig out a butterscotch candy from her apron pocket and pop it in her mouth. A loud, self-satisfied slurping sound emitted from her lips. She nodded, giving the girls a grin that would make a Cheshire cat jealous.

"Are you stupid? Look at it again."

This got Pet steamed. She was getting more than a little tired of Mae Delight's smart-ass attitude, but before she came back with a wisecrack, she counted to five before she spoke. She did not want this woman to get too defensive. She needed her as an ally.

"If you know something, I want to hear it now, Ms. Reddick. We're not playing a game of hide and seek here. I want to know where the ring is. If you do know, please tell me."

Mae Delight crossed her arms over her chest. She liked being in control like this. "Oh, I seen it. Seen it many times, bright shiny, really pretty. She wouldn't exactly let me see where she hid it, but I know it's somewhere in that desk, and I think it's really close to you. She's tryin' to tell ya somethin'."

Pet picked up the address book again and read the letters slowly in her head. Suddenly, Judy grabbed it from her. "Let's see. What sounds like greebx? The green box, Pet. It has to be in there. Why else would Grace keep those letter tabs on the address book?"

Pet shook the box. "Son of a bitch, you're right, Judy. Yes, hmm, let's see if this plastic is loose."

She dug her fingernail around the plastic holder. With a little prodding, the glued felt pulled away, and she was able to lift out the pen holder. The ring was wrapped in a piece of fine tissue paper. She unwrapped it quickly.

"Oh my God! It's beautiful! Look at it, Jude. It is the exact description written on the sales receipt. It IS the pink tourmaline ring."

"Wow!" Judy said excitedly. "It's stunning and valuable, look at its color. Put it on, Pet. It looks like it would be your size."

Pet was thinking the same thing. She was more than ready to slip it on her finger. Her finger tingled as she slipped it on easily. Stepping over to the window, she held it up to the light. The brilliance of the diamond-studded ring took her breath away. It gave her a sense of power. Judy grabbed her hand and stared at it, too.

"It feels magical, Judy, and to think it's all mine! I'm never going to take it off my finger."

"I know I wouldn't. I wonder how much it's worth today?"

"It doesn't matter, Jude. I'm never going to sell it. It could be worth a million! Who cares?"

"Insurance people, if your dumb self loses it!" Mae Delight piped up.

"Oh, yeah. She does have a point there. Could I try it on?" Judy asked, holding out her hand.

Mae Delight gave Judy an angry scowl that changed her mind instantly. Pet was lost in thought, talking to herself, and didn't catch the power play. Judy felt uneasy.

"Well, I will call my agent tomorrow, but now I'm going on a witch hunt for Mr. Prattmore. I wonder if it could be with Mr. Hyde? Wanna come, Judy?" Pet walked away from the window.

Judy turned to answer, but Pet was already on the cell phone.

"Mr. Prattmore, please. Oh, do you know where he is, or when he will return, Christine? I see, thanks."

"Well?" Judy asked

"He's not in his office, and she is not sure when he'll be back. Boy, that makes me mad. Suddenly, he's Mister Evasive! I'd like to know what he's up to. Another thing, the secretary, Christine, acted as if I were prying into Anthony's business. He's my lawyer, for heaven's sake. She's a pure bitch!"

Judy immediately followed her. "I think you're getting a little paranoid, Pet. Lawyers do this all the time." Judy smirked.

"Yeah, but that doesn't make it right, especially when I need him now."

With a determined march, Pet walked quickly back into the living room, picked up her purse, and was on her way to the front door.

"Do you mind, lady? Wait a sec, you're moving a bit fast. Aren't you going to say 'good-bye' to Ms. Mae Delight?"

Pet stopped dead in her tracks, "Oh, yeah, I should. Thank you, Ms. Reddick. You have been a real help in finding this ring. I do appreciate it very much."

She started to turn away, but stopped, "By the way, did Anthony, I mean Mr. Prattmore, retain you to reside in this house until the rightful owner moves in, or are you renting this mansion until someone moves in?"

"Girl, you must be out of your mind. Don't be simple. Miss Grace said I have a contract for five years to care for this house, and that's exactly what I'm gonna do. Mr. Prattmore wrote it up! The money came from Miss Grace's personal account for me. 'Sides, nobody knows this house as I do. I've been here long enough to know every crack and squeak of this here place. And my time ain't up yet!"

Pet stepped back a bit, "Uh, well, I guess so. Good, I'm glad you are here to take care of it."

Pet sincerely thanked Mae Delight and reiterated that she was glad the manor house was not always empty. Mae Delight gave her a noncommittal "whatever" and slowly closed the door behind them.

Pet mused to herself in a half-whisper. Judy kept quiet and watched her. "Why hadn't I seen her before? Was I so entangled in my life that I wouldn't see a maid in the lower part of the house?"

Judy plopped behind the wheel of her car. "You were in La La Land with Neil, hun. You probably went from newlywed bliss to the cringing miseries all in a very short time. Didn't you ever wonder who cooked all those fancy meals? You ate with Grace in the formal dining room, didn't you? Grace surely didn't cook it. Mae Delight was there, sweetie. You were spoiled rotten and didn't even know it."

Judy started the car. "Well, shall we go, madam?"

Pet smiled at Judy, "Okay, driver, I might as well give orders like a spoiled brat. On to Briar Town Furniture Company, and step on it!"

Chapter 51

Aloysius Spots the Ring

Pet did not have a plan in mind to find Anthony, but asking Bunny Haskell might be a good start. That girl knew everything without even trying. As they walked up the marble steps to the second floor, Pet desperately tried to remember where Bunny's office was located. She did not want to come off as stupid, aimlessly wandering around. She picked the administration wing and headed for it.

A tall, slender woman in a Vogue business suit immediately walked up behind Pet. "Mrs. Traffortelli, do you need assistance? Are you looking for anyone in particular?" Pet spun around and came face-to-face with Catherine Hartwell.

For an instant, it was deer-in-the-headlights time. Pet had no time to think. Who the hell is this? Shit, Catherine somebody. "Oh, yes." Pet stepped on Judy's foot, trying to get her balance. "I'm looking for Bunny Haskel because she'd most likely know where Mr. Prattmore would be, I think."

Catherine Hartwell winced in agitation at Pet's ineptitude. "That is not necessarily the case, Mrs. Traffortelli. Exactly whom do you wish to see? Mr. Prattmore, or Miss Haskel? And, for your information, Mr. Prattmore does not occupy an office at Briar Town Furniture Company. He may do some consulting for us now and again, but that wouldn't be any of your concern right now. As to Miss Haskel, I doubt if she would know his daily routine."

Pet felt intimidated by this witch and fought for all she was worth not to stammer like a schoolgirl. She had to think fast, so she made up a lie, "Mr. Prattmore suggested that he and I would meet sometime today, possibly with Mr. Buford or Mr.

Wingate, to determine when I would be introduced to the duties of the executive branch of this fine company. I assumed he might be here now. He is not at his office in town."

"You may come with me to my office, Mrs. Traffortelli. I'll see if Mr. Prattmore is here. Follow me, please."

Catherine turned her back to them and started walking briskly to the Administrative Wing, putting a little distance between her and the two women who followed like two puppy dogs in tow.

"Why did she do that," Pet thought. "She acts so superior. I don't care if she is an administrator. She doesn't have to be such a bitch. I feel like I'm ten years old and have jelly on my face. I can't wait to take charge of this place. I'll put her to work in the mail room till she's ready to retire."

While deep in thought, James Wingate came toward them in the hall. He passed by the trio. Judy caught his eye immediately. His big brown eyes locked onto her curvy bottom as they headed to the administration office. Judy could feel his eyes on her. Turning around, she gave him a flirtatious smile. Whatever James was thinking flew out of his mind while his imagination fantasized on Judy's tight skirt all the way down the hall. His mouth began to water.

Judy whispered, "Who the hell was that? What's his name?"

"Who?"

"Him, tall, brown hair, gorgeous eyes, just passed by."

"Tall? Oh, that's Mr. Wingate, I think."

"Hmm, very nice. Now, who's this witch in front of us?"

"I think her first name is Catherine, and she is Mr. Hyde's administrative assistant. Her last name doesn't come to mind right now. But she seems to know everything about me. I don't like it. I bet ten to one she knows exactly when Anthony comes and goes and his importance to the company."

After being led inside to the inner offices, Pet and Judy found themselves sitting in a very plush office. The décor spoke money with deep leather armchairs and a huge maple desk.

A few seconds later, they heard voices coming from the inner office. Catherine came out first, Aloysius Hyde followed, and then Anthony. Anthony spoke first, "Yes, Catherine, that will work out fine. Thank you."

When he looked at Pet sitting in the armchair with her hands resting on her lap, his jaw tightened. He was annoyed and grimaced, "That woman is at it again. This situation is getting old. Why did she have to bring this other irritant with her, too?" What a pair!" He resisted the urge to make a smart remark and instead gave her a warm smile.

Aloysius gave no indication of cordiality. He looked in Pet's direction for more than a few seconds as his eyes caught sight of the ring. The ring that ruined his life forever, and she had the nerve to be wearing it. He seized the chance to make her feel uncomfortable by staring into her eyes and then looking at the ring.

He enjoyed throwing his weight around as the man in charge and walked over to Pet, extending his hand as he did so. Her jaw clenched tensely as she rose to greet him and did likewise. He held her hand firmly, engulfing the ring with his meaty fingers. It was only for a few minutes, but long enough to dominate the moment. "This is an exquisite ring. It looks lovely on your finger, Mrs. Traffortelli. I hope it is insured. It would be a shame if you lost it." Pet felt uneasy, immediately withdrew from his painful grip, and stepped away.

An evil smile came over his face. He enjoyed inflicting a little pain on inferior people. He felt underlings should feel intimidated by powerful men. He looked down on her, continuing to speak.

"Mrs. Traffortelli, you've surprised us again. What can we do for you today?"

"I came here to see Mr. Prattmore, and I think Mr. Wingate. To be direct, sir, I feel it is time I learn my duties as the new owner. My college courses have been a great help in understanding how diverse the economy and consumer powers are in the world of commercialism. As I've said, Mr. Hyde, I'm very anxious to begin. I'm sure Mr. Prattmore would agree with me. He has been so much help already."

She finished talking with a big smile. Her voice bubbled with feigned enthusiasm. "I have so many ideas for this company! I can't wait for the next board meeting. I hope that is going to be very soon."

Aloysius let out a nervous cough. Anthony came to Pet's side. "Yes, Mrs. Traffortelli, we were kicking around some ideas a while ago. I was just thinking we could go over a few things later on at lunch today. Are you free?"

Pet nodded affirmatively, watching his eyes, trying to read his mood. Anthony walked close to her as he ushered the women out of the building, making small talk along the way. He even smiled and laughed when Judy made a sarcastic comment about Catherine's voice. She knew he was acting and was very adept at playing the role of goodwill ambassador. She loved this friendliness and enjoyed his attention, but she did not completely trust him. She learned all too well that his mood could change on a dime. His next statement surprised her when they got to the parking lot.

"Pet, are you going to be home tomorrow?" asked Anthony.

"Yes, I think so, why?" Pet replied.

"You are most likely going to get a registered letter tomorrow morning, so I wouldn't go anywhere until it comes."

She didn't hesitate in answering him but spoke slowly and carefully, "Okay, I will stay home until the mail comes. Is it important?"

His face was expressionless. "You might think so." He didn't elaborate. He just walked away, got into his Jaguar, and left.

"What a segue to get us the hell out of the office! In one minute, he's Mister Congeniality, and the next, he's a cold fish. I don't get him," Judy said, shaking her head.

"I don't either, Jude. Ever since the awful bedroom disaster, he's been hard to read. I think we're finished. So, we might as well go home. Lunch did sound good, now it's gonna be a cheese sandwich, the SOB."

"If you're talking about you and Anthony being finished, how do you feel about that? Are you upset?" asked Judy.

Pet shrugged her shoulders, "Eh."

Aloysius immediately went into his office after the two women and Anthony Prattmore left. He began barking orders, "Catherine, get Wingate and Buford in here now! I don't care what they're doing. Just get them in here. If they're at lunch, call or text and have them call me ASAP. If they don't answer in five minutes, call them again!"

Catherine walked to Aloysius' desk and picked up the phone, but before she dialed the phone, she barked a few orders of her own, "Okay, Al, settle down. You'll have a stroke if you keep huffing about. Sit down. I'll get them, don't worry. Don't let that twit get to you. You are smarter and meaner than anyone I know in the business world. You'll think of something to clip her wings." She reached into her purse and grabbed some antacid tablets. "Here, chew on some of these. You don't need a bleeding ulcer and a stroke at the same time."

Chapter 52

The Happy Letter

Pet was comfortably slouched on the couch watching her favorite rerun of Frasier, when there was a sudden knock on her door. Two seconds later, there was a louder knock. "I'm coming, I'm coming! Geez, gimme a chance will ya!"

She opened the door and saw the mailman standing in front of her with a letter attached to a clipboard.

"I have a registered letter for Mrs. Patrice Elyse Traffortelli. Are you her?"

Pet smiled at his diction, "Yes, I am she."

The young man jutted the clipboard in front of her. "Sign here, ma'am."

Pet quickly took it and signed the small postcard-like paper; he, in turn, handed her the letter, "Thank you, Ma'am. Have a nice day."

"You are very welcome. Have a good one yourself."

She thought to herself that the last time she signed for something official, it was a summons for court. Out loud, she prayed, "God, let this be good news!"

TO: Mrs. Patrice Elyse Traffortelli
FROM: Whalen Falls City Court House
Division of Wills and Probate

Dear Mrs. Traffortelli, Upon this court's decision, Rutherford Manor is now in your full and legal possession. As of November 1st, the said property and all of its confines inside and out are hereby bequeathed to the above-mentioned. The transfer of title will take place on November 6, 2018, at 2:00pm sharp at the office of Anthony J. Prattmore Esq. Whalen Falls, Pa.

Division of Will and Probate
John Ireland, Director

She read the letter three times. Yes, it looked legal, but she still couldn't believe what she read. She laughed and cried at the same time. "After all this time, and now with a few legal words, Rutherford is mine. All mine!"

She sat down again on the couch, composed and a little more rational. Anthony entered her mind on a negative note, "Why, that stinker. He knew what was going to happen and yet never said a thing. He wanted to make it a surprise for me. But, if he really loved me, he would've said something more than just 'be here'. He could've been here with me. He missed an opportunity to make up for the way he's been acting, the scrounge."

She thought for a few minutes. "Well, I'm not going to worry about his motives now. I'm too happy."

Her first impulse was to call Judy, but out of respect, she called her parents instead. Her parents were happy for Pet and couldn't wait to see her new home. They asked if Uncle Mike would live with her, too. Pet told them no, not in the immediate future. She did not need Mae Delight tangling with a big Swede every morning. Please, what a combo! She called Judy. Then, a half hour later, she let Bunny know the good news, too.

"You know, you will have to throw a big party after all this waiting. It will be a great time to celebrate."

"Yes, my dear friend Judy said the same thing,"

"Hey, you could have a costume party. What better excuse for excitement? After all, it is an old mansion. I bet there were many a masquerade ball in that place. I'll come as a tavern wench," said Bunny.

Pet laughed. "Bunny, that doesn't surprise me at all. The

party would be rated G, but some of the characters would be rated X! Oh, also, no one can wear masks."

"Why not?"

"I want to see everyone's face pea green with envy as they step inside my door."

The next day, she decided to call on Mae Delight Reddick. With her finger, she pushed the doorbell, and with her head held high and her eyes straight forward, she greeted Mae Delight warmly, "Good morning, Ms. Reddick. How nice to see you today!" Mae Delight just rolled her eyes.

Chapter 53

Pet's Announcement

"Come in. Come in. What are you so excited about? You're so bubbly, you look like a balloon ready to pop! Quiet down, girl. Let's go to the sitting room," said Ms. Reddick.

Pet could not contain herself any longer. She burst into conversation immediately. "Oh, Ms. Reddick, I'm so happy. It's finally happened, I'm moving in. I signed the papers on November 6th. Then this house will be mine. Isn't it wonderful!"

"For you, maybe, not me. Do you know what it takes to git a house like this ready?"

"No, but I'll help, and Judy will help too. I can get…"

"You'll get no one. No, sir, not in this house. Miss Grace had her own people to move things. I don't want just anybody trapesin ' in my house, seein' things they oughta not see. You have to be careful, girl!"

Her enthusiasm was quelled for a moment as she looked about this room. Her eyes wandered, looking at the high ceiling, the dark oak window frames, the lace curtains that flowed gracefully to the floor, and the delicate chairs that begged a lady's form to recline in. "Oh, guess so, I wasn't thinking for a minute, but the rooms, they are the same, nothing has changed them, except time and emptiness."

"Yes, a lot of time and too much emptiness. Now, how much time do I have? I got to call my people. Manny knows them all. He'll be here to set your piddly stuff into storage down below. And don't keep callin' me Ms. Reddick. I told you to call me Mae Delight!"

She was elated and saddened at the same time. "Mae Delight, could I have some of my things put upstairs? After all, there is the clock that Grace gave to me. Wasn't it in this hall down from the library? And is that Manny who helped move the clock to my house? Couldn't I keep my bedroom set and my bed?"

"Girl, you ask a lot of questions. I'll see about that bed of yours. I don't need any clutter in those bedrooms. And, yes, that's the man, why?"

"Well, I'm glad he knows his profession. Getting the clock in my apartment was not an easy task. Oh, and since you know all the movers and since today is the 7th of October, can we move in the weekend of November 10th? That's more than a month from now."

Mae Delight stood up, putting her hands on her hips. She looked at Pet like a mother about to scold a petulant child. She didn't like confusion in Rutherford Manor. Miss Grace wouldn't stand for it, and neither would she. Now this scrawny girl wanted things her way and right now. Her tone of voice was not friendly when she answered, but she didn't say no to her requests.

"I'm not saying anything until I talk to Manny. He got a lot of responsibility, and he has to do the movin' on his time. It depends on him, his men, and when. It'll cost ya. He doesn't work outta the goodness of his heart, and doesn't haggle with the man. The price he gives you is final. He won't cheat ya, he'll answer to me if he does. I'll take a look upstairs in the bedrooms to see what might suit you."

"Okay, I won't bother the man about price. I think he is an honest man. He's worked for Briar Town long enough." Then, as an afterthought, Pet almost begged her, "Oh, Mae Delight, can I have the flowered room, the one that looks out to the garden and the woods? It's so beautiful."

Mae liked throwing her weight around and being in charge, but she also knew sooner or later, Pet was going to rule the roost. Her voice softened, "I'll see, maybe, not promisin' mind you. I don't want any bureau or vanity scratched; that furniture upstairs is worth much more than anything you got."

Pet got a big smile on her face. She wanted to hug Mae Delight, but was afraid of an instant rebuke. "Thank you. I'll call you in two days. Is that okay?"

With a scowl on her face, she answered defensively, "Girl, you've got no patience. Do you always bark orders like that? Call me in three days and no sooner. These things take time. Now, git so I can work things out."

Chapter 54

The Big Kiss

She practically skipped down the front steps and into her car despite Mae Delight's attitude. The day couldn't have been more glorious, so she decided to forego studying for a test and check out Martha's Pearls. It was an established antique shop situated right in the middle of 3rd Street. It had been part of Whalen Falls scenery for a long time.

Shortly after her divorce, Pet walked in the city a lot. Looking in the different store windows took her mind off Neil. For some reason, she spent a lot of time in front of Martha's Pearls. The storefront was beautifully displayed with delicate antiques. Sometimes a little lamp or vase tantalized her curiosity and pulled at her purse strings, but she never had extra money to spend. Now she had the money to buy anything that caught her fancy.

She pulled into the parking space and got out quickly, not noticing the police car right behind hers.

A strong male voice startled her. "Are you sure you want to leave your car there, Ma'am?"

She spun around, almost closing her fingers in the door, "Wha…?" Then she laughed, "Officer Jones, do you always startle young women with a loud voice and a question?"

She came forward, and he got out of the squad car. Their eyes locked. They smiled at each other and walked quickly, ready to touch hands. He had the look of love in his eyes, and she had the excitement of a seventeen-year-old on prom night.

When they were inches apart, Pet took a big breath and began talking rapidly, "Guess what! Guess what! I am moving in! The house is really mine. I can walk right up to the front door, put the keys in the lock, and boom, I'm there! Oh, David, I am so happy! "

David didn't say anything but motioned her to follow him to the alley a few yards away. She obediently went with him around the corner of the building. David walked into the shadows and again motioned her to come closer. As soon as she got within arm's reach, he pulled her quickly to his chest. She felt his belt, his holster, his pants, his shirt, and then his lips on hers in a split second. She breathed in his cologne and didn't fight the sensuous warmth of his tongue.

Pet circled her arms around David's neck as she pressed her body into him. He was breathing hard, kissing her again and again. She responded quickly and passionately. He didn't care that his superior could suspend him for this unprofessional behavior. He didn't care if the mayor himself caught them necking in the alley. All he wanted to do was to show Pet he loved her and wanted her.

Slowly, he pulled away from her with a kiss on the forehead. "I have to go, but you look so damn good in that pink sweater and those tight jeans, I had to show you how I felt and say Hi."

Pet finally took a normal breath and looked up into his handsome, tanned face. Smiling, she pulled away from David, "That's some way to say Hi. You literally took my breath away. I like it."

"I'll come over tonight, 'kay? Now, I really have to go." He walked in front of her as they both exited the alley. Then he adjusted his hat and then his belt. David nodded to her as if he had been on official business and got back into the squad car.

Chapter 55

The Down and Dirty

THE TUNE was just outside the city limits. It was an old rectangular building that once had some historical value, but time and poor maintenance made it more of an eyesore than anything else.

There were other derelict properties: a café, a shoe store, and a pawn shop, which were boarded up. Separated from the stores, the road sloped down to railroad tracks. There, an old brick train station stood alone. It was built in the early 1900s. A faded white sign with iron lettering attested to its age, stating WHALEN FALLS WELCOMES YOU EST. 1909. Now it welcomed no one at this end of town. The Tune, unfortunately, was the only welcome wagon there, and its clientele were mostly bums or drifters of most dubious character.

Tonight, the Fall mist shrouded the derelict building, isolating it even more. The only distinguishing feature of the bar was its door. It was once a bright fire engine red, adorning this façade like a beacon of glory. Now it was faded and chipped. There was one small, dirty window in the center of it, about five and a half feet up, where a man could peer inside to check for occupants or gain the proprietors' nod to come in. In scroll lettering, THE TUNE was written above the cracked window frame.

The inside looked like a cluttered hallway. It was full of tables and chairs strewn haphazardly along the wall. The air was smoky. Dim lighting from two ceiling fans, spaced too far apart to provide any appreciable illumination, made it hard to distinguish the men from the women huddled around small tables. Three men stood at a long mahogany bar, resting their feet on a highly polished brass foot rail. It stood out in contrast to the sorely cared-for mahogany behemoth that otherwise dominated the room.

Above the wall was a huge moose head overlooking the room. The palmate antlers stretched the length of the seven-foot bar. Its incongruous presence was either meant for conversation fodder or displayed as a contradiction to the dismal ambiance of the room.

The walls, once a cream color, were filthy brown from years of cigarette and cigar smoke. The patrons didn't seem to care about the smell of cooking grease that permeated the room or the additional pock marks from ketchup and mustard etched into the chair rails along the walls.

There were scrape marks and small chips in the wooden floor as if tables were dragged across it, or the corner of the metal tables had fallen hard on it in drunken brawls.

The din of waitresses shouting orders, sudden raucous laughter, dishes clattering, and drinks being plopped down on tables gave an atmosphere of a 1920s speakeasy. A person running from the law could hide here for hours without getting caught.

James Wingate and Harold Buford walked to the table where Aloysius sat. James brushed off some breadcrumbs from a previous customer. Harold watched as some unsavory characters argued at a nearby table.

"Why do you come in here? It's a shittin' pigsty," James said, wiping his hands on his pants pocket.

Aloysius looked up at them in irritation, "Because they have the best cheeseburgers in town. So, shut up and sit down."

"Did you call him?" James asked abruptly, picking at another crumb stuck to the table surface.

"Yeah, I called him. Why do you think I called you two bozos to meet me here?"

"Oh, I don't know, Al, nothing good on TCM tonight?" Harold smirked, still watching the two men.

Before Aloysius could utter a vicious comeback, a waitress

came up to their table. She gave them half a smile, "What will it be, guys? Just thirsty, or do you want burgers?"

She was cracking her gum and holding a pencil and a small white pad in front of her. She was an attractive woman in her late thirties. Her thick auburn hair was cut short and framed her face. She had beautiful dark brown eyes, which she outlined with black liner and a little too much mascara. The attempt at a younger look, unfortunately, was lost by the early wrinkles and dark circles under her eyes. Most men could probably overlook the gum cracking and attitude, because she might give men other ideas.

She began to tap the pencil on the pad impatiently. Harold looked around for a possible menu. James didn't speak.

Aloysius looked up at her. "Another Miller draft and a cheeseburger for me.

He looked at the other two. "I don't know what they want."

James said, "Could you give us a few minutes?"

She put her right hand on her hip and cracked her gum as she said in a sarcastic tone of voice, "Honey, you won't find a menu here in this place. You either order a hamburger or a cheeseburger with or without."

"With or without what?" James asked.

Aloysius was getting impatient, "Onions, you jerk! Do you want one or not?"

"Okay, gimme one, hold the onions," Harold said gruffly.

James found her attractive and was eyeing her up. He stared at her uniform. The top button of the blouse was open, and it definitely had his attention. He decided to put on the charm.

"I'll pass on the burger, just the beer, please. What's your name, honey?" he asked with a smile, although his voice was very condescending.

"It's Sweeney to my friends; to you, it's ma'am."

Harold and Aloysius watched with cruel amusement as he failed to impress the waitress.

Aloysius stopped Harold with a glaring look from adding

another jibe to James's failure. This back-and-forth nonsense was getting on his nerves.

"Cut the crap. I need you two to pay attention!"

Harold leaned over closer to Aloysius, "Sorry, Al. So, you got hold of him. How did you know he was the right man for the job? Did you know him before Briars Town? Did he seem interested?"

Al said, "No, I didn't know him personally, and yes to the third. I'll tell you about your first question in a minute. I kept thinking something about his face looked familiar. I found out he works in our finance department. I have observed him during business hours. He keeps to himself a lot. His projections are perfect. When he turns them in, he is courteous and professional. He will only enter into conversation when spoken to, or if he needs info on a financial report."

Just as Harold was about to say something, Sweeney came back with their beers and burgers. She put the tray on the table and distributed their orders.

"Will that be all, guys?"

"Yes, thanks." James smiled again.

Sweeney picked up the tray, turned to go, gave James half a grin, and left. He watched her hips sway back and forth as she walked back to the kitchen.

James kept watching her as he sipped the beer, "She's not a bad looker for her age, but she can't hold a candle to that brunette number that was with Mrs. Traffortelli. Man, she is hot. I'd definitely do her. I think she'd be easy."

"You scum bag, James. She's nothin' but a tease. You'd jump her, though, wouldn't you? I know you."

Harold had a nasty look on his face when he spoke to James. He knew his work partner's morals all too well, and it was getting old.

Harold focused again on Aloysius. "Al, your description of him sounds like ninety percent of the people in our firm. His behavior is nothing out of the ordinary. Do James and I know this potential assassin?"

"No, I'm not going to divulge his identity to you yet. To continue, let me just say one day I saw him reading the morning paper at his desk. He didn't see me, so he didn't hurry to put it away. The newspaper's front page was typed in bold letters telling about a home invasion and another brutal murder. He studied it as if he were taking an exam. He read that same page for ten minutes. Later, I saw him sitting at the counter in the employees' cafeteria on the first floor. I intended to get just a quick cup of coffee, but he caught my attention again. I sat down next to him. He is still poring over the story, looking at the victim's picture on the next page. I said to him, 'Some story, huh. Poor woman. She was a pretty one.'"

"So, still nothing?" James commented.

"Well, after I said that, he got agitated. He looked at me very briefly and looked down again at the page. This guy said 'she was probably a nagging bitch and didn't know when to keep her yap shut. No woman knows when to quit naggin'."

"Well, now. He's got a few issues there." James let out a low whistle. Aloysius had his complete attention now.

"The next day, I saw him at Scotty's Pub having a beer. I casually went over to him. You know, it was just one of those days. I needed to shoot the breeze with someone and have a pint before facing the old lady. Also, he seemed to want to talk. We ordered two more beers and a couple of shots before he began to let loose. The conversation was more of a rant on how he hated controlling women, their nauseating voices, and their stupid demands.

"He was going on and on. I agreed with him, and he liked that. I led him on, saying, 'Yeah, I like to get rid of one myself. Then he laughed out loud; 'Yeah, I'd do it too!' Suddenly, he shut up and got quiet. I stopped talking and didn't provide anything else to entice him. I was feeling the booze and decided to leave. I had to be careful that night because I was driving the company car."

Before Aloysius continued, he looked over toward Sweeney.

He caught her attention and held up two fingers for more beer. She gave him a quick smile and disappeared behind the bar.

"So, after seeing him at the bar, I did a little snooping. About ten years ago, there was a news story of a murder on Commerce Avenue. A well-to-do woman was horribly mutilated in her home with a utility knife. The weapon was never found. The paper ran pictures of the possible suspects. Her boyfriend was one of them. He was described as good-looking, with sandy blonde hair and a well-built physique. All of them were questioned and released. The investigation continued for over a year, but nothing came of it. The case went cold."

Harold looked at his watch, "Does this story have an end, Al? Those assholes over there are getting rowdy. I don't feel like being part of a bar fight tonight. Let's wrap this up quick, okay."

Al continued, "Yeah, so, the bottom line is I'm sure that suspected boyfriend is my beer drinking buddy. I thought about this a lot. He has the personality of a woman hater and has the potential to do harm without regret. So, I called him, and he's definitely interested in getting rid of that Traffortelli woman. But first, I'm going to try to scare her out of town, the usual scare tactics, bricks through the window, that sort of stuff."

James raised his eyebrows with skepticism, "Sounds okay, Al. Do you think she'll scare easily? She does not look like the crybaby type. Anthony says she lives in an apartment building right now. You'll have to adjust your plans of scaring her at home. This will take time. I thought you wanted this done quickly. Also, you don't want to lose this guy. He might get disinterested and leave."

The beers were starting to work on Aloysius. His manners and speech were getting sloppy, "Nah, this guy's hungry. He'll take the job and the money I give him. I'll decide if I want to do that other stuff in a day or two."

James laughed. There was a bit of larceny in his sarcastic little chuckle. "Good, I like that, no hesitation. What do you think, Harold?"

Harold's voice was just above a whisper, and he leaned in closer. "Makes no never mind to me, that Trafforteli woman is going to be trouble. Once she gets a taste of power, she'll be a pure bitch. Yeah, I say get rid of her, but let me make one thing clear. I'm not taking the fall for anyone. Al, James, you got that?"

Aloysius wiped his mouth with the back of his hand and let out a belch. "Don't be an old lady, Buford, it'll be a piece of cake. Besides, this joker works for me. What can go wrong? If he screws up, I'll fire him. Are you guys with me?"

Harold and James looked at each other and then nodded in agreement. With a satisfied grin, Aloysius drained his glass of beer and was about to put it on the table when suddenly all hell broke loose. Two men stood up from their table, swaying in a booze infused shouting match. They were big men. The momentum of the argument propelled them into the crowded tables as they jabbed and swung at each other. Their drunken bodies moved wildly, heading toward the seated trio.

Out of nowhere, a huge arm went smashing into the other guy's face. The beer mug he was holding flew toward James. It crashed to the floor, spewing beer all over James.

Next, two drunken women got into the mix and began to swear at the men. Somehow, they got pushed aside by the drunken fighters and started fighting each other.

"Aw, for the love of Christ, I knew this was gonna happen," Harold said and quickly ducked to avoid another wild punch. "Let's get the hell outta here," Aloysius said to them. They didn't waste anytime and headed for the door.

Dodging the other onlookers, they each pulled twenty-five dollars out of their pockets and threw the bills on the end of the bar. Sweeney watched the men hurry out the door. She smiled, hoping they enjoyed the local entertainment.

And so, their plan began.

Chapter 56

The Contract

Charles and Aloysius came to an agreement over the phone. They would meet at an inconspicuous place and at a convenient time for Aloysius' business day. He didn't care how it affected Charles. After all, he would be the man in charge in this instance, and he complimented himself on the planning of it. So, three o'clock was the agreed time with the College Board members, and then he would deal with Charles.

The young man's eyes nervously darted about the Faculty lounge as Aloysius sat down with a cup of coffee in his hand.

"I don't like it here. We don't belong in a teacher's lounge. I feel conspicuous. It would've been better meeting at Chauncy's Bar and Grill than here."

"I've been in this lounge many times, meeting with other faculty members. I'm on the Advisory Board here, too. Don't worry. We won't be here that long. Quit looking like a nervous schoolboy, and things will go a lot smoother. I wasn't about to do this at a bar. There are too many listening ears," Aloysius informed him.

Charles looked around again, "Did you bring the money?" he asked Aloysius. Aloysius tensed at his brash attitude. He didn't need a snot-nosed kid getting the upper hand.

"Look, Charles, you may think you're running the show and have a plan on how you're going to pull this off, but I'm the one calling the shots. I won't pay any money until I know the details. You got that? Now start talking."

"Okay, I'll make my move at the Annual Whalen Falls Christmas Festival after the parade and before your speech. Put her in a booth with big Christmas trees in front and behind it so I can sneak up on her. Also, I don't want any shittin' bright or blinking lights in the booth. I don't want anything shining on me. She'll know by the sound of my voice and the warning I give her that I'm not fooling around. Is that good enough for you? There'll be no screw-ups. I'll be in and out before anyone knows I was there."

Aloysius watched with enthusiasm as Charles outlined his plans, "Okay, I like it so far. When are you going execute your plan if she doesn't believe you?"

"One or two days before Christmas, maybe even Christmas Eve. I hear from the office gossip that she is moving into Rutherford Manor very soon. I have been by that mansion many times. There are woods and big bushes in the back. I am sure I can get close enough to the house and get a kill shot. I will be inspecting the area tomorrow night. The weather forecast is calling for wind and rain. That kind of weather will make it easier to nose around."

"Around Christmas, you say. Couldn't you do it sooner?"

Charles was getting irritated with Aloysius. "Are you going to micro-manage me the way you do everything else at that god-forsaken office?"

Aloysius gave Charles a cold stare, "Don't get smart, asshole. I just want this job done soon and with no problems. That holiday is almost a month and a half from now. All I am saying is, are you sure you want to wait that long? The rest of your plans sound good. I will give you half of the $50,000 now. The cash is in an envelope under this napkin."

"It's $75,000, or it's no deal, I'll walk out of here in a heartbeat."

His eyes were steady, unwavering, and determined to have the upper hand in this agreement. He waited for the older man to bluster an insult and balk at his confident demand.

Aloysius said nothing. He thought how shrewd it was to ask for more than what was necessary. He'd agree and play his game for a little while.

"Okay, Mr. Franklin, you've got moxie; '75' it is. But, I guess you don't want this money. It's only $25,000."

"I'll take it. I never leave a deal empty-handed. It's bad business, you might say. To show you I have class, I'm not even going to count it in front of you." With a slight curl of his upper lip, Charles smirked at Aloysius, "I know you're good for the rest of it."

Aloysius got up wanting to punch him in the nose, but he didn't. He calmly pushed the chair back to the table. In a gruff voice, he said, "I'll be in touch."

Charles sat motionless, knowing the old man was visibly upset as he walked toward the door. A cynical smile crossed his face. He liked it when The Man squirmed.

Aloysius walked fast, his head down, muttering to himself, agitated over the meeting. He grew more disgruntled as he buttoned his coat, for a cold wind blew against him. Also, he didn't see the group of kids standing near the steps.

Suddenly, a young man called out, "Hey, man, watch it! Ya almost plowed into us."

Aloysius looked up and went around the group. He hated young people and couldn't resist sneering at them, "Aah, watch yourself, asshole."

This made him mutter even more, and he quickened his pace. By the time he reached his BMW, he was out of breath, coughing in hoarse spasms. He gunned the car's engine and, in two seconds, was out of there, making mental notes to call Wingate and Buford. He didn't like being on the other end of the stick. The tables had to be turned quickly.

Another student up a flight of steps saw the heavyset man's near collision and called out, "Hey, Pet, did you see that fat guy in the Beemer? He almost knocked Kim to the ground! What an ass. Talk about us students being ignorant!"

"Yeah, I did, the jerk." She didn't tell them she knew him.

* * *

Aloysius pressed the Bluetooth call button and said, "Call James Wingate at 888 599 8080."

"Hello."

"James?"

"Yeah, Al, what do you want?"

"Put a tail on Charles Franklin. I want reports on every move he makes. I want to know where he goes at night and how long he is out. Do not ask me any questions now. Just do it. Tell Buford what's going on, but emphasize that he is not to be approached, understand?"

"Yeah, yeah, sure, Al." Then James chuckled under his breath, "So, Charles Franklin, eh?"

"Okay, now, you and Harold be in my office early, and I will fill you in on what's happening. Also, I've been thinking about Traffortelli's friend. Let's see if we can put a wedge in their friendship. Is she a good influence on Traffortelli, or can she be bought? See if she will talk about money. Anthony must know her friend's name. Find a way to get her in here."

"Yeah, Al, sure."

Chapter 57

The Big Move

Pet stood in the middle of her living room, surrounded by a dozen boxes big and small. She looked at the empty place, remembering the day she moved into the Carrollton Apartments. These rooms seemed so big to me, and now they feel so small. I am ready to leave, though. I've finally got my wish!

Judy came into the living room screeching her tennis shoes on the bare wooden floor. She cracked her gum as she talked, "Well, chickee, are you ready? And yes, you left the door open again, but this time doesn't count; it's moving day. What goes first?"

"Gads, all that in one breath, Judy. Yes, every box is labeled. And by the way, I asked, no, I begged Ms. Delight if you could come today. I had to promise her you wouldn't be in the way of those men, that you would put the boxes exactly where she told you to put them, and that there would be no sass from you or from either of us."

"Wow, what a tyrant! Did she really hassle you that much?"

"Kinda, I think she was more frustrated with Manny because they couldn't agree on the day and time."

"But?"

"I know it's my party, but she's going to be the mistress of ceremonies on this day. There was drama, of course, between her and Manny. I wanted to laugh while she told me, but she was dead serious."

"Ooo, what'd she say? I can just see her with her hands on her hips smarting off to the hired help."

"The scenario went like this, so to speak. I called her; she called Manny; then Manny had to get back to her. At first, Manny wasn't sure that this particular weekend would work for him, and he had to call Mae back. Mae Delight told him she didn't like postponements. She wasn't about to have this move drag on or move this girl's pitiful furniture in the dead of winter. The move would take place Saturday, November 10th at 8:00 a.m. sharp."

"Well, I guess she told him! I am happy for you, Pet. You know that, don't you?"

Pet gave her a hug. "Yes, I do, my friend."

"What time is it?"

"Five minutes to eight."

As if it were a stage cue, Manny and Jimmy walked through Pet's door that very moment.

With the authority of a true professional. Manny greeted Pet, "Good morning, Mrs. Traffortelli. Is everything ready to go?"

Pet immediately turned to greet him with a smile, "Hello, Manny. Yes, everything is ready. I didn't touch my grandfather clock. I figured you would know how to move it this time."

"Yes, ma'am, I do remember your clock and this here door. If it's all the same to you, I'd rather not call your super. It won't be a problem now that we know how to tilt it an' all."

Pet thought a minute, "Oh, what the heck, Manny, I trust you."

"Thanks, ma'am. Jimmy, bring in the dolly and cart."

And so, it began, one box after another. Her meager belongings were piled onto a dolly and whisked away. The clock took a bit longer, but even that procedure went smoothly once the door was removed. A minor miracle occurred because the superintendent, Mr. Santorini, didn't come to inspect the move.

Pet drove behind the moving van, and Judy followed Pet. It was like a tiny procession to the castle. Pet's emotions rose and fell like a wave. She was elated moving into Rutherford Manor. As the new owner, she could do anything she wished, and she had the money to make those dreams come true. With Rutherford Manor came the furniture company, and that meant power. She wouldn't abuse it, but she vowed to strengthen her potential.

She lowered the car window, feeling the cool air on her face. She wanted to continue these happy thoughts. The Tourmaline ring caught her eye, sparkling in the sunlight. She believed that it brought her good luck and David Jones into her life, hopefully to share her dreams. Her fantasies about him in the house with her were endless.

The happiness dimmed for a moment when a troubling thought crossed her mind, and Anthony Prattmore's face appeared. She thought he would always share her dreams. She felt a heaviness as she remembered their last conversation. Pet realized that maybe Anthony was looking for someone more compatible, maybe more intelligent, but certainly not her. She decided to put him away in a box forever, like a discarded ragdoll destined for the Goodwill truck.

A tear trickled down her face when she thought of the friends she would miss from that apartment building. She thought about Harry and his sister Clementine. How often did she see them walk down the hall together? She whispered a prayer for Harry and begged him to look down on her from time to time. Lastly, she thought of the excitable apartment owner, Mr. Santorini, with his blustering temper, punctuating every word with a hand up in the air.

Finally, rolling up the long driveway, Pet relished the sound of the tires on the gravel path. Judy stopped her car right behind Pet. Both women got out of their cars and headed up the steps.

"Well, are you ready to face the commandant of Rutherford Manor?" Judy asked.

"Now stop that. You're making me laugh. I can't act like a smart ass right from the start, laughing in her face when she opens the door. She'll hate me forever!"

Mae Delight opened the door before their feet touched the doormat.

"Come on in. I been waitin'. Manny called me, gave me the heads up that you was on your way."

"Judy, I'm home. I'm really home!" Pet exclaimed.

Chapter 58

Footsteps

Pet felt safe around the campus and never gave taking evening classes a second thought. The last class ended between 8:15 and 8:30pm. This gave her plenty of time to walk to her car before the campus was completely deserted. To promote these classes, students were permitted to use the first well- lit row of the upper parking lot. But on this night, there was a free concert in the auditorium, and every space in both upper and lower lots was filled. Consequently, Pet had to park in the back lot near the maintenance building.

She looked at the big hall clock as she headed to the exit door. Now it was 9:30pm in an empty hall full of shadows. She admonished herself for talking so long with the professor. It could have waited till next week, but no, she had to get her point across. She regretted her folly and thought about how eerie and silent the building had become.

When she opened the door to the outside, she felt the sting of the wind and sleet on her face. The thin suede designer jacket gave her little protection from the sudden change in weather. She quickened her pace and ran down and around the long sidewalk in the back of the campus. There was one lone light on the maintenance shop door. It gave very little light, casting shadows barely into the parking lot. It caught her eye for a second, but it was just enough time to lose her footing and slip onto the blacktop. Her car keys flew from her hand, and so did her books.

The sudden contact with the slushy surface stung her hands. Now, the situation worsened. Not only did she have to retrieve the books, but the keys slid underneath the car. She got down on all fours and inched over to it. Sarcastically, she began muttering to herself, "What happened to all the beautiful crisp Fall moonlit nights the weatherman promised?"

Pet stretched both arms under the driver's side as far as she could. Her hands scraped over slush and pebbles, trying to locate the keys. Sleet pelted heavily on her head, and in her eyes, she couldn't see or feel them at all.

It was then that she saw a shadow from under the car. She also heard footsteps coming toward her. They slowed down and stopped a few yards away. Pet strained to see if it was a man's shoes or a woman's shoes while still trying to find the keys. "Hello? Can you help me?" she called out.

The light was so dim that she couldn't be sure of anything. Who was there? "Hey, can you help me?" Pet asked again. No answer came as the intruder came closer. His shoes dragged on the wet surface, making each step sound more threatening. Terrifying thoughts crept into her mind. No, not here, not now. Rape is out of the question. This can't be happening. She began thrashing her arms in every direction, stretching, and grabbing for anything metal. A silent prayer escaped her lips, "Dear God, help me, help me."

In one last sweep of her right hand, she felt the point of a key and grabbed it. With keys in her hand, she pressed the key fob to unlock the door and immediately got in. She started the engine, locked the door, and was about to pull ahead. Suddenly, the stranger appeared in front of the car. He held his arms high above a wide-brimmed rain hat. In a loud voice, he yelled, "Leave this county before you die!"

Pet turned on the headlights. The glare of the lights on his coat, combined with the sleet, gave a macabre vision of a ghost, but she knew this menacing figure was real and meant to harm her. She did not have to think twice. She quickly put the car in gear and got out of the parking space, nearly missing the specter by inches. She was doing sixty miles an hour by the time she got to the intersection.

She ran the red light, daring anyone to stop her. Where was a cop when you needed one? If she did get stopped, she'd tell him what happened. Her mind raced on how she would explain that terrifying moment.

She looked briefly in the rearview mirror to see if anyone was behind her, but the only thing she saw was a bedraggled, soaking wet head, a shivering, blotchy, red-faced woman who wanted to rant on about some guy looking like a ghost yelling at her.

Would any officer believe a hysterical woman like that? she asked herself. No, not even Officer David Jones would believe that story. It was a second later that she realized she had left her books in the slushy parking lot. "Damn!" she exclaimed out loud. Now, not only did she feel horribly defeated, but she had the agonizing task of retrieving her soggy books. A dire hope went up toward heaven that someone would find them because she wasn't about to turn around and go back.

Pet pulled in the driveway just as the sleet turned into a heavy snow. She was shivering in her soaking wet clothes when Mae Delight opened the door even before she got the key in the lock. Shaking her head, Mae Delight blasted into a tirade, "Where have you been staying out so late on a nasty night like this? You don't have the sense God gave a goose. I've been waitin' on you for the last hour!"

"Mae, please, it's been a horrible night. I lost my car keys and a stranger scared me half to death."

Mae busied herself helping Pet out of her jacket. "Hmmph, that ain't nothin new 'round here. There are a lot of scary people in this town. Now, let's get you out of those wet clothes, then come sit back down on the couch near the fire and put that throw around you. I'll bring you some hot tea."

As Mae Delight pulled and tugged at the soggy clothes, Pet stood there like a bewildered child. Her body became limp, and she moaned. "You don't believe me, do you. I was threatened tonight. It was horrible. He was big, ugly, crazy, and fierce-looking." Her outburst fizzled to a whisper. "It could have been much worse."

"You're not makin' sense, girl. Now do as I say, and we'll talk in a minute.

With the last tug of her shoe, Pet obeyed the housemaid's order and started up the stairs, but then turned for a second, "Oh, and could you put a special shot of Maker's Mark in it too, please. That should quiet me down some."

She heard Mae Delight mumbling to herself as she lumbered to the kitchen. A few minutes later, Pet returned to the sitting room. Slowly, she began to feel more like herself in her warm bathrobe, snuggling under the soft throw. The fire crackled in the old stone fireplace, giving a soft, warm glow to the room. It was exactly the salvation she needed right now, but a familiar pall came over her.

She felt very alone, as if she were in a round box with no windows, no doors, no ceiling, or corners to dig out of. Did she call for help? Who would hear her? Was she worthy of help? Her husband, Neil, didn't think so, and her parents wanted to smother her, coddle her, in their own special box. She didn't need that either!

Mae Delight came in with the tea and handed her the special brew. "You still ain't makin' sense, child. Tell me what's troubling you."

"Sorry, I didn't realize I was talking out loud, Mae Delight." Pet related her feelings about Neil and her parents. "Mae Delight, I feel like I have been left on a railway platform in the middle of nowhere. I have no one. I'm alone, totally alone. I hate it, because I feel like a failure."

She took a big sip of tea and continued. "At my age, shouldn't I know what to do? Why can't I rely on myself? Tonight, I thought I was going to die of fright when this boogie man jumped in front of my car, yelling at me to get out of town or die!"

Mae Delight scowled at her, "Die? Scared? Troubled? Do you think yer the only girl that has worries? Yer not alone in this world of trouble. I lost my husband a month after we were married back in 1971, when he was in Vietnam. A month later, my mother was beaten, robbed, and died alone in an ambulance before the paramedics could get her to a Baltimore Hospital. You want me to go on?"

A tear escaped her left eye, trickling down her cheek. Then Mae Delight quickly checked her emotions.

Pet gasped, "Uh, no, Mae Delight, I am so sorry. I didn't know. What did you do?"

"Well, I did a lot of things that got me here, listening to your pitiful story! Girl, in this world, ain't nobody gonna help you but yourself. You got some spunk, but you're whiny. You gotta have a game plan. If you screw up, you screw up. The world will not come crashin' down on you for a mistake or two. That jackass you married tore you down to nothin'. That was your first mistake, but you can make it. Build yourself up!"

Pet sat there, realizing Mae Delight was making sense, and decided not to fight her advice. She watched this old woman in the fire's light. Her warm brown skin showed her age, but her character did not. The lines around her eyes and forehead gave a softer appearance that Pet never noticed before. Dark coal-black eyes were piercing and stern, but her mouth had laugh lines that could break into a heartwarming smile in an instant. Whisps of silver-gray hair that escaped from a tight bun at the nape of her neck softened her austerity. She was a wise woman and knew it.

Finally, she said, "Well, I believe you were scared, but why didn't you call the police? I'd have run him down, m'self, but you're a mouse and probably would've missed him."

Pet shook her head and, by this time, halfway laughed, "Not helping, Mae Delight, not helping."

After a few minutes, Mae Delight got up and said good night. "You'll just have to figure it out yourself. Just don't go doing something brainless you can't get out of right away. Good night, child."

Pet smiled at her and said, "Goodnight." She watched Mae Delight walk down the hall. She snuggled further into the soft blanket and thought over the conversation. Quietly, she realized Mae Delight Reddick was right again. The message became crystal clear: Believe in yourself.

The hot toddy was working its magic, and she finally felt relaxed. Her mind trailed off. "I've got to call Bunny Haskel. I know she won't believe what happened tonight. Wonder if she knows any boogie men. Aloysius Hyde, maybe?"

Chapter 59

The No Go

About three weeks later, Bunny and Pet hatched an idea to meet at the factory again. It was a hasty plan, but it was their only chance to gain more information. They decided to drive in separate cars. Something was off the minute Pet entered the old road. The warehouse's look was more desolate, foreboding. Not one car was in the parking lot. Newspaper and pop cans were strewn along the edges of the blacktop. The lights above the overhead sign were busted out.

Closer to the warehouse, she encountered an obstacle course of pine branches, potholes, and rocks. The car bounced and weaved all over the road. Her concentration while driving through the debris almost caused her to hit a person approaching her with a bright flashlight. Fortunately for him, his huge frame made her come to an immediate stop. He shone the light into the windshield, blinding her instantly. When she hit the down button for the window, huge feathery snowflakes fell on her face as she leaned out the window.

"Hey, buddy, shine that someplace else. I can't see!"

The silent giant said nothing but pointed with his flashlight, urging them to keep moving past the corrugated metal building. She put the car in park but kept the motor running. He walked up and stopped beside the car door. His manner was curt as he asked her why she was here.

"I own this company now, and I need to take inventory of the remaining contents inside," Pet said authoritatively.

A few seconds later, she saw Bunny Haskel's car coming up the gravel road. The guard did the same, showing the newcomer where to park directly beside Pet. Bunny pressed the driver's side window button. Pet did the same to the passenger window, "Hey, what gives? Why are you still in your car?"

Then Bunny impulsively tossed the factory keys through the window. "Here." Pet jerked when they hit her in the chest.

"Ouch! What the heck?" Pet grabbed them before they fell on the car seat. "Hold on, Bunny, I don't know what's going on yet."

With the factory keys firmly in her hand, Pet looked up at this giant as she was ready to get out of the car, but before she could move a muscle, he put both hands in a palms-up position. "I'm afraid you are going to have to stop right there, ma'am. I have strict orders from Mr. Hyde not to let anyone come in here."

"But I have keys to this door, Mr. What is your name?"

"Bernardi, ma'am, Officer Bernardi."

"Officer Bernardi, you must let me in. I am Mrs. Traffortelli, the new owner of Briar Town Furniture Company."

"I am aware of that, ma'am, but you will have to discuss that with Mr. Hyde. He's still the C.E.O. of this place. Now, you will have to leave, and those keys you're holding will be a waste of time. The locks to all doors around and in the building have been changed."

By this time, Bunny had gotten out of her car and was edging up to the guard to get in his face. "Why, you son of..." escaped from her lips.

The guard immediately stopped her in mid-sentence, "I wouldn't say another word, ma'am. I am the authority here. This badge you see, and the sidearm at my hip, prove I can shut up anyone and remove them from the premises. Now, I don't think you want to tangle with me unless you'd like to end up in jail for trespassing and resisting arrest."

Bunny realized she was put in her place and got back into her car. Both women drove away in defeat. Pet drove to the end of the long driveway, where it met a wide lead onto the four-lane intersection heading south to 376. Bunny again pulled up beside her.

"Well, Pet, that was a lot of nothing. What are you going to do? Are you going to storm into his office and demand those keys?"

Pet grimaced, "Yes, another face-off. These situations are getting old. I'm going to call him tomorrow and give him a piece of my mind."

"Talking over the phone won't get you anywhere. We must find out who is moving money around and changing keys. It just doesn't add up. Catherine will stone-wall you. She loves the power play. Just go in there and cause a ruckus. He hates scenes in his office. Don't beat around the bush. Be assertive!"

"Yeah, smart ass, I guess you're right again. You will see me sometime tomorrow. We'd better get going. It's starting to snow harder."

Chapter 60

Stranded

Pet let Bunny go on ahead of her. Bunny wasted no time getting on her way as she stepped on the gas. The car swerved slightly on the slick pavement, then disappeared from sight.

Then, Pet turned left and went down the ramp to Route 376. The once-feathery light crystals of a few minutes ago, and the dropping temperature, turned the ramp into a treacherous, glazed slope with no guardrails. The car rapidly accelerated, and for a few seconds, she had no control over its direction. She pumped the brakes lightly and headed for the berm of the road. Her right front tire caught the gravel, and so did the right rear. Finally, the car slowed down.

She crept down the ramp, hoping that once the road leveled off, the driving would be easier. Pet muttered, “Damn, this is not going to be fun. Dear Lord, get me home safely.”

She kept the car at a steady forty MPH. After a few minutes, she felt more confident and gave the engine a little more gas. “Okay, now, going faster, getting closer, gotta get to that next exit. Go on, Pet. You can do it. Almost there!”

Suddenly, out of nowhere, a vehicle appeared right behind her. The high beams shone in her rear view mirror. It was a big vehicle with a powerful engine. She could hear it even with her windows closed. It was moving fast, coming up on her rear bumper. Every time she went a little faster, the tailgater went faster too. Her tires spun and swerved on the ice.

Pet was beyond panic. She got angry and started cussing. “You’re not gonna get me, you idiot!” she yelled. Now her only hope was to accelerate and find the road’s berm to gain traction. Then the car behind started to pass. It moved closer and closer to her. She looked out her window through the heavy snow and saw headlights and a front grill ready to ram her door. The muffled bump sent her car spinning to the right. She screamed "Noooo!" and turned the steering wheel to the left and then to the right again. The assailant got closer, fishtailing and striking Pet's left front fender as it passed. This was enough to send her car careening down a small slope. Pet turned the wheel as hard as she could to the left as the car slid sideways. It came to a sudden stop in a mound of dirt, inches from a guardrail.

There, in silence, Pet sat, alone, not thinking, not moving, just stunned, thankful to be alive. A few seconds passed as she oriented herself, "What happened? I survived. That's what happened. Why isn't the car running?"

Pet put the car in park and tried to start it again; thankfully, the engine turned over. The comforting swish thump of the windshield wipers glided rhythmically back and forth. She pushed the down button for the window, hoping to get an idea of what was out there. By now it was dark. No one was on the road. An eerie silence surrounded her. She wondered if anyone was out there. All that she could hear was the snow hitting the roof and windshield. It also fell on her face as she stretched her head out to see where the edge of the road was and where the slope began.

The view before her wasn't promising. She decided not to get out of the car because she had no boots. Wet feet and a light jacket weren't really the best survival clothes, but she couldn't stay here either. So, with crossed fingers, she put the car in drive and tried to ease up the slope. Her tires spun, and instead of going forward, the car slipped backward. She quickly tried to turn the car left to get it out of the rut, but the tires had no traction on the dead grass, mud, and snow.

Pet slumped down into the seat, feeling helpless. "Don't cry. Don't cry. Text David. It'll be quicker," she told herself. Digging into her purse, she grabbed the phone. It came on dimly, showing no signal. "NO signal! What do you mean, no signal? It can't be!" She waved it all about the front seat, trying to get it to come back up. Nothing worked.

Up to this point, Pet hadn't been too scared, but now the options of getting out of this mess were slim. She wondered if the state snowplows came out this far. She tried once more to get the car off the slope and onto the road. She thought if she put the 370Z Nissan coupe in low and gunned the engine, the power would get her out, but the sudden thrust pushed the car's back tires into a thick mass of bramble bushes growing on the edge of the slope.

Pet sat there, hands shaking, and scared that the sports car could be damaged underneath. She berated herself for not taking her good old front wheel Equinox tonight. She just wanted to show off as the young, powerful exec with an expensive car. "A lot of good this car did you, Missy."

Her thoughts raced on. "Who was going to see a small car stuck in a bunch of bramble bushes off the road? Why didn't I wear warmer clothes? I should've worn heavier shoes. No, I had to be a show-off and wear a fancy jacket and sling-back shoes. God, I'm so stupid!"

She made jerky movements to the right and to the left, but nothing was there, no street signs or lights. There was no use in looking behind her because the wooded hills overshadowed this highway. Her vehicle was hidden by nature's obstacles. It might as well have been hidden in a cave.

She cried out in panic, "I have to get out of here. What if I die out here? No one knows where I am. I could be buried alive in this blizzard." Those scary thoughts quickened her breathing, and she felt her heart beating faster. She took a quick look at her gas gauge. The needle was barely on a quarter tank. Pet figured the car could keep running for at least forty more minutes. She dug out her cell phone again, moving it in every angle she could think of.

"Finally, one bar! Oh, please let me get through to David. Let's see, I gotta make this short," she whispered. Her fingers shook as she punched his phone number and the message, STUCK ON 376 HELP! She waited in agony, hoping for his answer. Impulsively, she attempted a second message, but on the third letter the phone clicked off before she could finish. It went completely dead. "Aw, come on, don't do this, not now!" With a deep sigh, Pet became acutely aware she was totally alone in a blizzard.

Suddenly, an eruption of emotion overtook her. She screamed like a hysterical child. "Dear God, I don't want to die!" as she pounded the center of the steering wheel so hard with her fists that the horn went off in multiple blasts. At the same time, her leg muscles tensed up, pushing her foot between the brake pedal and the car floor mat. She didn't hear the noise of the horn because her sobbing turned into spurts of erratic breathing, coughing, and choking.

As the car's interior closed in, a darkness began to overcome her. She began to feel faint, and a ringing sounded in her ears. She was going down for the count.

"Hey, in there, roll down that window!"

Pet faintly heard pounding on her window.

"Hey, you havin' a fit or something? Wake up!"

His sudden voice made Pet look up. Her mind reeled as if waking up from a drunken stupor. She had no clue how long she had been in this desperate condition. She squinted at a big white blob yelling at her. "Why is he yelling at me?"

Slowly becoming alert, she realized that a real person was on the other side of her door.

He showed a flashlight in her face, "Lady, roll down yer winder! It's cold out here. We gotta get you moving fer sur, eh!"

This snowman started to look and sound familiar. Only her uncle Mike said "fer sur." She put down her window.

"Uncle Mike, is that you? What are you doing out here?"

"I got me a big snowplow to clean these here roads. You don't look too good. Are you hurt?"

"No, just scared. My car is stuck. I tried to get it out, and I don't know if I have enough gas to get me home. The car's been running a while. The gauge is showing less than an eighth of a tank. When I slid down this slope and then into the bushes, I don't know if I damaged anything underneath it. Can you send someone to help me?"

"Well, heck, I can take you into Whalen Falls myself. The salt shed is right behind the municipal building, and I can get a top off for my spreader. I'll take you right up to your door and plow your driveway at the same time!"

"You are a lifesaver, Uncle Mike. I'll turn off the engine and get my purse. You won't get into trouble taking me home, will you?"

"Nah, I'll call my boss, Ole Tom, on the radio. He'll understand, I'll plow this highway up to the exit and then some. I'm just doin' my job and saving my niece at the same time. Ha, we'll have this big boy clearing the way in no time."

Pet pushed the car door open as far as she could and stepped into the deep snow. The sudden sensation of the cold, wet stuff sent a shock through her body, and stiff legs and feet made it impossible to navigate up the slope. Three seconds later, Pet fell in the snow with a groan and a thud. With his big hands, Mike swooped her up so quickly it was as if he leaned down to pick up a rag doll.

It was quite a sight. Mike Yoderman's huge frame was a magnet for the falling snow. In the few minutes he was out in the elements, a layer of white completely covered his oversized jacket and big floppy lumberjack hat. He looked like the abominable snowman with a dwarf in tow. A few seconds later, he hoisted Pet up into the cab of the huge vehicle.

"I'm gonna make this here cab nice and comfy for you, Pet; don't cha worry! The heat will be on full force, and my country music will be nice and lively. I'll have you toasty warm in a minute. Alistair would be proud of me, helpin' his little girl."

Then, with a big grin on his face, he leaned over to her ear, "Hold on, Missy. We're goin' for a ride!"

Mike put his foot down on the gas pedal, and the sound of the plow's powerful engine came alive with a deafening growl louder than a grizzly bear on steroids. Then he skillfully engaged the gears and lowered the plow to the ground. Its massive metal blades pushed the snow away in waves of white as it rumbled down the highway.

Pet slumped down into the seat and leaned on the window. The warmth of the heater was making her drowsy. She watched the snow-covered road and side rails go whizzing by. In seconds, the cold glass fogged with her warm breath, and her drifting thoughts sent her into a fitful sleep. In a dream, she saw herself running down the highway, in the headlights of the snowplow, waving her arms frantically to make it stop.

With a sudden jolt of the truck, Pet sat up quickly. He looked over to her. "Hey, don't be scared. The plow hit a bump on the road. Things get all covered up when it snows so much. You were crying. Were you having a nightmare, Ladybug?"

Pet dug out some Kleenex and blew her nose. "No, well maybe." A sudden thought occurred to her. "Uncle Mike, if you hadn't come along, I would still be out there. How did you know I was there?"

"Well, Ladybug, out here in the dark, any flashing light far off catches your attention real quick, and those brake lights were a blinkin' like a flood light with hiccups!"

"Oh, I'm so glad you were alert and saw them. I have to admit I was scared, and you spotting me was a miracle. Please don't call me Ladybug. I haven't heard that nickname since I was five. It, well, kinda makes me feel small and helpless."

"Well, you were, Pet. Ever since that day you fell in that tulip bed, all I see is you in all those yellow flowers floppin' around like a bug on a petal."

She couldn't be angry at him. He was being so kind, but she had to nip this in the bud. If David Jones or Mae Delight heard this nickname, they would tease her forever.

Chapter 61

Safe Again

Mae Delight's eyes got big as saucers when the huge snowplow pulled up the drive. She opened the door just a crack at first, making sure no invaders were storming the castle. Then, when Mike eased Pet out of the truck's cab, she flung it open and started yelling at Pet. Of course, she was mad, scared, and relieved at the same time.

Pet wearily came through the door, heading toward Mae Delight with Mike right behind her. He stopped and stood at the door, feeling very awkward in the big house. He watched the maid in amazement as she fussed over his niece. He smiled at the two of them and could tell this older woman loved Pet beyond all the concerned chattering. She fussed with Pet's wet jacket. "Look at you. Just look at the wet!"

She eyed Mike Yoderman up with a quick look of disdain as his big boots dripped slush on the foyer's highly polished floor. With the wet jacket in her arms, Mae Delight put her mouth in gear, and the tirade got louder, "You done forgot everything I told you the last time you was late! I told you to call me. Look at you, sopping wet, with your clothes on. You're gonna catch your death! I swear you can't think fo' yoself! And who is this troll dripping on my floor?"

Mike attempted to take up Pet's defense, but Mae started in again. "Are you gonna just stand there? Close the door or get out!"

"I'm leavin', ma'am. I don't have time to stay and talk. I'll be seein' ya, Ladybug. This here woman will take good care of you, fer sure." He then backed up to the door and let himself out. Leaning against the upstairs banister, Pet smiled as he slid out the door. After Mae Delight helped get the muddy shoes off her feet, she silently went up to her room.

She knew Mae Delight would follow shortly with a warming toddy, a solace that was needed hours ago. Now that she was once again safe in her home, she began to feel alone and insignificant. Yet again, she got herself into a situation she couldn't control. She wondered if she shouldn't just give up on being Wonder Woman in the business world. Pet decided to think about that later. Fatigue was beginning to close in on her.

She immediately snuggled down into her soft, velvety comforter and pushed against the satin pillows until she was in her own bed, feeling secure.

This cozy feeling was like being a little girl again, hiding under the covers during nightmares. She wanted everything bad to go away. She wanted a knight in shining armor to fight her dragons. No, she thought, not fight the dragon, kill the dragon.

The thought of being stranded made her shiver. "I could have died out there. How awful. If I wasn't sure a while ago, I'm sure now; someone wants me dead." She put her head between her knees.

A few minutes later, Mae Delight came through the door. She gave the bewildered girl the toddy, muttering to herself, "I swear, child, you're gettin' outa hand. You're gonna git yourself killed. Mae Delight doesn't need this, no, sir."

"Oh, Mae, maybe nothing else will happen. I'm home now. I'll be okay. I'm going to bed after I drink this."

Mae Delight stood beside the bed, arms on her chest. "Girl, you don't know how many times I looked out that window, not knowing where you were. And those calls, good gracious to mercy. The same cop called three times, and so did Mr. Anthony. "They'd say, is she home yet? Where is she? Do you know when she'll be back? I was so tired of answering, I didn't want to pick up anymore. Then your silly girlfriend would call with an attitude. She likes to git on my nerves. I told her the same thing everyone else did. I don't know where she went and quit callin'! Also, where do you want those flowers put?"

Pet looked up from her toddy. "Flowers? What do you mean?"

"I said, Mr. Anthony sent you some big fancy flowers and asked me to put them where you would see them right away. I knew you couldn't miss them. The vase is all glass, swirly, with colors and flowers I've never seen before. They're so fancy, it's like to be seen at a funeral parlor."

"When did they come?"

"This afternoon, then he kept callin' like all the rest of those people."

"Was there a note with them?"

"Do I look like I'd care? Girl, I don't poke my nose in anybody's business!"

Pet shook her head and waited for another curt reply. Instead, the maid's attitude softened, and she waited attentively for Pet to finish the drink.

"Are you finished, child?"

After one last gulp, she handed over the mug. "Uh huh. Oh, Mae Delight, I'm so tired. I'm not going to think of anything else right now. Everything will just have to wait until tomorrow."

The stern façade she put on was all pretense.

Mae Delight just shook her head, picked up the rest of Pet's wet clothes off the vanity seat, and headed for the door.

Before Mae Delight's foot touched the hall rug, Pet said softly, "Thank you for being here. I know now why Grace loved you so. You care about people. I'm sorry I worried you. I promise not to do it anymore."

Mae Delight didn't return the sentiment. The head nod was the only acknowledgement Pet got. She heard familiar mumbling as Mae Delight walked away, "I swear to mercy, that girl doesn't mean what she says. She was born trouble, and she always be trouble!"

She smiled, laying her sleepy head on the soft, cozy pillow, and drifted off to sleep.

Chapter 62

An Epiphany

A soft light shone through her curtains and streamed into the room. She opened one eye and saw the moon peeping below the lace valance. Its soft glow made delicate shadows on her pillow. "It's the moon," she uttered groggily, rolling over on her side. Then she rolled on her back and stared at the moon. It made her think how different the night was now, calm and beautiful compared to snowy and terrifying.

She began to retrace the events in her head. Was the vehicle that passed me silver, white, or gray? The wind was so strong I couldn't see. The only thing I know is that it was big, and it hit my car. Pet closed her eyes for what she thought was a second. A sickening face came to her, vague at first, then clearer. She saw an old man approaching, his face twisted with hatred. It was Aloysius Hyde coming to get her!

She sat straight up in bed, and the clarity of it all amazed her. It was Hyde on the road. He wants me dead and gone. Why didn't I think of it before? Duh, how stupid can I be? He wants to remain as CEO forever. Well, guess what, Jack, your ass is out of here!

Pet's eyes were wild with excitement. I'll get that jerk, but I'll need a plan. I have to prove that it was him on the road. Surely his car was scratched or dented. He hit me hard. I wonder if David could help me? Without thinking, she reached for her bedside phone and called his cell phone.

"Officer David Jones speaking. Can I help you?"

Pet gasped, "David, you sound wide awake. Are you home?"

She looked over to her clock. "Oh my God! David, I am so sorry. I just realized that it is three a.m. Did I wake you?"

His voice sounded professional with a bit of irritation in it when he answered her back. “Pet? Why are you calling at this hour? I am not home. I am on a stakeout. Is something wrong? Are you okay?”

She realized immediately that this was a bad move and began apologizing.

“Oh, David, I am so sorry! I took a chance that you might be awake. I didn’t think that you would be working now or that it was three am. Everything is okay now, but it wasn’t a while ago. Can I call you, or maybe could you call me later today? I really have to talk with you.”

“We’ll talk, Pet. No harm done. I’ll see you later today. Good night.”

Pet wrapped the covers around her. She lay back down on the pillow and groaned, “I am such an idiot. I hope he was alone. I shouldn’t be so impulsive, because it always gets me into trouble, just like Mae Delight said.”

* * *

“Hello. What? Who is this? You’re mumbling. Oh, it’s you, Al. What happened? Why are you calling me so damn early? It is only six am. Hold on, let me get my robe.”

“No, honey, it’s not important,” James said to his girlfriend.

James got out of bed, tying his flannel robe about him, and sat down in his recliner across the room. He switched the phone from his left ear to his right.

“Now that you’ve got my attention, what’s the matter?” James asked.

“I’ll be out of the office, maybe one or two days. I’ll need you to cover some important meetings for me,” Al said.

James sat straight up in the recliner, “And this couldn’t have waited till later? What’s going on, Al?”

“Just listen to me, James. That dock worker, Manny something or another, is questioning the invoices from overseas. I encountered him once, and he's no dummy. If he starts putting two and two together about those imports, he'll go straight to accounts payable. We have to stop him. Do you understand me now?"

"Yeah, sure, Al. By the way, where were you last night? You didn't pick up on your cell, and your old lady was no help when I called your home. She didn't even know where you were."

"Don't worry about her," Aloysius continued, a little out of breath. "Also, Jimmy Kennedy from Herald Financial is flying in at 10:00 am. I'll need you to pick him up at the airport."

James was starting to hate Aloysius' demands, and his attitude turned sarcastic. "Aw, come on! Why do I have to do this? I'm not gonna be your fetchin' gopher while you're gone just because you don't feel like coming in the office today. Get some other jerk to do it."

"Don't question me! You'll understand once he gives you some very important documents. Do not break the sealed portfolio. Offer to take him to the Shelburn for lunch. If he declines, Jimmy will give you the portfolio, bid you good day, and leave. Once you get back to the office, make sure you are alone, and put it in the drawer safe, the one behind my desk with the wide drawers. You have the key I gave you, right?"

"Yes, I do."

Al turned sideways in the chair he was sitting in and gave out a sudden groan.

"What's the matter? You okay, Al?"

"Yeah, my ribs hurt, I might have to see my doctor. Don't say anything to anyone. Do you hear me? By the way, have you got a name on that woman yet?"

"Yes, we do. Her name is Judith Mackie, but I haven't got a plan yet."

"Well, get one soon."

"Sure, Al. Take care."

Chapter 63

David Comes Over

She awoke suddenly from a pounding on her bedroom door. Mae Delight's voice was incredibly loud.

"Are you going to open your door, or are you dead? I've been hollerin' out here like a fool for the last five minutes waiting for you to answer me! You've got company downstairs!"

Pet blinked awake, "Damn, I really zonked out. Is David downstairs, Mae Delight?"

"Well, it ain't Rhett Butler. Are you comin' down, or should I tell him to leave?"

"Oh, no! Tell him I'll be right down."

Pet ran to the bathroom and splashed the sleep from her eyes. She tried to comb out the rat's nest that circled her head, but loose ends had a mind of their own. She took a scrunchy and pulled her curls into a topknot, then found a Steelers jersey and a pair of black sweatpants. Looking in the mirror for a split second, she groaned at her appearance. "God, I could scare the dead right now. I hope he doesn't scare easily."

She decided not to fool around, put in her contacts, and shoved her glasses on her nose.

There was an immediate smile on his face when he saw Pet rush through the kitchen door. David stopped talking and observed a frantic girl caught by surprise. Mae Delight also looked up from their casual conversation and was ready to burst into laughter when she saw the bedraggled girl. Pet nervously pulled at her jersey as she came forward to greet David.

"Good morning, David. I hope you haven't been waiting too long, and if you have, I'm sorry. I wasn't awake when you came here. Can you stay? I have so much to tell you."

Mae Delight got up from the table, turning toward the stove. "Don't worry, child. He's not going anywhere soon. Take your time and sit down now. He's enjoying my coffee and cinnamon rolls. He's good for another cup and one more just ready to come out of the oven."

Pet smiled and sat down at the informal kitchen table. Mae Delight handed her a cup of coffee, and after the second sip, her nerves began to settle down. She couldn't keep her eyes off David, looking so good coming off a midnight shift.

She began at the very beginning, one detail at a time. He listened, and when he saw how scared she was, he held her hand but said nothing until she had finished speaking.

"Are you sure the person in that vehicle was out to get you, Pet?"

"I'm positive, David. What fool would deliberately ride my bumper in a snowstorm?"

David thought for a minute. "That might explain the call last night about a car in a ditch near the Shipingport Exit."

"Really? I hope the son of a bitch froze to death," Pet said.

David chuckled. It was funny hearing this rant from a young woman with the face of an angel and the temper of a caged tiger. Pet arched her eyebrow skeptically, "David, are you making fun of me?"

"Oh no, Pet, you took me by surprise, honest."

"If you had been there, David, you would know why I was so terrified. He was out to kill me. I know it."

"Hold on, Pet. I believe you, but before you start making accusations, you have to be sure. Would you like me to follow up with the State Police to see who owned the vehicle? I have a buddy working that sector of the county."

"I'd really appreciate it. David, I want to nail this creep to the wall."

Over another cup of coffee, they talked casually. He smiled, listening to her talk about this fine manor house that was finally hers. Pet's enthusiasm was animated and entertaining. She felt like a schoolgirl when David was with her. All the bad thoughts vanished in his masculine presence. He made her feel different from all the other men she had known. A combination of security and sensual titillation buzzed her emotions. She liked that.

Mae Delight even chimed in from time to time while busying herself cleaning up the pans from the cinnamon buns. This scene was too good to miss, and she wanted to hear every word.

Finally, David slowly got up from the table. "I hate to break up this coffee klatch, but I've got to get some sleep, Pet. I will call you soon."

There was a disappointed look on her face as he slowly pushed his chair to the table.

She got up too, "I wish you could stay longer, David, but I do understand. I'll show you out." She followed behind him and impulsively put her hand on his back.

There in the foyer, they stood facing each other, his arms gently resting on her waist. Suddenly, he reached up and lightly touched the rim of her glasses, tilting them downward.

Immediately, Pet put her hand up to his. "What's wrong?"

He gave her that impish grin again. "I've wanted to do that ever since you came into the kitchen. Your glasses weren't resting properly on your nose. They were crooked, and I wanted to set them straight for you." He put both hands on the rims, "There, that's better."

They both laughed.

He was waiting for the right moment. She was anticipating the feel of his lips. Mae Delight was peeking through the crack of the door, wanting to see them kiss.

Pet knew she was behind the door and cleared her throat, hoping Mae Delight would get the hint. Reluctantly, she did and closed the kitchen door. On that cue, David couldn't stand around any longer. He bent down slowly, reaching Pet's mouth and kissed her tenderly. In an instant, he was out the door, but not without a pat on her butt as an added goodbye.

Chapter 64

Decisions

Pet was on her way back up the stairs when she saw the flowers. It was not only big, but it was the most audacious Christmas arrangement she had ever seen. It sat right in the middle of the coffee table in the sitting room. Coming closer, she felt compelled to stare at it. Each piece of greenery was strategically placed. The brilliant white spider mums were centered among bright, multi-looped red velvet bows. Frosted pine cones were nestled among long pine needles that cascaded over the edges of a swirling scarlet crystal vase. A small pure white envelope was neatly attached under one of the pine cones. She carefully lifted it up and pulled out the card.

Because I truly love you, Anthony.

"How extravagant," she sighed. "It's obscene to imagine the cost of this arrangement. Knowing Anthony, the vase is most likely imported. It looks like Murano crystal. Now I know he'll call me, expecting praise and gratitude for this monstrosity. Why can't he let go of me? It is over. He has to see that."

Her happy mood changed as she dreaded a most certain call. She almost got to the hallway when the house phone rang. She picked up before Mae Delight did.

"Hello, Anthony. Yes, I did. They came late yesterday afternoon."

His voice was cheerful and light. "Do you like them, Pet? I put a lot of thought into the arrangement. I wanted everything to be perfect and beautiful as you are. Christmas has so much meaning for us. It is such a wonderful season of fun and fantasy. We were so close last year and had some good times. I hope we can renew our love. I meant every word on the card."

Pet was speechless, unable to echo his happiness. Her stomach churned with nausea. She felt emotionally trapped. She should rip his heart out now and say goodbye forever. The words "leave me alone, I don't love you anymore" were on the tip of her tongue.

All she could say to him was, "I don't need big expensive flower arrangements from you. You should have given the flowers to a nursing home, Anthony. I know they would have appreciated it more. I will ask Mae Delight to take it into the formal dining room. It will look prettier in a bigger room."

Her indifference didn't anger him. He tried harder to entreat her. "You sound different. Are you tired? I thought you would enjoy the flowers, especially now with the holidays just around the corner."

"That's it," she thought. "I can't go on with this prattle."

"You are not getting the picture, Anthony. I am very tired, I didn't sleep well last evening. I was nearly killed on the expressway during the snowstorm. I was terrified! Please leave me alone!"

Pet hesitated whether to tell him all the details, but then decided to let him know how awful her experience was and how she got out of her dilemma. She just wouldn't tell him the whys and wherefores of her mission. Just seconds after she started, he interrupted her.

"Do you realize you put yourself in serious jeopardy? Don't you listen to weather reports? You could easily have been killed on that desolate highway. You weren't using common sense, Pet. Only idiots would be driving around in a blizzard alone."

Her voice was flat, her expression solemn. "Are you going to call me more names and add to my misery of being stranded out in a blizzard, Anthony? Can't you be sympathetic to what I went through last night? You say you still love me. This doesn't sound like love to me. Don't ever call me again. Goodbye!" She hung up the phone and walked out of the room.

She muttered to herself as she rationalized their conversation. "What a shit. First, he gave me flowers and then berated me without knowing all the details of my experience. He expected me to get all gooey over his supposed thoughtfulness. He is so egotistical!"

Pet found herself in the middle of the staircase and sat down on the step. With elbows on her knees and her hands supporting her chin, a smile came to her face. "I'm done. Yep, it's over. I am not even going to discuss it with Judy. Nope. All gone. Bye-bye, low life. David is the better man."

Pet did not see Mae Delight at the bottom of the staircase. "Have you totally flipped your lid, girl? What are you saying?"

"I have made a decision. He will never darken my door again!"

"Who? You're makin' no sense at all, child. I think the snow mashed your brain some. Start talking right now. I got to get some work done around here."

"Oh, I'm just thinking out loud, Mae Delight. I don't trust Anthony anymore. I don't think he cares about this company, whether I take charge or not.

"Hmph, ain't no man tellin' me what to do, and I never liked him anyway. When Mr. Anthony and that Mr. Hyde person came here that day, he kept saying under his breath what he was gonna do with this house and what fancy stuff he was gonna put in this place and all. Oh yes, he had great plans for you too, Missy."

"Really, he's got a lot of nerve! Well, I am not going to waste any more time. I am going to Briar Town Furniture Company today and seek out an ally. I should think the roads will be clear enough now. What time is it?"

"Almost 11:00. Are you goin' to be out long?"

"Please, Mae Delight, don't start."

Chapter 65

Meeting with Marshall

She prided herself on knowing exactly where to go. After enough time, she did learn something. She searched out Marshall Kochmann's office, finding it down a secluded hallway. There were no expensive prints on the walls or fancy light domes in the ceiling illuminating his office door. There was no pretense of importance, just simple black lettering with his name and Controller right under it. It was the only office that didn't have an enormous philodendron guarding the door.

She walked in slowly and saw a pleasant-looking white-haired woman feeding receipts into an auto-file device. She immediately looked up at Pet, smiling in recognition.

"Good morning, Mrs. Traffortelli. My, isn't this a pleasant surprise! How are you?"

Pet was at a loss, and her expression probably showed it. "Good morning, um, Mrs…"

She laughed softly, "Oh, I should have said who I was. You met so many people that night at the Shellburn Room. I'm Eleanor Milner, Mr. Kochmann's secretary. You made such a nice impression on everyone there that night. We all liked you right away. I hope you are feeling part of the company by now."

"Thank you. You are very kind. Is Mr. Kochmann in? I'd need just a minute of his time."

"He is in, but he stepped out of the office for a moment. He won't be long. Would you like a cup of coffee while you are waiting?"

"Yes, I would like a cup if it's not too much trouble."

"Oh, no problem," she nodded and left the office. Pet tapped her fingernail on the armchair and prayed that no one from the higher executive branch would suddenly barge in too. How long should she wait, five minutes, ten minutes? Will he laugh at her and be like all the rest of the Yes Men to the old coot? She needed his alliance. The insecurities of her bold action started to mount. She was halfway out of her chair, ready to bolt out the doorway, when Marshall Kochmann and Mrs. Milner came through the door laughing hysterically.

Marshall was still laughing when he held out his hand. "Well, Mrs. Traffortelli, how nice to see you!"

She gave him a big smile back, "Hello, Mr. Kochmann. It is nice to see you, too."

"Please, you are going to have to call me Marshall, or we can't do business. The whole name is just too formal. I knew from our first meeting at Shellburn that we would be friends. Now what can I do for you?"

Pet instantly felt at ease as he ushered her into his office. He told Mrs. Milner to hold all calls as she gave Pet the cup of coffee.

Marshall spoke first. He was face-to-face with her, both of them sitting in dark green leather armchairs. "Now, tell me, Mrs. Traffortelli, what can I do for you?"

"Well, as long as I'm going to call you, Marshall, I will insist that you call me Pet. By and by, I'll give you the explanation for my nickname."

She liked him immediately. His demeanor was neither intimidating nor holier-than-thou. He presented himself as just one of the guys. Taking a deep breath, the words came slowly, with a little hesitancy, but as Marshall listened to her, Pet became more confident.

"I hope I won't sound like a tattle-tale, but I've felt ever since Anthony Prattmore brought me to meet the board members and the illustrious CEO, I have been stonewalled in claiming my rightful ownership. I've been humiliated, even been told I don't know or will never know anything about business. Mr. Kochmann, I am pursuing a degree in Business Administration, and I find the world of economics fascinating. I've been getting good grades. In due time, I know I can run this company. Grace told me many things about it, so I'm not completely ignorant of the workings of this business! Could you possibly help me learn more about it?"

Pet paused to catch her breath. Marshall didn't interrupt and waited patiently for her to continue.

She continued a little more excitedly. "Miss Haskel and I found some discrepancies in the old books from the warehouse near Chippewa. Some of the books had pages ripped out, and I found all these loose receipts stuffed in a file, and a picture of a bank on some Caribbean Island. It didn't make any sense to me, and neither did it to Bunny, I mean Miss Haskel."

The last two sentences raised an eyebrow. "When did you go there with Miss Haskel, Pet?"

"We went there this past fall. That was some adventure. I think someone didn't want certain pages found, but of course, I can't prove it. And another thing, I don't trust Mr. Hyde, Mr. Wingate, or Mr. Buford. If I'm going to be the true owner of this company, I need people I can trust. That's why I came to you.

"I also heard rumors that Mr. Hyde demoted you over something shady and blamed you for it. I didn't think that was right. Other people said you were railroaded out of the inner circle, but that he couldn't fire you because of your tenure here. I can imagine you have your reasons for not liking him. His business dealings don't sound very ethical. Is the company sound financially? No one will tell me. Can I select a new board? Can we call a special meeting without Mr. Hyde there?"

Marshall took his glasses off and put them on the nearby desk. He spoke quietly and soothingly.

"That's quite a lot of questions all at once, Pet. To answer one important question, yes, the company is solvent and doing well. You won't have any financial worries coming on board. Be cautious with Mr. Hyde. He is a formidable adversary. He always plays to win. The same is true for the other two board members. The answer to your last question is yes, I can help you and start on that right away. I know some very worthy men dying to oust Aloysius Hyde."

Pet sighed a long breath of relief. "At last, you are someone who can help me without a lot of empty promises. I trust you, Marshall. When can this procedure start?"

He smiled at her ambition, "Soon, Pet, there are a lot of details to work out. First, I must call these men and apprise them of what is happening. These are intelligent professional men with important jobs. Some are in this company, and some are bankers in high positions. I don't think I will have any trouble asking them to become members of this board. They've never liked Mr. Hyde's ethics. Give me at least ten days to contact and meet with them. The day we are all on board with a sound plan. I will call you."

"Good. I will wait for your call."

Pet stood up and offered her hand. She wanted to give him a hug goodbye, but she knew that would be inappropriate. As they clasped hands, both of them smiled at the same time.

"Again, thank you, Marshall. I'm glad I came here today. You've made me feel like my life is headed in the right direction again."

He still held onto her hand. "No, it is I who should say thank you. I've wanted this opportunity for a long time. I wouldn't mention this meeting with your lawyer friend, Mr. Prattmore, today. The fewer people knowing about this plan, the better."

Pet laughed softly, "Oh, don't worry about him. He's completely out of the picture. Trust me." She left with a smile on her face. Mrs. Milner said, "Come back soon, Mrs. Traffortelli. You will always be welcome." Pet had a comforting thought. I think I've found my old friend Harry again. Marshall is just like him.

Chapter 66

Zookies

Pet practically shouted over the phone, "Judy, Judy, Judy. Let's go out tonight and celebrate. Christmas is coming!"

"No shit, Sherlock. It is only two weeks away." Judy hesitated, not wanting to commit right away. "Today's Tuesday. Don't you have that meeting with Bunny tonight, you know that girl in charge of the Christmas Festival?"

"Oh, yeah. Well, we will just have to invite her along, too. Then she can tell me everything I need to know over drinks at The Shellburn."

Judy gave in, mentally changing her plans. "Okay, give her a call, and I'll pick you up in five minutes."

Bunny was more than willing to step out with the girls, but she said The Shellburn would be too quiet, and Zookies was the "in" place to go now. Since Pet was still a newbie with the bar scene, she took Bunny's advice without questioning it. Judy knew exactly where it was.

The atmosphere was lively. Over the din of loud voices and laughter, country music blared from where a DJ was manning the music in the far corner of the restaurant. As they walked through the door, the girls drew smiles from eager male onlookers. Couples passed by calling to their friends while waitresses said hello to the girls as they busied themselves with customers.

Judy scanned the room, hoping for a familiar face or a place to sit. "I don't see an empty table anywhere, Pet. Mind if we sit at the bar? We're still in the middle of the action."

She laughed, "No, I don't mind at all. It will be fun."

Pet looked around and caught the looks that they were getting from the men at the bar.

"Man, I feel like we are the main attraction tonight. Do you two know any of these guys?"

Bunny leaned over to Pet. "Nah, honey, these out-of-state plant workers are eager for some new meat. You get used to it after a couple of times. Just ignore them."

Judy nodded in agreement. "She's right. Don't worry, Pet."

"Okay, if you say so."

Bunny raised her voice an octave to be heard over the noise of the bar scene. She told Pet an abbreviated description of what she had to do for the "Hats for Santa's Helpers' Booth." The whole time she talked, her eyes were on a tall sandy-haired guy two seats down. She had barely finished talking when he came up to her and asked her to dance.

"Ooo, yes, I love this song," and off Bunny went, hips swaying and her curls a-flying.

With a surprised expression on her face, Pet turned to Judy. "Well, I hope she'll have a few more details than that! I don't want to screw up anything on my first festival. After all, we are hoping to raise $20,000 for the handicapped children's fund."

Judy nodded nonchalantly, gazing out into the crowd as she spoke to Pet. Her mind was on the dance floor and the guys sitting at the table in front of them. "Same old Pet. You've got this. I'm tellin' ya. It's easy. Collect the money. Write children's names on the furry hats, put them on their cute little heads, and point them to jolly old St. Nick. You'll have fun."

"Yeah, I guess so. Marshall was telling me about it. His wife really gets into decorating the booths."

Judy swished her long auburn hair over her left shoulder and took a sip of her Corona. "How is the company doing, Pet? Did that controller guy answer your questions?"

"Yes, he did. Briar Town is doing quite well in fact…"

"I heard that the stockholders were skeptical of a new president taking over the company and that its stock experienced a slight dip in the third quarter. Paul Dean's article in *Business Today Magazine* questioned the stability of Briar Town's yearly earnings."

Pet whirled around to see a rather rotund bald man standing close to her. She was about to ignore his statement, but his beady little eyes and raspy voice commanded her attention.

"I beg your pardon. Who are you to interrupt a private conversation, sir?" Pet asked.

"I'm the sales manager for Stoyer's Furniture Factory, and I've been keeping up on the financial growth of your company. I know what I'm talking about."

"What interest is it of yours, Mr…?"

"Charles Duggan, Ma'am. I mean no disrespect, but I keep up with the financial records of a lot of companies, which are common knowledge, you know, and I've always wondered who puts out your releases. I've never seen a company like yours that always shows huge yearly sales/profits with only a minor percentage increase in their gross national sales."

Pet had to catch her breath for a second. His demeanor slightly intimidated her.

"Well, Mr. Duggan, I assure you that our company's financial policies are sound and above board, and, for your information, I'll have you know I am the new owner of Briar Town Furniture Company, Mrs. Patrice Elyce Traffortelli."

He raised his pudgy cheeks into a half smile. "Nice to finally meet the competition in person, Mrs. Traffortelli. Your company has gone through quite a change. From my sources, I know this is a new experience for you. I knew of Miss Grace, as we called her, her good-for-nothing son, and likewise her grandson. I also know, on a professional basis, Aloysius Hyde. You are in for quite a ride, Mrs. Traffortelli, so I suggest you better buckle up and hold on."

He stopped talking and from his wallet handed her his business card. "If you ever want to talk real business, call me."

Pet watched Mr. Duggan walk away into the crowd.

"Judy, did you hear him? Of all the nerve! Hmmm. Ballsy bastard, isn't he? I've got to tell Marshall about him tomorrow."

Judy stepped away slightly from Pet with her eyes on another handsome man coming up to her. "Yup, hon, a real smart shit. 'Scuse me. I think I'm gonna be busy in a second." Judy gave the young man one of her gorgeous smiles and took his hand.

Pet turned to the bar and sipped her beer, feeling very left out. She mumbled into a half-empty glass, "Thanks, Jude. Thanks a lot. Why do I always seem to be the wallflower?"

James caught Judy's outstretched hand and nodded to her surprised partner.

"Mind if I cut in, guy?"

With the resignation of a cavalier, Judy's first partner disappeared into the gyrating crowd. James put his arm around her waist, not missing a beat, and continued dancing. Judy laughed out loud and kept up.

The upbeat music played for a minute or two, then slowed to a classic love song. James held her close to him, whispering in her ear, "Hope you don't mind me cutting in. Will you continue the dance with me?"

She smiled at him. Judy didn't mind. She was used to the guy's familiarity. It meant nothing to her because everybody danced with everybody else. It was no big deal.

After the music finished, James asked Judy to have a drink with him, but she told him she better not. James was insistent, so she said she might. He nodded okay.

Two dances later, the girls came back to Pet laughing and out of breath. "Wow, that was fun! Those guys can really dance!" Bunny and Judy said at the same time.

"Yeah, I'll bet," Pet grumbled. "Ready to go, Jude? I have an early day tomorrow."

"Guess so." Judy gave Pet a questioning glance. "What's up?"

Pet grabbed her purse and made her way to the door. Bunny's eyes followed Pet for a minute. "What's with her?"

Judy slung her purse over her shoulder, and she rolled her

eyes at Bunny. "Dunno, but knowing Pet, I'll find out soon enough."

"Hey, Jude. Coming back? It's early."

"I'll see. I might stay for at least another 20 minutes."

There was no conversation between them on the ride home. Judy had the radio turned up and was singing. Pet was lost in thought, questioning her paranoid mind. When the car pulled up to the massive front door, Judy didn't talk at first. Then she blurted out, "What's with you tonight? I could have had a lot more dances and a lot more fun, but you had to come home. Are you sick?"

"No, I just felt left out. How did you happen to dance with James Wingate?"

"Oh, is that who he is? He did look familiar. He's very nice."

"Yes, you certainly knew how to latch on to him. I thought you two were gonna do the grind."

Judy ignored Pet's remark. "Pet, I can't help that. You had your chance, but you sat down. I saw you. Get out there. Don't shy away. You're not married or attached to David. Have some fun. Guys can read your body language. Smile, flirt a little."

"I'm not that type of girl, looking like I've got a price tag on my butt. I probably got my signals crossed about tonight's agenda. I thought we would catch a bite to eat, listen to the music, and talk, something like that. You know Bunny didn't hear much of what I said. You two were concentrating on men, not business. Now I have to go back to Briar Town, get those Santa hats, and find out if there's anything else I have to do. Bunny's mind was totally on those guys at the bar. And you weren't any help."

"'Scuse me, Miss New Executive, but when you go to a sports bar at happy hour, you're not going to talk business! Are you calling me a pickup?"

Pet studied Judy's defiant expression. Now she made her best friend angry and had to apologize instead of asking what was really on her mind. She changed her attitude and tone of voice. "Judy, I am sorry. I wasn't judging you. I guess I did have the wrong idea about tonight. I wanted to accomplish a lot, but I got upset when it didn't happen. Please forgive me."

Judy's face softened when she accepted Pet's apology. "You know I can't stay angry with you. Call me tomorrow, hon'."

Pet gave her a quick hug and got out of the car. "You be careful going home."

"Uh huh. Yeah. Sure." Judy waved and disappeared.

Pet thought, "Well, maybe I am reading her wrong. I'll give her another chance."

* * *

Judy breezed through the door at Zookies and made her way to the bar, scanning the crowd for Bunny.

Bunny came up to Judy laughing. "Oh my God! You did come back!"

"Was there any doubt?"

"Yeah, we had a bet."

Before Judy could give her a come-back, James Wingate was right behind her.

"Time's a- wasting, pretty girl. This dance is mine."

James led her to the dance floor. Excited couples followed them. The Latin-tinged music was intoxicating. Judy immediately stepped in front of James, and their bodies were immersed in the rhythm.

Minutes into the dance, James deliberately slid his hand down her back to her butt while she inched her left leg up to his right leg. Without missing a step, he twirled her into a slow spin. Twirling, gyrating, and swaying, the dance continued for several more minutes.

When it was finally over, Judy broke away and headed for the bar. "Man, I really need a drink. You're killing me."

"No, I'm not. You're loving it. Where did you learn to dance the Rumba?"

"Oh, is that what it's called?" she laughed lightly.

"What's so funny?" asked James.

"Well, I was wondering if you take dance lessons," Judy asked.

"No." James smiled and said, "But, if you wanted to come up to my apartment for a waltz and some champagne, that would be nice."

Judy smiled and looked directly into his eyes. Her expression was less flirty and more friendly, "Look. I really enjoyed dancing with you, but I have heard that line once too often. Did you really think it was going to work, Mr. Wingate?"

James feigned a look of contrite disappointment. He took her hand gently, "I'm sorry, Miss Mackie. I did not intend to insult you. We got along so well that I wanted to get to know you better. You are an exceptional dancer, and I'd like to say, without being flip, also very beautiful. Please accept my apology."

She was taken aback by his sincerity and didn't know what to say. Hesitating for a second, she blurted out, "How did you know my last name? Did Bunny tell you?"

"She didn't volunteer it at first. Then I asked her because I do want to get to know you better, Judy."

Judy looked at her watch. "Thank you, Mr. Wingate. It is getting late. I will think about it."

"May I walk you to your car?"

Judy nodded. They walked out into the parking lot. As she looked for her keys, she took out one of her business cards. She smiled and handed it to him. When they got to her car, he held it up and said, "When I call your number, I sincerely hope you will answer, because there is something important I want to tell you."

As she got into the car, Judy asked softly, "How important?"

James stood by the car door waiting for her to roll down the window. "Well, if you'd let me in for a minute, I will tell you."

Judy thought to herself, "Eh, what the hell. This might be interesting."

James slid into the seat and faced her immediately. "Did you know your friend is wearing a very valuable ring that she has no right to have?"

"No."

"Did you know it was bought and paid for by Aloysius Hyde, only to be disgraced and taken away from him?"

"No! I don't understand. It was in Miss Grace's house. I thought it was hers to give to Pet."

Without too much drama, James told her the story of Aloysius' past. "So, you see, Judy, Mr. Hyde should rightfully own that ring. Can you see how awful he feels whenever he sees that ring?"

"Well, I guess so when you put it that way. Why are you telling me all this?"

"Because we need you to explain the circumstances to her and get back that ring."

Judy almost laughed at him. "Really, you guys expect me to do your dirty work?"

"Think about it. I don't need your answer right now, but I'll need it sometime in the near future. It could mean a lot of money for you."

James got out of the car and walked back into the club. From that point on, Judy had a lot to think about.

Chapter 67

More Details

Bunny stood leaning against the office desk with an armload of red and white Santa hats, "Oh yes, I danced at Zookies for a good while. You should have stayed, Pet. Judy even came back for a while, and danced up a storm with Mr. Gorgeous."

"Oh? Wonder why. She told me she was tired."

Pet took the bundle of hats from Bunny. "Oh well. I'd better get going with these. Let's see, hats and a marking pen, and a Santa sign, right?"

"Yup, you got it. Don't worry. I'll be floating around that night. I'll stop and check on you."

Pet smiled warmly at Bunny. She was good at her job and meant what she said. Pet believed her even though she was an incorrigible flirt. "Thanks, Bunny."

Just before she reached the main foyer, a young man came up to her holding a manila folder in his hand. "Um, Mrs. Traffortelli, I need some help. Mr. Buford isn't in his office, nor is his secretary, and neither is Mr. Hyde or his assistant, Mrs. Hartwell. Mr. Buford oversees the weekly ad campaign, and he signs it before I send it for a printout. Could you sign the approval sheet for me?"

He awkwardly handed her the folder. Pet looked at the advertisement intently, reading the descriptions of the dining room table and chair combinations on sale for 25% off. The recliners and love seats at the bottom of the paper read mix or match, buy one, get the other half price.

She answered him professionally, "Does a different ad go out every week, Mr… what is your name?"

"Oh, excuse me, ma'am. It is Ed, Ed Prittcher. Yes, every

week for three weeks, then we stop it. Next week, we make up a new set of discounted items and send them out. I think it's a waste of money, to tell you the truth."

She smiled at him, looking up from the folder, "I think you are right, Mr. Prittcher. I will sign this approval sheet, but I will write a note to the advertising manager to let me know to see me in Mr. Kochmann's office on Tuesday morning. Could you make sure he sees my note, Mr. Prittcher? By the way, what is his name?"

"Michael Farley."

Pet spotted a bench and quickly walked over and sat down. She quickly looked for her cell phone. "Darn. I left my phone at home on charge. Hmm. Oh, good. I have a packet of index cards." She then took out a 3-by-5 index card she kept handy for class notes and began writing.

Dear Mr. Farley,

Could you please meet me in Mr. Marshall Kochmann's office Tuesday morning at 9:00 a.m. for a brief meeting? I am concerned about our advertisement schedule. I have some ideas and would like to discuss them with you. I am looking forward to meeting you. I hope this meeting will not be an inconvenience to your workday.

Thank you,

Mrs. Patrice Elyse Traffortelli

Owner, Briar Town Furniture Co.

After reading it twice to herself, she signed the sheet, attached her note, and handed the folder back to Ed.

He grinned at her, accepting this new responsibility. "I'll give this to him right away, Mrs. Traffortelli. I'm sure he'll be glad to see you."

Pet walked out of the building feeling quite proud. All the

way to her car she thought, “Of course, Mr. Hyde will be pissed when he hears what I’ve done, but I have to start taking charge soon, why not in advertising. There I did it. Now I gotta call Marshall and tell him what I did. Come to think of it, I need an office, a big one, bigger than Hyde’s!”

Chapter 68

Different Ideas

The meeting in Marshall Hoffmann's office went better than Pet expected. Michael Farley wanted to change the ad campaign months ago, but his idea was always put on the back burner. Pet began the conversation with one question about circulation, and Michael Farley took it from there.

His first idea was to put the company's ad in the local paper instead of individual flyers. This would save a huge amount of money in bulk postage because the local Whalen Falls Press had a big subscription base. Secondly, he wanted to show the new seasonal furniture coming in and when the sales would begin. They would appear on the first Monday and Friday of each month, and separate items and two-fers would appear mid-month on Wednesdays.

Marshall thought it was a sound idea, and so did Pet. Now, all they had to do was to sell it to one of the three administrators. Pet perked up, "Hey, I'm one of the administrators. I own this place! Marshall, I'm going to okay these changes. Mr. Farley, do you think we could get this new ad ready? Even if it appeared one or two days later than the usual advertisements, I think our new format would make a big difference in appeal and information. What do you think? Is the seasonal layout ready for print?"

Michael Farley thought for a few minutes, checking his iPhone. The ad might be a day late, but I am sure it won't be a problem. I'm going to leave now and get things rolling. Thank you, Mrs. Traffortelli. Good day."

After Michael Farley left Marshall's office, Pet laughed out loud. "WHEW, what a rush! This is the beginning, Marshall. I feel it, and it's good. I wonder why Mr. Hyde or Mr. Wingate allowed that situation to go on for so long a time?"

"My guess is that he needed a write-off for some reason."

Pet could not have been in a better mood on the drive home. "She knew it wouldn't be hard to take charge. So, move over, Mr. Blow Hard Hyde!" exclaimed Pet.

Driving down Weston Avenue, a navy-blue Cadillac Escalade caught her eye. It looked like Anthony's vehicle, but it was parked a block from her house. She took a quick glance and saw two people kissing in the front seat. She thought she saw the back of a woman's head. Pet couldn't slow down because another car was behind her. She decided to drive around the block again to get a better look.

This time, no one was behind her, and she could get a good look. Moving closer to the car, she saw the couple in question release their embrace. The man looked directly toward the street. Judy did the same.

"Oh my God! It is her and Anthony, too!" Pet wanted to blare her car horn at them, but instead stepped on the gas and drove away.

She slammed the door behind her, swearing out loud, "Of all the frickin' nerve! I trusted her. I trusted that bitch with my life. My good friend. My back-stabbing buddy!"

Mae Delight heard the commotion and met her in the foyer. "I know you were a flighty girl, but now you've flipped out again! What are you yellin' about, child? Come and sit down. You'll have a stroke in a minute if you don't."

Pet sat down on the library sofa, crying. Her body was rigid with agitation. She held her fists tightly on her lap. "Why would she kiss Anthony? Has she no shame? He's against me. Judy knows I don't trust him. She can't do this to me. She's betrayed our friendship. Why would she make out in a car in broad daylight? That is so immature."

Mae Delight waited a minute for Pet to take out a hanky and blow her nose.

"She's the flirting kind of woman. Don't you know that by now, girl? Oh, she might be a friend to you and all, but she's the type that likes her men. She's not dumb 'cause she likes them rich, too. Now, didn't you tell me you and that man were over? So why shouldn't she get some of the gravy, hmm?"

"Yes, but Judy didn't tell me anything about Anthony. She went behind my back. She should have told me something."

Mae Delight shook her head. "You still have a lot to learn about men and women. They don't have to tell you nothin.'"

The housekeeper patted Pet's hand and rose to go out of the library. "I suppose you won't want dinner after this little episode. I'll just fix you your special tea."

"The tea would be nice, and maybe a piece of your blueberry pie if there is any left over from last night. Oh, and would you bring it upstairs for me, Mae Delight? I'd really appreciate it."

Mae Delight turned and nodded her head, mumbling, "Yes, Missy, upstairs tea and pie, making my feet work hard all day long, always upstairs."

Pet smiled and grinned when she said, "Thank you, Mae Delight."

Chapter 69

The Plot Sickens

With the Whalen Falls Press laid out in front of him, Aloysius Hyde could feel his blood pressure rising as he waited for James Wingate to answer his call.

"James, what smart ass put this ad in the paper?"

"Not sure, Al. I'll check on it. Harold was covering that sector for you while you were out last week. He didn't mention anything new happening, but it's possible Michael Farley handled the layout and processing. He's the head of that department. Aloysius queried a little further,"What do you mean, Farley? He has no right to change that! Get him in my office right away and get Buford in here, too!"

"Yeah, will do. Oh, by the way. I haven't seen your car in your parking space. Is it still in the shop?"

"No, they can't get it in for another week, and it's taking up space in front of my house like a road hazard. My wife gives me grief every day about it. What a pain in my ass."

Over the next hour, conversations grew heated as the three principals scrutinized the full-page ad.

Harold Buford rubbed his chin, still staring at the paper. "I rather like it. The printing is bold, the text is concise, and the furniture layout is clear. Look, even the color is good. I like the wording of the sale dates. What more could you ask?"

Aloysius got up from his chair and stood right in front of him. Harold's face, "What more could I want, Harold? I wanted it okay'd by me, that's what I wanted! Peons don't make major changes in my company! Get Farley in here!"

James had a bad-boy grin on his face when Michael Farley knocked on the door. He didn't hesitate to usher in the new victim. Aloysius looked away from Harold and scowled at Michael, "Are you responsible for this ad?"

Michael looked directly at Aloysius, "Well, I guess you could say I am."

Aloysius' right eyebrow arched, "What kind of answer is that, Mr. Farley? Are you not in charge of that division, and don't you always come to one of us to get a change okay'd?"

"Yes, I am, Mr. Hyde, but the new owner of Briar Town furniture approved this new change. You know Mrs. Traffortelli. Since I am the head of the department, I thought it was a good idea, and I put it into motion."

He looked at Michael Farley for a second. Then, in a deadly tone of voice, said, "Thank you. That is all the information I need. You may go."

On his way to the door, he hesitated for more commands from Aloysius, or at least a reprimand for not waiting for an official go-ahead. Receiving none, Michael Farley casually said, "Have a nice day," and walked out of the office, leaving it at that.

"Have a nice day, my ass," Aloysius said out loud. His face was turning that brilliant, puffy red, and he began to bellow for Catherine Hartwell. "Catherine, get me some Advil tabs now and get Mr. Franklin on the phone, in that order!"

Harold Buford casually walked into Aloysius' office. "Kind of a spunky move for a young kid, eh, Al?" he said with a sarcastic chuckle.

Aloysius leered at him, "What are you chuckling about? You want to take orders from that nitwit? I still run this place and don't forget it!"

James Wingate was a little more serious. "I thought she was going to be trouble. I just didn't think she was going to get her hands dirty this quickly. We can't let her think this change has gone unnoticed, Al. Want me to call her in here now?"

"No, don't call her. Very soon, she'll know she screwed up big time."

Aloysius's deviant mind flooded with ideas, but he kept to just one. Charles Franklin would help him carry it out.

* * *

One evening before the Christmas Festival, Charles walked along 3rd Street casually smiling as he passed the busy ladies scurrying about decorating the tents for the big event. He slipped unnoticed around to the back of Pet's assigned tent, hoping for a split in the canvas material. There was none, but just like the old "carny" tents, the back panel was tied by a cord through a metal ring, one at the top and one at the bottom. One swift cut at the bottom would get him in there. Going to the front again, he saw the elaborate garlands around the entrance of Santa's Workshop. He was glad of the clutter, knowing it would be that much easier to slip in and out without being seen.

Charles planned on an easy gig that night. He figured his time in the tent would only be a couple of minutes. He hated her beauty, all fluff and no brains. He mumbled, "She's like all the rest of those office women, a total airhead. I'll be able to control her easily. I'll drop her to the ground and slip away. In no time, I'll be sitting at The Tune sipping bourbon and waiting for my money."

Chapter 70

Christmas Festival

Pet saw lights of every color on the decorated Christmas booths lining both sides of 3rd Street. Whalen Falls was out tonight in throngs of all ages, laughing, shouting, and spending money, all for a good cause. That realization made Pet happy, hoping this event would reach its expected goal.

As she pushed through the crowd, she recognized many workers from Briar Town. Some of them waved to her, and she waved back. Suddenly, a woman came into view. It was Catherine Hartwell. Pet tried to remember her name and took a weak stab at it, nervously blurting out, "Hello, Mrs. Haskell!" Catherine looked at Pet as if she were a revolting trash picker, replying with a venomous hiss, "I'm Mrs. Hartwell, you twit! You should know that by now. Don't ever confuse me with that bimbo you hang around with!"

Before Pet could get a "Merry Christmas" out of her mouth, Catherine plowed through the crowd and was gone. After that little encounter, Pet angled her way between baby strollers and darting kids to get to her assigned area. She smiled in approval at the job Marian Hoffmann did on the Santa booth. It was a true Christmas fantasy workshop decorated with toy elves nestled in Christmas Trees, holly garland hanging around the entrance, and Santa hats strewn on the mantle of the fireplace behind her table.

Her table, festooned with more hats, was close to the trees, making the scene inviting and ready to beckon children into her workshop. Pet immediately busied herself, making sure everything was ready. She pulled a money bag out of her coat pocket, counting out fifty-one dollar bills and four rolls of quarters. She also found the money box Marian left her with a receipt pad.

"Do you think you'll have enough change, hon?"

Judy's voice startled Pet. A thousand angry expletives were on the tip of her tongue as she slowly gazed up at her unfaithful friend. Judy waited for Pet to comment, and when she didn't, her warm smile faded.

"Did you hear me? I came over to see if you needed any help. You might get busy. If you don't want it, I'll leave. What's with the attitude?"

"Oh, nothing. I'm surprised to see you here at my booth. I thought you'd have other plans with someone else who could take you to classier places, Jude. I saw you two making out in the Escalade. I thought you were my friend."

"Look, I'm not going to discuss this now, not here. I'll call you when you're in a better mood."

Without looking up, Pet's tone of voice was expressionless, "I don't think I will be in a good mood, at least not for a while after your flagrant disregard for our friendship. Jude, that was so inappropriate."

With an air of bravado, Judy pulled in her imaginary claws and turned to walk away. She didn't want to end their friendship by causing a scene, but halfway out of the Santa Shop, she turned, "Okay, suit yourself, lady. Just remember the old cliché. 'Don't always believe what you see. You might only have half the story.'"

After Judy left, kids and adults flooded Santa's Shop. She heard voices all around her, "Oh, how pretty!" Mommy, can I have two? I want my name in big letters! Is Santa's hat just like this one?" One little boy pointed at Pet, asking, "Can I have a hat just like hers?"

She laughed. Parents complimented Pet on her beautiful red Christmas dress. She looked like young Mrs. Claus, complete with her hat and black patent leather boots. Then they began buying hats two and three at a time, shelling out money by the handful.

Slowly, Pet got back into the Christmas spirit. The children were so innocent and adorable. They all wanted the perfect Santa hat. They weren't afraid to talk to her and wondered if Santa came down her chimney, too.

As the night progressed, the big pile of hats had dwindled down to five. She admonished herself for not keeping up with her merchandise. Now she had to replenish it quickly. Still seated, she looked around to see if Marian stashed extras. Her eyes darted to every corner, desperately searching for any kind of box or bag. After a minute, she spied something brown behind the middle tree and made a dash for it.

Crouching down with both hands stretched under the tree, she searched for anything resembling a container. Her concentration was suddenly interrupted by a commotion outside the tent. A man and a woman were arguing. At first, she heard muffled interjections, then heated exchanges. One accusation led to another. Pet started to stand as the voices grew even louder, wondering to herself, "What the hell. Damn, I wish I could go out and see the "goings on." She laughed out loud, "Oh man, I can see the front-page headlines now: KNOCK DOWN DRAG OUT FIGHT IN THE STREETS OF WHALEN FALLS AT CHRISTMAS TIME!"

Chapter 71

The Attack

About the same time, Charles Franklin entered the festival grounds. He perused the teeming crowd. He hated crowds, especially women with baby strollers and youngsters running about, giving little care to whom they ran into. His plan was in motion as he glided stealthily through the crowd, anxiously wanting to get this job done.

He headed for the back of the tent. A confrontation caught Charles' attention. He tried to hear what the two people were arguing about, but dismissed the commotion and thought, "This public exchange couldn't have come at a better time. It is a good distraction." With that thought, he studied the back of the tent, realizing the Santa tent seemed to be the busiest one on the street, so he better act quickly. He immediately slid a ski mask over his head and put on a pair of black leather gloves. With his steel utility knife, he bent down, cut the cord at the bottom of the tent pole, and eased inside. He was surprised to see her so close, crouched down at the back of the tent. He heard her laugh as she looked for something behind the trees.

Charles hesitated, studying her movements, calculating which way to grab her and take her off guard. In a split second, he was about to lunge when she began to stand. He couldn't take the chance of her turning around, so with one swift movement, his body leaned forward, and he clamped his hand over her nose and mouth.

Pet felt an immediate searing pain as leather fingers pressed her lips hard against her teeth. The action was deliberate and rough, making it impossible to breathe. Then she felt his breath in her ear as he hissed, "That will be the last stupid thing you laugh at, Missy, if you don't get out of town now! You won't get another chance!" What made the threat even more terrifying was the sharp blade pressing on her ribcage.

Her assailant pressed the blade a little further into her side, saying, "You got that?" His grip tightened on her mouth, pulling her neck and left arm closer to his chest. A whimper escaped from her lips as she felt a sharp blade cut into her side and prick her skin. Pet's heart raced in terror. Her emotions reeled with words screaming in her head, "I won't be a victim, not again!"

Her stomach muscles contracted in a violent spasm. "I'm gonna be sick," she thought. "I'm gonna faint. No, fight, idiot, fight!" And fight she did. Her movements were erratic. She had no time to think anything through. It was all on impulse. With the assailant's left arm over her chest, she took a jerky step forward, squirming her torso spastically to the left. The sudden twitches loosened his grip on the knife, giving her a second to bend her knees downward. Her left arm got free, and she tried to brace herself, but the move pushed her forward. She lost her footing. This action pushed her buttocks into his hips. Suddenly, both of them fell down on the cement. He was on top of her for a few seconds. He swore while getting up and pushed her head into the cement. He quickly grabbed the knife and left. Pet couldn't move. In a state of inertia, she watched him escape as if watching a surreal movie clip of him hitting tables, pulling down Christmas trees, tearing at his mask, and clawing at the back of the tent, making his exit into the darkness. Suddenly, out of nowhere, a loud, piercing scream escaped from her mouth.

"HELP ME! HELP ME!"

A man and his son heard Pet screaming and came running in to help. She was still on the ground, dazed. Her forehead was cut and bleeding. A dark purple bump was forming over her right eye. The father took one arm, and the son took the other. Slowly, they eased her to a chair.

"Gosh, lady, what happened? You look bad! Did that guy hit you? Did he rob you?"

The father admonished the boy for asking so many questions and then instructed him to stay there while he went to get the police.

A crowd began to form all around the tent. Some of them began putting the Santa shop back together. Four teenage boys hoisted the Christmas trees back to their upright positions. Women straightened the mantle while saying what a shame it was that something like this should happen. It never happened before in all these years. How awful.

A Briar Town employee recognized her and knelt down beside her, "Mrs. Traffortelli, you've got a nasty cut on your forehead. I'm going to get a doctor or at least a paramedic for you. There should be a medical unit for an event like this. Are you hurt anywhere else?"

"I don't think so," she lied.

"Okay, don't move. I'll be right back."

The crowd kept milling about her tent, pretending to clean up. Their feigned concern was just curiosity about what really happened to cause such a commotion. Pet was about to tell them to please go away when Judy came running up to her.

"Pet, I just heard you were attacked! You're bleeding. I feel awful. I am so sorry I didn't stay and help you. This wouldn't have happened if I stayed to help you. I'm…"

Pet put her hand up to Judy. "I'm fine. It's okay, Jude. Do you have a clean hanky?"

"Oh my God. You're bleeding more now." Judy immediately dug in her purse for anything clean.

Before Judy could get her hand out of her purse, an ambulance came on the scene with Officer David Jones' squad car right behind it. The paramedic got out and went directly over to Pet to administer first aid. Meanwhile, Officer Jones shooed everyone away, telling them, "Nothing more to see here, folks. The festival is still going on, plenty of things to do at the other tents. Please go so we can do our job here. Thank you."

Judy didn't budge. "I'm her best friend, Officer Jones, and I'm not going anywhere until she tells me to go."

Pet smiled at her and nodded a yes to David.

Paramedic Stark was efficient and caring at the same time. After cleaning up the abrasion with antiseptic wipes and Betadine ointment, all Pet required was a large bandaid on the widest part of her wound.

"Mrs. Taffortelli, you were fortunate that your fall didn't put a deep gash in your forehead." Then, in an authoritative manner, added, "I will be making out my incident report for tonight, and I advised you to get a tetanus shot at the hospital emergency room, and also to follow up on your head wound." He stopped speaking for a second and then smiled at her to lighten the request, "You know, ma'am, city streets aren't the cleanest places in town. Are you hurt anywhere else?"

She looked up at him, and her upper lip began to quiver. "I'm okay, I think. I promise I will go later tonight. I don't want a scene. I just want to go home. David, could you take me?"

"I can do that, Pet." David bent down to help Pet up. He looked at her table and saw the closed metal money box.

"Pet, were you robbed? Do you know if he took money from the box? If money is gone, we will have to ascertain how much was there."

Pet shook her head, "No, there wasn't time. He just grabbed me and threatened me." She fought back tears and looked at David's serious face, "Please, can we go now? I need to get away from this place."

Judy was right behind them. "I'm coming. I'm right behind you. Okay? Not letting you out of my sight, girl."

David looked at Pet as if to say, "Do we have to let her come?"

By this time, she wasn't about to split hairs as to who wanted to be with her as long as it was away from 3rd Street and all of its ugly confusion. She whispered to David, "Let her come. It's okay. Oh, and bring the money box."

Once in the car, Pet knew David was talking, but the sound of his voice was very far away, even though she sat right next to him while Judy sat in the back seat, prattling on about something. She thought it was odd to be in a police car. Low-life scum should ride in the back seats behind the wire mesh, not Judy. Then she heard Judy say "newspapers."

Pet said to herself, "God, no headlines, please! It would be just too much." She slumped deeper into the car seat.

"Pet, did you hear me? Are you feeling faint?" asked David.

"No, David. I was just hoping that I won't be tomorrow's headlines."

Judy muttered sarcastically, "Fat chance on that one."

David shot a warning glance to Judy in the rear view mirror. "I didn't see any reporters roaming around afterward, Pet, but I will have to file a report at the station sometime tonight. Joshua Iverson has surely heard about it by now from one of the council members."

Pet looked at him, frowning, "Oh no, really?"

"Oh yes, there's a snitch at every corner of this town, an official could burp, and two minutes later Joshua knows about it in detail."

Mae Delight seemed to have radar when things went wrong for Pet, and tonight was no exception. She was opening the front door before Pet, David, and Judy were on the porch.

"Another night of mayhem, being brought home by the police. I saw the car pull up in front. Can't you stay out of trouble for at least a month? Look at your head. Do I have to call a doctor for you?"

David gently assisted Pet through the door with his arm around her shoulders. When Pet didn't answer Mae Delight, he continued guiding her to the living room. Mae Delight scurried in front of them, "Glory no, you ain't comin' in this room with those nasty work shoes an' all. Go into the kitchen and sit on the padded deacon's bench in the breakfast nook. Officer Jones, Lawd, every time she comes through my door it's somethin' else. I'm afraid to open it half the time."

The obedient entourage went down the hall a little way and turned into the warm kitchen.

Chapter 72

Information

"Third Street Police Station, Officer Hanley."

"Hi. Is Officer Jones there? This is Smiley's Body Shop."

"No. I'll take a message for him, though. He'll be back later tonight. Is this Bud?"

"Yeah. Sam, that you?"

"Yeah. All right then. Can you tell me what it is about? If it is important, I can get him on his cell phone."

"Sam, just tell him a car with a banged-up rear fender came in this morning. There's damage to the right back fender, and the left rear fender and wheel well are smashed in, too. It's gonna be in my shop for a while."

"Okay, Bud, nice talking to you. He'll be in touch."

"Thanks."

Officer Hanley jotted down the message for Officer Jones. As he put down the receiver, Joshua Iverson walked through the doorway with a young reporter on his tail.

"What do you think, Detective Iverson? Do we have a sexual predator on the loose? This situation can't happen again and ruin the Christmas season. People want to feel safe in this city. They have to..."

Joshua spun around, pointing his finger at the man. "Look, I don't want any mention of potential anything in this city. No predators, no hoodlums, nobody to incite fear or chaos. You got that? It was an unfortunate incident, and it will be investigated thoroughly. I will have to speak with the woman involved to see if she can give me any reason why this happened. I'd better not see anything in the newspaper until I have all the facts."

The reporter flipped his notepad shut and shoved it in his

pocket. "Okay. Okay, no story yet, but I think the people of Whalen Falls should be aware of 'low lifes' lurking in the city."

Joshua headed for his office, dismissing the obnoxious news hound, "Get outta my sight, Mac, or whoever you are, and don't call here for at least a day or two. Is that clear?"

"Yeah, yeah, sure."

Detective Iverson walked down the hall to his office, slammed the door behind him, and slumped in his chair. He hated news reporters because they always sensationalize the circumstances.

Officer Hanley waited a couple of minutes before making the trek down the hall to his superior's office. He knocked softly on the glass and walked in.

"Begging your pardon, Sir, but do you know when Jones is coming in?"

"No, I don't. He was working the festival. If it's something important, get him on his radio. What's the message about?"

"Well, he was checking up on a hit and run the night of the snowstorm, and Smiley called to let him know a vehicle came into his shop."

"Oh, put it on his desk. I think he's early shift tomorrow. But if he does call in, switch it over to me."

Officer Hanley had no sooner closed Detective Iverson's door when David came into the station.

"Hey, speak of the devil, got a message for you and …"

Jones walked quickly past him, opening the door, "Yeah, thanks, Hanley."

Iverson looked up at Jones, "What's up? You look a bit uptight. What went on over there?"

David sat down. "Pet was brutally attacked tonight. The assailant caught her from behind, sliced her side with a knife, pushed her face into the pavement, and left."

Joshua listened intently to the young officer who was visibly upset over Pet's attack. "Does she know why? Christ, sounds like déjà vu all over again. Poor kid." Joshua grimaced for a second, then asked more seriously, "How badly was she cut?"

"Well, not that badly. It looked like a surface cut like you'd nick yourself with a paring knife. You know sorta like that."

"That's pretty vague for a police report. What did it look like? Did she need stitches?"

"No, like I said, just deep enough to pierce the skin and to make it bleed a bit. The laceration was about an inch long. Pet didn't want to come down here. She hates this place and wasn't even going to show me the cut, except her maid saw the bloody spot on her dress and raised all kinds of hell. She got really mad at me, yelling, 'How could I let something like this happen to the poor girl?' So finally, I persuaded the girls to come back down here. I couldn't wait to get away from that house. That Reddick woman is mean!"

Joshua had a smile on his face while listening to David's confrontation with Mae Delight Reddick. "Must have been something. Who's with Pet?"

"Judy, her best friend. I drove them back to the parking area to get their cars. Then they are coming here so Pet can make a statement about the incident."

"Good. Oh, by the way, Bud from Smiley's Body Shop called. Hanley left you a message on your desk."

Joshua Iverson watched this young officer get up hesitantly as if he didn't know what to do next. Then, with a more determined movement, he went to the door.

"Thanks. I'll get on it, among other things."

David walked out of the office, heading for his desk. Anxious thoughts filled his mind. He checked his watch again, thinking the girls should have been here by now. He realized he was becoming a worrisome mother hen wanting to shield Pet from the creeps around here, but these days it is impossible. Never had he known anyone who could get into more dire situations than she did in the blink of an eye. He made a vow to keep her safe forever because, at that moment, he realized he loved her. "Yes," he said quietly, "Now and forever."

His fears immediately subsided when he heard a sudden

bang of the huge outer doors and spontaneous laughter from Pet and Judy as they walked into the station.

A warm smile came on her face as she saw the look in David's eyes. Pet embraced him tenderly and kissed him on the lips.

"I love you, David, and want you madly," she whispered in his ear.

* * *

A day later, James Wingate's cell phone suddenly bleated, and another sinister conversation began about Pet's demise.

"Just like that?" James asked.

"Just like that. Clean, swift, and precise," Aloysius said smugly.

"When?"

"The 23rd"

"It's already December 18th. You can't make any mistakes with this. Are you sure? It will all come back to you if you screw up, Al," James cautioned.

"Nothing will be proven. Trust me."

"Yeah, uh-huh. I've heard that before."

"I've covered my tracks," Aloysius assured him.

"I hope so," James whispered.

The two clicked off, and the conversation ended as abruptly as it began.

Chapter 73

Judy's Confession

With the ordeal of the police station over, the ER visit and the tetanus shot done, Pet didn't unwind until she was seated comfortably in the study on a soft leather recliner, sipping a glass of her favorite Chardonnay. A glow from the fireplace gave the needed warmth and relaxation. The wine was also doing its magic in lulling Pet into a dreamy haze. Judy talked on about one of her college capers.

"And then, Janie threw the joint out the window. Prattymore dove for the damn thing and almost fell out of the car window. I tell you, Pet, you should have seen Pratty hanging there with his butt in the air and..."

Pet sat straight up and looked directly at Judy. "What did you say, Prattymore? Who is Prattymore?"

"Oh, he was some guy my girlfriend Janie dated." Judy laughed out loud to make light of the name and continued. "Funny. He was a pure cut-up. He could get you any drugs and a good time, night or day. He was..."

Pet's voice sounded irritated, "Who are you talking about? Is that a nickname, or is it someone I know? Judy, that name sounds too familiar to be a coincidence." She broke off quickly and stared into the fire for a minute. Then she looked at her friend. "You're talking about Anthony, aren't you? Did you know him in college?"

"Well, yes, I did. What about it?"

"All this time you never told me you knew him. Were you lovers? How much of Anthony is in your past? And you said drugs. What kind of drugs? Judy, I thought I knew you. What is going on?"

Both girls stared at each other. Pet took a deep breath and then let it out slowly. Judy's soft sigh exhaled a minute later.

"Look, hon. It's like this. I only knew Anthony in college because of my roommate, Janie. He was a pretentious bozo, but he was a likable guy, and Janie adored him, so we hung out sometimes. He would do the most bizarre things because he had the money to do it. We all did pot back then, and he could get the good stuff from a connection overseas. It was fun. Just a laugh, and for the record, I'm no druggie. I have this stenosis in my lower back resulting from a bad car crash. It happened in the late '90s. My pain gets so bad that my left leg goes numb, and I'm down for at least two days. So, when I can't stand it any longer, I call Anthony, and he helps me out. I don't ask where he gets it, or from whom, or how much. I know he will get whatever I need with no strings attached. What you saw that day was me thanking him. He's been good to me, Pet. And considering everything that has happened in the last year and a half, he has been good for you, too. You loved him for a while, didn't you?"

Pet didn't speak as she carefully considered her next words. Her attitude toward Judy softened, and her facial expression softened. "Yeah, I thought I loved him, until I got to know David. I'm sorry I misjudged you, Jude. But at the time, I saw what I saw. What else could I have thought? I do believe you about the drug thing. Maybe if I had gone to college, I would have understood the student life back then. Maybe I would've understood people a lot better, especially Anthony."

Judy looked at her watch as she got out of the recliner. Pet stood up and came to her friend. Judy put her arm around Pet. "It's late, and I have an early meeting. Don't worry, we're still best buds. I can't be angry with you. You came into my life at a good time, and we became friends. We need each other, no matter what our past was like. I told you the other night not to jump to conclusions. Now don't cha feel a little dumb knowin' the real facts?"

Pet gave Judy's arm a squeeze, "Yeah, I do. I'm glad we talked it all out. There will be no more misunderstandings. I'll call you tomorrow."

Pet showed Judy out the door, and they said good night.

Chapter 74

Connections

In the early days, as Mother Prattmore put it, heads of the household in polite society were either predisposed to wealth or had the propensity of obtaining it. These less fortunate offspring were taught by their parents to do well, seek knowledge, and manipulate underlings anyway they could to fill their desperate coffers.

Anthony Prattmore's family line fell somewhere in between. He was brilliant enough to gain admission to college through scholarships, but living an affluent lifestyle at the University of Kentucky was hard.

He did the usual odd jobs during his college years, but even that wasn't filling his pockets. Anthony had a keen sense of humor and the gift of gab. Students and professors liked him. This gift enabled him to schmooze professors and lackeys into getting him practically anything he wanted, but it still wasn't enough.

Soon, he got into a bartering scheme and sold anything for a profit. This little game went on well until his roommate, Ken Stucky, told Anthony he was wasting time with the small stuff.

"Hashish is the way to go, man. You'll be able to live in style sellin' this high-class weed. Why, we could be filthy rich business partners. Jes' listen to ole Ken Stucky from Kentucky. I'm your hick from the stick with the tricks."

Anthony laughed at his country twang, but his easy talk and business smarts paid off. Their alliance was cemented at that point, and they became pretty good friends. Anthony eventually learned that Ken's Uncle Cletus had somehow acquired the "good seeds" from another connection while he was in Vietnam during the war.

He was captivated listening to Ken's story. He would say, "Made it really convenient, too, that my father and Uncle Cletus worked in the fields down home, all perfectly legal like. Why, you never saw such a beautiful sight, seeing that special weed just a growin' right beside the other hemp with nobody knowin' the difference."

Ken didn't stay at school once he realized he had a solid connection with Anthony. Why study for a career when he could keep his persona of a country hick and live like a king at the same time? The rest was a very profitable history.

Anthony was doing his postgraduate work when Ken was killed in a car crash. He was stunned and utterly lost by the news. He thought to himself, "How could that lovable hick get himself killed? Was he high on that weed?" Anthony thought he would live forever, wheeling and dealing his commodity as if it were a gift from the gods. Now, he was afraid his profitable source was gone for good.

It wasn't until the day of the funeral that Anthony's fears were relieved. A distant cousin of Ken's came down for the funeral, a Mr. Chastain Franklin, and introduced himself to Anthony. Ken didn't talk much about other relatives in the "business," so he was surprised when approached.

During their conversation, Mr. Franklin assured Anthony, "Don't worry, Mr. Prattmore, Ken told me a lot about you. Our family is a tight-knit clan and has many contacts. There will be no trouble with the shipments. What you two settled on stays that way."

Anthony told him of his plans after grad school and then head north to a firm in Pennsylvania. He was pleased to learn that the Franklin family lived in western Pennsylvania, too, and there would be no problems. His son was also advancing in the ranks and learning the distribution process. Details would be worked out. Anthony mused, "Things always work themselves out. What providence!"

Chapter 75

Manny's Road Trip

At eight a.m. on December 19th, the call caught Manny blind sighted on his way up to Erie.

"Manny, is this Manny Holmes?"

"Yes, who's callin' me?"

"This is Harold Buford, Manny. Look. I've got a situation here. I need you back at Briar Town ASAP. Jake Haney just had a heart attack a couple of hours ago, and I have no one else to replace him. His assistant is in Europe on vacation and won't be back for two weeks. We have all these orders to get out before Christmas. Can you get back here in a couple of hours?"

"No can do, Mr. Buford. After I unload this order in Erie, I'm going on to Punxsutawney. My semi is fully loaded. I won't be back till after midnight, and that's pushing it, providing the weather holds."

Harold took a long draw on his cigarette and exhaled, "Well, see what you can do. I know it's a long haul. There will be a bonus for you if you can get here before midnight. Call me when you get back to the docks. Good luck."

"Does that mean one for Jimmy, too, Boss?"

"Yes, Manny, Jimmy too."

"Thanks, Mr. Buford. I'll call you when we get back."

Manny was thankful that his deliveries went smoothly, but the traffic in Erie was backed up. Once they got to their destination, he and Jimmy worked well together. While Manny handled the paperwork, Jimmy supervised the workers doing the heavy lifting.

On their return trip, snow began to fall outside of Clarion. The intensity was enough to make the road slushy and visibility poor. Manny pulled into a rest station. He got out and checked the tires.

"We might as well take a leak and gulp down some coffee while we're here. We'll eat those sandwiches your wife made us on the way back."

The road was treacherous. Manny slowed his rig and added another hour to his trip, wanting to be safe rather than on time. As he pulled into the loading dock, Manny called Harold Buford.

"Sorry to call you so late, sir. Just doing what you asked me to do."

"That's okay, I'm glad you are back. Any trouble?"

"No, sir. Everything was in order. The snow didn't help, but nothin' I couldn't handle. I'm going to shut this rig down, close up the office, and call it a night."

"Good. Get some rest, and I will see you later in the day. I will help you as much as I can. Jake Hanley ran that place well and never asked for anything. I didn't have to worry with his leadership. I hope he can get back here soon."

"Yeah. Thanks, Mr. Buford. Good night."

Manny checked his watch after talking with Harold Buford. It was 1:00 a.m. He was tired and his eyes burned. Just once, he thought to himself, he wanted to get home at a decent hour with a hot meal waiting for him. Now that the added responsibility of the whole shipping department was dumped in his lap, his life wouldn't be normal for a while. The job weighed heavily on his shoulders. He glanced over at Jake Haney's desk. It was a supervisor's nightmare: several clipboards with shipping manifests, overseas invoices, and warehouse reports were strewn all over the desk. Nothing was in order.

"Screw it. I'm not even goin' to look at that mess till morning." Then he looked at his watch again, "Christ, it is morning."

He closed and locked the office door and was about to proceed down the short hallway to the rear exit when he thought he heard whispers coming from the men's bathroom. The door was slightly ajar, and a shadowy gray light emitted from the room.

Then he heard the unmistakable raspy voice of Aloysius Hyde. "Did you get it? Is the armoire listed?"

"Of course, it was on there, Al. Was there any doubt? Haney's heart attack just made it easier to swipe the Will Call slips right off the pegboard. There was so much confusion, poor guy. Why don't you put me in charge of the department? We could furnish the apartment like the Biltmore Castle."

"Stop rambling, Gibby. I need you to transfer those items to the miscellaneous delivery sheet early tomorrow morning. Don't make a big deal out of it either. They are going to expedite Christmas deliveries as quickly as they can until 4 p.m. Christmas Eve. Nothing is going to be left in the warehouse, so that means all slips and merchandise have to be accounted for. Do you understand?"

Gibby's answer was almost a whine. "I know what I'm doing. I could be an executive, you know. When will I get promoted?"

"Not now, dick head. Get outta here before the night guard comes around."

Al poked his head out of the men's room door and eased himself out, motioning Gibby to do the same. Their footsteps clumped down the hall to the exit. When Manny heard the heavy door close behind the two men, then and only then was he able to breathe a complete sigh of relief. The second he heard the voices, he ducked beside a coffee vending machine and pressed his body against the wall. Fortunately, the night shadows of the place were still enough to hide a big man like Manny, especially if no one was looking for him.

He moved out into the hallway and stood there thinking out his next move. The fluorescent light over the exit door sputtered. It blinked several times, made a popping sound, and went out. Two seconds later, Manny was in complete darkness. He had to leave. Walking straight ahead, his outstretched hands searched for the door handle. He suddenly found himself smacking the back of his hand against the metal handle, "Shit!"

When he got home, he was physically drained. He dragged his body into bed, wanting desperately to unwind and go to sleep. Unfortunately, his mind was full of questions. He wondered why a shipping clerk and the CEO would be in the Company's shipping department at one in the morning. The two made an odd coupling.

Hearing Gibby's whining voice didn't surprise him, though. He was a tattletale and a snitch who always stirred up trouble among the dock workers. Manny recognized Aloysius Hyde's gruff commands right away. Why would he be concerned with a Will Call Sheet? It did not add up. He sighed heavily and rolled into his pillow, mumbling, "I'll find things out tomorrow."

Chapter 76

Mounting Evidence

The brass door knocker slipped hesitantly out of David's hand. With a loud clank it bounced loudly on the metal plate twice. He winced at the alarming sound. It only took Mae Delight two seconds to open the door to the early morning intruder.

She stood at the door perturbed and grumbling, "Don't you ever come at decent hours of the day? It ain't even eight o'clock and you're rappin' at my door. Y'all like to wake the dead. Missy ain't even outta bed yet. What do you want?"

David took a slow step inside. "I'm very sorry, Ms. Reddick. I know it is early, but I have important news for Pet. It's something she's been waiting for. Could you please wake her for me? She won't be angry with me or you after she sees this report."

Mae Delight scowled at David. "All right, you can come in and go into the kitchen where you were the other night. I'll put a pot of coffee on when I get back downstairs. And, close the door behind you. I'm not heatin' the whole damn city!" She turned her back on David and headed up the stairs.

David sat at the kitchen table looking over the report shaking his head thinking, "One day I'd like to see her in a good mood. I wonder if she gives Pet a hard time."

A few minutes later, Mae Delight came into the room. She didn't speak. She busied herself measuring out coffee for the Mister Coffee Maker. She told David the last time not to expect those individual sissy cups of coffee. Her brew was the real thing and much better.

Then to David's delight, she took out some homemade cinnamon rolls from the freezer and proceeded to put them on a cookie sheet for the oven. Enduring her tirade would be worth it just to munch on her homemade rolls.

Pet breezed into the room, face scrubbed and all smiles. She gave David a hug and sat down close beside him. "HI!"

David leaned over and kissed her on the cheek "Hi, yourself!"

Mae Delight poured the steaming coffee and handed one cup to Pet and then one to David. She leaned over to him slightly. "Well, what news did you bring? I hope it's gonna be good for a change."

"I think it is, Ms. Delight." David took out the work order from Smiley's garage and laid it flat on the table.

"This is the exact information that puts Aloysius on the road the night of the blizzard. The license number matches the trouper's report of a stranded vehicle on Route 376. It describes the needed repairs corresponding with your story where he hit your vehicle. Also, the address given from the vehicle registration is Hyde's home address."

Before Pet could get her hands on the sheet of paper, Mae Delight put a hot plate of cinnamon rolls in front of them. Each grabbed one and bit into the gooey goodness. Then she reread the sheet of paper. "David, this is wonderful! I got him! Do you think this info would stand up in court?"

"It would have to be investigated further and verified by the garage owner that it was truly Hyde that brought the car in to be repaired. Are you pressing charges, Pet?"

There was no hesitation in Pet's voice. "Yes, I will. I'm not afraid of him anymore. Marshall Kochmann called me the other day to let me know he had found more incriminating evidence about Mr. Hyde. Now with your help, David, we've got him right where we need him, out the door!"

Mae Delight made her comment as usual. "That's good. Now you can go ahead with your life, and, girl, you better not back down!"

"You don't have to worry about me, Mae Delight."

David and Pet got up at the same time and walked arm in arm from the kitchen to the front door. David started laughing. Pet looked at him funny. "What are you laughing about now?"

He leaned close to her. "Well, we seem to have a pattern going on here. We always leave the kitchen. Mae Delight waits behind the door and I want to take you upstairs and make love to you and can't. Can you understand my frustration?"

She smiled and kissed him passionately. She pulled away slowly. "Well, I guess I do, but you don't have time and Mae Delight wouldn't get any work done wondering exactly what you were doing to me, as if she wouldn't know already!"

David slid his hands down her back resting them on her butt. "You, missy, are a little minx. You will get your turn. Seriously, I have to go. When are you meeting Marshall?"

"Not really sure, in a day or two. I am going to call him the minute you leave. I am relieved and apprehensive at the same time. I don't want anything to back-fire."

David said confidently as he kissed her cheek, "Don't worry, Pet, it won't."

She shut the door behind him and headed for the library to call Marshall.

Chapter 77

The Preliminaries

Pet took the liberty of calling Marshall at home. She didn't like making early morning calls. To her, early calls before nine always meant disaster was coming, or that it had already happened. But, in this case, Marshall welcomed it.

"I'm glad you did call now. I have gathered enough evidence against Aloysius and James to convene a meeting with you and your new board members. With your permission, I'd like to do that this morning. Can you be in my office in forty-five minutes?"

"Yes, I can do that, Marshall. Thank you."

Never had Pet felt so focused. Finally, she felt things would go her way. The company was going to have a new board and a new CEO, Mrs. Patrice Elyse Traffortelli. She would be able to protect Grace's legacy and keep the company out of Aloysius' contemptible hands.

Marshall was sitting in his office when she walked in. Pet started talking immediately. "Marshall, I am so excited. Do I have to say anything? Can I say you're out of here, Aloysius Hyde? Can we call the cops and arrest him today? I want to see him squirm."

Marshall quelled a belly laugh. "Hold on, young lady. This isn't an episode of *Law and Order*! The protocol has to be followed. Nothing but the obvious evidence from the old file books, my deposition from the First Fifth Bank of Detroit, and the Alton Paint Company deal debacle will be charged against them today. More evidence from the auditors will follow. I am calling in Catherine Hartwell and James Wingate and..."

In her usual exuberance, Pet interrupted before he finished speaking.

"Wow, fraud and embezzlement are something else. Bunny told me about the Alton thing. I'm sorry those guys got you demoted. That was just plain mean. I didn't know Mr. Wingate was that sinister. Catherine must know about those accounts. Do you think she will stay if Mr. Hyde is convicted? Could she face charges, too?"

Pet broke off suddenly. "Sorry, Marshall, I'm ranting on. I'll stop talking and listen to whatever you need me to say."

Marshall was still smiling at her when he spoke, but soon got down to business. "Don't worry. We, meaning our new board, have enough evidence to file criminal charges against them, and they will no longer be employed at our company. I know Aloysius will deny and challenge these facts, but that's okay. Our lawyers will rebut their arguments. But remember, Pet. Do not be intimidated if they start yelling at you. You are the lawful owner of Briar Town Furniture Company. You have the authority to fire administrators and anyone else found in criminal activity."

For a second Pet pouted. "I'd still like to see Catherine in handcuffs. I want to put them on myself."

Marshall almost laughed out loud. "Now, Pet. Don't get mean. You'll have your last laugh soon enough."

Chapter 78

The Ambush

James Wingate's secretary stood at his door looking like a squirrel ready to run into traffic. Her eyes blinked nervously as he passed by. She followed him into his office. "Sir, you are wanted in the boardroom now. There is a meeting at nine a.m. sharp."

"Says who?"

"Um, Mr. Marshall Kochmann."

"Miss Spence, what does he want? Did he ask Mr. Hyde, too?"

"I don't know, Sir. Mr. Hyde isn't in his office, nor is Mrs. Hartwell. Mr. Kochmann has called twice for you to come."

James immediately took off his coat. "Get me a coffee, two creams, two sugars." James coughed in irritation, "Please."

Miss Spence answered, "Yes, sir," and quickly scooted out the door.

The mere fact that he was caught off guard by this meeting irritated him, but not hearing from Al in two days infuriated him even more. James was about to siphon off $500,000.00 from the company's consulting fund to another offshore account. This new broker guaranteed him an annual interest rate of 10%, but he wanted two signatures on the policy before the 24th of December. He couldn't do a damn thing without Al's presence. The thought of losing that much money made the bile rise up in his throat. He racked his brain for an alternative plan. He thought about this all the way to the boardroom. By the time he got to the door, his stomach was beginning to rumble. He almost ran into Harold Buford.

He stopped abruptly and eyed Harold up and down, "What are you doing here, Buford?"

Harold shrugged his shoulders slightly. "The meeting, same as you."

James didn't move. "You haven't been over to my office lately. What are you doing, working for a change?"

Harold didn't say a word and opened the door for him to pass. All eyes were on the two men as they walked to the front of the boardroom.

James was about to sit down in his usual seat, but Marshall motioned him to take an empty one three chairs down. Harold sat down next to Marshall.

Looks could have killed as James sat down. His eyes slowly took in unfamiliar faces, except for Pet, Marshall, and Harold. They likewise looked back in noncommittal appraisal. He wondered who these people were. Why were they here, and where were his friends from the old board?

As he cleared his throat, Marshall looked at each member around the table. He fingered the legal pad in front of him. "Now, gentlemen, I think we can get started with this meeting. The agenda is before you."

James spoke harshly. "You can't start this meeting. Aloysius Hyde is not here, and neither are any of the board members."

"I beg your pardon, James. These people you see here are the new board members of Briar Town Furniture Company: Mrs. Traffottelli, Harold Buford, David Higby, our attorney, and I, along with these other fine ladies and gentlemen, are the new regime."

In a fit of rage, James got up out of his chair, ready to charge Harold.

"Why, you back-stabbing son-of-a-bitch! What did you tell him?" He pointed his finger at Pet. "You wanted her out of here, you said so yourself. You had your chance to get money. Your record ain't that clean, Buford. I'll sue you for libel!"

James then faced Marshall. "Where's Al? Why isn't he here? If he thinks I'm taking the fall for this, he's full of crap!"

"I'm afraid your threats won't hold water. We have hard

evidence of the illegal offshore accounts being siphoned from the company payroll, with both of their initials on it. I wouldn't carry on so much, Mr. Wingate. Hysterics don't become you. I think it would be best if you sat back down, sir."

Pet watched James' expression to see if he would accuse her of anything. Fortunately, no words came from his lips.

With the formality of a judge, Marshall read the charges against him and Aloysius Hyde.

"As of this date, December 20th, 2019, Aloysius Hyde, CEO, and James Wingate, CFO, are accused of multiple counts of fraud and embezzlement. An IRS audit found discrepancies in accounts payable, bogus consulting companies, and illegal transfers of funds to offshore Caribbean accounts. Due to these charges, Briar Town Furniture Co. will be under further scrutiny by the IRS and an independent auditing firm. Because of these actions by said persons, they will no longer have the title of CEO and CFO or be employed by this company."

Marshall's demeanor stiffened. "Getting back to your question, Mr. Wingate, Aloysius Hyde is nowhere to be found. His wife doesn't know where he is either. A warrant for his arrest has been issued by the local police. He will be put in jail immediately when found. You will be escorted to the county jail by the sheriff standing outside this door. I suggest you call your lawyer. One more question: were you the last person to speak with him?"

James straightened his jacket and rose slowly, his voice solemn and his complexion ashen. "As of this moment, I won't answer to anything. Go through my lawyers. Not even my secretary will answer you, Marshall."

"I understand, Mr. Wingate. The sheriff will also escort you to your office, and you will hand over to him all documents pertaining to this company's financial books. Mrs. Bows, our legal stenographer, will assist the officer and make notes of what is handed over."

Chapter 79

The Headache

In a foggy daze, Manny heard the phone ringing. He rolled over and sat up on the edge of the bed, praying for consciousness. His wife handed him the phone. It was one o'clock in the afternoon, December 20th. One call after another came in from the dock supervisors and truckers wanting to know about their schedules, overtime, and special deliveries. By three o'clock, Manny's head was about to explode with a ferocious migraine. He didn't know what was worse, being home or being at work.

His wife, Minnie, stood by his side. "I wish I could help you in some way, Manny. All these calls are makin' you crazy."

"Don't worry about it, Minnie. Being promoted is gonna come with a price, and it is gonna be a big one. Right now, I gotta call the boss."

Toward the end of their conversation, Manny said, "I'm sorry, Mr. Buford. Things just didn't work out. I tried to straighten out as many of the calls as I could."

"That's okay, Manny. All hell broke loose here in the administration office, too. We fired the CEO and the CFO simultaneously. Mr. Hyde is no longer the man in charge, and no one knows where he is."

"That is something. By the way, Mr. Buford, do you have a minute?"

"Yes, what is the matter?"

"I was going to tell you this when I came in, but I might as well tell you about it now."

Manny related the whole incident of seeing Hyde and Gibby the night before in the warehouse. Harold listened intently.

"That son of a bitch. He couldn't be satisfied with money.

He had to have the expensive pieces of furniture for himself, too! Well, Manny, get some rest. I will see you early tomorrow morning, right?"

"Yes, sir."

Chapter 80

Cleaning Up

It was just getting light as Manny approached the warehouse the next morning. He saw the night guard making his routine rounds, opening the outer dock doors for the 6:30 shift. The day was cold with a bone-chilling wind blowing in his face. The clouds overhead were heavy and unpredictable. Manny believed in the clouds, and gray was never a good sign.

When he got inside, he flicked on the corridor light. The area was quiet. Fortunately, the day's rumble of activity hadn't started. Suddenly, he heard a door slam shut. In the shadows of the hall, he saw a tall, slender man walk quickly out of the shipping office and down the hall. He vanished around the corner before Manny could catch a glimpse of him. In a vain attempt to get the intruder's attention, Manny yelled, "HEY YOU, STOP!"

Naturally, the man didn't stop. Manny picked up the pace and walked straight to the office, finding the door unlocked. He wondered for a few seconds who else could have a second key. His musings came to a quick stop when the overhead lights came on.

It was a hellish scene, like a bomb had gone off, and this shit hole was the only thing left. He didn't know where to begin. Every desk had piles of paper on it. Nothing was in order. What made it worse was a sickening smell coming from some hidden space reeking of grease and cigar butts.

He walked over to one corner of the room and gingerly lifted a loose-leaf binder hiding a box of Kentucky Fried Chicken with a half-eaten chicken breast smashed on top of mashed potatoes. Manny dropped the binder immediately and almost puked.

He walked out of the office and picked up a wall phone. He pressed the PAGE button. "MAINTENANCE TO SHIPPING, MAINTENANCE TO SHIPPING."

A few minutes later, a kid in gray work clothes approached Manny. "What? What do you want this early in the morning? I just punched in and haven't gotten my worksheet yet, or a cup of coffee."

"Your coffee is going to have to wait. I need this office cleaned up right now! And bring a room deodorizer too. It stinks in there!"

The young man lifted his head up to look at this big, unfamiliar face in front of him. "Why the hell do I have to do it? I always get caught doing the shitty jobs. Besides, you ain't my boss in this area. Haney is."

"Mr. Haney to you, son, and if you haven't heard by now, he's had himself a heart attack, and you're looking at the man in charge now."

The kid backed down on hearing about Jake Haney. "Well, we, the younger guys, usually get the cleaning lady to do the dirty jobs. Sorry about Mr. Haney."

Manny's voice wasn't as gruff when the kid softened his attitude. "When does the cleaning lady come in?"

"She's part-time and comes in at 10:00, sir."

"That won't do now, will it? What is your name, son?"

"Terry Smith."

"Terry, I am Manny Holmes. I'll be acting Department Head until Mr. Haney gets back. Now that we know each other, I would appreciate this office being cleaned up quickly without any fuss. Is that understood?"

The kid wasn't happy, but agreed to obey Manny's order with a nod, saying, "Okay, Mr. Holmes."

"Thanks. Did you see anyone in this department earlier?"

"Yeah. That was Gibby Seethaler. He always comes in early."

Manny didn't have a chance to return a comment because Harold was coming down the hall.

"Good to see you. How are you feeling, Manny?" said Harold.

"A lot better, sir. Thanks. Did you see inside that office? It's a pig sty. What went on in there?" asked Manny

"I'm not sure. The trucking and forklift men must have taken advantage of the situation, using this as their private mess hall and dispatch area. I spent the last two days trying to find Aloysius Hyde. I should have had more supervision over these guys, but there just wasn't time. Hey, see what you can do with the paperwork, Manny. More orders are coming in today. I would start with the shipping manifests in Haney's computer. I have his password."

Harold handed Manny a small black leather notebook. "Don't let anyone use this. I will be back down here as soon as I can. I have another situation to take care of. Sorry, I can't stay."

Manny took the notebook, went back to the office, and delved into the computer while a crew cleaned the office. It didn't take long for him to realize something was terribly wrong. He compared the shipping manifests in the computer with the physical delivery sheets. Many items were duplicated with different dates and destinations.

On paper, it looked like an easy scheme to move a lot of furniture to different places and hide other merchandise in unmarked holding areas. He fixed that situation and got the deliveries moving to the right people.

He was about to close the files when a glaring figure caught his eye. Yesterday, December 20, $15,000.00 worth of cherry wood secretaries and armoires were delivered to the West Side warehouse. No destination sheet was with the order. Manny thought this had to be another screw-up. In all the years he worked there, he had never heard of the West Side warehouse. It stumped him.

Manny thought for a while, going over the surroundings of this shipping building in his head. He remembered one place tucked far back on the original side of the warehouse. It hadn't been used since the renovation twenty years ago. Only certain people would know about this area. It was a good hiding place because it was out of sight from the building's regular traffic, and it could handle a large order.

Manny headed down the hall. "Well, looks like I'm on the move."

As he walked down and around several corridors, he thought someone had a lot of balls stealing that much furniture right under Jake's nose. The curiosity was killing him in wanting to find the thief and the merchandise.

Finally, he came to the original part of the building. It wasn't an easy place to find, and he was amazed at how narrow the halls were with each corner he turned. The lighting also dimmed, giving another advantage to hidden goods.

As Manny approached the huge double doors, he noticed that one side was slightly ajar. He was about to open it wider when he caught a whiff of cigarette smoke. Then he heard someone talking on a phone.

"Yes. Yes, that's it. You'll find me waiting here outside at the west wing door on the platform, Mr. Eddie. The merchandise is in the crate right beside me. Yes, that is the price we agreed on, $3000.00."

Manny's first impulse was to find out who the sneaky SOB was, but immediately after that call, he heard a cell phone ring.

"Yeah, Gib speaking. Okay, I have your stuff. Okay, meet me here in 15 minutes and don't be late. Have the cash in your hand."

Manny opened the door slowly and saw Gibby standing on the landing with his back to Manny. He watched the little man nervously pace back and forth for a few seconds, and then he lit a cigarette.

With the force of a giant, Manny lurched for Gibby and pulled the scrawny man back through the double doors and into the hall. He grabbed him so hard that Gibby landed on the floor flat on his back, stunned.

Standing over the cowering thief, Manny restrained his size twelve shoe from stomping on Gibby's chest. "You dirty rotten son of a bitch! I could squish you like a bug. I should beat the living crap outta you. Did you really think you were gonna get away with this?"

Gibby attempted to get up and run, but Manny caught him, lifted him up by the shirt, and pressed him against the wall with both arms.

"Talk! Who's in this game of yours?"

"I don't have to tell you a thing."

"You do if you want to live."

Before Manny could utter another threat, he heard through the cracked-open door a vehicle's horn beep twice. Gibby started grabbing at Manny's muscular arms to get free.

"I have to go. He'll leave!"

"Good. Let him go, asshole."

On the outside, someone was revving up an engine. It sounded like a big truck. A minute or two went by. Manny waited, hoping they would come in to complete the theft, but nothing happened. They were impatient and blasted the horn twice more. After a short wait, they drove away.

Gibby was going spastic. Manny let him squirm for a few more seconds before he questioned him some more.

"Is Aloysius Hyde in on this?"

Gibby's voice was defiant, "Maybe."

"Like he doesn't know where $15,000.00 worth of merchandise went to?"

"Oh yes. He got his armoire and the Louis XIV chaise lounge, but I was smarter in acquiring the old-world cherry secretaries. He had no imagination, now see..."

Manny pushed his head hard against the wall. "Shut your hole! Save it for the police. Now, tell me where the rest of it is, or I'm going to bash your face in!"

In defiance, Gibby twisted and turned his body, swinging his puny arms at Manny's face. He was like a Jack Russell Terrier going against a Bull Mastiff. With a sudden jerk, he kicked Manny in the shin. The blow caught Manny off guard, but it didn't hinder his reaction to plant a solid fist to the side of the pipsqueak's head, putting him to the floor again.

He was about to kick him in the ribs when Terry Smith came running down the corridor. "Hey, boss, do you need any help?"

Manny had no time to answer because another vehicle outside the doors bleeped two quick honks. Manny leaned down to Gibby and shouted, "Hey, how many more you got comin'?"

Gibby moaned, saying nothing. Manny looked at the kid and took a chance. "Watch him. Don't let him move. I do not care if you have to sit on the son of a bitch! Can you do that?"

"Yes, sir!"

By the time Manny got out to the platform, the car was speeding down the road. He was frustrated that he couldn't make out the license plate. He was about to go back inside when his foot kicked Gibby's cell phone. Picking it up, he saw a missed call on the screen. He saw A. Prattmore.

Manny read the text. "Hey, where the hell are you? You said to be ready. I don't have time to wait. You and Charles better not be screwing with me. You won't live to enjoy my payment!"

Manny didn't have time to figure out what the message meant, but he took a second to think, "Yes, it was him. Wonder why Prattmore would be involved in a scheme like this?"

Inside, Gibby was just coming to and cringed at the sight of his assailant coming toward him again. Terry was sitting on Gibby's legs.

"Thanks, Mr. Smith. You can get off him now. I need you to call the police and get them down here right away. Tell them this is not an ordinary theft case. Also call Marshall Kochmann and ask him to come down here as well. Tell him all will be explained when he arrives. Got it?"

"Yes, sir, I will."

"Good. Tell them to meet us in the shipping department office. I'll be in there with this jerk."

All the way to the office, Manny shoved Gibby down the hall while he spilled his guts about the furniture scheme. He also mentioned that Aloysius was acquiring expensive pieces for his home and city apartment with company money.

"Who set up this 'Got It' app?"

"Oh, that was so easy. Al doesn't think I have a brain in my head, but I fooled him. Two clicks on the smart web link and you're in, baby. Worked instantly. I needed money, too, ya know."

Manny shook his head in disgust. "What a shit you are. Now, who was that second call from? Don't lie to me."

Gibby's smirky attitude changed, stopping him in his tracks. He stared down at the cement floor. Manny hit him in the back with his fist. "Come on, asshole. You're not going to clam up now!"

"Ow! That hurt! Um, I can't say. He'll kill me!"

"I'll kill you myself if you play me. Tell me who the second caller was."

"I don't have to say anything until my lawyer gets here."

Manny was in Gibby's face and running out of patience with this scrawny smart ass. Grabbing the shirt collar with his meaty fist, he said, "You're not arrested yet. You are under my thumb now. All I have to do is pull this shirt tighter around your neck until your eyes bug out. Do you feel me, asshole?"

Gibby gulped hard. "It was that lawyer. Everyone knows him in administration. I just can't think of his name right now."

When they finally got to the shipping office, Manny dismissed Terry Smith, warning him not to breathe a word about what had just transpired. He liked the boy and promised him a few days' paid leave for his cooperation.

Detective Iverson and Officer Jones were there to meet them. And so the process began.

Chapter 81

Al the Drunk

In the Whalen Falls Holiday Inn motel room, Aloysius swayed toward the table and sat down. His beefy hands tipped a bottle of Jack Daniels over, but caught it before it fell to the floor. With a shaky hand, he poured himself another drink, straightening up just enough to gulp down the numbing liquid. Aloysius belched loudly and slumped down, resting his head on his folded arms on the table.

A wallet-sized picture of a girl fell out of his other hand. He stared at it for a few minutes with bleary eyes and began to mumble. He let loose a tirade of anger and incoherence. "Aah, go on. Fall out of my life. I don't care anymore. You ruined me. You broke my heart, promisin' to marry me. You liar! You promised me the business too, but you gave it away, gave it to that little bitch that didn't deserve nothin'! Don't worry, Gracie, she'll get hers. I'll fix her!"

Afterward, a fitful sleep overcame him until he heard the buzz from his cell phone vibrating on the table.

"Go away, you son of a bitch! I'm tired. Let me sleep."

The phone stopped buzzing, but then five minutes later it buzzed again. Aloysius was coming out of his stupor and clutched the phone, fumbling to answer it.

"What? Who's this?"

"It's me, you son of a bitch! Why didn't you answer your phone? I've been trying to get you since Friday. That was two days ago," said James.

"I don't care what day it is," Aloysius said sarcastically.

James pressed on. "Al, it's Sunday, the 22nd. Where are you? Do you know what you are doing? You left me holding the bag.

They have got evidence against me. You said you covered our tracks. Buford spilled his guts to Kochmann. Now those two are in charge down there. They are pinning all the blame on us. They've found the books, plus I couldn't get the Kennedy contract out of your desk. My wife had to post bail and get me out of jail. What a freaking mess. I'm not going to swing for your screw up!"

"Aw, shut up! I got it covered! Nothing's gonna happen to you, so leave me alone. You're whining like a little girl!"

Before James had a chance to shout a comeback, Aloysius clicked off, throwing the phone across the room. It landed right in the middle of the bed instead of falling to the floor.

Chapter 82

In the Woods

Charles' footsteps crunched in the snow as he stealthily crept among the pines behind Rutherford Manor. He took care to check the distance from her bedroom window to his seating position. It was a perfect place for a sniper because this secluded area was on a slight grade and away from other homes.

Charles aimed his 308 Winchester rifle at the house and adjusted the scope. He focused on the bedroom window again as he had done for the past seven nights. He got to know her predictable pattern. At 5 pm, the bedroom light came on, the window shades were pulled up, and she stared into the yard. Then he could see her going to a dresser and taking out an article of clothing. She never changed her pattern. He was slightly amused watching her come back to the window, brushing her hair for several more minutes. He thought it odd but didn't question a woman's prerogative.

When he was satisfied with his position, the distance between him and his target, a smile came over his face. Distance and a deadly weapon were on his side. He thought to himself, "A few hours from now, I'll be on a plane to Jamaica."

Then he decided to get warm before completing this sinister contract and laughed out loud as he walked out of the woods. "Aloysius Hyde, you pompous ass, I won't have to take your crap anymore, or listen to your lawyer stooge once he gives me the money you promised. You don't even know I stole $50,000.00 in bonds from your desk. Yeah, I'll be sitting pretty."

Two days earlier, Aloysius called him. The request was simple. "Charles, I need you to leave the area immediately. Get out of Whalen Falls as quickly as you can and meet Anthony in the back of the old warehouse. He will be waiting for you."

Before Charles answered Aloysius, he thought about this change. "What the hell. It would be less complicated than meeting in town for the payoff."

"Sure, I'll be there. He better not stiff me."

"Don't worry. He'll be on time, and he'll have your money."

"Okay."

Chapter 83

In the Kitchen, December 23rd

"Now what are you doin' knockin' at my back door? You look stupid with that raggedy ass hat on your head, all snowy and wet," said Mae Delight.

"Please don't get mad at me, ma'am. I know my big snow boots just wouldn't be right dripping on your nice floor mat."

She sighed and extended her arms toward Mike Yoderman, pulling him out of the cold. "Get on in here. You look pitiful. You don't keep good hours either, do you? It ain't even eight o'clock yet. Are you plowin' at this hour?"

"Yes, ma'am, and I forgot to get me a cup of coffee. When I was passing your home, I told myself you're a good woman. Surely, you would be kind and give ole Mike a cup to keep his belly warm."

Mae Delight tried to look mean, but she couldn't help smiling inside at the big hulk of a man standing before her. "Hmmpf, you musta been a beggar before you was a trucker, 'cause you do it real good. I guess there's still a cup or two left in the pot."

"My stomach would surely appreciate it, you betcha." Mike hesitated as he stood looking around the kitchen. He sniffed the air like a bloodhound. "Do I smell cookies baking? Something sure smells like sweet heaven in that oven over there. I could smell something baking clear out on the porch. Are they sugar cookies?"

Mae Delight shot Mike a look of impatience. "Well, you might as well sit down for a second while I fetch the thermos and a container for some cookies. You sure want a lot this early in the morning. You're keeping me from my Christmas baking.

Another thing, why are you out so early plowing? What's the highway people gearing up for?"

"Well, as far as I know, they're expecting a big snowstorm again starting now and a goin' till late tonight. We'll be out on 376 all day. That's where I saved my little Ladybug, you know. It's gonna be mean out there fer shur!"

Mae Delight chuckled to herself, "Ladybug, huh. I can't wait to call her that."

She fixed Mike a big thermos of coffee with rich cream and sugar. She also filled a large container with sugar and oatmeal cookies, placing it next to the thermos.

He smiled when she handed them to him. Mae Delight put her finger up, "I'm warnin' ya. Don't go telling every soul you meet that my kitchen is open to every highway trucker in the state. I don't need beggars like you at my door at all hours of the day. You hear me?"

"Oh, yes, ma'am. Ole Mike wouldn't give you away. I don't want to get on the bad side of you! You'd lick me with that wooden spoon of yours."

Mike Yoderman thanked Mae Delight with a big bear hug and ran out the kitchen door laughing. She pretended to be upset, yelling at him until he was out of sight. He was right about the snow. Big fluffy flakes were already covering her back-porch steps.

Mae Delight wondered what the night would bring. She felt the cold coming from the windowpane. A shiver ran down her spine. "Oh Lord, bad things are a comin'."

* * *

December 23rd

Late Sunday afternoon, from the motel room, Aloysius decided to call Anthony. In his inebriated state, he brought the phone up to his face to read the numbers more clearly. His voice was slurred and guttural. "Hey, Tony, how you doin'?" He belched loudly over the phone. "You told him where to meet you, right?"

Anthony was stunned at the call and irritated at the same time. He was about to settle down in his recliner and watch the Steelers' game. At first, he didn't recognize the drunken voice, but then realized it was Aloysius. "Yes, Aloysius, for the fifth time, I know what to do. You picked a bad place for this meet. I hope to Christ I don't get stuck out there. It's going to be a real mess if the snow gets deeper."

A grunt escaped from his lips. "You're smart, Tony. You'll figure it out, don' complain and don' choke up. I hate that scrawny bastard. After you kill him, drag his body under those pine trees. He won't be found for days."

"Thanks for nothing, Aloysius. This plan better be worth it. I'll call you. Don't worry. I'm meeting Charles at six. You said the guard doesn't make rounds around the perimeter till eight every night. We should be long gone by then."

"Yeah, yeah, I'm good. Don't be late, Tony. I ain't that drunk."

"Yeah, right," Anthony mumbled. He thought for a few seconds, then said, Fine. See you at the airport on the 24th, Gate 14, Delta Airlines."

"Good." Al clicked off and poured himself a tall one.

Chapter 84

The Treacherous Rendezvous

Sure, he could get in a lot of trouble for doing this, and he could get demoted for an act of stalking, but David didn't think of it that way. It was merely an exercise in surveillance at Rutherford Manor. David felt it was a matter of protecting the woman he loved. Each night, he hoped to see Pet coming home from somewhere so he could get ten minutes alone on the back porch and give her a long, tender kiss. Unfortunately, it didn't happen.

His rationale seemed valid. He was going nuts not being with her. She was becoming his entire world. Their lovemaking was tender and exciting. She enticed him to want more. "Soon," he thought, "soon I'm going to make her mine." He was tired of Mae Delight's ridiculous interruptions when he was at the Manor House. It was as if she had to chaperone his every visit. This situation was getting old.

David's simple plan couldn't miss. It had few details, and Mae Delight's pattern never varied. She came out while putting on her coat, checking her left pocket for cigarettes, and ambling across the portico over to the rhododendron bushes. This night was perfect and right on schedule. The snow was just an annoyance David had to put up with. Next, the activity upstairs changed rapidly from one scenario to another.

Tension mounted. He watched the maid from the driveway as she followed through with her routine. Mae Delight didn't look about. Her mind was on the first drag of a cigarette. She enjoyed her evening smoke break alone, but little did she know that someone was watching her from a bedroom on the second floor.

Simultaneously, another scenario was taking place. Charles' plans were finally in motion. He came back into the woods and sat on the snow-covered log he selected last week. The thick wooded hill gave him the right elevation and cover for his intended shot. He focused intently on the window through his scope, watching Pet's routine, a pattern that never varied. She flitted about the room and, every so often, looked out the window. His stiff fingers were aching to pull the trigger. "Now put your head up to the window like you always do, stupid bitch, so I can plug you and get out of here," he mumbled.

Meanwhile, the falling snow and early winter darkness gave David the advantage he needed as he jumped onto the low end of the wall from the driveway. He pulled his body over the wall and onto the sloping backyard. The snow was wet and crunchy under his feet. Getting up was very tricky, so he crawled like an invading commando to the porch steps as fast as he could. Getting to that first step, David searched for Mae Delight, who was nowhere in sight. He stood up, brushing off the snow, and took two giant steps, making it onto the porch and through the partially opened kitchen door.

Down the hallway and around the corner to the stairwell, David took the steps to the second floor like a gazelle. It was easy with his long legs. He hummed, mounting the stairs, "Almost there, my Pet. Comin' through. Gotta see my baby tonight!"

As Charles was about to squeeze the trigger, he saw another person come in through the bedroom door and ease in right behind Pet. He cursed, "Shit, someone's in my sights!" He waited anxiously as they embraced. Then they parted, and the woman put on a robe. The man was close to her.

The unfolding scene was inviting, and David took advantage of it. Luckily, the bedroom door was halfway open. He sneaked in quietly, closing the door behind him. Pet was singing happily, brushing her hair. Her back was to him. In one swift move, without thinking how cold and wet his coat was, he leaned forward, grabbed Pet around the waist, and pulled her to his chest.

All she had on were slacks and a bra. Pet screamed, "SON OF A BITCH! LET GO OF ME!"

She squirmed around, facing him, ready to clobber her assailant with the brush.

"Shhhhh, Pet. Don't yell, please. It's me!" David was laughing softly. "Don't hit me!"

Pet stepped back and grabbed her robe. "I should, you're an icicle. Where the hell were you?"

"Don't worry where I was. Aren't you glad to see me?" He spoke penitently as he took off his wet coat. "I don't have much time, Pet. I had to be with you tonight. We have three precious hours, just the two of us, now, alone. Tell Mae Delight if she calls you up that you want to be alone and that you'll come downstairs later. Be convincing."

Pet melted in his arms. He engulfed her with a passionate kiss. They clung to each other, holding on, not wanting to move. Pet snuggled into his shirt. She smelled his cologne. Then their bodies swayed gently to a love song from the radio for a moment longer until they could no longer resist the strong temptation of her bed.

David whispered, "I'm going to turn out the light."

"Wait, David. I want to remember this night forever. Look out the window with me. The snow is coming down so beautifully."

When the man clung to her, not letting her go, Charles' finger cramped up. It was agonizing keeping the light tension on the sensitive metal. In exasperation, he hissed, "Come on. Move asshole! Let me get this shot!"

David sighed. "Pet, you're killing me. You know that, don't you?"

She smiled, took his hand, and the two watched the snow transform the yard into a fairyland of ice and snow. David could only bear the anticipation for a minute or two. He slipped from her arms and headed for the light switch.

Charles perked up when he caught David's sudden movement. "Finally," he mumbled. "I can pull off this shot." The pelting snow was getting into his eyes. He quickly relaxed his right forefinger for a split second, readjusting the rifle. Seeing the man move away from her was an answer to his silent command. She was in his sights. He squeezed the trigger just as the bedroom lights went out.

In the immediate darkness, David screamed, "Pet!" and a body fell to the floor.

Chapter 85

The Deadly Double Cross

Charles sat motionless. He did not try for a second shot. If the bullet met its target, the deed was complete. He figured there was no time left to analyze the moment. Time was of the essence for his getaway.

He left undetected, walking cautiously. He listened for any unusual noise, but the only sound was the snow pelting down on his coat and the swaying trees around him. His tracks going out of the woods were just slight indentations. With luck, no one would ever know a crime had occurred in this quiet place.

As Charles drove out of town, he realized it would be no easy task to get to the warehouse on time. The streets were snowy and treacherous. There was no way he could do 60 mph on 376. He shoved his hand in his coat pocket, fumbling for his cell phone.

"Prattmore, are you there yet?"

"Yes, Charles. I'm coming up on the back road now. It's getting pretty deep out here, too. Don't piss around. I don't want to be here all night."

"Believe me, I'm not. These roads are shitty. Ice is under all this snow, and visibility is nil. I'll get there as soon as I can to get my money. You hear me?"

"Yes, I'll be waiting."

Both men hung up their phones at the same time. Anthony didn't want to hear any explanations. Charles wasn't about to give him any details.

On the last twenty yards to their rendezvous, Anthony's back wheels spun wildly as he gunned the sports car forward in the mounting snow. He was making his own path to the back of the warehouse. Suddenly, the car came to an abrupt stop. He turned the steering wheel to the right a little and gunned the engine to see if he could maneuver the car farther, but the wheels, unfortunately, would not budge.

Anthony pounded the steering wheel with his fist. "Son of a bitch! Stuck! Damn! I knew I should have brought the Escalade. Didn't think the snow would be this bad. Guess I'm stuck for a while." Anthony turned off the engine and checked his watch. It was 6:15. "That weasel better not be too late."

For a few minutes, Anthony sat there. In the silence, the area's darkness became as desolate as an ancient tomb. His mind wandered, and he began to think of Pet. The thoughts at first were pleasurable. The delicate features of her face and body were before him. He could hear her soft laughter and ached for her sensuous body next to his. He still wanted her. It was the absence that drove him nuts. His angst turned to anger.

His pleasant fantasy turned ugly. She betrayed him by dating that cop. It wasn't right. Why did she break all those promises to love him forever? She mocked him. In his reasoning, he had to get rid of her. He heard his mother's words warning him 'not to trust blondes. They're fickle twits. They will rob you blind. Trust money instead.

The thought of her lying on the bedroom floor, dead, put a wrench in his stomach. Sweat began beading on his forehead, and a lump formed in his throat. Anxious moments heightened his breathing. He felt the urge to leave and go back to her.

Then, for some reason, he leaned his head on the car window. The sudden jolt of cold brought him back to reality. He pushed back any reminders of Pet and concentrated on his present situation.

He began to think about this meeting with Charles, the two-bit hustler with beady eyes. To Anthony, Charles had the look of a rat nibbling on yesterday's garbage. In retrospect, Anthony never trusted him, recalling a couple of heated arguments when Charles stiffed him on a weed delivery. Anthony smiled grimly,

"Tonight that vermin will be exterminated permanently." The more he thought about Charles, the angrier he got, but he told himself to be calm. Nothing could go wrong, not tonight.

Finally, after twenty more minutes, Anthony saw the headlights of an SUV. The vehicle slowed down and stopped short a few yards behind him. He leaned over and got the .38 caliber revolver out of the glove box. His thin calfskin gloves held the grip snugly. It felt good. Then he checked the clip and made sure it was loaded. He put it in his inside coat pocket.

Charles didn't hesitate to get out of the SUV. Although he turned off the engine, he kept the headlights on as a precaution. He wanted to see what would happen next. He stood there stamping his feet in the snow, waiting for Anthony to do the same. The car door scraped the snow into a mound as Anthony got out of the car. He was amazed at how deep it had gotten in such a short time.

Even though the two men were only yards apart, he tried to determine if Charles had another weapon on him. Blowing snow made it difficult to confirm his suspicions. Anthony prepared himself for the inevitable. Charles cautiously took a step closer. "Well, you got my money?"

"It's not your money yet, pal. Did you kill her?" asked Anthony.

"Yeah. Why are you doubting me?"

Anthony's next question stuck in his throat, dreading the obvious answer. "Did you see her fall? Is she really dead?"

"Yes, I'm pretty sure she's dead. The bedroom light went out just as I pulled the trigger."

"What do you mean, the light went out?"

Charles was getting frustrated with his questioning. "She was in my cross hairs, and the bedroom light went out the instant I pulled the trigger. Believe me. When I aim at a target, I don't miss!"

Anthony was yelling now. "You screwed up! There is no guarantee now that the job is done."

Charles took another step closer. "Pay me, Prattmore. I have a contract with Aloysius. Now hand over the dough!"

Anthony shouted, "Stop right there!" But Charles didn't stop. He lunged forward in the snow, putting one hand up to his jacket. Suddenly, a gust of wind stung Anthony's face. Snow got in his eyes. Space and timing were critical. He couldn't hesitate a second. He wiped his eyes quickly and drew the gun from his coat. The next sound Anthony heard was the echo of his gun's pop. He shot Charles Franklin squarely in the chest.

In the SUV's dim headlights, a motionless body lay before him. Anthony watched blood ooze from the bullet wound onto the snow. It turned pink, then dark scarlet. He turned the body on its back and surveyed Charles' face. There, in the dim lighting, he saw a grotesque, wild expression of complete surprise.

Compelled to say something, Anthony said without remorse, "Well, it's done. My summation of you is simple, Charles. If you hadn't been so crooked, you'd still be alive. You deserved everything you got."

Anthony didn't waste any time getting rid of the body. He remembered Al's cryptic instructions. "Drag the SOB under those pines behind the warehouse. Don't try to bury him because the ground will be frozen. There are a lot of loose pine needles to cover him up and low branches at the base of the trees to hide him. With any luck, no one will be back in that area for at least two or three days because of the holiday. We'll be long gone before anyone spots him."

From Anthony's quick perusal, he surmised it was only about fifteen or sixteen yards to the base of the pine trees. He bent down and proceeded to drag the body backward. After a few feet, he stood up. A fierce wind blew snow into his unprotected eyes, adding to his misery. The meager light and now drifting snow had distorted the contours of the land. He soon found out that this job was not as easy as Aloysius had predicted.

He had to get this done and continued the task. With every

inch backward, the body seemed to get heavier and more cumbersome. Suddenly, halfway to the pines, Anthony fell down a hidden slope. This slowed his progress even more. He cursed Al's suggested place of rendezvous while crawling back up to the body.

"Sure, Al, piece of cake. You didn't warn me about the hill, and you didn't account for the snow factor, did you? You better have my money, old man."

Several minutes went by until he finally reached the deep trunks of the pines. He had no shovel or broom to combat the snow-laden branches, so he batted his arms about to dislodge the snow. One branch sprang up in front of him, spewing the white stuff in his face and down the collar of his coat.

Finally, Anthony got under a large branch and pulled Charles close to the tree's trunk. It was eerily silent. The arms of the huge pine protected him from the wind and snow, forming a natural barrier that kept him safe from the elements. In a way, he felt safe here. He didn't want to leave, but he knew he couldn't stay. He worked diligently, gathering the loose debris and small branches covering the body, then wrapping it in a pine-scented blanket. With the last handful of needles, Anthony gave a final farewell, saying, "Rest in Peace, you son of a bitch," and left the shelter of the pines.

Chapter 86

Ironic Justice

Anthony stood there, getting his bearings on his next move, and immediately looked for landmarks. Straining his eyes, he saw the faint glow of the warehouse floodlight. It looked miles away in the blinding snow. Once he got a bead on the surroundings, his eyes searched for the cars. He muttered to himself, "Why can't I see them?" Then he spotted two dark clumps of snow on the slope. He realized, with a sinking heart, that the SUV's battery had died. Now he no longer had that guiding light to help him climb up the slippery mound.

No situation had ever intimidated Anthony J. Prattmore, Esq. He stood up to criminals and put them in jail without a snag. Using his brain was his forte. This storm, on the other hand, was totally out of his comfort zone. He hated the outdoors and had literally no experience in survival skills. He had to hope his common sense and physical strength could get him out of here. The logical plan was to get into his car and call for help.

All this time, adrenaline pumped through his veins, keeping him warm. The short respite from the elements brought relief, but now the winds attacked him, stinging his skin mercilessly. He had to move and move quickly. Indecision at this point would kill him for sure.

With determination, he trudged back up to his car. Again, he fought the mounting snow to get inside. Once inside, Anthony fumbled for his cell phone. Finding it, he placed it on his lap. He blew on his numb fingers, cupping them to his mouth, and reached for the phone. It was like a square ice cube.

He tapped it to come on. Nothing. Tapped it again. Nothing. He blew on it. Still nothing. He hit it against the dashboard and waited. Nothing.

"Shit. It's dead! I didn't realize the battery was so low."

He turned the ignition key. The car groaned. He put it in reverse. It didn't budge. All he could hear was a muffled whine of spinning tires. The car stalled.

"Dammit to hell." His frustration engulfed him.

He sat encased in the frigid darkness, pondering his doom, when a faint rumbling sound caught his attention. Was it a truck? Was it close? It had to be a snowplow. Desperation turned into a glimmer of hope that it would come close to the warehouse and save his dumb ass.

Anthony suddenly realized he must get out and hail that driver to come closer to the building. Using all the strength he had, he forced his body into the hostile night again. The snow was deep, up to his knees. By the time he rounded the corner, the winds had blown a short, uneven path to the front of the building.

Although his feet kept slipping on the uneven terrain, this narrow path made running a little easier. He couldn't see any vehicles but kept yelling toward the road. "Help! I'm out here! Stop! Please stop, anybody!"

Panicking, he ran faster, waving his arms wildly, turning his body to the right, then to the left, looking for any signs of help. With this precarious momentum, he began to stumble from the path. Suddenly, his right foot slipped off the road. He lost his balance and fell headlong onto a pine log that had a dead branch sticking straight out from the trunk. The jagged weapon pierced deeply into his chest.

Nature's weapon could have been more kind and just graze the vulnerable mass with less severity, but the whims of fate often play upon a most tragic end. Anthony J. Prattmore, Esq. died shortly after falling onto the branch in excruciating pain, alone in the snow. The last conscious words he uttered were "Oh, God."

Chapter 87

A Shot Through the Window

It was a short sound between a plink and a crack, a shot in the dark aimed at Pet, but serendipity intervened to wound its victim in the back. The searing pain sent David falling to the floor.

She screamed, "David, are you okay? What happened?"

He lifted his head up slightly from the floor and whispered a hoarse reply, "I'm shot! Get down!"

"David!" She frantically got down on all fours and crawled toward him. She was scared. Her voice was hesitant. "David, why? I don't understand."

"Someone wants you dead! They're not kidding around this time."

As she crawled to him, Pet reached for his shoulders. He let out a sudden groan, "Ow, careful."

"David! What can I do?"

"Find my phone in the right pocket, then get a towel before I black out."

Her whole body shivered, but it wasn't from the cold. Fear made her wonder if the shooter would strike again. On her hands and knees, she crept to the bed. Her movements were awkward, and she fumbled with the coat, trying to find the phone in the dark. Her actions were clumsy. After some anxious moments, she found the phone and jerked it out of her pocket. She almost dropped it, fumbling for it. The awkward search annoyed her because she couldn't do anything right the first time.

After handing him the phone, Pet was able to see better and crawled again to the bathroom for a towel. She helped David onto his right side and gently placed the towel over his shoulder. He leaned against her thigh, clutching the phone in his right hand. "Pet, I'm getting weak. Call the number for me. Here, take it."

"Okay, ready. What's the number?"

"777"

Every move sent a blinding pain through his chest. David could feel the blood oozing from his wound. It was hard to stay alert long enough to make the call and wait for Clancy to answer the station hot line.

"Hello, Clancy. This is Officer Jones. Get an ambulance to the Rutherford Manor ASAP. Call it in as a shooting, officer down."

"Who is shot?"

"I am."

"Son of a bitch, Jones. Hang in there. I'll tell Iverson, too."

"Yeah."

Then David put the phone beside Pet and rested his head on her knee.

Pet quickly cradled his head gently in her hands and began screaming at the top of her lungs. "Help! Mae Delight, help!"

David's body went limp. She began to cry, pleading to God, "Oh, God, don't let him die!" She yelled again with all the strength she had. "Mae Delight, help! Come up here, now!"

She didn't know whether to leave and get Mae Delight or keep screaming. Why wasn't she coming? She must act quickly. She yelled one last time.

Just as she was about to get up, the disgruntled maid burst into the room, flicking on the light.

"Lord God Jehovah, what on earth are you screaming about, Child?"

Pet screamed, motioning for her to get down. "Mae Delight, we have to save him. He's shot! Turn off this light and then turn on the hall light until we know it's safe in here."

Mae Delight crouched down, and Pet walked over to them.

She thought for a minute and then started giving orders in rapid succession.

"We'll have to take a chance and get him into bed. Get under his right arm. I'll take his left side, and we'll get him on the bed as gently as we can."

In the dim light, Mae Delight stooped down and got under his left arm. With one arm around his waist, she grabbed him by the belt and had him on the bed in two seconds. She tore away the pillow and lay David face down on the bed.

"He's lost a lot of blood. Get me another towel. Did you call an ambulance? Turn that light on. I can't see nothin'. If the sniper was gonna shoot, he'd have done it by now."

Pet quickly turned on the bedroom light.

"Yes. He called it in."

"How long ago?"

"Um, right before I started yelling for you. Oh, Mae Delight. Why didn't you come? I was afraid you didn't hear me. Panic was setting in real fast." While they talked, Mae Delight covered David with blankets, fearing he would go into shock.

"Of course, I heard you. That blood-curdling scream came all the way down to the kitchen. You sounded like a dyin' screech owl! Now go downstairs and open the front door so those men don't have to pound on it. But first, you'd better put on a shirt. You don't need to be showin' everyone what you got. Ida liked to know how he got up here!"

Pet looked down at herself, stunned at the sight. Her partially opened bathrobe was stained with David's blood.

"Oh, my good Lord. Yes, I'll change my clothes."

"Now don't fuss, girl. Just put something on. The sooner they can come upstairs, the sooner they will get him to the hospital. I will see to him. Don't worry."

Pet did as she was told. She put on a Steelers sweatshirt, ran downstairs, and opened the front door. Waiting there, she felt helpless and inadequate.

She cursed whoever did this, hoping he would skid off the

icy road and die a horrible death. She also prayed that the ambulance would come soon.

Finally, she heard the siren in the distance, soft, then loud, and then blaring as vehicles drove up the driveway. She expected just one vehicle, but three SUVs drove up first, then an ambulance. Four officers jumped out of them and ran around both sides of the house. An officer standing beside his vehicle spoke into his radio, directing the men to circle around to the back and check out the wooded area. A moment later, a paramedic ran up to the front door.

"Good evening, ma'am. I'm Medical Commander Edwards. Where is the officer?"

Pet pointed upward, "At the top of the stairs, keep on going." She had a puzzled look on her face.

He read her mind. "Don't worry. The other paramedics will come as soon as the officers secure the area, Ma'am."

"Okay, understood."

Not two minutes later, other men with a stretcher came through the doorway.

Pet called out to them as they passed her by, "Top of the stairs and straight ahead." But her directions weren't really needed. Mae Delight was already ushering them into the room.

She was about to run up the stairs herself when she heard a familiar male voice.

"Mrs. Traffortelli, are you alright?"

She turned and saw Joshua Iverson coming toward her. She was stunned and surprised to see him.

"Captain Iverson, I didn't think you would be here on a night like this."

"No, neither did I, but when I found out David Jones was shot. I had to come. Can you tell me what happened?"

And so, it began, a line of questioning that was tedious and impossible for Pet to answer exactly. He asked her what time it happened. She didn't know. Who watches the clock when one is about to make love? She didn't say that, of course, and hemmed and hawed a bit and then gave an approximate time of six o'clock.

There was question after question: Who? What? Where? Joshua was polite and very professional. His questions seemed endless, though. She wanted to go. David might need her. Couldn't he see that? "Let's wrap it up," she said to herself.

Joshua's voice got a little more insistent. "And then what happened, Pet?"

"I was standing at the window with David, watching the snow. It was so beautiful. I wanted to see it in the darkness, and he then went across the room to the light switch." Despite her emotions, she decided to omit many passionate details.

Captain Iverson was about to ask another question when Pet saw the paramedics bring David out of the room. He was lying on the stretcher, all covered up except for his head. The paramedics rounded the corner to the stairs, picked up the stretcher, and slowly brought him down. She wanted to run up to him. Joshua saw it in her eyes and gently held her back until they got David to the door and stopped.

She bent down and gently touched his face. He was groggy but smiled. Her eyes welled up with tears when she saw how pale he was. Joshua gave Captain Edwards a nod so Pet could have a moment with David.

She looked into his eyes. "David, I love you." She kissed him gently on the lips.

An impatient paramedic interrupted their goodbye. "I'm sorry, ma'am, but we have to go."

Pet reluctantly stepped back.

David turned his head to look at her once more. "I know, Pet, I know."

The paramedics took hold of the stretcher and whisked David away into the ambulance. Pet walked closer to the open door. Teary-eyed, she watched the ambulance's blazing lights going down the driveway.

Once they were out of sight, Pet darted to the hall closet,

reached for her coat, and proceeded to pull it over her shoulders. Joshua stepped toward her. "Pet, we haven't finished the questioning."

By this time, she was out of patience. Nobody was going to stop her from getting to the hospital. "Look, Joshua, no one is going to tell me that I must stay here while the man I love is in critical condition and about to have surgery."

With a resigned smile on his face, he said, "Okay, Pet, we will let the questions go for now. You win this round. So, bundle up, and I will drive you to the hospital. You don't need to be out there alone tonight. The streets are treacherous."

Her expression calmed down immediately after Joshua said that. Just like old times, she thought Joshua was still on the sidelines looking after her like a big brother. She liked that.

She looked up at him. "Thanks, Joshua, but can we hurry, please!"

Joshua held the door for her and nodded in compliance.

Chapter 88

The Ill-Fated Escape

Still in a fog, Aloysius found himself standing in front of the bathroom mirror. He splashed water on his face. It was 5:30 pm when he looked out the window at the persistent storm. It was coming down hard. He thought to himself, this is going to be hell getting to the airport, but nothing was going to keep him from that flight. The alcohol from the weekend kept him drunk, and his arrogance kept him stupid, thinking he could make the forty miles to the airport on time.

An hour later, he was finally approaching the ramp to Route 376. His Escalade made its own path to the highway. Different levels of snow made it hard to maintain a steady speed through the drifts.

Finally, he came to a section of the expressway that had been plowed into a hard mix of sand and packed snow. He was almost euphoric cruising at 45 mph for the next five miles, but the good times did not last. A fierce wind blew against the windshield, making visibility almost impossible. Cursing the conditions, Al leaned forward as far as he could, pressing against the steering wheel, trying to see better. His actions made no improvement. Then a sudden dip in the road slammed his stomach against the wheel, bringing up an unpleasant reminder of the weekend booze.

The sudden jolt reminded him he was coming to the big hill that made a sharp turn into Pemberton's Valley a mile ahead. He felt the ascent and floored the gas pedal, giving the V8 engine the needed power to reach the crest. He joyously laughed, slamming his hand on the wheel, "I knew I could do it! Come on, baby, get me there!"

He opened the window and breathed in the cold air. That proved to be a bad idea. The air caught in his throat, and he started to cough, belching up the stew pot of alcohol and Cheetos still wrestling in his stomach. His eyes blurred, and for a few dangerous seconds, he couldn't see the road.

He was now on the steep descent. Without warning, the Escalade picked up speed, and the road turned into a treacherous sheet of ice, holding Al hostage behind the wheel. The tires were losing traction, spinning all over the road. In panic, he jerked the steering wheel in a hard right, over-correcting the direction of the spin. Suddenly, he found himself leaning over the console between the seats. By the time he got up and faced forward, disaster loomed ahead; a huge snowplow was only yards away.

* * *

Fierce storms never bothered Mike Yoderman. They excited him and tested his road savvy. He loved this challenge, driving the powerful snowplow down the highway. One day, he told Pet that he finally found his calling, "keeping roads safe for these here travelers."

During this night, Mother Nature got mean. The howling wind blew against his plow. Controlling the huge blade and steering the monstrous vehicle became a nightmare. Mike was starting to get tired. Driving under the pressure of these conditions kept him on edge. He constantly wiped the inside of the windshield with the back of his hand to keep it clear. He mumbled, "Never seen a storm this bad. No, sir, I gotta keep alert, and my eyes peeled on every inch of this road."

Out of habit, he looked at the side view mirrors, first left, then right. He was just about to grab one of Mae Delight's cookies when a black speck in his left mirror caught his eye. It was getting bigger by the second, coming up from behind, out of control, and heading right for him.

"Holy shit! He's gonna hit me!" Mike yelled.

Mike felt the ice underneath as he veered the plow to the right, giving the speeding vehicle a wide berth. The plow dug into a huge snowbank, spewing chunks of snow and ice into the air. He kept his wheels rolling steadily as this speeding car behind him barreled down Rte. 376. He looked at his side view mirror and caught a glimpse of a crazed man passing him, careening off to the left and back again, gaining speed with every jerky move.

A sudden realization broke out in a sweat on Mike. Disaster was on its way, and it was coming up in a matter of seconds. They were nearing the bridge over the vast expanse of Pemberton Valley.

Even on a good day, cars had to watch out for the narrow approach to the bridge. There were no signs to warn unsuspecting drivers of an uneven surface, low guardrails, or impending doom. The locals knew about this and automatically slowed down. The unsuspecting ones spilled their coffee mugs as tires met the uneven cement and bumpy blacktop. Also, there was a wide gap before approaching the narrow bridge. The rails were low and inadequate. Now, the drifts obscured them altogether, and Mike realized sadly that this should have been fixed long ago.

* * *

For the first time in his life, Aloysius Hyde had no control over a situation. The Escalade was in command now. Pumping the brakes was useless at this point. Weight and momentum were against him. He was still all over the road on a downward slide headed for a collision with a monstrous snowplow!

Al heard himself scream as he made a hard left, missing the snowplow's spreader by inches. The move got him away, but by accelerating, gravity pulled him into a deep rut in the ice. He then turned right, swerving sideways and somehow righted the Escalade to the middle of the road.

A brief elation came over him. "Ha, you thought you could lick me, didn't you. I got this now, baby!" He aimed the SUV as best he could down the center of the road, still going 50 mph.

For a second, he averted disaster until his tires hit the icy dip before the bridge. All four tires hit the ice and bounced up the mound of ice like a ramp. Evel Knievel, the wild stunt driver, would have been proud to see the Escalade sailing over the ice-covered guard rails. It hung in the air for a second and then made its dive, somersaulting down into the valley, into the dark, into the great abyss, and into eternity. A muffled crash was the only sound of finality for the life of Aloysius Hyde.

Chapter 89

David's Surgery

Tonight's blizzard held no fear for Joshua Iverson. His big SUV plowed through the streets with no trouble. He let Pet off at the main entrance in fifteen minutes. She got out of the vehicle without ceremony or a handshake and hailed the first orderly she saw.

She was pointed to the second-floor family waiting room that was all too familiar from this past summer. Pet took a deep breath and entered the room. When she saw the older couple sitting quietly in a corner, an immediate feeling of guilt washed over her. She was the reason his parents were here. Dare she tell them the whole story of passion gone horribly awry? She quickly dismissed the urge, moving hesitantly toward them.

"Mr. and Mrs. Jones?" Pet asked softly.

"Yes," Helen said, looking up at her.

"I'm Mrs. Traffortelli, David's friend. Have you spoken with a doctor or surgeon yet?"

"No, we were told an hour ago that someone would be in to give us some information, but no one has come yet," his father said rather curtly.

Pet bent forward.

Mrs. Jones looked at Pet and tried to smile reassuringly, "This waiting is very upsetting. Alex does not like being lied to."

Pet nodded in agreement. "It is hard for a family to wait in critical situations."

Then Mrs. Jones asked suddenly, "Are you a nurse, dear?"

"No, unfortunately. I've had a little experience waiting in hospitals, Mrs. Jones."

She had a kind face with a soft, refined voice. Instinctively, she held out her hand to Pet. "How nice to meet you. Please, dear, you can call me Helen. What may I call you?"

"My friends call me Pet, Helen. It is a nickname. David laughed at me the first time I told him that." Pet sat down beside Helen.

"I know, David talks about you all the time. He told me your Christian names and the reason for your nickname. I think they are beautiful."

The women smiled at each other as Pet thought to herself, "She's trying to console me when I should be the one putting her at ease. Would she be this nice if she knew how David was shot in the first place?"

Helen and Pet talked in whispers. Pet related to how she and David met. She also told her briefly about her inheritance while David's father sat in silence. By the end of Pet's story, they were friends.

At 2:00 a.m., a tall, dark-haired man entered the room in surgical scrubs and walked directly toward Mr. and Mrs. Jones. He wasted no time in talking to them.

Looking at Helen, he said in a heavy Russian accent, "I am Dr. Vas Dalezki. You are his mother, yes?"

Helen stood up, looking afraid. "Yes, I am his mother."

"Surgery is going to start very soon. I will operate on your son. The nurse will update you on his progress. It won't be an easy surgery. Please be patient."

Then Dr. Dalezki took Helen's hand, looked into her eyes reassuringly, and said, "Don't be afraid; it's okay."

He left the room as abruptly as he had appeared. All three of them looked at each other, wondering what would be next.

David's father stood watching the door for a few minutes. He whispered something to Helen. She, in turn, shrugged her shoulders.

Walking away, he said, "I'll be back."

Helen whispered to Pet, "He hates waiting. He feels he has to do something, so he walks."

After that brief bit of activity, the room went silent. Some twenty minutes later, Mr. Jones returned and sat with Helen. Pet felt a little out of place and picked an armchair to sit down and gather her thoughts.

The night dragged on. She decided to pray silently by saying some "Our Fathers" and "Hail Marys" punctuated by her pleas, "Please, Lord, let him live!" After half an hour, she stopped praying because she couldn't concentrate. She kept seeing David holding her in his arms one minute, then lying on the floor bleeding the next.

She looked at her watch and got up. It was 4 am. Nervous boredom moved her to the windows and the storm that was still howling outside. She played with the metal chain that opened and closed the vertical blinds, feeling very isolated. She wondered, had the nurse forgotten about us? Why hasn't she called?

She looked around the room. It wasn't a very comfortable place to wait. The walls were painted a pale gray. The furniture was adequate, but there was nothing to distract, no television or even a magazine rack. There was a simple wooden table with a phone on it. On it was a sign encased in plastic stating: HOSPITAL USE ONLY. PERSONAL CALLS NOT PERMITTED. She said to herself, "Ring, damn it, ring!"

Pet stood there for quite a while, thinking of Harry Potter, as she often did when she was scared. A mental conversation ensued. "How am I going to tell David's parents I am responsible for this awful happening, Harry? Should I tell them now? Would they understand why David was in my bedroom?"

In her head, she could see his kind face, with those laughing eyes, and hear him talking to her softly. He would be whispering something like, "You will know what to tell them. Don't fall apart on me now, dear lady. You must be strong. Think of David. How are you going to help him get better, crying like that? Get a game plan going. You have your future ahead of you, the company, his job, your wedding, 'cause you know he's gonna ask you, Pet."

She felt a tear stream down her cheek as she looked out to the storm, "You're right, Harry, I've got to take charge of myself." She looked at her watch again. It was 6 am. Suddenly, behind her, she could hear footsteps entering the room.

Dr. Vas Dalezki walked with a deliberate stride, heading toward the older couple still seated on the couch. He was tall with dark, wavy hair. He looked at them with confident blue eyes. He took off his surgical mask and spoke softly.

Helen stood up. "I am Dr. Vas Dalezki, remember?" Then he looked at Mr. Jones."Your father, yes?"

They nodded, "Yes."

"He is seriously injured. How did the bullet get inside him?"

They looked at each other, stunned. "We're not sure, Doctor."

Pet practically ran to their side and blurted out, "He was shot in my bedroom through the window. It was an accident! I don't know who did it!" She immediately put her hands up to her mouth, "Oh my God, that sounds so horrible!"

Helen started to cry. Dr. Dalezki looked at her. "The bullet is out, but there is an issue with his lungs. Does he cough much?"

Mr. Jones stepped closer and asked solemnly, "What is it, Doctor? Does he have cancer?"

"We found a tumor in the lungs, which we removed and sent to the lab for testing. We found a spot on the CAT scan, which we did before surgery."

He bowed slightly to Helen. "Sorry, it has taken so long, but we did quite a bit of repair work to save his life. He is stable now. Do not worry."

With those words, he started to leave the room. Pet took a step toward him. "Um, Dr. Dalezki, can you give us some more information on his condition? We know so little, and..."

Dr. Dalezki looked a little irritated but spoke only to Helen. "There will be more time later to discuss details. The nurse will answer your questions. Go home and sleep. I will make rounds in the morning."

After the doctor nodded to Helen, he turned and left the room. A nurse in OR scrubs met him at the waiting room door. She wrote down notes as he spoke to her. After a few minutes, she came to them, carrying a white plastic bag with the hospital's logo.

Helen was on the verge of a teary breakdown. The experienced nurse guided her to a couch.

"Now, now, Mrs. Jones. Don't cry. Your son is fine."

"I have to see my boy. Please, nurse, he is my only child."

Chapter 90

Waiting

Frances Dannelli let Helen compose herself before she started talking. She held Helen's hand the whole time.

"I am Frances Dannelli, OR Supervisor. You can ask me anything. But first, let me tell you about David. Doctor Dalezki told you the bullet was taken out of your son's lung. It was a tricky surgery because of where the bullet was lodged. The bullet entered through the left back and into the left lung. As the Doctor operated to remove the bullet, he found a tumor close to the pericardial sac of the heart. It was quite large. Dr. Daleski had to be careful not to destroy the lung tissue. It was a very delicate surgery. Now, with all that said, David will be in the intensive care unit on the third floor. We are on the second floor now. When he gets out of recovery, I will come and get you if you still want to wait and see him in his room."

His parents said yes immediately. Pet nodded hopefully.

"Now, don't be upset when you see him because he will have tubes hooked up to him. Is there anything you want to say or ask me now?"

At first, Mr. Jones' tone of voice was sarcastic. "I hope his surgical skills are better than his English. He was very abrupt."

"Alex! Please! Please don't take offense, Nurse Dannelli. He's just nervous. Will this surgery affect his heart?" asked Helen.

"Let me just say, David was lucky the tumor was found now, and that Doctor Dalezki is the surgeon. He is one of the top surgeons in the county. He can be abrupt at times because his main concern is his patient. The tumor looked benign, but he sent a section of it to the lab. Then Dr. Daleski removed the tumor so David would not have complications as he got older."

Helen and Pet looked at each other and said "Oh my" at the same time. Mr. Jones looked impatient, saying, "How long will he be in recovery?"

Nurse Dannelli said, "That's not an easy answer. It will depend on David. Some patients wake up quickly, and some take a longer time."

Mr. Jones said sarcastically, "My boy doesn't wake up for anyone. He can make the dead look lively."

Helen turned to Mr. Jones. "Alex, please! Don't be insulting!"

Frances smiled at the couple. "I know this isn't where you want to spend the Christmas holidays, Mr. and Mrs. Jones, and it is a stressful time for all of you. I know you will get through this night when you see your son and talk with him. I wish we could wave a magic wand and make him better, but please be patient. I assure you. He will be fine."

The supervisor reached for a white plastic bag. "These are your son's personal belongings. Please look inside to make sure these are his clothes. I have a paper for you to sign stating that these are his belongings."

Mr. Jones quickly reached for the bag and looked inside. "Yes, this is David's uniform jacket. His name is on it. I'll sign the paper."

With that duty completed, Nurse Dennalli gave Helen a big hug and walked to the door. Before she disappeared, she said, "Now don't worry. I will be back."

Pet smiled at the nurse, thinking how nice she was to David's parents. But then she felt very awkward in their presence, watching them pick out each piece of blood-stained clothing. The urge to leave was strong, but seeing his bloody shirt drew her to the macabre events of last night. Helen whimpered when she saw it, too.

Pet became so anxious that her stomach cramped and churned until she finally excused herself and headed to the restroom. Once inside, she leaned against a sink. The emotions of fear, guilt, and uncertainty overcame her. Before she knew it, she was sobbing uncontrollably. She did not hear footsteps or the door open, but she did hear Joshua Iverson's deep voice.

"Pet, are you okay? What's the matter? Are you sick?"

"Huh? Joshua? How did you get here? I'm scared to death about David. His parents are so worried and..."

Compassionately, he said, "Come here." He extended his arms.

Pet went to him sobbing. Joshua shook his head and handed her a handkerchief. She took it immediately and blew her nose.

"Why are you crying? The worst is over. David is strong. He is going to recover, Pet. Have faith in these doctors. Don't worry about his parents. They understood what happened."

"I'm not crying about that, Joshua. How am I going to tell his parents I am the person who got him here in the first place? It's all my fault. What if David dies? It's just too horrible to think about."

With that last word, she continued to sob on Joshua's shoulder. He slowly ushered her out of the restroom and into the hallway.

"They understood everything; don't worry."

She looked up, "What do you mean? Are you talking behind my back? Do you know all the details? What did you tell them?"

"Now, don't get paranoid, Pet. I told them the bullet was intended for you, and you have had threats on your life. David was patrolling the area for a prowler and came upstairs when you did not answer your phone. He was in the wrong place at the wrong time." He hesitated for a second. "Well, that is the condensed version anyway."

"Did they believe you?"

"Yes, Helen became quite upset and wanted to come and get you, but I said I wanted to talk with you first on certain matters."

"Oh, I should go to her." She turned away from him.

Joshua turned also, "But, Pet, I have to tell..."

Without giving Joshua a chance to say another word, Pet left him and went to Helen. They embraced. "Oh, my dear, you have been through so much. Detective Iverson said anything could have happened tonight. Wasn't David brave? He said the department will surely apprehend the man who shot my boy."

Mr. Jones looked at Joshua skeptically. "So, you think you've caught the man who shot my son? Who is he? I will press charges. David is too critical to do that now."

"In due time, Mr. Jones. I will keep you informed on the progress of this case. Our focus is on getting David better. He will need your support and understanding."

Mr. Jones turned away, his expression dissatisfied, mumbling to himself. Joshua thought he heard the older gentleman say, "Figured you'd say that."

Helen and Pet walked to a couch, whispering to each other. Joshua stood in the doorway when his cell phone rang. "Iverson. Yeah. I will meet you at the morgue."

Pet looked up and gave him a quizzical look, but Joshua didn't attempt to come over to the couch. He looked at his watch and then wrote a note on a small pad.

Finally, at 6:50 a.m. Nurse Dennalli appeared in the doorway.

"Mr. and Mrs. Jones, I can take you to his room now."

They stood up and walked immediately to her. She looked at Pet, "Is she coming, too?"

Pet asked Helen, "Please, may I see him?"

"Of course, dear, you're almost family."

Pet almost started crying again. They walked behind Nurse Dennalli to the elevator. The whole time, Helen held a little white box tightly in her hand.

Chapter 91

Grizzly Facts

No one talked in the elevator. When the door opened, David's parents and Pet walked quickly to the outer door of the CCU unit. Joshua caught up to Pet, grabbing her arm. "Pet, can I see you for a minute? I have to get back to the station immediately."

Pet wrenched from his grip. "What could be more important than David's life? What is the big rush?"

"I'm sorry, Pet. I know you want to see David, but this is important. It concerns Anthony Prattmore. Besides, don't you think his parents should have this moment? Anthony was found dead last night."

Instantly, all the color drained from her face. "Oh my God! Really? Are you sure?"

"Pet, please, no sarcasm. Do you know where his mother lives? Does he have brothers or sisters?"

Pet's attitude changed slightly as she absorbed the fateful news. "No, I don't, but why should I care about him or his mother? He turned out to be a two-timer and a jerk."

"Do you know if his mother lives in Whalen County?"

"Joshua, what kind of questioning is this? I never met the woman, so I don't know much about her, except that she is really old and possibly living in a swanky nursing home, maybe in Pittsburgh. Why?"

"The County Coroner always has to notify the next of kin when a body is brought to the morgue."

Pet looked straight into Joshua's eyes and became more serious. "I can't help you, Joshua. Sorry. Did he have a heart attack?"

"No, something a bit more grizzly, but we'll know more after the autopsy tomorrow, or perhaps later today." Joshua stifled a yawn. "We all have been up way too long. As I said, I must get back to the station, but I suggest you get some sleep soon. I may need you down at the morgue."

"Morgue? Why?"

"If we can't contact his mother, we try to find the nearest relative or close friend."

Pet's eyes opened wide. "Oh no, I'm not going down there. No, absolutely not! I don't want any part of his death." The more she talked, the more agitated she became. "Joshua, don't make me do this. I can't see him dead."

Joshua came closer to her, whispering, "Don't be afraid. We will make every effort to contact his mother. We probably won't need you, but Homicide wants to wrap this up before the newspapers get wind of this situation. I wanted to brief you, just in case, you know, you get a call. It is just police business, Pet."

Pet needed a minute. Turning from him, she walked slowly down the hall. She didn't know what to do. The idea of being in a morgue terrified the hell out of her.

"Pet, aren't you going to see David?"

She stopped and turned to Joshua. Her voice was flat and soft. "Yes, yes, I am." Then she asked, "Do you know where Anthony died?"

"Yes, at the Briar Town Furniture Warehouse off 376. Do you know where it is?"

His words startled her. "Uh, yes, I do."

A minute later. Helen burst through the doors with a big smile on her face. "Oh, honey, he's asking for you." Helen waved her on excitedly.

Chapter 92

The Proposal

He watched her through slitted eyelids. Groggy and barely coherent, David smiled. Going to his side, Pet choked back a cry. Nurse Dannelli was right. His body was invaded by tubes and electrical wires. Both arms had IVs in them. Pet tenderly caressed his cheek.

"David, I was so worried, I had to see…"

David's voice was just above a whisper. "I know, Pet. You don't have to talk. Just seeing you is good. Mom told me all about you. She likes you."

"And I like her, too. Oh, David, you are so pale. Are you in pain?"

Alex mumbled under his breath, "Of course he's in pain. They just took a hunk of lung out of him."

Helen shot Alex a look of annoyance. "For the last time, Alex, please, shh!" She continued in a soft whisper, "I think you have picked out a very lovely girl, David. We have been talking like old friends waiting for you to come out of surgery. Your dad likes her, too."

David looked over to his father. "Dad, are my clothes here? I need something in my jacket."

David barely got the last word out when the unit nurse came into the room. "I'm sorry, folks, I must ask you to leave. My patient must get some rest."

David put up his right index finger. "Please, nurse. I need one minute to ask the girl I love a question."

Reluctantly, she said, "Okay, one minute," and stood in the doorway.

Alex searched in the bag for his uniform jacket. "What do you need in the jacket, David?"

"Give it here, Dad."

"No, you're too weak to hold it. Just tell me what it is."

David lifted his head off the pillow. In short breaths, he said, "A little white box."

Alex fumbled through the heavy black jacket. "It's not here. You must have lost it."

"No, it has to be there! Look for it." His voice was strained and panicky.

Helen came closer to the bed and held out the box. She then gently put it in his hand.

"Is this what you are looking for, David? I found it loose in the bag. I thought it just might be important, so I held on to it for safekeeping."

"You sure know how to be helpful, Helen. The kid was panicked," Alex chided.

David motioned for Pet to lean closer to him and whispered to her, "Please, open the box and take out what's inside."

Pet's hand was shaking as she opened the box. She gasped and immediately put the ring on her finger.

"Oh, my God. It is the most beautiful ring I've ever seen, David."

"Will you wear it forever as my wife, Pet? I love you and want you to be with me for the rest of my life. I'd like us to get married very soon. Is that okay with you?"

"Oh, David, yes. We can get married whenever you want. I will wear this ring forever. I love you very much. I will never leave your side."

Pet started to cry. Helen started to cry. Alex shook his head, smiling down at his son. "They always cry. Why do they always have to cry?"

Lying back down, David closed his eyes. His voice was weak. "Dunno, Dad. They just do."

The nurse came over, insisting that they all leave the room. Pet kissed David on the cheek and gently squeezed his arm. "I love you. I will be back later." But David was already fast asleep.

Walking out, Helen put her arm around Pet's waist. "Happy, dear?"

"Yes, Helen, very."

Chapter 93

Airport Gate 24

Judy walked quickly through the Air Side terminal. Noting that the flight was on time from the arrival/departure board, she denied herself that Starbucks latte and kept heading toward Gate 24.

When James spied her in the distance, a smile crossed his lips. "Well, I'll be damned. She didn't chicken out."

"Hi. Have they announced a boarding time yet?" she asked nervously.

"No, you're fine, relax. We still have a few minutes. Let's sit down." James ushered her to a nearby row of seats.

"Did you get it?"

"Yes."

"Take off your gloves and let me see it."

Her hands shook as she took off the fine black leather gloves, exposing the ring on her right fourth finger.

"Does Pet know it is gone?"

"Knowing her, I don't think so. I went over to visit on the 23rd. We were in the kitchen having a good old time making sugar cookies. I noticed she left the ring on the counter, so I had to create a diversion by tipping a tray full of cookies onto the floor. Then, with a quick grab, I put it in my pocket. After that, I gave her some excuse to meet Bunny at Zookies, and practically ran out the door."

"You are a devious bitch, aren't you? I like a girl who can think quickly. I wish I had met you sooner. We coulda pulled a lot of shit like that and made some real money."

"Don't make me feel cheap. I feel terrible if I think about it too long. Pet has been a good friend, too trusting, maybe. Now she will think the ring is lost, not that I stole it. I hope Mr. Hyde appreciates what I've done."

"Oh, believe me, he will. I appreciate it, too." With a cynical smile, James whispered in her ear, "I'll show you exactly how much when we get to Nassau, baby."

She winced when he said baby.

James smiled. "I like the color of your hair. You matched it perfectly to my cousin Sonya's. Did you have any problem going through customs?"

"No, the inspector didn't flinch. I was surprised. I could almost be her clone, but if I'm using her passport, won't she miss it?"

"No. She's dead."

"Good God, what kind of creep are you? You did not tell me I was impersonating a dead person! Are you using your own passport?"

"No, it's my cousin Ivan's passport, and you are his wife. Unfortunately, they are both dead. That is all I am going to tell you. Don't get crazy on me, and don't think about what I just told you. I will tell you more later. The only thing you must think about is that in a little over 6 hours, you will be out of this hellhole and flying into the sunny beaches of Nassau. Just keep calm."

James didn't have time to explain all the details of his elaborate plan for this getaway. His focus was on wondering where the hell Aloysius was. The son of a bitch promised to be here. James wanted to see the satisfied expression on Aloysius' face, cementing their criminal brotherhood and knowing they had pulled off the perfect crime.

Five minutes later, the JetBlue gate attendant opened the door and announced boarding instructions. James looked around one more time for his friend. He was not going to wait or look back. It was Al's loss.

Chapter 94

A Sobering Meeting

There was no conversation between Joshua and Pet on the way back to the manor house. Pet sat, looking out the window, holding back tears from emotional and physical exhaustion. She thought life was not fair. The whole night made no sense except for the exquisite engagement ring on her finger. How could she be so happy floating on clouds of joy one minute and the next minute insecure, fearing if David would completely recover from this delicate surgery?

As the SUV pulled up the driveway, Joshua promised to keep in touch with her. She smiled, thanking him with a kiss on the cheek.

Mae Delight scaled down her voice and didn't give her the usual orders. She knew Pet would ignore them anyway. She followed her up the stairs, picking up discarded clothing along the way, and helped her get into bed.

"I'm so tired, Mae Delight, too tired to worry about David and too tired to talk at all. I can't believe it will be Christmas tomorrow." She lay her head on the pillow and fell asleep immediately.

At one p.m., the phone rang. Mae Delight rolled her eyes, answering in a gruff voice, "Hello."

"Good afternoon. Is Mrs. Traffortelli there? I hate to disturb the household on Christmas Eve, but I must talk with her. It concerns the company."

"Yes, sir. Who is calling, please?"

"Mr. Marshall Hoffmann, Acting Assistant CEO for Briar Town Furniture Co."

"She is still in bed. It was a long night, but I'll see if I can wake her."

"I understand. We've all had a very long night here, too."

She put down the phone and plodded upstairs, grumbling as to why people just didn't leave the poor girl alone.

"Pet, wake up. You're wanted on the phone. It sounds important. A Mr. Hoffmann wants to speak to you."

"Huh? Phone? What? Go away."

"Honey, you have to wake up. I know you're tired, but this man ain't gonna take no for an answer."

"Hoffmann? Marshall?"

"Yes, I said that."

"Good God, what now?"

His name brought her to a semi-coherent state as she put the phone to her ear. "Yes, Marshall, is anything wrong?"

"Yes, Pet, a lot has happened to the company and its administration within the last twenty-four hours. I think you'd better come down to the office. I am here now. I will have our security guard come and get you since the roads are still hazardous. I would feel better about your safety if Emmerson were to drive his truck. Could you be ready in half an hour?"

"Sure," she said slowly. "I will be ready."

"Now what was that all about? Are you goin' out again? Are you goin' to be here for Christmas Eve? I already put the turkey in the oven. Christmas ain't no time to be traipsing around town. You have people comin',' don'tcha?"

"Mae Delight, please! I don't know what's happening! I must get ready. The security guard is coming to take me back to Marshall Hoffmann's office. I'm in charge now. I must go."

Mae Delight continued her mumbling while getting Pet's boots and heavy coat out of the downstairs closet.

An hour later, Pet was holding a steaming cup of coffee, watching Marshall Hoffman and Harold Buford furiously writing notes on the legal pads before them.

Marshall looked up. "Pet, thank you for coming here. The events of the last 24 hours have been bizarre to say the least. A short while ago, I was called by Trouper John Milestone, who said they had found Aloysius Hyde's vehicle at the bottom of Pemburton's Valley, with him in it. The vehicle evidently nose-dived off a bridge in that sector of Brighton Township. A PennDOT snowplow driver named Mike Yoderman saw the whole event. There was nothing he could do to prevent the accident."

"Oh, my God, Uncle Mike, how horrible! I didn't like Aloysius, but I didn't want him dead. Why was he out in such a storm?"

"Well, we are trying to piece together this event and two other deaths that took place in the same area. Charles Franklin and Anthony Prattmore were found dead behind our warehouse by a part-time watchman."

"Yes, I know about Anthony, but Detective Iverson didn't tell me about Mr. Franklin. How did he die? How did Anthony die? I'd like to know. And now David was shot, too. Three deaths in less than 24 hours? Do you think they are connected?"

Marshall looked at Harold, who nodded back to Marshall, drumming his pencil on the pad. "Go ahead, she might as well know all the details. Start at the beginning of November," Harold said, looking a little sheepish, knowing his name is going to come up, too.

Marshall took a sip of his coffee and cleared his throat. "Pet, you do remember the last meeting when James Wingate was arrested, right?"

"Yes, I do quite vividly."

"Well, from that time on, we've discovered that more money in the retirement fund was siphoned off by Aloysius and James. Mr. Buford informed us that during that time, Aloysius paid Charles Franklin to kill you. We have just learned that James Wingate has skipped town after his wife posted bail for him.

"Also, Manny caught an assistant dock manager selling armoires filled with bundles of marijuana for the last six months. Anthony Prattmore was involved in buying the merchandise also."

Pet had a panicky look on her face. "Marshall, this is terrible! How could two men, no three, do such a terrible thing to our company?" She hesitated for a second, then looked at Harold Buford. "Pardon me if I seem a little judgmental. I really don't know you that well, but you were in on it, too, right? Is anyone else in this devious scheme? This isn't going to leak out to the media, will it? We are responsible for that retirement money. Drugs, good God. How low can a person go?"

Marshal intervened immediately, saying, "One panic at a time, Pet. Don't worry. We have a detective tailing Wingate. He won't get far. We got a tip from one of our bank managers that Aloysius and James initiated a line of credit from yet another offshore bank a few months ago. Their plan would have worked nicely if they had not been so greedy. Don't worry about Harold. He is one of the good guys now."

Pet raised her left eyebrow. "Good guys now? What is going on, Marshall?"

"It is a long story, Pet. Harold was party to the plan but came to his senses when your permanent demise was formed. Al was the main culprit. He wanted you gone in the worst way, believe me."

Marshall's short affirmation for Harold was a disappointment. She expected more of an explanation. Shrugging her shoulders, she said, "Okay, now what?"

"We will convene an executive meeting to decide on all the changes to be made. Once that is done, the shareholders will receive a letter detailing the new board."

As soon as Marshall finished speaking, Harold turned his back to Pet and began whispering to Marshall. Pet sipped her coffee. Her whole body felt tired, and her mind slipped into a sleep-deprived fog. Suddenly, she heard her cell phone ringing.

She fumbled frantically until she had it in her hand, "Hello? Yes, OH MY GOD! I will. I'm on my way!"

The startled men spoke at the same time. "What's wrong, Pet?"

"I have to leave. David took a turn for the worse. I'll get Emerson to drive me to the hospital."

"Then go!" Marshall said quickly.

Pet ran down the corridor shouting orders for Emmerson to come with her. Her footsteps pounded on the marble floor. Shrill calls for Emmerson's help echoed in the empty lobby. With each step, a desperate prayer, "David, don't leave me."

Chapter 95

Déjá vu

Pet met Helen in the hallway. She was in a heightened state of panic. "I can't explain it. We were talking with David, and the nurses asked us to go into the waiting room for a few minutes while they checked the drainage tubes. Alex got me a coffee while we waited. A few minutes later, the nurse said, "Please stay here. David is spitting up blood, and the doctor had to be called." Nurse Danelli said, "Don't worry. It can happen sometimes."

Pet's voice wavered, "Spitting up blood? Don't worry! Good God, this can't be an everyday occurrence. When can we see him? Has anyone come out to you?"

Helen held Pet's hand. "No, dear, not yet."

Pet nodded and became silent. She stared at the CCU door. She watched Alex mumbling to himself. He looked in her direction for a split second with an evil scowl on his face. His expression was angry enough to kill someone, and she figured his mumbles didn't sound like prayers.

An agonizing wait turned into forty-five minutes. Finally, Alex exploded and charged through the CCU doors. "I don't care what anybody says. I want to know what is going on with my son!" Two seconds later, Mrs. Dannelli walked him out into the hallway where the two women stood.

"I am so sorry this happened. David's condition is grave but not hopeless. I'm not going to give you a lot of medical terminology, but the simplest way for me to tell you is that his blood is very thin, and he began bleeding internally. This situation can happen sometimes. We have given him medication to reverse the bleeding. He is in stable condition now, Mr. and Mrs. Jones, believe me."

"He better not die because of a situation, nurse, or I will sue this hospital for every penny it has!"

No one spoke after Alex's tirade. They stood motionless like park statues in front of the CCU doors, silent and waiting. A few minutes went by. Then Pet's cell phone jerked them into reality once more.

She looked at the caller ID. "Hi. Mom. What's wrong? I can hear you breathing funny. What's the matter?"

"Pet, me darlin'. You have to come home. Your father is bad off in the hospital. He didn't want to tell ye when we were there this summer that the leukemia came back and took hold of him real fierce. Poor man, he's so weak now." Her voice was barely a whisper, "Please come right now, Pet, and bring yer Uncle Mike too. He will take care of you. Just ask. He will bring you straight away."

"Okay, Mom, but what hospital is he in?"

"Oh, Pet, he is in the big one, you know, by the river. I'll be seein'..."

She was about to ask another question, but Fiona's voice trailed off, and she apparently hung up the phone.

Pet was visibly shaken. To comfort her, Helen put her arm around Pet's waist. "I couldn't help but hear your mother's voice. She sounded desperate. You must go home, dear. I would normally ask a lot of questions about your father's condition, but you have no time for conversation. Go. Go now."

In a strained voice with tears welling up in her eyes, she answered, "How can I leave David the way he is? He lives minute by minute! Our future together is dangerously uncertain. What if he dies? I would never forgive myself for not being here."

Helen took Pet's hands in hers. "This is where your inner faith comes into being, dear. If you believe there is a God who is watching over us, then David will survive this crisis. Your parents need you right now. No one will think less of you. I will tell David what happened. He will understand."

A grateful tear trickled down her cheek. Helen was right.

She had to have faith that David would survive. With a quick hug to Alex and Helen, Pet walked quickly down the hall to the elevators.

Chapter 96

Chaos

Judy looked out the window from high above. She saw a halo of blue and white surrounding the white sandy beaches of this tropical island. Then she heard the captain say, "Welcome, ladies and gentlemen, to Lynden Pindling International Airport." A few minutes later, she felt that unmistakable thump of the jet's wheels touch down on the runway.

For a moment, conflicting emotions engulfed her. She was excited to be in the warmth of Nassau with all its luxury and beauty. She even fantasized about being pampered by handsome cabana boys with margaritas in their hands, ready to serve her, and the remote possibility of hot romantic nights titillated her female appetite. On the other hand, she began to feel ill at ease from the way James barked orders but never answered her direct questions. He could have given her some reasons and a purpose for the trip. Was it really a vacation? Are his motives on the up and up, and would he be honest about Mr. Hyde's part in this adventure? After all, she ended a friendship because of his effective persuasion and tantalizing offer of money.

Nervously, she twisted the tourmaline ring. It felt tight, and twisting seemed to help. She could never figure out why her limbs swelled on a flight. It weighed heavily there, shining ominously, a murky collaboration of her and Pet's once cemented friendship. A bittersweet memory came to her the day they found the ring. The excitement of finding it and now the deceit of wearing it depressed her. Also, the irony of having to give it away to Aloysius Hyde intensified her guilt.

James watched her study the ring, letting out a soft whistle.

"That is some ring! It does look beautiful on your finger. No wonder Al wanted it! Anyway, are you ready to experience the island life of Nassau, Judy? We have some good times ahead of us. I know you will enjoy the island life."

Then he changed the subject abruptly. "Listen, I've been thinking. Do exactly what I tell you. When we get off the plane, don't dilly-dally. You will have to go through Customs. The overhead signs are easy to follow. Don't be nervous or bring unnecessary attention to yourself when the Customs Officer asks you your reason for this trip. You are here for pleasure, that is all. Now, once you get past Customs, go to the exit. Look for the shuttle to Margaritaville Beach Resort. I will follow you ten minutes later, taking another shuttle."

Judy smiled at the hotel's name. She thought a minute, then raised her eyebrow quizzically. "Why the cloak and dagger act? You're spouting off a James Bond scenario. Have you got a Rembrandt under your coat, some company funds tucked in your jacket pocket? Is Mr. Hyde on vacation, too, or will he stick around just long enough to get the ring? Somehow, I can't picture him on the beach taking in the sun. We are just tourists, right?"

James was impatient with her. "Judy, don't ask questions that don't concern you. Just do what I tell you to do."

She frowned in irritation, but obeyed his request with, "Okay, you're the mastermind of this little jaunt."

After the plane arrived at the gate, Judy tried to ignore James' attitude and focused on retrieving her baggage from the overhead compartment. The flight was packed, and the din from the passengers surrounding her was chaotic. Everyone was in a rush to get off the plane. Soon she acted in the same panic mode, feeling very ill at ease. All the while, she thought about what kind of situation she gotten herself into.

Judy followed the signs, pulling an old carry-on suitcase with rusty squeaky wheels. It was awkward navigating through the crowds. She was tugging at it, constantly trying to walk faster, but the wheels kept holding her back. People were coming at her from all directions, and dodging them wasn't easy. Many people were casually dressed in brightly colored shirts and Bermuda shorts. They greeted each other as her fellow passengers headed toward Customs. She felt out of place in her heavy coat, wishing she were casually dressed like these carefree islanders.

Once she got to Customs, she saw the agents behind a small window. People pushed and shoved to get in line in the small area. The noise level rose so high that the agents had to yell for the next person to step up to the window. She looked for James. At first, she didn't see him at all and started to panic, but shortly she spotted him walking slowly toward Customs. She watched him take his time, then something caught her eye. Four men seemed to be following James several paces behind. They stuck out in the crowd because they were dressed in business suits.

Suddenly, just as she was about to take another step forward, a couple holding two children moved up to the line. Both children were crying and thrashing about. The young parents were juggling backpacks, shoulder bags, and two toddlers. The woman looked anxious as she fired back in rapid Spanish to a man yelling back at her while the two toddlers screamed and pulled at their parents. The scene was quite intense. Judy was inadvertently shoved, and she stepped back, giving them some space. Out of the corner of her eye, she noticed the men ease closer to the crowd.

After waiting several minutes, Judy approached the Customs Agent. She answered the perfunctory questions. He seemed to study her face, looking up several times as he inspected her passport. She became unsure of herself and started to fidget. Her breathing became slightly irregular as she shifted her weight from one foot to the other. She took off her coat and transferred it from one arm to the other. Becoming more uncomfortable, a nervous cough sputtered from her throat. Paranoia set in. She wondered why this was taking so long. Then Judy heard herself saying "Yes, sir, no sir" to the COVID-19 questions. She thought the agent was purposely drawing out the procedure. Judy flexed her right hand in anticipation of attaining the passport.

With feigned politeness, the agent said, "Have a nice day. Welcome to our island." She muttered under her breath, "Finally," and quickly grabbed the passport. She walked to the overhead signs pointing to the exit and shuttle buses.

She said to herself, "Good, almost there. Margaritaville, here I come!" By this time, fatigue was setting in. She saw a travel kiosk, walked a few more feet, and leaned against it. She bent down and rubbed her right foot. Tugging the suitcase, she was glad she just brought her carry-on.

Before heading to the exit, Judy looked over her shoulder. The ensuing scene startled her. The men in suits closed in on James as he left the Customs window. She watched as their voices got louder and angrier. She could see the panic in James' face. His body movements showed agitation, his eyes darting back and forth. He saw her standing at the kiosk. Their eyes locked on each other. Suddenly, James bolted from the men. His actions were so abrupt that they caught the men off guard. He darted in and out of the crowd, and running past Judy, he yelled, "Run! Get out of here!" His escape became more desperate. He pushed people out of his way as the "suits" tore after him.

Fearing for her life and capture, Judy looked for an escape route. She was afraid to head for the exit, so she calculated they would go there first and looked for a public restroom to hide in. Spotting one, she grabbed her luggage and sprinted to it as fast as she could. The crowds intensified, filling the terminal with clumps of men, women, children, and people in wheelchairs, slowing her down immensely.

She yelled at them, "Please get out of my way! S'cuse me, pardon me."

Finally, she saw the door of the women's restroom just a few feet away. Then, out of the corner of her eye, she saw another suit and an airport security guard heading toward her. "Damn, they're gonna cut me off!" She darted quickly to the left. They were running to the right. Just as she was putting space between them, she hit a very large woman head-on. The woman landed on the cement floor with a heavy thud. The irate woman screamed. Judy was thrown off balance but she didn't touch the floor. She ran faster, hearing another man shouting and blowing a whistle.

On impulse, she ditched the carry-on. She just threw it down and didn't care if it wasn't the right thing to do. She had to get out of there, anywhere. She could see uniformed police running in the opposite direction, pursuing James. She was the fox with hounds at her heels. She saw a vending machine and ducked behind it for a second, but a security guard spotted her. Changing plans again, she ran blindly trying to get to any exit she could.

Just as she was gaining speed, she bumped into the father with the screaming kids. Understanding the situation, he called out, "Policia! Policia!" Two guards heard the shouts and headed her way.

She saw another exit sign a few feet away and headed for it. Unfortunately, she didn't see the giant coming up beside her. In the deepest voice Judy had ever heard, he said, "I don't think you are going to make it to this exit, Judith Mackie. You are mine now. Your running days are over."

Chapter 97

Judy's Downfall

Pet was about to push the down button of the elevator when Joshua came to her side.

"Did you get to see him, Pet?"

Joshua's deep voice startled her. "Oh, Joshua, no, I didn't. I talked to Nurse Dannelli, who is in charge. Her explanation of David's condition sounded like a vague description of his physical condition morphed into an apology. I don't feel very assured that he will pull out of this. How could this surgery go so wrong when Dr. Dalezki said David would be fine?"

"You have to believe him, Pet. Trust this doctor and the big Man upstairs."

Joshua's words brought a half smile to Pet's lips. "So now you are going to get religious on me?"

He looked a little exasperated "You know what I mean, Pet."

She hesitated a minute, then gave him a real smile. "Yeah, I do. Why are you here again?"

"I circled back because I was hoping to get a report of David's first assessment of the gunshot wound and, hopefully, get the bullet from the OR nurse. I didn't have any luck, unfortunately. You know, just tying up loose ends. I see you are alone. Do you have a ride home?"

Panic engulfed her, "Oh, my God, I didn't even think about that. I didn't drive. Joshua, everything bad is happening at once. My mother called and told me that my Dad is in critical condition. Mom was crying so pitifully over the phone that I could hardly understand her. She said he didn't have long to live and that she needed to hurry. So now, I must get to my parents' home in Minnesota. Also, I will corral my Uncle Mike and ask him to drive me up there in this crummy weather. Joshua, could you please take me to Rutherford Manor?"

"No problem, Pet. I'm here whenever you need me."

The ride home was quiet. Joshua turned on the radio for a distraction. Pet was lost in thought. Her thoughts bounced from one person to another. She was angry at her Dad for not telling her how sick he was and angry with Fiona for not telling her the truth. She was agitated with the situation of still being coddled as a fragile child and her father's perpetual tactic of sparing her from death's reality.

Then she thought of Helen worrying over David. She worried about David and prayed, begging God for mercy. She prayed Uncle Mike would get her home to see her father before he died. Lastly, she wondered how in the hell they would get there in this awful weather. She wondered how Uncle Mike felt about this situation. His relationship with his brother-in-law was always so stormy.

As Joshua pulled up the driveway, Pet busied herself unlocking her seatbelt and grabbing her purse. Just as she was about to open the door, a news bulletin startled them. The announcer spoke with a clipped British accent.

"Now, at the top of the hour, here are the world headlines. Today in Nassau, an incident occurred at Lynden Pindling International Airport. Two Americans suspected of embezzlement of Briar Town Furniture Company funds attempted to flee from several island police and FBI agents. It was a chaotic scene, with a man and woman running helter-skelter through the terminal, pushing people down as they tried to flee.

"The wife of one of Nassau's dignitaries was pushed to the ground and vowed to press assault charges. The two were finally apprehended and taken into custody. More news to follow in the next hour."

Pet looked at Joshua. "What the hell!" she exclaimed." I kinda figured it would be James Wingate, but who is the woman?"

Joshua looked at Pet. "Well, Pet, my men who were on the case have every reason to suspect your friend Judith Mackie. They have been seen together several times in the last two weeks."

"I can't believe it. Judy? No. Not Judy. I don't understand. She never mentioned anything."

"It was quite an elaborate plan. They even assumed different identities in order to obtain their visas. The Feds really did their homework well."

Without saying goodbye, Pet opened the truck's door and bounded up the steps. She reached the door and impatiently banged the door knocker instead of fumbling for her keys.

"I'm comin', I'm comin.'" Pet passed by Mae Delight in a flash with the maid following right behind her. "Wait, I gotta tell you something. It's important."

Pet ignored her request and headed to the living room. She took off her coat and immediately sat down in front of the television. There she saw the lettering at the bottom of the screen: BREAKING NEWS COMING UP NEXT. Two seconds later, she saw reporters pushing and shoving with police surrounding two people. The commentator listed the names as the camera again showed Judy and James being pushed through the door. "Today, Judith Ann Mackie and James Wingate were apprehended at Lynden Pindling International Airport. Their alleged attempt to embezzle company funds has been confirmed by acting CEO Marshall Hoffmann of Briar Town Furniture Company."

The man and woman tried to shield their faces from the camera. Pet recognized James right away. At first, she wasn't sure of the woman. She scrutinized the screen, hoping she was wrong, but then she saw it. The ring, her ring, was on Judy's finger. She cried out, "Why? Why did you do it? How could you! You betrayed me!"

Then, with bitter sarcasm, she cried out, "My so-called friend!"

Pet put her hands in her lap. She touched her left ring finger and felt the diamond, realizing it was her engagement ring. She hadn't missed the tourmaline ring in all the turmoil. She fought back the bitter tears welling up in her eyes and continued to stare at the television, which had already changed to another story. Her voice was flat when she asked Mae Delight what was so important when she came through the door.

"That's the news. I told you she was no good, Missy. She had big ideas on money, gittin' it the fast way and breakin' your heart in the process!"

Leaning over slightly, Pet brought her hands up to her face and covered her eyes wearily, and she said, "I know Mae Delight. She did it on purpose. She can't resist a handsome man's attention, no matter what happens. I'm done with her."

Suddenly, someone was banging on the door. "Lord A Mighty. Who's that now?" Mae Delight asked as she walked toward the foyer.

Uncle Mike stood in front of her, his snow-covered boots dripping as usual on Mae Delight's highly polished floor. "Is Pet ready, Ms. Mae Delight? We have to head up to Minnesota real quick. Time's a wastin'!"

Pet heard Uncle Mike's voice and jumped off the couch. "Oh, my God! I have to get ready. Mae Delight, I need your help. Need my suitcase, and I must get..." Pet rambled on as she dashed up the stairs to the bedroom.

Chapter 98

The Long Ride Home

In Pet's bedroom, Mae Delight folded clothes while Pet gathered toiletries. Soon her suitcase was packed. Mae Delight studied Pet. She tried to caution this headstrong girl against anything else hellbent for disaster. "Are you sure you want to git on the road now? It's Christmas, and Lord knows what restaurants are gonna be open down the road. What if no gas stations are open? You haven't slept much these last few days, and you haven't eaten right either! You'd better not git yourself sick carrying on all hours of the day and night. And, as for that overgrown bear downstairs, will he git you there safely? What if the roads are blocked? What if you slide off the road?"

"Mae Delight, please don't mother me now. I'll be fine. Nothing or nobody will prevent me from going. My parents need me. I must see my father one more time before God calls him home from this miserable world. Mom is a strong woman, but I won't let her go through this ordeal alone. As for Uncle Mike, he has always driven in bad weather. We're from snow country, for God's sake! Knowing him, he probably has a monster of a truck fully tanked up, ready to go. He is the least of my worries right now."

"All right, I guess you do know what you're gonna do, child. I'll make up a basket of food for you and him t'a git you started on the journey." She turned and left. Halfway out of the room, though, she said in a soft and caring voice, "You better call and let me know how things are goin'. You know I won't sleep a wink. You hear me?"

"Yes, ma'am. You know I will call you."

Mae Delight gave her a slight "humph" and quickly hurried

downstairs mumbling to herself, "That child is gonna be the death of me yet."

Uncle Mike hoisted Pet's suitcase in the back of the Humvee, helped her in the front seat, went around the vehicle, jumped in, and buckled up. He took a road map out of the middle console and traced their route with his right index finger. He then looked at the GPS in his left hand. "That's after Ohio I-80W onto I-90W. Yup, uh huh, here we go."

Uncle Mike looked at her with a seriousness in his voice that Pet had never heard before. "Buckle up, Ladybug. We have fourteen hours of road ahead of us. It'll be a long haul, but I know we'll get there."

"Fourteen hours! That's an eternity! Can't there be a shorter route?"

"Well, it's like this, Pet. We have 3, almost 4 states to travel through until we get up north to Duluth. The only other way would be by air, but the airports are just digging out now. Also, we would have to backtrack into Pittsburgh to get you on a train, and I really don't think that way would be any faster in these conditions, fer shur."

She knew he was right, but the thought of fourteen hours was agonizing. She sat further into the seat. Then, with a wave of her hand toward the driveway, with as much bravado as she could muster, she said, "Play on, McDuff, you are at the helm of this colossus. Let's get this sucker on the road!"

Mike Yoderman turned the ignition key, and the Humvee rumbled into gear and down the driveway. He looked at Pet. Her head was turned forward, and her eyes were alert and expressive with determination. It brought back memories of the feisty little girl he remembered from Duluth, proud and full of spunk. "You sure do have a lot of big words in that head of yours. How do you know all that stuff?"

She faced him with an impish smile, "Let's just say I got me some book learnin'. By the way, where did you get such a big vehicle? I didn't know you drove one like this. It's a beast! I hope it will get us there."

"Ladybug, don't you worry about this here Humvee. This beast will crawl up a mountain and back down it, you betcha. After I told my boss, Ole Tom, what I was up against, he lent me this Humvee. He sure is the salt of the Earth, and he said this baby will get us to Duluth real safe."

A hundred miles later, hunger growled in their stomachs. Pet wondered what goodies Mae Delight prepared for them. She opened a thermos of coffee and poured the steaming, rich liquid into mugs. The hearty chicken sandwiches she found were filling and comforted their need for something good. The food was strong for the journey.

Uncle Mike turned the radio to a country station. John Denver's voice came in loud and clear, singing "Country Road Take Me Home." Uncle Mike joined in, and so did Pet. They sang with gusto, giving their all to the familiar chorus lines. It was a needed lift to their spirits and made them laugh. For some reason, that song opened a door, and Uncle Mike began to talk. He talked about growing up in Duluth, about his exciting days on the high school hockey team, and later playing in semi-professional teams. He related the events of a bad accident during a game that shattered his kneecap and how it changed his life completely.

With a sudden sadness, he said, "Pet, I almost had that big break. I was practically signed up for the major leagues. A talent scout for the Minnesota Wild Ice Hockey Team wanted me, wanted Mike Yoderman to play on his team. Then fate stepped in. Life has a funny way of pointing ya in very different directions."

He went on to tell her about his personal life that she had never known before. Some of the stories were hilarious, some were bittersweet. Like the time he was engaged, married, and divorced all in six months. Uncle Mike was becoming a real person to her, not just the incorrigible brother-in-law of Alistair Teaseling.

Two hours later, with a little smirk on his lips and a twinkle in his eye, Uncle Mike said, "Well, there you have it. I've told you everything about me, Ladybug. I'm kinda interesting, huh."

Calmly, Pet said in a supportive voice, "I can understand you a lot better now. I guess Daddy was just being a protective brother-in-law. I think you are a very interesting and good person. I love you no matter what your crazy past was like, Uncle Mike. You have been good to me, and that is all that counts."

He smiled at her. "Well, thanks, Ladybug. I love you too."

After their conversation, there was a comfortable quietness. Pet scrunched around in her seat until she got comfortable and peered out into the bleak darkness. She felt the rumble of the tires digging into the ice-packed road while sporadic bursts buffeted the Humvee, moving against the wind. Blowing snow had piled up drifts high enough to make a wall in some sections of the road. She thought how desolate the night was out there, and if it hadn't been for her steadfast driver, her mood would be ten times worse.

Uncle Mike studied the road, watching the cars in front of him. Chicago was behind them now, and Skokie was coming up.

"Pet, we are coming up to an interchange, and a rest stop is just ahead. Do you want to make a pit stop?"

"Yup, you read my mind. Mother Nature calls. Maybe a vending machine will have some hot chocolate for two weary travelers."

"Good idea. I will pull in there right now."

As soon as the Humvee stopped, Pet jumped out and headed for the ladies' room. She hadn't realized how badly she had to go until Uncle Mike mentioned stopping. Opening the door to the rest station, she was amazed at how many people were milling around the large open area.

She wasted no time entering the stall. A minute later, she chuckled to herself, ah, sweet relief. Before she could get out of the stall, her cell phone went off in her pocket. She pulled it out. "Hello. Oh, Mom. Yes, we are approaching the city of Skokie, Illinois. How is Dad? Um, hmm. Please don't cry, Mom. Please tell him to hang on till I get there. Don't let him die. I have to tell him how much I love him."

Before she could properly end the conversation, she heard the call waiting beep. "I have to go, Mom. I love you."

"Hello. Marshall. Yes, we are nearing Skokie now. What's up?"

"Well, Pet, the dock workers are set on striking tomorrow."

"But the whole factory is off 'till New Year's. I thought unions didn't strike unless they could walk off the job?"

"They just want to make a point of the bonus they never got and the pension fund issue that Al and James siphoned off. I am going to call in the shop stewards and negotiate these issues before the workers dig in their heels for bigger demands. I just need your approval for a 3% across-the-board raise. If they get hard-nosed about it, I'll maybe go 4%, but only if I have to go that high. I will also call in the financial planning head, Will Cranston, to see if we can boost the profit-sharing benefits, if that's okay with you."

"Yes, sure. You know the ropes better than I do. Oh, what…"

Call waiting beeped in again. "Marshall, I must go. I'm getting another call."

"Sure. Thanks, Pet. Take care."

By this time, Pet was walking to the vending machines, and her phone kept ringing. A little exasperated, she mumbled, "How am I going to juggle two cups of hot chocolate and a phone at the same time? They will just have to wait until I get back in the Humvee. Geez, can't even enjoy a rest stop!"

She didn't have to check her missed calls because her phone rang again.

"Hello. Oh, Helen, HI! How is David? Is he awake yet? Can he talk? Is he alert? I hated to leave him in the ICU. Please tell me he is better."

"Pet, dear, slow down. David is getting more alert when he wakes up from time to time, and the internal bleeding has stopped. That is the main thing Dr. Daleski was worried about.

The nurses say his vital signs are good. Dr. Daleski has come in twice now to check the drainage tubes and is pleased that they are looking good. David said he wants to FaceTime with you tomorrow, if he is up to it. Will you be able to talk tomorrow?"

"I, I don't know Helen. I want to with all my heart, but I don't know what kind of situation I will run into once I get to the hospital in Duluth. My mother keeps calling and crying over the phone. My father is gravely ill. Please tell David I love him."

Before she had a chance to buckle her seatbelt, the cell phone rang again. Uncle Mike shook his head, glanced sideways at her, and headed the Humvee down the road. Pet cried out in anger before she answered it, "Son of a brick! Why won't people leave me alone! Hello! Who? Joshua? What's the matter now?"

"I know you're stressed, Pet, but don't bite my head off just yet. I must ask you something important."

Pet took a long sip of the hot chocolate before she answered. She wasn't looking forward to his question.

"My detectives have been led on a merry chase. We have searched three different places where Anthony's mother should be residing. Every lead was the wrong person. I hate to ask this, Pet, but could you please identify the body? Let me assure you that there have been improvements to the viewing process. The identifier doesn't have to be in that small room anymore, and the body is viewed from behind a window, totally draped except for the head, of course. I would be with you the whole time. We would like to wrap this case up as soon as possible."

Pet took a deep breath and wished that she was holding a good stiff drink instead of a mug of hot chocolate.

"I really don't want to see the face of a man I once loved on a steel table in a morgue. No. Joshua, it's too personal. The idea is grotesque. Are you sure you can't find anyone with the last name Prattmore?"

There was a resigned finality about his voice. "Okay, I have one more weak possibility, Pet. I'll call you if I find someone." With her answer, he ended the conversation.

Joshua was just about to say his last word when her cell phone beeped again.

"Who's callin' you now, Ladybug?"

"I don't know. I don't recognize the number, probably some jerk. Oh, good, it quit."

Pet began to fiddle with the radio station when the phone rang again. "What a nuisance!"

This time, she looked at the number on the caller ID, "Hmm, it looks like an out-of-the-country phone number. There are a lot of zeros and ones." Pet shrugged her shoulders and pressed talk. Her tone of voice wasn't polite. "Hello. Who is this?"

The whimpering voice was soft between sobs. "Oh, Pet, I'm so glad you answered."

"Speak up, I can hardly hear you. Judy? Is this you? Judas!"

"Yes. Pet, I am so sorry, I didn't mean to hurt you or betray you, honest. James was so convincing. He turned out to be a real creep."

Pet was about to hang up on her, but then paused. "Yeah, tell it to the judge, Jude. It doesn't help me now, does it?"

Between sobs, Judy tried to talk. "Pet, I'm scared. It's awful down here. I'm in a cell among hookers and drug addicts, and I don't know if I'll be able to get off this island. I'm literally by myself. I don't trust anyone. I don't know anyone. I'm so sorry, Pet. Please help me. I will give you the ring back, honest. Please, Pet, I'm begging you."

Pet almost felt sorry for her. Before speaking, she swallowed hard and hesitated, fighting the urge to punish Judy by hanging up and letting her fend for herself. She thought, "Damn, Judy, why do you put me in this position?"

"Hell, Jude, do you really expect me to bail you out?"

"No, can you just get me a lawyer? I will do exactly what he says, no games, honest."

Pet's voice was harsh, "I'll think about it. You don't deserve my help, but maybe I'll call Marshall and see what he says about this situation."

Still crying, Judy thanked her and hung up. It took a while to analyze the feelings she had for Judy. She was waffling back and forth, hating Judy for what she did, but remembering the good things Judy had done for her.

She looked at Uncle Mike. "I don't like this situation! I'm so hurt that Judy could be swayed by a sweet-talking con artist over our friendship."

"Honestly, how do you feel towards your friend? You gotta dig deep down in yer soul an' think, is she worth yer love? Would she help you in a jam? That's the question you have to ask yourself, Ladybug."

Pet thought long and hard for an hour or so as the Humvee headed toward Duluth. She then decided to call Marshall. She told him about Judy. He was surprised Judy called her.

"Well, Pet, I am glad you called. I know this situation is hard to take emotionally, but if we do get her a lawyer, it might benefit the company by giving us information on how extensive James and Al's plans were. We can find out if there are any other monies they attempted to steal. I will contact our corporate lawyer, Henry Winesapp. He is also very knowledgeable in international law. I will keep you informed."

"Thanks, Marshall. I am glad you understand. Yes, please keep me posted. Goodbye." Pet sighed in relief when she put the phone in her lap.

"Do you feel better now, Ladybug?"

"Yes, you said all the right words in making my decision. Thank you. By the way, where are we? I haven't paid much attention. It's getting light out. Are we near Duluth yet?"

Uncle Mike scratched his head. "We're makin' pretty good time, but we still have a ways to go. In 50 miles, we will pass the outskirts of Minneapolis – St Paul. So if all goes right and these here roads aren't treacherous, we just might be there in about 4 hours."

Pet sat straight up in her seat. "Four hours! Oh, my aching butt! Four more hours in this seat? This trip is agonizing! I wish I had flown. Why can't things go my way? You are doing a great job, Uncle Mike, don't get me wrong, but it's such a long way to go!"

Uncle Mike tried to soothe her frazzled nerves. "I know, Ladybug. This ordeal will be over soon. You'll see your Papa soon and be able to give him a big hug. Why don't you try to call that young man of yours? Maybe he will feel like talkin' to ya. That would make ya feel better, fer shur."

Almost like magic, Pet's FaceTime app pinged, and David's face appeared.

There, propped up on pillows, her beloved's face appeared. Her voice was a mixture of pure delight and relief. "David. Oh David! You look wonderful considering what you just went through."

"Yeah, well, it took some doing, but I had to see you and hear your sweet voice, Pet. I know now I'm going to make it. Every minute I am awake is a true gift. I still have trouble taking deep breaths, but it's nothing I can't handle. Listen, I want to marry you as soon as I can walk out of here. My Mom said she could handle much of the planning for a simple home wedding. Whata ya say?"

Her voice was a squeal of happiness. "Yes! Mae Delight would be in her glory showing off Rutherford Manor. David, I don't need fancy. I just need you close to me. I'll have to give Mae Delight at least two weeks to get things together. Oh, David, for a second, I forgot about my father. His condition is very critical. I don't know what will happen within the next 24 hours."

"Forgive me, Pet. I got caught up in our plans. Of course, I understand. You want Rutherford Manor for the wedding? My mom was thinking about her home. No worries, Pet. It will be your day. I don't care if we get hitched at Brewster's! Helen is the perpetual planner. When she comes in today, I will tell her."

Before Pet could answer him, Pet's phone beeped. She sighed, "Damn, here we go again. David, I must answer this. It might be my Mom. I will call Helen. I love you so much, and I'm glad we aren't going to have a big wedding."

"Hello, Mom? Please calm down. What's the matter? Yes, yes, we are only 4 hours away. Mom, please, there is nothing more we can do. Uncle Mike is driving as fast as he can under the circumstances. Please don't be scared. I'm anxious too. Please whisper in Daddy's ear that I love him and I'm on my way." Fighting back tears, she abruptly said good-bye.

The seriousness of Alistair's condition weighed heavily on her heart. She wanted to burst into giggles and tell Fiona about the wedding plans, but that wouldn't be right, even though Fiona needed some good news right now. For a minute, she thought she might find the right time to tell them that their daughter's future would be a happy one.

On and on, the rugged Humvee ate up the miles by passing big cities and plowing through small towns. Her mood lightened. The GPS counted down the hours to their destination. Duluth didn't seem so far away now. She was uncomfortable and began to fidget, stretching her back and extending her legs as far as the seat would allow. Pet wished the vehicle had more creature comforts. Sitting all those hours in the sparsely padded bucket seats, her hips felt every bump in the road. Luxury padding and back support must not have been a priority. Her bum was numb. This discomfort brought her back to the days of sitting on the gymnasium bench in high school.

At one point, as they headed due north, Uncle Mike needed a stretch. Nearing the city of Eau Claire, he saw a signpost for Arby's. "Well, Ladybug, I need a stretch, and I need to fill my belly. I'm starved. I could down a couple of 3 or 4 Beef N' Cheddars fer sur."

Pet echoed back, "Me too. Maybe I'll get something to take the edge off." The two got out of the Humvee and headed inside the fast-food oasis.

They were greeted by an energetic young man of about 18. His voice was welcoming, and he smiled, asking how he could serve them.

"Yes, ma'am. We'll have that order ready in no time. Help yourselves to the coffee. It's on the house today."

"How nice. Thank you." Pet didn't care if it was company policy or not, but it made that moment special. Uncle Mike tipped the lad even though he knew it wasn't company policy. The coffee tasted especially good, and the Beef N' Cheddars were tasty and hot.

Back on the road, Pet finally began to relax now that her stomach was full and she was sipping on the free coffee. Taking out a pen and a notepad, she decided to make some wedding plans. Fatigue was setting in, and it became harder and harder to concentrate. Soon, the rhythm of tires and hum of the engine lulled her into a restful nap.

She woke up with Uncle Mike's booming voice coming at her over the radio's music. "Hey there, Ladybug, wake up! We're gettin' close to Duluth! I need a favor. Look up the hospital where your Papa is. I don't know if I put the right one in the GPS." Pet googled it immediately. "Let me see. Here it is: 915 East 1st Street."

"Yup, that's the one I put in. Well, we should be there in about 20 minutes. We are only 2 or 3 miles away from the exit ramps. Almost there, Pet. Just hang on."

To her elation, she saw an overhead sign reading "Duluth Business Exits 31A 32B 2 miles." "I can't believe it, finally! I really must have zonked out."

"Yup, you were really snoring up a storm, Ladybug."

Before she could utter a retort, Mike suddenly slammed on the brakes. A semi stopped abruptly in front of them. After a couple of minutes, the semi-truck crept along at 10 mph. Mike did the same.

Then, the inevitable happened. Traffic came to a complete stop. Pet screeched. "What the heck is going on? Oh no. I hope it isn't an accident. We'll be here for hours!" Pet wailed. She immediately rolled down the window and stuck her head out, trying to see beyond the semi. "I can't see anything, Uncle Mike. How's your side, anything?"

Uncle Mike leaned out his window as far as he could. He

couldn't see anything past the semi. After not moving for ten minutes, Mike said, "Don't panic yet, Pet. Let me see if I can find out what's goin' on up yonder. Traffic is backing up fast. I'll be back in a jiffy."

Mike unbuckled his seatbelt, opened the door, and swung his long legs out of the Humvee. Pet watched Uncle Mike's big body lumber up to the truck and then disappear into the truck's shadow to the left. The wait was excruciating. She wanted to know what the news would be. "What's keeping him? I can't wait here too long. I'll go nuts. I know I will. Dear God, let my father still be alive." She moaned and prayed at the same time.

Fifteen minutes later, Uncle Mike startled Pet by opening the driver's side door. His voice was loud and excited. "Well, I found out what happened. That there driver in front of us said a SUV smashed up right before the ramp to Exit 31A. He's a real nice guy. Why does he know my old boss from..."

"Uncle Mike, please. I don't care who he is. Just tell me what we can do!"

"Well, we were talkin' about the roads, and he told me about the old Bent Fork Road about twenty yards up the way. It runs right along the lake and up to the hospital. It's not traveled much since the highway came through. I thought some, and don'tcha know I remembered it fer shur. If we can get on the shoulder of this here highway, we can sneak outta this mess. Although it will be a dangerous way to get to the hospital. We gotta go over mounds of snow, under a low bridge, and through a section of road real close to the lake. Since it hasn't been traveled in a while, I'm not sure just how good the surface is, Pet."

Pet began to panic at the thought of staying put, waiting endlessly for traffic to clear. "Are you talking yourself out of this solution, Uncle Mike? Look, Mom is by herself. She is waiting for us all the while watching Dad slip away. It will be agonizing for her. We have to try to get there as fast as we can. I'm willing to take this chance."

"Well, Ladybug, I know ye got a sense of adventure, but if

I harm a hair on yer head, Fi will never speak to me again, you betcha. But I think this Humvee can do the job. We'll put'er to the test!"

"Okay, let's go. I have faith in you, and anything will be better than just sitting here. If you think this Humvee can make a path to the hospital without getting us killed in the process, let's do it."

"Okay, buckle up and hold on!"

Mike put the Humvee in low gear and moved out slowly, inching the vehicle past the semi tractor-trailer and a three-foot wall of snow. As they passed, the trucker gave Uncle Mike a thumbs-up.

The chosen escape route tested a driver's nerve on a good day. On this day, it verged on suicidal. The Humvee plowed through drifts four feet high, but that challenge didn't scare Mike. He pushed harder and drove up over mounds of snow, not knowing what was going to be on the other side of the winding slopes. At one point, both of them came out of their seats as the behemoth plunged down a steep grade, landing onto a low field that edged the dunes of the lake. Finally, the roller coaster ride ended when the road smoothed out and came to a stop behind a Walmart parking lot.

"How did we do that, Uncle Mike? Why, I can see the blacktop." Pet was astonished and glad to start breathing normally again. A couple of times, she thought eternity was just around the bend.

Mike smiled, "Well, I was pretty sure we could do it, Ladybug. Are ye in one piece? That treacherous adventure brought us where we needed to be. Look, the hospital is straight ahead."

Chapter 99

Sorrow and Resolve

Two minutes later, the Humvee sat in front of St Luke's Hospital. The two weary passengers unbuckled their seat belts, stretched their stiff bodies, grabbed jackets, and made motions to climb out of the Humvee. Suddenly, Pet froze. A state of inertia held her in the seat. A mental battle ensued as to whether to stay in the vehicle, shielded from reality, or run through the entrance, desperately trying to find a dying man. She envisioned her mother wringing her hands and pitifully crying over Alistair. This made her feel helpless and alone. She went through it with Harry, and now she has to face those gut-wrenching feelings of loss with her father.

Impatiently, Mike said, "Pet, Ladybug, move. Open the door! We've come all this way. Ye can't stop now!"

With a hesitant sigh, she decided to accept whatever God had in store for her. She got out of the vehicle and walked to the hospital's entrance. Then, in a spurt of panic, Pet's pace quickened, almost jogging to the elevators after asking the information clerk where her father was. She checked the floor listings and pressed the 4th floor button for critical care.

The unit secretary pointed them to Alistair's room. Entering, Pet heard the unmistakable soft whimper from Fiona's lips, praying over Alistair. She turned, greeting Pet with a tearful hug. "Yer here! Oh, me Darlin'. His spirit's nearly left him. He hasn't said a word these last two days. He's been waitin' for ye. Talk to him."

Pet fought hard to compose herself and crept silently beside Alistair. She watched his chest rise ever so slightly and eyed the monitors that barely registered his life signs. She leaned close, whispering softly in his ear, "Daddy, I'm here. I love you. I have some good news. David asked me to marry him. You won't have to worry about me anymore. David is a wonderful man. I love him so much!"

Then Pet leaned even closer. "I am carrying David's child, Dad. You're going to be a grandfather! Don't worry about Mom. I will take good care of her. She will be with us from now on. Oh, Daddy, there was so much I wanted to tell you, I..." She couldn't go on. Tears welled up in her eyes. She heard the last rasping breath escape from his mouth. On impulse, she kissed him quickly and whispered, "I love you."

Suddenly, the room got very quiet. Uncle Mike gently placed his big hand on her shoulder. "He's gone, Ladybug. He's n'a of this earth no more. The angels took him up to heaven."

She started to rise from the chair, but she couldn't leave her father's side. She smoothed the hair around his ear and put her head on the pillow. Pet smelled that familiar "father smell" of Old Spice still clinging to his skin, mixed with a tinge of perspiration. It was that little intimate part of him she would never smell again. This final realization brought tears gushing down her cheeks.

She felt Fiona patting her arm. Bleary-eyed, she saw the flat line of the monitors and the nurse easing into the room. The nurse put her hand gently on Fiona's shoulder and, in a quiet voice, said those inevitable words. "He's gone, Mrs. Teaseling." Fiona nodded and began to sob into her hanky. There were no dramatics, no heroic last-minute effort to bring him back to life. Alistair's time had come. His life was now complete, and he peacefully slipped away from them.

All three of them sat motionless in the small room, not wanting to leave. Pet watched the nurses unplug the cords from the monitors. Mike sat next to Fiona, patting her hand comfortingly. Fiona stared at Alistair and whispered, "Goodbye, my love. I'll miss ye."

Alistair's nurse came in with a clipboard in her hand. In a

soft voice, she asked if they were ready to leave. With a slow nod, Fiona whispered a resolved "Yes." Then, after the tedious formality of signing final papers and designating which funeral home to be notified, Fiona, Pet, and Uncle Mike walked slowly out the door. They made their way to the main lobby.

Sunlight flooded the immense lobby from huge bay windows surrounding it. Pet gazed out in wonderment. The storm had subsided. It was like God parted the clouds like the Red Sea and turned a raging storm into the most beautiful day she had ever witnessed. She felt peaceful seeing such a beautiful day and whispered to the heavens, "In your mercy, Lord, I hope my father heard me. You took him on a sunny day, and for that I am thankful. Please help my mother. Amen." Fiona dabbed her eyes and felt calm for the first time in two weeks.

Pet affectionately looked down on Fiona. Slowly, with a smile, she said, "You are all mine now, Mom. We will be strong together. With God's help, we will get through this sadness even though we'll miss him something awful."

As the threesome walked to the Humvee, Pet stopped before she opened the vehicle's door. She looked at Fiona and spoke pleadingly, "Mom, will you come to Whalen Falls with me? Could you leave Minnesota and live with me? I'm going to need your help with the wedding. There is so much to do, even though we are getting married in Rutherford Manor. Will you help me pick out a dress? If the dress needs altering, you could do it. I would trust only you."

Fiona put her hand up, "Now, lass. Don't be puttin' too much in me head at once. I can't leave Alistair's house tomorrow! We built the homestead, ye know."

Pet tried not to sound demanding. "I mean, it won't be tomorrow, trust me. Oh, Mom, please come and live with me. The manor house has many rooms. You will live in a suite fit for a queen! If you come, we will have good times again. And besides, I can't leave you up here all alone. I would be worried sick every minute of every day just wondering about you."

With a half-smile and sigh, Fiona said "yes" with the promise she could bring the "forever things" Alistair made for her. "Only a few things: a rocking chair, a cedar chest, an ebony fern table, and a maple cradle. The memories are so precious, I must take them with me, lass," Fiona said with a finality that wouldn't budge.

"Okay, Mom, I understand, but please, there is only so much room in a moving van. We can't bring the whole house." Pet chuckled to herself, "Manny is gonna love this job."

It was fun packing with Fiona. Pet revisited her childhood, going through her special clothes. For some reason, Fiona kept every one of her prom dresses. When she asked Fiona why, she replied, "My beautiful girl looked like an angel, and I couldn't give away an angel to anyone!"

With a tear in her eye and a smile on her lips, Pet said, "You're killing me, you know that, but I do agree with you. I did look good in them, didn't I!"

The two of them tackled every room, sorting and pitching. Some days were quite tedious, but they persevered, rejecting the urge to keep things pulling them further into the past. Tackling each job, Pet's life slowly got back to normal. A moving company was contracted to take Fiona's precious items to Whalen Falls.

A few days after the funeral, Uncle Mike, the eternal optimist, calculated the quickest way home with the responsibility of getting his two favorite ladies back safely in that Humvee. It was decided later, though, that Mike should go alone, with the exception of Fiona's yellow cat named Gizzy and the handmade cradle. "We'll be great pals by the time we get to Whalen Falls, Fi. Just you wait and see. Yes, sir, buddy!"

And so, another chapter of Pet's life had closed. She looked ahead to a brighter future with David's everlasting, constant love and their child. These separate people would finally be a family now.

Epilogue

All the Details

The journey back to Whalen Falls didn't happen for quite a while. The matter of selling the house was more complicated than expected. Slapping a "For Sale" sign in front of the yard and accepting the highest bidder were far from the ideal reality Pet had imagined. For two months, real estate agents haggled with potential buyers over price and upscale remodeling. Finally, a young couple proposed an "as-is special."

Pet wasn't too sure about that kind of deal, so she consulted with Marshall. Thanks to his input, she agreed with the buyer's offer. The house sold. A week and a half later, papers were signed. Five days after that, Fiona Teaseling was stepping onto a plane for the first time in her life, and to Pet's amazement, Fiona enjoyed every minute of the flight.

Mae Delight welcomed Fiona with open arms. Over hot coffee and cinnamon buns, the wedding plan conversations never ceased. Mae Delight made it plain, though, that she was running the show, and that this Helen woman could make suggestions here and there if she wanted to, but it would be her final decision on everything.

Mae Delight had saved all the papers about Judy, James, the airport fiasco, and Aloysius Hyde's grisly demise. The Whalen Times also had a field day with all the details of Aloysius stealing company funds and his spectacular death driving off the bridge. Every day, the paper posed different questions as to how Briar Town Furniture Company would handle the thefts. What would the new owner do? Each day, the headlines got more bizarre.

Judy's jail experience in Nassau preyed on Pet's mind. After her second call, more pathetic than the first, a twinge of compassion seeped into Pet's heart.

"Well, what do you want me to do, Jude? You got yourself into this mess. Didn't Henry Winesapp meet with you?"

"Yes, but the Nassau Authorities couldn't tell him when I could come back to the States. Pet, it is horrible down here. There are rats in my cell, and there is absolutely no privacy! Can't you do something, anything to get me to a hotel, maybe?"

"You don't deserve any real consideration, but I imagine living with rats is pretty horrible. I will call Henry. Be patient."

"Oh, thank you, Pet. I will make this whole thing up to you, honest. If it takes me a lifetime, I will make things better." Judy was about to hang up, but started to sob, and with a heavy voice said, "Please get me out of here."

Henry Winesapp knew his way around the foreign system and finally managed to spring Judy from jail after a month's time. Then it took another week until she was extradited back to the states to a women's minimum-security prison until the trial. Another melee of stories covered the front pages of the Whalen Times. Pet tried to ignore the whole situation, but it wasn't easy with Mae Delight's mouth running every time the phone rang. The reporters' inquiries were relentless.

The best day of all was when David came to Rutherford Manor. Pet felt as if she was floating on air. She laughed constantly, talked incessantly, and made one plan after another. David was almost as giddy as she was, and he couldn't keep his hands off her. Mae Delight threatened to hog-tie both of them and put them in separate rooms until the wedding.

One night after dinner, Pet and David were alone in the library. They talked quietly and embraced each other. After a loving kiss, Pet whispered to him, "Oh, David, I feel so content. Mae Delight should've known she couldn't keep us apart! I can't wait for this child to be born! Let's tell everyone tomorrow. Who woulda thought making love in a library would be magical!"

David tenderly kissed her forehead. "Yes, those special encounters are the best! I love you, future Mrs. Jones!"

www.ingramcontent.com/pod-product-compliance
Lightning Source LLC
LaVergne TN
LVHW041058080826
845145LV00007B/1619